Brenin's Crown

To Mary,
Happy reading!
Janet L Ruth

Brenin's Crown

A Celtic Romance

Janet Ruth

Writers Club Press
San Jose New York Lincoln Shanghai

Brenin's Crown
ACaslon Regular

Writers Club Press
an imprint of iUniverse, Inc.

For information address:
iUniverse, Inc.
5220 S. 16th St., Suite 200
Lincoln, NE 68512
www.iuniverse.com

ISBN: 0-595-20810-X

Printed in the United States of America

Thank you to all of my family, friends, and fellow writers who read this story and offered advice, information, and encouragement. And a special thank you to my husband, Steve, who bought me all those books about England and the Celts and encouraged me to dream.

Introduction

In the year 55 B.C., Julius Caesar first crossed the English Channel with the intent of conquering the vast island he called Britain. It took several major offensives and over a century of fighting, but eventually much of the island fell to Roman rule, from Hadrian's Wall in the north, west into Wales, and south into parts of Devon and Cornwall. Much more quickly than they had come, the Romans abandoned the island in 407 A.D, leaving behind roads, villas, walled cities, and a deep influence on the native Celtic people. Calling on Rome for protection from invaders, the natives were instructed in 410 A.D. to "look to their own defenses." And that is just what they did.

Chapter One

The Year of Our Lord 477. In Britain, the Kingdom of Dumnonia.

Addien had always been fascinated by the tunnels that ran underneath her house, even though she was forbidden to play in them. She had never seen the inside of the tunnels, only the metal grates on the floor of each room where the tunnels opened to the world above. She knew, from being told, what the tunnels were for; but she could no more understand that information than a rabbit could understand the purpose of wearing clothes. The tunnels were a part of her house, but they were not a part of her world. They were a reminder that the house had not always been her father's house, or the house of her grandfather. There had been someone else there that was gone now, someone who had been replaced but not entirely forgotten.

Stuffing her small fingers through the narrow openings in the grate, Addien tugged at the stubborn metal once more, still without success.

"Trevilian," she whispered, putting her head down close to the bars where she could smell the stale earth beneath. "I know you're down there. I can hear you buzzing. Do come out and play with me."

She paused before putting her ear next to the grate. The sound that she had heard before was gone, leaving nothing but an annoying silence.

"All right," she pouted, "don't come back. I didn't want to play with you today anyway. I have much too much to do."

Addien pushed herself up onto her hands and knees, then stood and shook the long skirt of her sleeping dress away from her ankles. Stepping to the one window in her room, she pushed open the wooden shutters. The morning sun, still hidden behind a high stone wall, threw its light through the opening, illuminating white-washed walls, a sturdy oak bed-frame, and a pile of blue and green blankets in a heap on the green tile floor. An autumn breeze rustled the branches of a primrose bush just below the windowsill, blowing a faint scent of decaying blooms into the room. Addien took a deep breath and smiled.

"Addien, are you awake yet?" a voice called from the hallway. "You're going to miss your own birthday if you sleep all day."

A thick tapestry woven of yellow and brown stands of wool was swept back from the doorway, allowing a tall woman to enter the room.

"I haven't missed anything, have I?" Addien asked, running to her mother and throwing her arms around her.

Morveren laughed.

"Of course not," she said. "The feast isn't until this evening. But our guests will be arriving throughout the day. I want you to be up and ready to greet them."

A short while later, Addien was dressed. Her mother sat beside her on the bed brushing out the mass of red hair that fell in waves almost to the child's waist. Then she gathered whole fistfuls of it into her hands to begin the long braid down the center of her daughter's back.

"I have some green ribbons we can tie into your hair later," Morveren said as she worked. "I know you like red better, but green will bring out the color of your eyes."

"Is that why you wear green?" Addien asked, trying to peer behind her as her mother continued to work on her hair.

Morveren leaned over to meet Addien's look. Her own neat braid of deep red fell over her shoulder and brushed the floor, and her eyes sparkled in a brilliant shade of emerald green. Her gown sparkled as well with golden embroidery at the neckline and waist, but the rest of it was green—a soft green made for touching, like the first leaves of spring.

Turning back again, Addien suppressed a yawn.

"Were you awake very late last night?" Morveren asked, continuing to work on the braid. "I know you were very excited after we finished decorating the room."

"Oh, I didn't go to sleep at all!" Addien replied. "I kept wishing it would be morning. And Trevilian came and sang to me, and he made my wish come true. It was morning, and I had never even closed my eyes!"

"It was morning, and you had never even closed your eyes? Not even a little?" Morveren teased. "Well, I suppose it is nice to have an invisible friend who can make your wishes come true."

"He isn't invisible to me," Addien corrected her, "only to other people. He lives in the tunnel under the floor. He said one day he would take me down there with him."

"I thought you said he was the size of a mouse? How can he fit through the grate to get into the tunnel?" Morveren asked.

"He can make himself smaller anytime he wants to. He can even disappear."

Morveren paused near the end of the braid. She turned Addien toward her and took her chin in one hand, forcing her daughter to look directly at her at.

"You haven't been trying to get into the tunnels, have you?" she asked. "You know that would be very dangerous."

"But why?" Addien asked in a small voice. "What's down there?"

Morveren sighed. "Nothing. Nothing at all. A long time ago, this house belonged to a Roman governor, before your great-grandfather, King Bryon came to live here. The tunnels were used to send heated air from the furnace room into the bedrooms."

Addien wrinkled up her face and stared at her mother. She had heard all of this before, but it still made no sense to her.

"Then why don't we use them anymore?" she asked.

"I don't know," Morveren laughed, reaching down to give her daughter a hug. "The furnace was taken apart long ago and locked away, and the tunnels are not to be played in."

Addien nodded her understanding and then stood to let her mother finish tying off the braid.

"Mother," she asked, looking down at the metal grate on the floor of her room, "who lived here before the Roman governor?"

"No one did. This house was built for the governor. Our people lived in this land before the Romans came, but not right here. The Romans built this whole city, the only one like it in Dumnonia."

Addien was silent for a long moment before turning to face her mother again. She clutched her hands together in front of her and tried to still the trembling of her lower lip.

"Will we have to go away some day, like the Romans did?" she asked.

Morveren sighed, then she pulled her daughter onto the bed beside her and wrapped her arms around her.

"Of course not," she whispered into Addien's ear. "This is the King's House now, and it always will be."

* * *

The hallway outside Addien's room was long and narrow and paved in white tiles with a colorful pattern of exotic flowers. Oil lamps sat securely in brass fasteners all along the white wall, and faded tapestries hung over the entryways to servants' rooms and storage areas. At the end of the hall, a wide opening led into the kitchen where the warmth of a large oven softened the air. Addien followed the sweet aroma of fresh bread into the bustling room and bobbed her way around busy serving women to reach the center table. A plate of bread and cheese appeared before her and a wooden cup of goat's milk. Addien emptied the plate and then raced back out of the kitchen into the cooler air of the hallway.

Across from the kitchen, the door into the Great Hall stood open. Addien skipped into the room with a broad smile and looked all around her. Evergreen garlands tied with red ribbons hung from the four high walls. The long tables and benches that ran in two rows down the length of the room had been pushed back a little to make a place in the center for the evening's entertainment. At the far side of the room, the Royal Table sat at a right angle with three high-backed chairs behind it, one for Addien's mother, one for her father, and one, completely covered in red ribbons, for her. Even the great tiles of grey marble on the floor had been polished to a dull shine in honor of the special day.

Before the morning had half passed, Addien was called into the garden to greet her first guests. There, surrounded on three sides by the Great Hall and the two wings of the house, a gravel path wound its way through an array of fruit trees and planting beds to the massive double-doors leading into the Great Hall. Local nobles and their families arrived first and crowded into the Hall, while other guests, who had traveled from further away, were shown to guest rooms in the west wing. Most brought a small gift of some kind for Addien. With great enthusiasm and well-taught politeness, she accepted carved wooden animals, cloth dolls, hair ribbons, and pretty stones. In return she handed out sweet treats and little toys for the children. As her nurse disappeared with each new gift, Addien ran around the garden or the Hall, playing with the other children or just nosing about into everyone's affairs.

Morveren glided effortlessly around the house, greeting old friends, providing food and drink, settling issues of mixed-up belongings and extra visitors with infinite grace. Addien's father was less visible, spending most of the day behind the closed door of the King's Court in the west wing of the house. It was rare to have so many nobles gathered together at one time, and the desire to discuss weighty matters of the kingdom was too great to ignore. But Addien didn't mind. She knew that her father would be sitting next to her at the feast that evening, and she was willing to wait for his attention.

* * *

By the middle of the afternoon, Addien was tired of the noise and the crowd and the games of the other children. Making certain that no one was watching, she slipped out of the Great Hall and ran past the kitchen to the solitude of her own little room. The tapestry at her doorway blocked most of the noise from the hallway, and the narrow walkway outside her shuttered window was deserted. She was finally alone. Uncertain what to do next, she looked around for something to distract her.

In addition to the bed, there was a table and a stool in the corner of the room and a chest that sat beside the wall to hold clothing and personal belongings. Addien's gaze fell on the table, where her nurse had carefully arranged her gifts. A few moments later she was curled up on her bed, surrounded by the dolls and stones and other trinkets she had received that day. The guests, the clamor, and the excitement of the day faded away. With a contented sigh, Addien closed her eyes and fell asleep.

* * *

"Addien! 'Ere you are!"

Red-faced and breathing hard, a stout woman stood over Addien's bed glaring down at her. Through the mist of dissolving dreams, the child looked back at her.

"Yes, nurse," she said with a yawn. "I am here."

"Well, it's 'ere that you aren't supposed to be," the nurse scolded. "'Ere we have a house full of guests for yer special day, and you slip away without telling anyone to come hide in yer room."

Unprepared for this lecture, Addien's eyes hardened and she drew her lips tightly together.

"I'm not hiding," she said between her teeth. "I was tired."

The nurse returned Addien's stare for a long moment, but finally looked away. With a slight "hrumph" and a shake of her shoulders, the woman addressed her charge in a calmer voice.

"It's only that I've been looking for you all over the grounds," she said. "Everyone is in such a state. Lord Finnen's wife has lost a brooch, and yer dear mother has been near to fits dealing with the woman. She has every servant in the house looking for the thing. I don't know what's going to happen if...."

The woman's voice faded away. Her eyes widened, and her jaw dropped. Puzzled by the sudden change, Addien followed the woman's gaze to see what had captured her attention. There, on the bed, half hidden by her skirts, lay a gold brooch that Addien had never seen before. Even with her mind still half asleep, Addien realized what it was. She looked back at the woman beside her, noting the deepening shades of red and purple that illuminated her face.

"Addien! 'Ow could you?" the nurse sputtered. "Today of all days! When yer father finds out about this...."

"But I didn't take it!" Addien exclaimed. "I never touched it, I promise!"

Her mind clouded over with fear at the thought of her father being called away from his guests to deal with her apparent crime. Brenin was a kind man, and a loving father, but he was also the king, and his anger was something to be avoided. He had already scolded Addien about stealing things, and he had restricted her to her room on more than one occasion. She didn't want to think about what her punishment would be this time if he didn't believe her.

"If you didn't take the brooch," her nurse asked, "then 'ow did it get into yer room?"

Eyes downcast, Addien answered quietly, "Perhaps Trevilian took it."

Her nurse threw her arms up in the air, looked to the sky, and shook her head violently. Addien watched her under half-closed lids. The reaction had been expected. The woman often behaved just so when mention was made of Addien's closest friend.

"Trevilian!" the woman blustered, when she could find her voice. "Trevilian again? When are you going to stop this childish pretending?"

"I'm not pretending!" Addien retorted angrily. "Trevilian is real! And he's my friend. I'm sorry he took the dumb ol' brooch. He was only playing. He just wanted to have a little fun."

Looking down at her blankets, she could still feel the nurse's eyes fixed on her. A sullen silence filled the room. Slowly, Addien picked up the brooch and, without looking up, handed it to her nurse. The nurse accepted it and clasped it tightly in one hand.

"Are you going to tell my father?" Addien whispered.

There was another moment of silence before the nurse responded.

"No," she said. "Not now, anyway. There's no reason to bother him. I'll tell yer mother that the brooch has been found, and that I found you asleep in yer room. But you stay here for the rest of the afternoon, until it's time for the meal. There'll be no more trouble from you today. And no more talk of pixies!"

With that, the woman swept out of the room, knocking the tapestry at the doorway out of her path, and stomping on down the hallway. Addien was left alone in the quietness of her room. A single tear crept down one cheek and disappeared at the corner of her mouth. She sniffed and wiped the dampness away. Her wonderful day had been ruined.

* * *

As is often the way with children, Addien's spirits had quite revived by the time of the great feast that evening. She had played happily in her room with her new toys until her nurse came to dress her for supper. Her birthday dress was as colorful as a garden, embroidered all across the bodice with gold threads in swirling, interlocking designs. Her hair was combed out again and braided with the green ribbons her mother had promised. She even had new shoes to wear, soft leather boots with fur lining to keep the chill of the tile floor away from her toes.

The feast itself was everything she could have wished for. Jugglers and acrobats pranced across the floor. Musicians played on drums and flutes. Then the Chief Bard stood to sing her favorite tale about the king's triumph in the battle of Killarney Springs. As the bard sang, Addien turned to look at her father. He was a large man, with straw-colored hair and a long beard. His red tunic and breeches were crossed with thin gold lines in a traditional plaid pattern. He was whispering something to Queen Morveren, while the Captain of the Guard stood expectantly behind his chair. Then the king rose and quietly exited the room with the Captain. The bard's song continued, but Addien was no long listening. She crept out of the hall after her father, hoping to persuade him not to leave her wonderful party.

Addien followed her father through the door leading to the west wing of the house. The first room along that hall was the King's Court, a large, sparsely furnished room, used for confidential meetings and the bringing of legal disputes before the king. She arrived in the hallway in time to see him stepping into the room, the Captain of the Guard and one other man behind him. The third man she recognized instantly as Lord Balchder, her father's closest friend and companion in arms.

Dark-haired and clean-shaven, Lord Balchder stood in striking contrast to King Brenin, who was several years his senior. Even the clothes that he wore set him apart from the people around him. Instead of the heavy woolen tunics and breaches more suited to the climate, Balchder wore a knee-length Roman-style tunic and a short cape. He shunned the bright colors and patterns worn by the other nobles, preferring black or grey instead. The only things that gave him any color were the gold chain that held his cape around his neck and the cool blue of his eyes.

Addien paused, hoping that he wouldn't see her. She hadn't seen him arrive earlier in the day, and she thought it was quite possible that he wouldn't come at all. Or perhaps she was wishing that he wouldn't come. Addien had long felt a dislike for Lord Balchder, although she couldn't say how it had started. She resented that his name was sung by the bards almost as much as her father's, and he never seemed to come except to take her father away. She had once heard one of the Elders call him arrogant, and although she had never heard the word before she was sure she knew what he meant.

"Princess Addien," Balchder chimed pleasantly, noticing her against the wall, "permit me to offer my best wishes on your special day."

She frowned at him as he continued, "I apologize for stealing your father away. We have important matters to discuss. I'm sure you understand."

She didn't understand, and her tight lips and wrinkled forehead were meant to show it. Balchder knelt down beside her to speak in a low voice.

"I did bring you a present though," he said, reaching into a hidden pocket within his black cape.

Retrieving a small object from the pocket, he held out his hand, fist closed. Slowly, he opened it to reveal a graceful silver ring. Addien stared at it without moving until he took her hand and placed the ring within it. Then he rose quickly and swept into the room, closing the heavily carved door before she had a chance to react. Addien was left in the hall alone and required to return to the feast without her father.

* * *

Later that night, Brenin came to find his daughter in her room. Even in the dim light of a single lamp on the table, Addien could see the creases on his brow and the frown beneath his beard. She wondered if he had been standing in the hallway for very long, listening to her through the tapestry.

"You've been talking with Trevilian again, haven't you?" Brenin asked, as he sat down on the bed. "Telling him what a horrible monster Lord Balchder is?"

Addien scowled at her blankets and said nothing.

"Addien," he said gently, "one of the most important things the daughter of a king must learn is how to keep her own counsel. Listening ears are everywhere, and an untimely word can bring destruction upon a whole house."

He paused and accented his last words with a raised eyebrow. When Addien made no response, he fumbled with a cloth he was holding, placing it on the blanket before her.

"I didn't have a chance earlier," he continued, "to give you your birthday present."

Addien's hurt feelings paled in light of the new gift. Gingerly, she reached for it, pulling back the corners of the cloth to reveal a beautiful gold necklace inside. Oval-shaped gold beads ran the full length of the necklace, interspersed by teardrop pieces inlaid with mother-of-pearl and deep red garnets. At the center of the beadwork hung a round charm of polished gold, embellished with a Christian cross. She gasped at the sight of it and grabbed it up into anxious hands.

"Wait," her father told her, reaching out to touch the center charm. "There's more. I had this made especially for you. There is a secret compartment here, inside the charm. This piece opens on a tiny hinge and then snaps shut again."

Addien watched with wide eyes as he demonstrated the workings of the tiny locket.

"It is for your most secret of thoughts," he said, laying the locket back in her hands, "and for your most secret of friends. You are a young lady now, Addien, and much will be expected from you. It is time to put away childish playthings and no longer speak everything you think or feel."

Although her father had not said his name again, she knew that he was talking about Trevilian. Her habit of speaking to her unseen friend at any time of day, often making blunt and unguarded comments, had begun to annoy even her father. Addien frowned at the gold and garnet necklace and said nothing. After a few moments, her father rose to leave. Still, she looked down, unwilling to meet his strong and commanding gaze. She heard him step into the hall and begin to walk away, softly whistling a merry tune.

Impulsively, she shouted, "Good-night, father!"

His clear voice rang back, without a hint of rebuke, "Good-night, Addien!"

Then she grabbed up the necklace, examining every bit of it and opening and closing the locket, until it was very late and the lamp in her room was nearly out. Laying aside the locket at last, she vowed that from that day on she would never take the necklace off, other than to sleep at night. And the silver ring that Lord Balchder had given her, she threw out of the window to be lost in the branches of the primrose bush.

Chapter Two

Five months later, Morveren was dead.

Winter had descended early that year, sending howling winds and ice-storms well before Christmas, leaving a clutter of fallen roofs, shattered grain-bins, and overturned wagons in its wake. The wind had died down in January, and the city had begun to rebuild. Frozen animals and blighted food stores where thrown out into the streets to be taken away some other time. A stench filled the air as one brutal storm after another forced the people back into their homes, while the refuse of everyday life continued to pile up outside their doors. Then the fever had come. So many families had been stricken by it, and Morveren had gone out into the city to do what she could to help. But the fever had no respect for rank or beauty, and the queen had fallen ill as well.

In her mother's absence, Addien took to following her father everywhere about the house and the royal compound. Together, they would walk and talk for hours at a time. And, when the needs of the kingdom called for his attention, the king never asked his daughter to go away and play or give him time alone with his advisors. He let her stay, sitting on the floor beside his chair in the Great Hall or in the King's Court, half listening to whatever was going on and half daydreaming. When he left the compound to go into the city or away into the countryside, she either went with him or wandered about the garden waiting for his return. And on the late nights when she fell asleep on the floor beside him while he finished some business or other, he carried her off to bed himself, whistling her favorite tune.

She was on the floor of the King's Court where she had fallen asleep one evening when the sound of her own name roused her from her dreams. She lay still with her eyes closed, hoping that whoever had spoken would go away soon and she might have a few moments alone with her father before being put to bed.

"She's asleep," Brenin was saying, his voice low and tired. "Leave her be. She sleeps almost as much on that hard floor as she does in her own bed these days."

"She has lost her mother," a voice replied from across the room.

It was a crisp voice, a soldier's voice, each word marching along in line with perfect precision. Addien drew in a quick breath and was instantly grateful that she was facing the wall away from her father and his visitor. Although she had not seen him since her mother's burial ceremony, she could not mistake his voice. She was in no mood to make polite conversation with any visitor just then, and especially not with Lord Balchder. So she pressed her eyelids closer still and willed her body not to betray the fact that she was now fully awake.

For a long moment there was silence in the room. Addien's legs began to ache from being curled up too long without a stretch, and what had started as a tiny itch on her scalp was growing more insistent and annoying by the moment.

"My king," Balchder began at last, driving forward as if the silence had never intervened. "I don't think that you understand the seriousness of this current threat. The Saxons have already taken over much of the north country and are setting up camps only a few leagues from Glastening."

Brenin replied in slow, measured tones. "I understand the threat perfectly well. And I have every intention of responding to Cormac's call for our assistance."

"Then we are taking our army into Glastening to reinforce their troops?"

"Not we, my friend," came the king's slow response. "Just you."

Another silence filled the room, as Balchder failed to answer.

"The Elders have agreed with me to send our army under your leadership," the king continued. "You know more about commanding an army than anyone on the Island. You were born to it. You have the blood of a Roman Centurion in you, and the men respect you."

"But you are their king," Balchder ground out, with less control than Addien had come to expect from him. "Your place is with your men in battle."

"My place is here!" the king retorted with a fist to the oak table in front of him.

The air shook from the blow to the wood and the strength of his voice, but then it calmed again, leaving the room seeming quieter and colder than it had before.

"I need an heir, Balchder. You know that. There's no one else. My only brother died in infancy. My father's brothers died in battle, and their fathers and uncles and cousins all left with Constantine to die in Brittany in some insane attempt to save the Roman Empire. I'm all that's left of my line, and I have no son."

Beside the wall, forgotten by the two men, Addien shivered and bit down on her lip to keep herself from making any sound. She was glad she could not see her father's face just then, and glad he could not see hers, as one disobedient tear slipped out from under a firmly closed eyelid and slid down to the floor.

"You're going to remarry then?"

Balchder's question was barely audible and received no better answer than a deep sigh.

"It's barely been two months."

"I don't need to be reminded of that," Brenin growled. "I loved Morveren. No one knows that better than you. If she had lived...."

"But she didn't," his friend interrupted, tight control regained. "And now I suppose the Elders are lining up every fertile young maiden in the kingdom for your inspection. What is it that they are so afraid of?"

"Afraid of?" Brenin huffed. "Civil war. Rebellion. The Saxons. What's not to be afraid of? But this is my decision, not theirs. I have made it, and I will not be swayed. I shall stay here and take a bride, and you will lead the army into Glastening and put a stop to the Saxon's encroachment.... And may God grant us both success."

Brenin's chair creaked as he pushed away from the table and rose. The light in the room wavered as the sole lamp on the table was extinguished. Another lamp on the wall went out, then another, and another, as the king made his way to the far side of the room. In the near darkness, Brenin stopped beside his friend.

"There is one more thing," he added, his voice so soft that Addien was forced to turn her head to hear him better. "I want you to take with you more than my blessing when you go."

In the following silence, Addien's curiosity finally overcame her caution, and she rolled over on the floor to where she could just see the chests and heads of the two men over the thick table. On top of the table, cradled in her father's hands, something shiny glowed in the light of the one remaining lamp.

"Your crown?" Balchder whispered, stepping back from the table and the circle of light.

"Not all of it," Brenin responded softly. "The Military Stone. I've decided to have it removed and placed in a smaller crown—a circlet, if you will. With you wearing it, whatever power it contains will go with you into battle."

"I thought you didn't believe in magic," Balchder replied.

Addien could feel Brenin's smile, more than she could see it. She knew what the crown meant to her father, and she was astonished that he wished to alter it in any way.

"Magic or no," the king went on, "it is a symbol of power. It will remind the men of your authority and give them something to follow....You don't approve?"

Even in the dimness, Addien could see the firm set of Balchder's jaw and the crease across his forehead.

"No, I don't," was his simple answer. "But I suppose you have already made up your mind about this as well."

Brenin pushed the crown away toward the center of the table. Leaning down, he pressed his hands into the firm oak and stared at the far wall.

"Let's not argue anymore this evening, my friend," he said. "Tomorrow we will face the troops together and tell them. You will need to leave as soon as possible."

With that, the interview ended. Balchder left the room without another word, while Brenin continued to lean against the table, eyes downcast, lost in thought.

* * *

"Father, tell me again the story of the crown."

Addien had at last been tucked into bed, and her father sat beside her smoothing her tangled hair. Although his fingers continued to move through the thick tresses, pulling one strand free and then another, his eyes were focused somewhere above Addien's head on something she couldn't see.

"The crown?" he mumbled.

"Please?" she whispered, adding a bright smile to her entreaty when his eyes at last lowered to hers.

"The crown," he repeated with a sigh. "It's a long story. Too long, if I tried to tell it like the bards do. But maybe a shorter version will do?"

Addien nodded her assent.

"Well," Brenin began, continuing to run his fingers through his daughter's hair, "a long time ago, long before you or I were born, when the world was young, the Dumnonii people had no king. The people were wild and warlike, always fighting amongst themselves and unable to fight together against their enemies. The elders of the people called out to the wise men, the Druids, and asked what could be done. The Chief Druid told the elders that the people needed a king, that without leadership, the people would each care only for themselves and there would be no peace.

"'What is a king,' the elders asked, 'and how shall we find one?'

"'Give us one year,' the Druids responded. 'We will discover the answer to your questions, and then you will have a king.'

"So the Druids left the land of the Dumnonii," Brenin continued, waving one arm broadly, "and traveled afar to discover what a king should be. One of the priests traveled east across the sea to Gaul where great ships of iron and wood sailed to every known port in the world bringing back jade and silk, gold and silver, and a multitude of spices. The King of Gaul told the priest that trade and commerce make a people great, and therefore a king must have the power to extend his kingdom beyond itself in trade with other nations and peoples.

"A second priest traveled to the Land Under Waves, where the immortals live in halls of coral and pearls. The King Under Waves told the priest that a great people must be a civil people, and therefore a king must have wisdom and discernment and the power of law.

"A third priest went north to the Holy Island, where priestesses once kept the mystical fires of the Druids. The queen of the Holy Island told the priest that respect for the spiritual world makes a people great, and therefore a king must have faith in what he cannot see and bow to power greater than his own.

"A fourth priest traveled to the Kingdom Under the Mountain, where the great warriors of the past gather together. The King Under the Mountain told the priest that greatness is reserved for the fierce and strong, and therefore a king must have the power to lead men into battle without fear.

"And a fifth priest traveled to the Land of Eire, where the Finnians and the Giants once dwelt. The High King of Ireland told the priest that wealth can produce greatness if a king has the power and wit to take what he needs from the people and use it to make them even better.

"And so the five priests returned to the Dumnonii, each bearing a blood-red stone that had been given to them as a reward for certain services rendered. From the King of Gaul came the Commerce Stone. From the King Under Waves came the Law Stone. From the Queen of the Holy Island came the Religion Stone. From the King Under the Mountain came the Military Stone. And from the High King of Ireland came the Tribute Stone. These five stones were set into a crown of gold onto which the Druids etched magical runes to bind together the power of the stones into one mighty talisman."

"Your crown," Addien interjected.

"Yes," Brenin smiled. "This crown has been handed down from the first king of the Dumnonii, from father to son, for many generations. My great-great-grandfather took the crown south across the Tamar River when the Romans first came, until we learned to live with them in peace. It continued to be passed on from father to son even under their dominion, and it was given to me by my father on his deathbed, only two years before you were born."

"And one day you will have a son who will be the next king of Dumnonia."

Addien realized at once that her words had not been wise. The smile faded from Brenin's lips, and his eyes grew weary. Untangling herself from her blankets, Addien sat up and put her arms around her father. His own arms encircled her, as he cuddled her against his chest.

"But no matter how many sons I may have, Addien," he whispered, "you will always have first place in my heart."

"And the first dance with you on May Day?" she asked, peaking up at his face.

"And the first dance on May Day," he answered. "Always."

* * *

The King's House sat at the very center of the city. Renamed Briallen after the Romans left, it was the largest city in the southwest corner of the Island. It was filled with potters, weavers, iron smiths, and farmers who kept small plots of land not far from the city wall. Briallen boasted a great market where people traded pottery for cheese, wool blankets for vegetables, and gold jewelry for daggers and long shields. Sea-traders still traveled to the city from all over the Roman world, and goods could be found in the marketplace from as far away as Alexandria.

A great festival grounds sat outside the city wall, with a huge fire pit in the center and a low stone wall surrounding it, providing seating for the spectators. It was on these grounds two weeks later that the king and his new queen took marriage vows before an assembly of elders, nobility, land-owners, and wealthy merchants. There had been little time for elaborate preparations, or even for new clothes to be made, so Addien wore the brightly embroidered dress that had been made for her last birthday. The gold and garnet necklace that her father had given her hung around her neck, and threads of gold were braided into her hair. In her excitement, the nurse had made the braid tighter than usual, which only added to Addien's discomfort about the whole affair.

The household guard, in long capes of bright blue, stood at attention behind the king and his guests. Noticeably absent was the regiment of red-caped soldiers which normally accompanied the king on important state occasions. They had already left for the northern border along with the rest of the kingdom's soldiers, under the leadership of Lord Balchder. Also noticeably absent was one of the garnet stones from the crown on the king's head. The stones, each at least three-fingers in width, usually encircled the crown and could be seen from quite a distance. If anyone had not already heard the story of how the king had given the Military Stone to Lord Balchder, they probably heard about it that day.

It was only one week before May Day. Although Addien had been only five the previous May Day, she held a vivid memory of the day, and she had been schooled in the meaning and traditions of the celebration. It was when the Celts had traditionally celebrated the New Year, before the Romans had imposed their own calendar on the Island kingdoms. In each town or territory, it was the highest ranking woman who declared the beginning of the festival and welcomed the coming of spring. All household fires were extinguished that day, and re-lit at the end of the day from a single torch born by the appointed lady, who represented the giver of life. In Briallen, that had been Morveren's place. When she closed her eyes, Addien could still see her mother, long red hair streaming unbound to her waist, dressed all in green with a circle of gold around her head, holding up a great torch from which many other torches would be lit and passed on to the waiting crowds.

May Day had been their special day for as long as Addien could remember—Morveren shining in all her glory, the center of everyone's attention, Brenin standing behind her, eyes wide with appreciation for his beautiful and graceful wife, and Addien in her own crown of oak leaves and twigs, waiting patiently for the music to begin and for her father to sweep her off her feet and twirl her around and around into the center of the festival grounds.

It was a time to think of new life and new beginnings.

"But I don't want a new beginning," Addien whispered to herself as the wedding ceremony ended and the crowd erupted into enthusiastic applause.

Within moments, the king and his bride had moved from the center of the festival grounds to a row of tables where meats, breads and sweets had been set out for the wedding guests. The king lifted a large cup and led the guests in a toast. Another round of applause followed, which was then replaced by the trilling of pipes and the beat of drums.

But Addien, forgotten for the time, wandered alone to the far side of the grounds. Finding a patch of cool grass beneath a lone tree, she sat down, clutching the charm of her gold and garnet necklace, and cried.

Chapter Three

"Stop pulling at it, Addien. You're going to pull out all of the stitching."

The king's new bride was a young woman with auburn hair and pretty dimples. She had little of the grace and maturity that Morveren had displayed, but she had quickly endeared herself to the servants and taken her place as the new mistress of the King's House. To Addien, she was little more than a nuisance, to be avoided whenever possible. But as her father spent more and more time away from the house, she had little choice but to endure the company of the new queen.

"It's too stiff," Addien complained, tugging at the frilly neck line of an elaborate linen gown.

The queen smiled patiently and set the child's hands at her sides. The deep purple of the gown did little for Addien's fair complexion, and she could barely move in the tight lines of the skirt, but the queen took no notice.

"You're just not used to such a grown-up gown," she said. "Why don't you wear it awhile until the material loosens up a bit. Your father will be home soon, and I want him to see you in it. May Day is only a week away. I want you to look your best for the festival."

It was another May Day, a full year after the king's wedding day. His new wife had fulfilled every expectation and hope, and her dimpled cheeks glowed with pride as her belly swelled beneath her dress more every day. In two months time, the queen would bear her first child, and prayers were said daily that it would be a son—an heir to the great kingdom of Dumnonia.

Addien had no hope of dissuading the queen once she had made up her mind about something, and she was left with orders to remain in her fancy purple dress until her father had seen and approved of it. The queen retired to her room to rest, and Addien dropped back upon her own bed, too constrained by the yards of purple cloth to return to her normal activities.

A short while later, she heard the horn blast that signaled her father's return to the house. Rising carefully from the bed, so as not to wrinkle the dress, Addien looked over at the large wooden chest that sat against the bedroom wall. Her gold and garnet necklace lay draped over one end, dropped there carelessly when her step-mother helped her change into the gown. In the year and a half since she had received it, the necklace had become smaller about her neck, but she still wore it everyday. Feeling the heavy lace ruffles around her neck, she discovered a new reason to dislike the dress—the necklace wouldn't fit over it. Sighing, she reminded herself that she only had to wear the dress a little while longer that day and then not again until the May Day celebration. So she left her necklace upon the chest and went out drearily to find her father.

The king was standing just inside the main door to the Great Hall. He had apparently been accosted by one of his advisors as soon as he stepped in from the garden. His deep voice echoed off the walls of the huge room.

"What do you mean he's bringing the whole army with him?" he bellowed. "I sent word twice that he should disband the army and release the men to their homes. It is already planting time, and it will be difficult enough to prepare the fields after so many of them lay fallow last year."

The king's advisor responded in a low tone, bowing repeatedly, attempting to appease the king's anger. The king ignored him and bellowed at another servant in the Hall.

"Send me a messenger at once!" he ordered. Then back to his advisor, "I want those men sent home!"

At this point, Addien was close enough to hear the advisor's response. Still bobbing up and down in little conciliatory bows, the man droned on in his self-important manner.

"There have been reports that Lord Balchder has become very proud," he said. "He has taken credit for the army's glorious victory over the Saxons."

"Of course he's taking credit," the king interrupted impatiently. "He's the commander of the army, the one that led them to that 'glorious victory.'"

"Perhaps," the man pressed on, "he is expecting some fitting tribute to his accomplishments. It may be his intent to march the troops through Briallen as a display of his success."

The king sighed.

"Then let him get on with it and then send those men to their homes," he said, trying to shoulder past the older man.

"Sire," the man continued, stepping once again before the king. His voice dropped and his eyes darted about the room for unwelcome ears. "A proud man with an army at his back, returning to the grateful acclaim of another man's kingdom, can be a very dangerous thing."

Brenin froze in his tracks and glared at the old man. His arms tensed, as if he was struggling to keep them at his sides. He drew a deep breath before responding between clenched teeth.

"Never again in my presence question the loyalty of Lord Balchder," he growled. "It was you and the rest of the Elders who convinced me to give him this commission. You wanted someone else to guard our borders while I remained at home. He did everything you asked of him, but you eye him suspiciously because he did it a little better than you expected. Well, if it's a show of appreciation that Balchder wants, it's a show he can have. And you can be the one to go out and tell him!"

The king motioned to the messenger who had been waiting nearby for his orders.

"Take Sarrug with you and ride to Lord Balchder's camp outside of the city," he commanded the young man. "Tell him that the city awaits his arrival with great expectation. When you learn of his plans, return and tell me. I myself will welcome him and his men at the city gate."

With one last withering look at Sarrug, Brenin marched out of the Hall. It was a few moments before Addien remembered her purpose and hastened after him. But she was too late. The door to the King's Court was already closed, and she had promised never to enter there unless the door was open. She had also promised to wear that ridiculous dress until her father had a chance to see it. So she sat down against the wall in the hallway and stared at the strange, interlocking beasts carved into the door, no longer caring about wrinkling the dress.

The moments passed slowly and quietly in the hall. Morning chores had been finished, and most of the servants were in the kitchen area, preparing the midday meal. Muffled voices from the King's Court escaped under the thick door, telling Addien that her father was not alone. She was beginning to think about returning to her room, when a commotion in the Great Hall made her wonder if the door at last was about to be opened.

The door into the hallway from the Great Hall flew open in the haste of the young man who barreled through it. Breathlessly, he stumbled to the door of the King's Court and demanded entrance. It was one of the king's messengers, but not the one that had been sent to Lord Balchder's camp. The door opened and Addien sprung through it in the messenger's wake. The king and the Captain of the Guard, who had been the other occupant of the room, took no notice of her but turned their attention to the messenger instead.

"Sire," he gasped, trying to catch his breath, "I have just come from the East Road. Lord Balchder has set up camp there within view of the city walls."

"We are aware of that," the king snapped. "I have already sent word that Lord Balchder may enter the city whenever he is ready."

"Sire," the man began again, wide-eyed with the weight of his message, "your messenger is dead. Elder Sarrug, too. Lord Balchder's men slew them without warning, before they had time to present your message."

Brenin whirled around and faced the poor messenger, who shrunk back from his look. A red tide swelled up over the king's face, and his eyes narrowed. For one long, tense moment, everyone else in the room held their breath, waiting for the explosion. But none came. Without a word, Brenin turned and stormed out of the room toward the Great Hall. The Captain of the Guard and the messenger followed swiftly behind him, while Addien crept along still further behind, hugging the wall like a frightened mouse.

Half-way across the Great Hall, the king was stopped again. Two guards came flying into the room from the garden, shouting their dark tidings. Townsfolk followed on their heels, crying out for attention. Servants, advisors, and household guards streamed into the room from every door, responding to the uproar. In all the confusion, Addien gathered that Lord Balchder's men held the East Road and were turning back anyone who attempted to leave the city. In addition to the king's messenger and Elder Sarrug, two other men had been killed, both soldiers guarding the East Gate. The small military force that was in Briallen had already been called together and was heading to the gate to defend it.

"Not the East Gate!" a voice called out from the crowd. "The North Gate! There is a legion of armed men approaching from the north and turning back all who attempt to go out that way."

The clamor of voices grew into a roar, but one voice could still be heard above them all. Pushing his way through the clinging townsfolk, Brenin shouted orders to anyone who would listen.

"Get these people out of here!" he yelled. "Everyone—go to your homes and stay there! If you offer the soldiers no resistance they will have no cause to harm you."

As the crowd began to thin a bit, the king fought his way over to the Captain of the Guard. In a lower voice, his orders continued.

"You've got to get your men back here at once. Balchder knows there aren't enough armed men in Briallen to defend both gates. We have to place all of our defenses around the House and hope that the townsfolk have the good sense to stay out of the way."

The Captain turned at once and strode to the door, yelling a few commands of his own to the soldiers in the Hall. Royal servants escorted townsfolk out the door, and, slowly, the din in the room lessened. Standing alone in the middle of the room, Addien's father remained motionless for a moment. Then he turned and started for the hallway door. He stopped when he saw his daughter, cowering behind the high-backed chairs of the royal table. He came and knelt beside her, placing his large, strong hands on her shoulders.

"Don't worry," he said gently. "We'll get through this somehow. Just stay inside the house and you'll be safe."

She looked into his steel grey eyes and attempted a timid smile. But in all the years she had known and loved her father, it was the first time she had ever suspected him of lying to her.

The lull did not last long. Only moments after the king retrieved his sword and returned to the Great Hall, shouting was heard again in the garden. The guards had been routed at the gate and were falling back to the King's House. Balchder's soldiers were in hot pursuit. The king ran to the door to survey his position, shouting for his Captain.

"The west wing!" he yelled, waving wildly in that direction. "Place your defenses at the west wing!"

The west wing, of course, was where the king and queen had their rooms and where the queen had retired some time earlier. Addien knew enough from the old stories she had heard to realize that the queen would be as much of a target as her father if Balchder intended to seize control of the kingdom. Her unborn child posed as much of a threat to him as the king himself, and Balchder's apparent plan could not succeed until they both were dead.

The clashing of metal swords and daggers could be heard distinctly in the garden. Addien remained in the Great Hall, riveted to her spot. Suddenly the garden door flew open wide under the force of fighting men. Royal guards in blue capes stumbled onto the tiled floor of the Great Hall as red-caped soldiers pushed past them. More guards engaged them from behind, and the clanging of iron swords and bronze shields echoed off the high ceiling.

After a moment, Addien could see her father in the midst of the fray. He thrust his way through the tangle of bodies and weapons to gain the open ground inside the Hall. His Captain still at his side, the two men turned again to face the enemy until a new alarm diverted their attention. From the hallway, screaming could be heard and a desperate cry for help.

"The west wing!" Brenin cried out in dismay. "It's been breached!"

The king and his Captain vaulted across the room toward the hallway door. Hardly breaking his stride, Brenin grabbed the arm of his daughter as he passed her and pulled her into the hall with him.

"Go into the Court and stay there," he ordered, pushing her toward the door.

She obeyed without a second thought, too afraid to watch him as he ran on down the hall.

The door of the King's Court was one of the largest and thickest in the house. It was also one of the few doors that could be locked. The heavy metal hinges squealed as Addien shoved the door shut behind her. Then she grabbed frantically for the long board that could be placed between two metal posts to bar the door. She struggled to lift the board and then let it fall into place with a thud.

Backing away from the door, Addien realized that she was alone. Outside in the hall, the sounds of the battle drew ever nearer. She clasped her hands over her ears and wished for the noise to stop. It did not. She turned away from the door and waited.

"Addien! Addien!"

A pounding at the door brought her back to her senses. The Captain of the Guard was calling her, hammering upon the door. As quickly as she could she pushed the heavy board out of its posts, dropping it to the floor in her haste. The door flew open from the Captain's weight. He stumbled into the room, bleeding from the arm and neck. Behind him, the king staggered in, holding back a river of blood that flowed from his stomach. He stepped toward her, opening his mouth to speak. Then he fell, crashing to the floor like a stone statue. The gold crown upon his head flew off from the force of the fall, rolling to a halt a few feet from his outstretched arm. Addien stared at him in horror and disbelief.

The Captain of the Guard managed to close the door again and drop the board into place just as the enemy reached it. Pounding and shouting were soon replaced by a new sound—the splintering of wood from the blow of an ax. The creaking of the door shook Addien into awareness again. The Captain took up his sword and stood expectantly before the door. Then he looked at the only other door to the room. Hidden behind a tapestry, a tiny servants' door led to a narrow hallway that ran behind the Great Hall to the kitchen area.

"The crown, Addien," he whispered urgently. "Take the crown and go. You must find a place to hide it where Balchder will never find it."

She stood motionless, still staring at her father.

"Addien, the crown!" he implored.

Breaking free from the terror that held her, she raced across the room, scooped up the crown in her arms and held it close. For one last moment, she looked at her father, tears streaming down her face. Then she turned and ran from the room, into the darkness of the unlit hallway, and away from the terrible sounds of pounding axes and splintering wood.

At the far end of the hallway she slowed to a cautious walk. There was no door at that end of the hall, only a left turn into the hallway of the east wing. She listened carefully for awhile, trying to calm her racing heart and still her sobs. As her breathing slowed and the tears no longer clouded her view, Addien realized that she hadn't much time to act. The door to the King's Court would soon be breached, and the Captain could not long hold back the invaders. They would find the servants' door and find her still standing there if she did not take some action.

Looking back down the hall, Addien wondered briefly if the queen was dead. She couldn't imagine her father leaving her if she wasn't. And he had left, retreating to the King's Court with his last measure of strength. That was a memory she couldn't bear to face, so she shook off the dreadful thoughts and concentrated on her immediate problem.

She needed to hide. Or run away. But the sounds of soldiers fighting and dying were all around her. They would search for her, she was sure. And if not for her, they would search for the crown. Where could she go to find someone to help her?

"Trevilian," she whispered, suddenly struck with an idea. "Trevilian can help me. If only I can reach him."

Peering cautiously around the corner, Addien assured herself that no one was within sight. The sounds of fighting and the screams of the wounded and frightened could be heard from the Great Hall. But if she could just get past the door without being seen, she could make it back to her own room. She had not only herself to think about, but the crown as well. And she knew just what to do with it. If only she could get up enough courage to step into the hallway and run!

* * *

To the north of the city, the land rose gradually to a tree-lined ridge that provided an excellent view of the city walls. A solitary man sat tall on a great roan horse, unmoving against the greying horizon. A bronze circlet wrapped itself around his head, narrow in the back and widening in the front to house one large blood-red stone. A dark cape was flung back over his shoulders, revealing a grey tunic beneath, only partially covering arms and legs which were muscular and tanned. The man's face was equally tanned, but so rigid that it might have been made from stone instead of flesh. One long, grey line ran down the left side of his face, from the hairline over his eye to just above his ear, the only flaw in an otherwise perfect figure.

Another man approached on horseback, a red-caped soldier with a long sword slapping against his boot.

"Lord Balchder," the man called, matching a salute to his words.

The man on the roan horse nodded, without ever taking his eyes off of the city below.

"You have a report?" Balchder asked.

"Yes, sir," the soldier replied. "I'm sorry, sir. I still cannot report success."

"You haven't found it?"

They were only words, but the soldier grasped the horse's reins and backed away as if he had been threatened by something more.

"No, sir," the man answered, tightening his knees around his mount. "He had the crown when he was cut down, we're sure of that. Somehow it disappeared after he got into the King's Court."

Balchder took a deep breath and then slowly turned his gaze to the soldier.

"Nothing disappears," he growled. "Someone took it."

"Yes, my lord," the soldier agreed in a tight nod. "We'll keep looking. The whole city is blockaded. No one will get past us."

"See that they don't."

Balchder's gaze returned to the city, now fading into the mists of twilight. The soldier waited and watched him.

"Sir."

The soldier coughed, then waited again until his commander turned back to him.

"Will you be going into the city now? It's been two days since Brenin died. The King's House is yours to claim."

For a long moment, Balchder sat quite still, looking past the man at the distant horizon. Then he turned to look back at the city. The skin over his cheekbones stretched as he clenched his jaws together, and a tiny blood vein hammered beneath the scar on his forehead.

"I will enter Briallen when I have Brenin's crown on my head," he replied at length in a voice as glassy as his eyes. "I will be king in every way. I will have the kingdom, and the city, and the house, and whatever else I choose. But first, I will have the crown."

Balchder's right arm shot up into the air, as if in defiance of the irony of his fate, but then came down on his horse's rump in a purely practical gesture. The horse vaulted forward, turning her head toward a small camp outside the city walls. The soldier watched them go. Then, leaving a respectable distance between himself and his commander, he followed.

Chapter Four

The day had been cold and misty. A thick layer of clouds lay over the canyon threatening at any moment to open up and send down a torrent of rain. The sheep could sense the impending storm and stood huddled against each other beside the canyon wall. The river that ran down the middle of the canyon could rise quickly when the water began to fall, making it a dangerous place for the slow-moving and slow-witted sheep, so their shepherdess had gathered them into their pen at the first sign of the storm.

Although it was only a few weeks after the festival of Saint Valentine, it was already too warm for snow. But the rain could easily turn to ice, and the girl didn't want to be out in it. Pulling her cloak tighter about her, she finished checking the wood railing that kept the sheep on the higher ground next to the cliff wall. Then she filled a water trough and unbaled some of the dried grasses that were kept for winter feeding, placing the grass all around the pen so that the stronger animals wouldn't prevent the weaker ones from eating. From the look of the sky, she guessed that they would have to stay penned up for the rest of the day, and she wanted to make sure that they had everything they needed.

Gennes was tall and fair, despite her daily exposure to the sun. A long braid of dark red hair ran down the back of her wool cloak. Roughly eighteen years of age, she was old enough to tend the sheep by herself, even for long winter spells. She enjoyed the solitude of the little canyon, with its tall leafless trees and high grasses. The river that shared the canyon ran from the center of the moor all the way to the sea, but it was usually slow and shallow at this point and gentle enough for the sheep to drink from it. If Gennes stood at the very edge of the river looking south, she could just see the walls of the St. Petroc monastery, clinging to the side of the steep valley. It was half a day's walk up the slopes to the monastery, and nearly as far in the other direction to the place where her family kept a permanent home. In the canyon, she was alone, and the protection of the sheep was her responsibility.

Even above the rising howl of the wind, Gennes heard the distinctive clip-clop of hoof-beats on the rocky slope of the canyon, and it wasn't the plodding footfalls of a moorland pony, either, but the striking beats of a riding horse. Men on horseback rarely came to that part of the country, and she couldn't imagine why anyone would be journeying on the moor on a day such as that. With great interest, she left the shelter of the cliff wall and walked toward the river, watching the rocky pathway that led from the moor down into the canyon.

At last the horse appeared as the pathway turned the final bend toward the canyon floor. When she first saw it, Gennes thought that the horse had no rider. Then she realized that someone was hunched over the animal, clinging to its mane. Whoever it was who had disturbed her solitude, he appeared to be injured. Gennes ran to the man to assist him, intending to help him from his horse and determine if he was sick or wounded. But as she drew near him, she could hear another sound. Higher on the path behind the man, more horses were approaching, at a much faster pace. The first man turned and looked back up the path, wincing in his pain. Struggling to push himself up in the saddle, he cast about him for something—a hiding place perhaps! Thinking quickly, Gennes motioned him toward a row of tall bushes across the river. He spurred his horse toward it and disappeared only moments before the sound of thundering hooves exploded into the canyon.

Five men galloped down the pathway onto the gravel bank of the river. Each wore a cape of dark red over black breeches and tall boots. Two of the men carried long spears, and one of the others carried a sword in his hand and a nasty scowl on his face. A swift pain in the pit of her stomach took Gennes' breath away. They were soldiers—Balchder's men. She knew it in an instant, though such men seldom came onto the land of her master, the Lord of Trevelgue. When they did come, they brought nothing but trouble, and Gennes had always reacted to them in the same, gut-wrenching way.

As the red-caped men pulled their horses to a stop at the river's edge, Gennes fought back the wave of nausea which threatened to overwhelm her. Ordering her limbs to obey, she walked over to the men with what she hoped was an air of mild curiosity.

"Have you seen someone ride through here?" the soldier nearest her barked. "Was there another rider that passed this way?"

Pausing, so as not to seem too anxious, she regarded the man in feigned awe. Then she pointed down the canyon where the river disappeared beyond a bend in the rock wall.

"He went downstream," she responded in her most timid voice.

As the soldiers scanned the valley, she added helpfully, "There is a monastery ahead. Perhaps he is going there to escape the storm."

She pointed again, this time at the high stone walls that peered down from the hill just over the next bend.

"The path is after the second bend in the river," she told them.

Without a word of thanks, the soldiers spurred their horses onward, splashing through the river, and rounding the bend a few moments later. Gennes returned to casually tending the sheep until the last muffled thud of distant hoof-beats faded away. Then, when she was sure it was safe, she ran to the bushes where the injured man had hidden and found him lying motionless among the tall, damp grasses.

The man was hardly a man at all, although no longer a mere youth. From his tousled, rust-colored hair and fair skin, Gennes guessed he was no older than herself. He was bleeding heavily from a deep cut on his arm. The straight edges of the slash across his sleeve suggested that he had been cut by a knife—or a sword. Whatever the cause of his wound, she knew that it needed attention quickly, or it was possible that the young man would bleed to death. Removing her cloth belt, Gennes unwound it and wrapped it tightly around his arm. Then she attempted to lift him to take him to her little hut against the canyon wall.

Rousing somewhat, the stranger was able to walk a little. Together they struggled to reach the lean-to made of thick branches and thatched grasses that Gennes called her winter home. Once in the hut, Gennes placed him on her straw-filled sleeping mat and removed his damp cloak and muddy boots. She covered him in coarse blankets and then went back out to find a safe hiding place and some water for his horse. Standing by the river, she listened carefully for any sound of the soldiers returning. The wind had dropped, and all was quiet except for the soft bleating of the sheep and the small sounds of the river lapping against its banks. The calm before the storm had begun, and the rain would not be long in coming.

Returning to her hut, Gennes looked at the young man lying so still on her rude mat on the ground. Even in the dimness of her tiny hut, his face appeared white and nearly lifeless. Blood seeped into the cloth she had wound around his arm. Too much blood. She wondered if he would survive.

Unexpectedly, he moved, struggling for consciousness. Eyelids fluttered, and his good arm grasped the ground beside him. With his jaw clenched against the pain, he rolled to his uninjured side and attempted to rise.

"The soldiers," he mumbled in his struggle. "I have to get away."

Gennes knelt beside him. She laid her hands on his shoulders and eased him back down onto the mat.

"The soldiers are gone," she assured him. "They're looking for you on the hill. They won't come back this way at least until tomorrow."

"It's too dangerous," he protested in a rough whisper. "I shouldn't stay here."

"You don't have any choice. You're injured and too weak to travel. I'm not afraid of the soldiers, and I'll make sure that they don't find you here. You can trust me."

His eyes opened to tiny slits. Blue, she guessed, glimpsing only a hint of color behind blunt red lashes. Wider still they opened, taking in her face, her hair, her eyes. Mostly her eyes.

"They're trying to stop me," he groaned between clenched teeth. "They want to stop us all. But they can't. We have to find it before they do. We have to find the king's crown."

Exhausted at last by this revelation, the nameless young man yielded himself to the mat and blankets. His eyes closed, and his features lost all expression. But he breathed still.

For a long moment, Gennes did not.

Outside, the wind was gaining strength again and the pattering of the first heavy raindrops began. The dim light in the hut faded as the storm arrived in full force. Sheets of rain pounded on the thatch roof, blocking out even the bleating of the sheep penned against the canyon wall. But Gennes heard none of it. The pounding she heard was not the sound of rain, but the crash of an ax against a thick wooden door. The chill she felt was not from the wind, but from the sensation of marble tiles beneath her knees. And the man she saw before her was not the stranger she had helped, but another man, lying so still, soaked in his own blood.

The king. The last king of Dumnonia. And his crown was in her arms.

* * *

Gennes had no idea how much time had passed before the dreadful vision faded. She roused from it as if from a deep sleep, uncertain of what she had seen had been real or only a dream. Shaking the last of the apparition from her head, she covered herself in her cloak and hood and went out to check on the sheep. The splattering of cold raindrops on her cheeks brought her mind back to the present and her unusual situation. The rain had started sooner than she had expected, and she could only hope that the soldiers would make it to the monastery and remain there. There would be no reason for them to return, since the rain would wash away any tracks left by the fugitive they were seeking. Looking up at the clouds that she had been scowling at all morning, she said a prayer of thanksgiving and then returned to her hut.

The rain continued all through the day and into the evening. Gennes lit a small fire at the door of the hut and sat beside the sleeping stranger, eating a simple evening meal. That night she slept fitfully, tossed between dark dreams and even darker awakenings. She rose with the first soft light of morning and sat beside the stranger until he stirred. After checking his wound, she heated some porridge for their breakfast, while her visitor carefully pulled himself to a sitting position and leaned against the rough tree limbs that made up the wall.

"Tell me your name," he said, shifting his weight away from his injured arm.

Unaccustomed to being alone with a stranger, Gennes felt a need for caution. Turning from the fire, she set his bowl before him and then withdrew the short distance to the far wall of the hut.

The stranger smiled.

"I won't hurt you," he said. "I promise. Even if I could move, which I'm not sure that I can right now."

He grimaced as he again shifted his sitting position.

"My name is Gennes," she said quietly, trying to draw his attention away from his pain. "My family calls me Gennie."

Smiling again, he reached for the bowl with his good arm.

"Thank you, Gennie," he said, with a hungry look at the steaming porridge. "You saved my life, you know."

She smiled in return and looked down at her own breakfast. There were so many things that she wanted to ask him, so much she wanted to know. But the stranger was obviously hungry and not yet ready to talk. So they sat in silence while he devoured two full helpings of the porridge and all of the dried meat that she had in the hut. After quenching his thirst with cool water that she brought from the river, he finally seemed ready to talk.

"I'm Colin," he said, smiling again as if they were old friends. "I've never been in this part of the kingdom before. Thanks to you, I may live long enough to leave it."

He paused for a moment, as if expecting her to answer, but then went on again.

"I'm trying to reach the castle of Lord Trevelgue, but I've gotten off my path. Can you tell me how I can get there?"

Gennes was amazed at his casual manner. It was quite obvious that, if he had gotten off his path, it wasn't by accident. He had been chased off of it by five armed and angry men, one whom had apparently tried to kill him.

"You aren't far," she answered at length. "The lord's castle sits between two rivers to the west of here. If you cross the moor, it's a half-day's ride, but you can easily get lost that way. When you're ready to ride, I can take you downstream and show you a better way from there."

"I'm ready to ride now," he said, trying to rise.

"You can't!"

She crossed to him swiftly and grabbed him by his good arm. Still weak from loss of blood, the effort to move had obviously been too much for him. He collapsed back against the wall, stifling a cry of pain.

"You can't move yet," Gennes said. "You're far too weak. Besides, what if the soldiers are there waiting for you?"

For a long moment Colin stared at her, as if trying to make sense out of what she had said.

"What makes you think they would wait for me at Trevelgue's castle?" he asked.

His eyes had narrowed, and his tone had been colder, even suspicious.

"You're in the middle of nowhere," Gennes said, answering cautiously. "Other than St. Petroc's monastery, there's nothing beyond here but the sea. Trevelgue is the master of all the land here, from the beginning of the moor to the sea and west to the Tamar River. Who else would you be going to see?"

Colin leaned his head back against the wall and stared at the roof, firmly woven of sticks and dried grass. He remained that way, deep in thought, for quite awhile before he looked at her again and smiled.

"Then I guess I'll stay," he said with a sigh. "But if anyone comes looking for me, you have to promise to stay out of the way. You can't try to help me again."

Gennes looked back at him with all the determination she could muster.

"No," she said. "I won't promise that."

Then she rose and went out to care for the sheep.

* * *

All that day, Gennes divided her time between the sheep and her guest. For all he had been through, Colin was a pleasant companion and eager to talk about himself.

"I've lived in Briallen all my life," he told her. "But it's changed. It's not the place it was when I was a child."

"Tell me what it is like," Gennes asked, anxious to hear about the great walled city of the last king.

"It's a Roman city, of course," he answered. "Most of the old buildings are still standing, but a lot of them are unused now. People that come from outside the city prefer the old ways, so they build their round huts right beside the Roman halls. I still remember when I was little seeing the great house where the king lived and the Roman Hall, before they were deserted. Now the King's House sits empty, with all the windows boarded closed. You can't even see it unless you know it's there. So many people lost their land to Balchder's soldiers these last ten years that the city is packed with makeshift huts. Balchder doesn't seem to care, as long as no one goes inside the King's House itself."

"Where does Lord Balchder live?" Gennes asked, surprised that she had never heard this news.

"At Cleddyf Castle, overlooking the northern sea," was the answer.

"Not in Briallen?"

"He has soldiers and allies all over the city, but he never visits there. Without King Brenin's crown, he has never been able to gain enough support from the nobles or the freemen to declare himself king. He just sits in his dark castle while his soldiers roam the kingdom looking for the crown."

"The crown," Gennes echoed, suddenly picturing again the strange vision of a dead king and a shiny crown in her arms.

"Balchder has the Military Stone, but he still needs the other four stones of the crown," Colin continued, apparently unaware that his audience was now barely listening. "The nobles and landowners refuse to pay tribute to him. Trade in and out of the kingdom has come to a standstill, and the people turn to the local nobility to solve their problems, since there is no king. If not for the threat of Balchder's army, Dumnonia might well have been carved into a number of petty kingdoms by now, ruled by the strongest of the nobles."

Leaning forward on his uninjured arm, Colin narrowed the little distance between himself and Gennes and recaptured her full attention.

"But not everyone is afraid of Balchder," he added with a hard gleam in his eyes. "Some of us in the city have joined together to fight the soldiers. Oh, I don't mean we've had any battles with them—yet. There are too many of them, and still too few of us. But we get in their way whenever we can. We help the people that the soldiers victimize. And we watch them, mostly to make sure that they don't find the crown. And our numbers are growing every day."

As Colin spoke, Gennes' eyes grew wide and she could feel her heart pounding in her chest. She tried to take a breath, to make some answer, but her throat had suddenly gone dry. But Colin didn't wait for an answer.

"That's why I was going to see Lord Trevelgue," he continued in a lower voice. "We need to know which nobles will support us in our fight. Someone has to stand up to Balchder and take the kingdom back, even if we never find the crown!"

"Let me go!" Gennes said suddenly, the words squeaking out through a tightened throat. "I can take your message to Lord Trevelgue."

Colin stared at her through wide eyes, his mouth dropping open in an unspoken reply.

"My father will be here tomorrow with supplies," Gennes continued quickly. "He can stay with you and watch the sheep. If I take your horse, I can reach Trevelgue and be back in a day. Let me take the message, Colin."

Colin looked at her for a long moment before answering. Finally, he shook his head and smiled.

"Trevelgue can wait a few days," he said. "I'll take the message. But you should be a member of our little group in Briallen. We could use someone like you."

* * *

Colin stayed with Gennes the better part of a week. Although both Gennes and her father, Evin, offered again to take his message to Lord Trevelgue, he insisted on delivering it himself as soon as he possibly was able. When, at last, he mounted his horse and left, Gennes felt as if she saying good-bye to a cherished friend.

"If you ever come to Briallen, look for me at the old Roman Hall," he told her. "I can't thank you enough for everything you've done for me. I'm going to miss you, Gennie."

"And I, you," she replied, waving to him as he turned his horse to follow Evin, who was taking him downstream to see him safely on his way.

Evin had remained at the hut with Gennes ever since he had arrived and found a strange man sleeping in his daughter's bed. Colin had offered to sleep outside with his horse, but Gennes was able to convince Evin that her visitor was trustworthy. At least, Evin trusted him enough not to throw him out of the hut, but not enough to return to his own place leaving Gennes and Colin alone together. Gennes smiled at the thought of it, and sat with the sheep waiting for Evin to return.

* * *

"He's a handsome young man," Evin mused, sitting beside a small fire that evening with Gennes.

The sky was clear, and the stars shone above the canyon walls like a river of light. Gennes stared at the stars without answering until Evin reached out and touched her on the arm.

"Your friend, Colin," he began again, "he's a friendly sort of man."

Gennes turned to her father and smiled.

"He is," she agreed, before turning her gaze back to the stars. "He's from Briallen."

Evin sat quietly beside his daughter for a long moment.

"Briallen is a long journey from here," he said at last.

Gennes turned to look at him again. Even in the dimness of firelight and starlight, she could see his faint smile and a crinkle of laugh lines around his eyes. She hadn't noticed before how much of his brown hair had been turning to silver or how deep the lines around his mouth and eyes had been etched.

"Don't look at me like that," he laughed. "Your mother and I can get along if you decide to go away. We never thought that you would stay with us forever."

"Go away?" Gennes echoed, wondering if Evin had been reading her mind. She had been thinking about going away, ever since the first day Colin came—and with him came the dreadful vision of a dead king and a shining crown. There had been a restlessness inside her ever since, pushing and pulling, forward and back, telling her there was something that she needed to do. If only she knew what it was.

"Father," she began after a long silence, "do you remember how you first found me?"

Evin looked into the fire and grinned.

"I could hardly forget that, now could I?" he replied. "It was up on the moor, inside the circle of standing stones. We were moving the sheep to new pasture grounds for the summer, your mother and I. We had always stayed away from the stones before, but some of the sheep had strayed. I found you curled up under one of the stones, half dead from hunger and cold. I never thought you would survive, but you proved to be stronger than you looked."

The two exchanged a loving look before Evin turned his attention back to the fire.

"Your mother, she thought you were an answer to her prayers—her not being able to have children all those years. She wanted so badly to have you as her own little girl."

"*Bachgennes*," Gennes whispered.

"Yes, our own little Gennie. No one ever came looking for you. And later we found out that an entire village by the coast had been wiped out by the fever. I don't know how you could have traveled so far, a child all alone, but Anna had family there, and she told everyone that you were the child of her cousin, lost to the fever. And in time, you just became ours."

"Have I ever said 'thank you' for saving my life and taking me in?" Gennes asked with a grin.

"Probably not," Evin replied.

Scooting closer to him, Gennes threw her arms around him. With a soft laugh, she rested her head on his shoulder, and together the two stared into the fire.

"Will Anna be very sad if I decide to leave?" Gennes asked at length.

"She will. But she will also be happy for you. You're not our *bach-gennes* any longer. It's time for you to make a life for yourself."

Gennes squeezed her adopted father closer to her and sat in companionable silence until the fire died down and it was time to go into the hut for the night.

Chapter Five

Colin had been gone for more than a month before Gennes finally made up her mind to leave. Without knowing why, she was certain that she needed to go to Briallen. There were answers waiting there to questions she didn't know how to ask. But before she could go to the city of the king, there was someplace else she had to go to first.

The day had been fair when she started out from Evin and Anna's round hut at the edge of the moor. She wore her old brown cloak, as it was the easiest way to carry it. The remainder of her belongings—a few changes of clothing, a blanket, a water skin, and some food—she carried inside a wool bag with a bright metal clasp which she slung over her shoulder. She stopped for a midday meal under the cover of some budding trees in a little valley before setting out onto the highest part of the moor. Briallen was to the northeast, but the path she took led due north and then west, across the very center of the high moor.

The rolling moor was covered in yellow-green grasses, in some places as high as Gennes' knees. There were no trees or bushes as far as the eye could see, only a bank of dark clouds in the distance. There were no signs or roads to lead her to her destination, only some vague directions from Evin and a little intuition. By mid-afternoon, she was foot-sore and tired and afraid that she might be hopelessly lost. But still she walked, looking for the circle of standing stones where Evin had found her such a long time ago.

When she first caught sight of the stones, Gennes could do nothing but stand and stare. In a great circle running around the center of a round hilltop stood more than a dozen grey stones pushing up out of the earth as if they had grown there. Each one was taller than a man with his arms stretched above him. They were not entirely smooth or entirely straight, but more resembling huge teeth plucked out of some great monster and planted there as a memorial. But whether true stones or the remains of some beast, they could not possibly have been placed there by mortal hands.

"This is it," Gennes whispered to herself as she walked slowly toward the stones. "This is where my new life began—and my old one ended."

On silent feet, she approached the stones, reaching out to touch the nearest one. It was cold and solid, as it appeared. She ran her hand along the rough granite, circling the stone until she returned to her starting place. Then she moved to another stone, touching it cautiously, then circling it. As she made her way around the hilltop, the sun dropped in the west and the shadows of the stones lengthened, completing parts of the circle. Gennes' own shadow merged with one of the stones as she leaned against it, putting her head back to look at the sky.

"What am I doing here?" she asked. "What is it that I'm looking for?"

In the center of the circle was a large mound of dirt about the same size as one of the stones. She walked to it and sat down, cupping her chin in her hands. A gust of wind blew a few loose strands of her hair around her face. There were no bird calls, no animal noises, just a persistent buzzing noise of some insect in the grass. The longer that Gennes sat still, the louder the buzzing grew until it was impossible to ignore. Rising, she walked toward the sound, which seemed to be coming from the base of one of the larger stones.

"A singing stone?" she smiled.

But the smile faded quickly from her face. She was certain she had walked around all of the stones in the circle. But standing there, just then, she felt as it she was seeing this stone for the first time. Or—not the first time. She had seen it before, a very long time ago.

Dropping to her knees, she began to dig into the hard ground, just at the base of the stone. Before long, she had dug a good hole, and her hands and arms were covered in the rich, dark soil. She stopped for a moment, but before she could even catch her breath she started again. When her hands were almost elbow deep in the earth, her fingers caught on something that wasn't dirt or rock. Digging deeper, she freed it and pulled a crumpled-up ball of cloth from the hole. It was caked in dark soil and badly frayed, and it looked as if it had been under the ground for a very long time. It was also heavier than it appeared, and Gennes could feel something solid inside the folds.

Sitting back with her legs crossed in front of her, she turned the ball in her hands, looking for a place to unravel it. Clumps of dirt and rock fell into her lap, and her eyes stung from a spray of dust when she finally pried open one stiff end of the cloth. More dirt fell as she slowly unwound the cloth freeing the prize inside it. Finally, she held it in her hands—a necklace strung with oval beads and teardrop-shaped pieces set with stones and inlaid with mother-of-pearl. Even beneath a heavy layer of dirt, the metal beads glowed in the light of the setting sun, especially the center piece, a large oval charm with a cross on it.

Gennes' dirty hands could do little to clean the ornament. She rubbed it against the sleeve of her dress, hoping to get a better look at the stones. They were red, like garnets, and she was sure that the beads were made of gold. The center charm alone would be worth a great deal. She continued to examine it, even as the sun was setting and daylight faded from the moor, until she found a little clasp on the side of the charm.

Using her thumbnail, she scratched off the grime that had settled into the groove on either side of the clasp. Breathing hard, she held the charm away from her face and popped open a little door to a secret compartment. Her eyes grew wide, and she held her breath. But nothing happened. Slowly, she began to breath again. Her shoulders sank, and she drew the locket closer to her to inspect it. There was nothing inside it, only the warm glow of polished gold still visible in the fading light.

She sighed and stared, unseeing, at the locket in her hand.

A sudden crack of thunder told Gennes what she hadn't realized before. The bank of clouds she had seen earlier in the day had moved in over her head. The dimness of twilight fled before the low rain clouds that stretched from one horizon to another. Lightning flashed across the sky and down to nearby hilltops, followed swiftly by the boom and crash of angry thunder. With each strike of lightning, the standing stones sprung out of the darkness and jumped toward Gennes like hungry beasts intent on devouring her. She clutched the necklace to her breast and threw her head down, trying in vain to shut out the booming noises and flashes of light.

Another flash of lightning exploded beside her, nearer than the others, followed instantly by a crack of thunder. The air itself seemed to split apart, like a piece of wood torn open by the crash of an ax. Again the thunder cracked—an ax against a wooden door. The wind roared, and the clouds opened, sending down a torrent of rain. There were voices yelling, angry men outside the door, and an ax pounding, biting into a heavy door, and the cracking of the wood as the door gave way.

"Trevilian!" she shouted.

She lifted her face into the rain and shouted again.

"Trevilian!"

Rain soaked her hair and clothes and ran off her face like a river. There was someone beside her, helping her to her feet. In the next flash of lightning, the stone beside her grew into a mountain. Even the grass around her feet, beat down by the streaming water, seemed to grow all out of proportion. It grabbed at her legs, tripping her as she tried to run with the unseen stranger beside her. Following a worn path through the grass she hadn't noticed before, they ran toward a wall of rock and ducked into a narrow cave at its base, away from the rain and wind.

Gennes was shaking in every part of her body when they finally came to a stop. Further inside the cave, a warm light glowed, inviting her in. She stepped out of the narrow entryway and into a cozy room where a fire crackled cheerfully. Drawn to its warmth, she stepped closer and watched the light of the fire dance across the smooth rock that made up the walls and ceiling and floor of the room.

"Ye look half drowned, lass," came a little voice behind her.

Gennes stepped around the fire, putting it between the stranger and herself. It was the first time she was able to get a real look at him. He was a small man, much shorter than she was. His hair was greyish and tightly curled, like a tuft of moss on a granite rock. He wore a brown tunic and brown breeches covered to the knees by green stockings, and a red cap sat jauntily on the back of his head. But it was his eyes that Gennes couldn't stop looking at. In the dancing firelight, they appeared absolutely black. There was no white around them, just tiny circles of solid color, twinkling with reflected light. If his nose had been longer and covered in long whiskers, he would have looked more like a mouse than a man.

"Sit down, sit down," the little man droned, with a slight hum in his voice. "Let the fire warm ye."

Startled out of her rude inspection, Gennes looked around her and then sat down on the hard floor next to the fire.

"I want to thank you for saving me from the storm," she mumbled when at last she found her voice. "It came up so quickly, and I didn't know where to go to find shelter."

The little man nodded. "'Tisn't much of a home, but it does keep the weather away," he hummed.

Gennes looked around again. There was nothing in the room except the fire, the little man, and herself.

"Do you live here?" she asked.

"Aye," he answered. "I've made my home on the moor for many a year. But this is only a part of my house, ye see."

"Oh," Gennes sighed, relaxing a bit as the warmth of the fire soothed her.

"And what were ye doing on the moor this evening, if I might ask?"

Gennes looked into the strange black eyes of the little man and felt strangely at ease. Then she looked down at the necklace she still clutched in her hand and tried to think of a believable answer.

"Did ye come lookin' for that?" the man asked before she could say anything. "It is yers, isn't it?"

Gennes held the necklace up to the firelight where they could both see it better.

"I'm really not certain," she answered truthfully. "You'll think this very strange, but I was here once before, as a child. I don't know how I got here, or where I came from. A man found me here, a shepherd named Evin, and he and his wife raised me. But I've never been able to remember who I was before."

"Why did ye come back?" the man asked.

"I'm not certain of that either. Perhaps to try and find out who I am and where I really belong." She held the necklace out with one hand before continuing. "You've been on the moor a long time. Do you know anything about how this necklace came to be here?"

The little man stroked his chin and tilted his head to one side.

"Not many folk ever wander up here," he answered, "and certainly not wearing fancy jewels like those. But there is something that I recall."

As the man paused for a breath, Gennes leaned forward anxiously.

"There was a girl," he continued, "a little thing of seven or eight, came up here all alone, many a year ago. She buried something under one of the stones. Something wrapped in cloth, I believe."

Gennes let out the breath she was holding. It seemed too impossible that this man could have seen her ten years before in such a remote and inhospitable place. But then, everything about the man, and his home, and their entire conversation seemed too impossible to believe.

"I did know where to look for it," she mumbled, turning her attention back to the necklace. "And I knew about the little door on the charm. But when I opened it...."

She stopped and drew in a quick breath. What had she expected when she opened the locket? What was supposed to happen?

"Nothing was there?" The humming voice of the little man broke in on her thoughts. "Ye were looking for something, and it wasn't there."

Gennes stared at the man for a long moment before dropping her gaze back to the necklace.

"I don't even know what I was looking for," she said, shaking her head slowly.

"Ah," the man droned, "sometimes we can't see what is right in front of us. Magic is like that. You have to believe in it to see it."

Gennes placed the necklace in her lap and warmed her hands before the fire. She was growing sleepy, and her conversation with the little man seemed less and less real.

"The brothers at St. Petroc's monastery say there is no such thing as magic," she yawned. "People only believe in magic to explain what they can't understand. Of course, there are miracles. And they say you have to believe in those to see them, which seems a little like magic. Except they call it faith."

As she spoke, she lowered herself to the ground, overcome by weariness. Cradling the necklace in one arm, she slipped the other under her head as a pillow. Breathing deeply, she closed her eyes and was nearly asleep when a thought suddenly struck her. Forcing her eyes open again with difficulty, she turned her head toward the man.

"The little girl who came to the moor all those years ago," she asked, "do you know where she came from? Did you see what direction she was traveling?"

The man smiled, and his strange black eyes twinkled more brightly than before.

"Aye," he answered. "She came from the east."

"Briallen is to the east," she murmured. Then she laid her head down on her arm and fell fast asleep.

* * *

Gennes awoke to the pale light of a new morning, shimmering through a thin fog. The ground beneath her was damp and cold, and dew drops sparkled on the grass in front of her face. Her clothing was wet where she had been lying on the ground, but the rest of her was dry and surprisingly warm. Beside her loomed one of the standing stones, with the hole she had dug at the base. And in her hand she still grasped the gold and garnet necklace.

There was no sign of the little man, or a cave in a rock wall, or a pathway through the grass.

"I must have been dreaming," she whispered into the still air.

She found her bag of clothes and food on the far side of the stone circle, where she had left it the day before. It smelt of wet wool and soggy bread. She didn't even have the heart to open it and see how much was damaged. Instead, she slung the bag over her shoulder, wrapped her cloak tightly about her, and turned to find the ball of saffron that glowed softly in the east through the morning fog. Briallen was in that direction.

For a moment she hesitated. Then she turned in a full circle, letting her gaze linger on each of the mighty stones that encircled the hilltop. When she was facing the sun again, she squared her shoulders and lifted her chin.

"Briallen is to the east," she said.

The rumbling of her stomach reminded her that she had eaten neither breakfast that morning nor supper the night before. But she didn't want to think about eating food that had been spoiled by the rain.

"I'll just have to find my breakfast somewhere along the way," she told herself as she started to walk.

She also needed to do something with the gold necklace she was carrying. It was dangerous to be seen in the wilderness with something so valuable, and she didn't want to attract attention to herself when she reached the city. But she also couldn't bear to hide it away. At last she decided to remove the beads of garnet and mother-and-pearl to use as barter when she needed them. Then she tied the string with the remaining gold beads and the center charm around her left wrist with a strong knot. The charm with the hidden door dangled safely over her hand within easy reach, but was hidden under the sleeve of her dress and the cover of her cloak.

Setting out again, she began to plan what she would do when she arrived in Briallen. She had no idea how to find the Roman Hall, and she didn't want to ask about Colin by name. The soldiers might still be looking for him, and she didn't know whom she could trust. She had heard of the great marketplace within the city walls and felt certain she could at least find that. There she could trade one of her beads for food and lodging and make a few careful inquiries about her friend.

The fog was already lifting, and her journey wouldn't take much more than a day. As she walked, she listened to the jingling of the gold beads around her wrist and she smiled. She would soon be seeing Colin again and the great city of Briallen she had heard so much about. She was beginning to trust in whatever it was that had brought her that far. She didn't know whether it was faith, or some kind of magic. But she had found one piece of her past, and she knew that there was more waiting to be found ahead of her.

Chapter Six

Gennes arrived in Briallen the following morning.

It wasn't difficult to find the marketplace. The commotion of it could be heard from several streets away. Wagons rolled along gravel pathways. Heavy baskets banged onto the stone walkways. Vendors shouted over one another the best buys of the day. There was a smell, too. Bread fresh from the oven, chickens and pigs, and the heavy dust that rose from the street in spite of the gravel.

The large courtyard that served as the city's main market area was not far from the southern gate. It was surrounded by four long, rectangular buildings built in the Roman style, each with numerous openings where colorful merchandise covered tables or hung from the walls. Food sellers stood beside baskets and carts outside the buildings or herded small animals into pens on the grassy mall in the center of the courtyard. All around her, people were busily engaged in haggling, trading, gossiping, and laughing.

Gennes knew that the few beads she had brought for barter wouldn't last very long, but she found herself drawn into the spirit of the marketplace. Soon she was haggling over bread and cheese and turnips, just like the other women who wandered through the courtyard, armed with baskets and followed by squealing children. The buildings were larger than she had ever imagined, and there were so many different ways to go! She started to wonder if she would ever be able to find the Roman Hall, even if someone told her the way.

Tired from her long journey, she sat down on the grass in the center of the courtyard and pulled out a few of the turnips she had bought. Their tangy taste did little to solve her problems, but at least they lessened the rumbling of her stomach.

It was a different rumbling, though, that suddenly caught her attention. Looking up from her snack, she saw a large covered wagon pulled by four black horses. It stormed into the marketplace through an entryway between two buildings barely large enough to permit it. There was a loud crash as the rear edge of the wagon plowed into a stack of empty crates and flung them to the ground. Women screamed with fright, men shouted, and a whole family of pheasants escaped from their coop and flew up into the air. In the midst of the chaos, Gennes saw a poor woman trying to flee from the path of the heedless wagon, one arm full of loaves of bread and dragging with her other hand a frightened child. Just then, the child stumbled and fell sprawling into the gravel. The woman, losing her balance, stumbled the other way, out of the road, but the child lay motionless right in front of the thundering black horses!

Throwing her bag to one side, Gennes jumped from the sidewalk and raced toward the child. Without thinking, she scooped him up in her arms and leapt out of the way, just as the wagon careened past. The roar of the heavy vehicle and the wind of its passing filled her ears, and her arms and face were stung by the tiny pieces of gravel that were shot up into the air. Miraculously, nothing else struck them. The roar passed on, and the wind settled. Then, startled at her own boldness and realizing just how close she had come to those horses' hooves, she fell to her knees, still clutching the little boy.

Within moments, the child's mother was frantically pulling him from Gennes' arms, crying, laughing, and thanking her all at once. Someone helped her to her feet, and others gathered around. At that instant, though, she was unable to hear anything but the beating of her own heart in her ears. Concentrating on breathing, she turned back to retrieve her bag, when she discovered that she had drawn another kind of attention. Mounted on black horses like the ones pulling the wagon, two red-caped soldiers eyed Gennes suspiciously. Her stomach lurched without warning, leaving her breathless and weak. She hadn't seen them earlier, and she wondered if they had followed the wagon into the marketplace, as an armed guard for some valuable cargo. From their apparel, they were obviously Balchder's men, apparently on some mission in the city, but heedless of the safety of the people there.

One of the soldiers directed his horse over to Gennes. The crowd around her thinned. It dispersed completely as the soldier dismounted. Ignoring her sudden queasiness, Gennes drew herself to her full height and faced him alone.

"I don't believe I've ever seen you before," the soldier said unpleasantly.

His eyes traveled from her face to her feet and back again, lingering at the bodice of her blue-green dress, which was rising and falling with the rhythm of her quick breaths. He stepped closer, narrowing his eyes like a snake ready to strike.

"What is your name?" he asked, almost hissing.

Evading his question, Gennes answered, "I've just arrived in the city. I'm looking for some work I can do and a place to stay."

An evil light came into the man's eyes, and a thin smile crept up one side of his face. He cocked his head toward his companion, still on horseback, but never took his eyes off of Gennes.

"You hear that, Cal?" he called. "She's looking for work and a place to sleep. I wonder what kind of work she does?"

The man chuckled and surveyed her again, this time stepping around her, like a hungry dog circling its prey. His friend dismounted to join the fun, ending up behind Gennes just as the first soldier ended his circle directly facing her again.

"I think we could find a place at our barracks where she can stay in bed and work all day," the man leered. "I'll let her start with me."

Laughing at his own sick joke, the soldier reached up with his right hand, cupping it under Gennes' left breast. She jerked away from him, but his friend was directly behind her, blocking her retreat. She winced as the first man raised his left hand toward her face, but it never made contact. A blur flew past her eyes, and something impacted on the side of the soldier's head, sending him reeling away from her. The second soldier pushed her aside to see to his friend, and suddenly she was free! Turning quickly to see who had delivered her, Gennes expected to catch but a glimpse of some fleeing figure. But in the midst of the street, one man stood alone, hands on his hips, defiantly waiting for the soldiers to recover.

His golden hair shown in the sun like a god, and his eyes flashed like an avenging angel. She gasped in amazement. Then she realized that the soldiers were moving, the one scrambling to his feet and the other nearly falling over him in his pitiful attempts to help.

"Get off of me!" the first bellowed, then gestured at the angel. "Get him, you fool! Get him!"

The second soldier stumbled away after the man in the street. Gennes gasped again and watched, but suddenly hands came out of nowhere and pushed her into the street as well.

"Run, child! Run!" cried the voices of the townspeople behind her.

Reacting more quickly than she had, some brave souls had reappeared from the buildings to help her escape. Awake to her situation again, Gennes ran across the road to the grassy area and grabbed her bag. She turned to look for an escape route, but it was too late. The first soldier was beside her again, grabbing for an arm to stop her. With every ounce of strength she had, Gennes swung her bag upward, striking him in the face and throwing him backward. His cry of pain rang through the street like a tremor. In horror, she realized that the metal clasp on her bag had left a great gash along his cheek, and blood ran through his fingers as he grasped at it. Stumbling backwards, she ran. Across the road again and onto a sidewalk she stumbled, past carts and barrels and boxes, but all the time his screams followed her.

Suddenly, the marketplace seemed to be swarming with red-caped soldiers. Two men ran at Gennes from behind a building, and another man on horseback blocked her path down one roadway. She skidded to a stop and wheeled around looking for a way out.

"Over here!" a voice called out, and Gennes swung in its direction.

There he was again, her golden-haired angel! Standing at the entrance to a narrow archway through one of the buildings, he motioned for her to come to him. Watching the mounted soldier out of the corner of her eye, Gennes ran toward the arch as fast as she could. The soldier galloped after her, but the entryway was too small for a man on horseback, and she reached it before he reached her. Her unknown friend pulled the bag from her arms and grabbed her hand, leading her swiftly to the far end of the tunnel. Someone was following them on foot now, but they were far ahead of him. As soon as they reached the other side, the man pulled Gennes down another side street, around a few more brick buildings, and across a small bridge. Finding a hedge of thick bushes, he pushed her into them and threw her bag in after her.

"Stay there and stay quiet," he whispered with authority.

Then he was off again, running along the bank of a stream like a fox trying to hide its scent from the dogs. Peering through the bushes, Gennes watched him disappear beneath a foot-bridge. Then the sound of thundering hooves sent her scampering back into the thickness of the hedge. A number of horsemen passed by—three perhaps. They rode on toward the bridge, where orders were called out. Then the sounds moved on, and Gennes was left alone in her hiding place, wondering why she had ever come to Briallen.

Time passed slowly within the little refuge. When her breathing returned to normal and she no longer startled at every distant sound, Gennes was able to close her eyes and remember the incredible events of the past half-hour: the carriage, the child, the soldiers, and then—the man. A desperate flight, a narrow escape, a place to hide, and never a moment to even speak to the man who had saved her from certain doom.

He wasn't difficult to picture. Over six feet tall, hair like a golden field of grain, pulled back and tied at the neck, with a trimmed beard the same color. His blue tunic hung open at the neck and was tucked into brown breeches at the waist. His tunic sleeves were rolled up to his elbows, revealing lean muscles beneath. And his face—it was difficult to describe in human terms. He could have been an icon, fashioned from stone or bronze, with a strong jaw, prominent cheekbones, and high forehead. She opened her eyes and peered once again through the branches, wondering where he had gone, and whether he would ever return.

As the moments lengthened and the shadows dwindled toward mid-day, Gennes began to wonder whether she had mistaken the order to "stay here". She had assumed that the man who left her there had intended to return as soon as the way was clear. For what purpose, she was uncertain. But the immediate area had been clear for some time, and her 'friend' had failed to return. No breeze could penetrate the thick bushes where she hid, and a damp heat radiated from every leaf. Cramped, hungry, and becoming very annoyed by the little white flying things that made their home among the leaves, she was starting to feel very foolish and, once again, very much alone.

Although she wanted to start out on her own without waiting any longer, she had no idea which way to go. The view from her hiding place was unfamiliar. Even if she could find her way back to the marketplace, surely there would be soldiers there waiting for her. She had no idea how to find Colin or the Roman Hall, and she still had no place to sleep that night. Waiting, and hoping that her unknown accomplice would return, seemed to be the best option for the time being.

Taking care to stay quiet, Gennes retrieved some bread and cheese from her bag and ate a solemn midday meal. She pushed her sleeves up over her elbows and folded her cloak into her bag. She thought again of her 'hero' of the marketplace. Where was he? Had something happened to him, or had he simply left her there, thinking his chivalrous deed for the day completed? She pictured him again in her mind. This time his eyes shone less brightly and the cut of his chin seemed less daunting. There was even something in the tone of his voice—was it impatience? Or even annoyance? He had been very high-handed, ordering her to follow him, dragging her through tunnels and down streets, then commanding her to "stay there and stay quiet" without another word. Of course, there hadn't really been time to discuss the situation. But still, he didn't need to be so imperious.

Something else began to bother her as well. Why had he come to her defense in the marketplace? Why had he risked his own welfare by attacking the soldiers and helping her get away? Had his motives been truly heroic, or was there something else which prompted his actions? His clothing identified him as a townsman, not a man of nobility or rank. He wore no weapon to indicate he was a warrior. And he certainly seemed to know the streets and pathways of the city. She knew nothing else about him, and she was at a loss trying to decide what might have motivated him. As time passed, however, she was less and less inclined to believe that he had helped her just out of the goodness of his heart.

An hour or more had passed since Gennes had first been thrust into the bushes when someone approached her hiding place. From what little she could see through the leaves, it appeared to be a monk, dressed in a long brown robe with his hood pulled down about his face. He walked slowly along the path, past the nearest building and then close to the hedge. When he arrived directly in front of her, he dropped something—a silver ring, which jingled on the tiny stones at his feet. Gennes watched him stoop down to retrieve his possession, and then, without warning, he looked directly at her!

She gasped involuntarily. But the eyes that looked into hers were not startled or alarmed. They were amused. And they were familiar.

"It's you!" she whispered, recognizing her ally from the marketplace.

The man smiled broadly and held out his arm.

"Give me your hand," he whispered back. "I'll help you out."

His hand was before her, waiting, but for a moment Gennes didn't move. Looking at that hand, she wondered again who this man was who so enjoyed ordering her about, and why he was there, helping her again. Then she looked into his clear grey eyes. He really was as handsome as she had at first imagined. Hesitantly, she put her hand in his, feeling his warmth and his strength. Then, before she was ready, he was pulling her upward and out of the bushes, using his free hand to push the branches away from her face. With her left hand, Gennes reached back for her bag and caught the sharp end of a broken branch along the forearm. Her arm stung, but there was no time to inspect it. She was being dragged upward, and there was only enough time to grasp her bag and find her feet before she was being led swiftly down the path.

A few moments later, they were in front of a decrepit shack, more leaning than standing at the end of a long brick building. Still holding Gennes' hand, the man pulled her through an opening into the ruins. Leaving her alone in the middle of the disheveled little room, he went immediately to the back wall and began moving some boards. The stillness of the dusty room was unsettling, and a cold shiver ran down Gennes' back.

"What is this place," she asked softly.

The man answered without stopping what he was doing or turning toward her.

"It used to be a potter's shop," he said.

Filtered sunlight found its way into the room through the broken roof. Littered around the floor she could see shards of old pottery. A long table lay tilted in one corner, its broken legs barely visible underneath. A clay oven lay smashed beneath the part of the front wall that had collapsed inward. There was no sign of fire, and she wondered what had caused this destruction.

"What happened here?" she asked, overcome with curiosity.

Gennes had been turning and looking about the room, and the man was now behind her. The sounds of his labor stopped, and he paused before answering.

"Those soldiers," he said at last. "Apparently one of them didn't like the pot he bought here once."

Appalled at his response, she whirled around to face him. She wanted to know more about the potter's shop and about the soldiers who had destroyed it. Her companion, however, was ready to move on again. Pulling off the monk's robe, he motioned to her to follow him as he stepped into a narrow passageway that he had uncovered in the wall.

"We go down this way," he said, without even the hint of a polite request.

This time, Gennes stood her ground.

"Go where?" she asked, viewing him through narrowed eyelids.

Her sudden reluctance seemed to take the man by surprise. He turned back to her with widened eyes, but he made no answer.

"I want to know where you are taking me," Gennes insisted, still standing in the middle of the room.

The man took a few steps toward her, then answered in a low voice.

"You said that you needed a place to stay," he said.

Saying nothing more, he held out his hand to her again. She didn't move. He had not yet answered her question. After a moment, he dropped his arm and shrugged.

"I know a place," he started again, "where you will be safe."

"With you?" she asked.

He laughed softly.

"Not with me alone," he answered. "There are a number of people there, mostly women in fact…."

Gennes was suddenly reminded of the dreadful suggestion made by the soldier that morning. She thought of her questions about this man's motivation, the strangeness of his behavior, and the peculiar manner in which he was entering his living place. Clutching her bag, she backed away.

"I'm not interested!" she interrupted him. "There must be some other way for me to make my living in this city."

The man stared at her and laughed softly again.

"I realize that you are quite lovely," he teased, "but do you think your beauty so overwhelming that I could think of no other place to take you than a house of harlotry?"

Gennes felt the blood rush into her cheeks. In a dizzying array of anger, embarrassment, disappointment, and loneliness, she whirled around and headed for the narrow doorway back to the street. Her head was down and her eyes clouded with angry tears, or she might have seen him coming. But she didn't. The man crossed the floor quickly and grabbed her left arm as she raised it to reach for the doorway. His grip was not hard, but it fell right on the scratch that she had received in the bushes. She cried out softly and tried to pull away from him, but he held her tight.

"What is this?" he asked.

The amusement was gone from his voice and replaced with genuine concern. He held Gennes' left arm in his two hands and looked closely at the wound.

"It's nothing," she said. "A scratch from the bushes."

"It's bleeding," he replied.

She looked down then and realized that her arm had indeed been bleeding, probably ever since she left the hedge. The scratch itself was two to three inches long, but there was a deep gash at one end that was still oozing dark fluid. A thin ribbon of dried blood ran down to her wrist, under the bracelet, and into the palm of her hand. Gennes tried again to free her arm, but he still held it in one hand, using his other hand to pull up the edge of his tunic and press it firmly against the wound.

"I didn't know you were hurt," he said. "I'm sorry."

His eyes looked up and met hers, holding them for a long moment. Then he looked down at her arm again, alternately pressing down and then lifting the cloth to inspect the cut. When the oozing appeared to have stopped, he released her.

"We can clean that at the house," he said, looking into her eyes again. "That is, if you are willing to come with me?"

She stared back at him in silence for a moment.

"I don't even know who you are," she said weakly.

He smiled—a radiant, disarming smile that soothed her anxious mind like a tonic.

"Michael," he said, leaning his head forward in a short bow. "Michael of Trevose at your service."

Timidly, Gennes smiled back at him. Michael—the Archangel—the name fit him. He offered his hand to her again, and this time she took it. Then he led her across the room, past the broken boards, and into the dark passageway beyond. She waited while he covered the entryway with the same boards, concealing their path and blocking out the sunlight. Willingly, Gennes took the hand he proffered and walked with him into the darkness. She still didn't know where they were going, but she no longer questioned it. For the first time in days, she didn't feel alone.

Chapter Seven

The passageway was not as dark as Gennes had at first thought. It appeared to be a narrow walkway between two long buildings. The top was boarded over in some spots and covered with cloth in others, enough to conceal the pathway, but not enough to block out all sunlight. After walking some distance, Michael stopped before a small door set back into one wall. Releasing Gennes' hand, he maneuvered a long metal bolt out of a rusty slot in the door frame.

"We don't use this entrance often," he explained. "But there are times when it is very useful. This bolt can even be reset from the inside and locked, if need be."

Michael looked at Gennes as if he expected some answer. Distracted by her own thoughts, she could only smile at him politely. He smiled back and opened the door wide, standing beside it to let her enter first. She did, stooping to pass through the low door frame. As her eyes adjusted to the brighter light inside, Michael closed the door and reset the bolt. Then he was beside her again, smiling warmly and just opening his mouth to speak.

He was interrupted by the sound of his own name being called from somewhere in the room.

"Michael!" a voice called out. "I was about to lose my bet about you never being late for a meal."

Gennes turned quickly at the sound of that voice. It was unbelievable, but true! Walking across the room in her direction was her rusty-headed friend from the canyon—Colin!

"I've been watching for you," he said to Michael as he approached. "I didn't expect you to use the back door today." He paused and gave Michael a teasing look. "Just who is it you have here?"

Peering around Michael's shoulder to get a better look, his eyes widened in surprise.

"Gennie!" he exclaimed, reaching out for her. "Is it really you?"

Colin pushed past Michael to embrace the unexpected guest. She hugged him back, happily.

"What are you doing here?" he asked.

Pulling back from the embrace, she locked her hands in his and they smiled at one another.

"I've been looking for you," Gennes said, her throat heavy with emotion. "I decided to take your advice and come to Briallen. I only arrived this morning, and I never thought I would find you so quickly. In fact, I wouldn't have, if it hadn't been for…."

Looking from Colin to Michael, she wasn't sure how to end the sentence. Were they friends? Relatives? Was it possible that Michael was a member of the resistance group who worked with Colin? That would explain why he had rescued her from the soldiers in the marketplace, and why his actions were so secretive. It also helped to answer her confusion over whether Michael's motivation was for good or evil.

Michael, however, did not seem to share in his friend's excitement. His face had become cold and hard like a statue, completely unreadable. Looking at him, Gennes felt her own enthusiasm began to ebb, and her smile faded. Looking from her to Colin, Michael shifted uncomfortably and cleared his throat.

"I see that the two of you know each other," he stated.

"This is Gennes," Colin told him, as if that would completely resolve the matter. "The girl that I met in Trevelgue," he prompted. "The girl who saved my life."

Michael nodded then, obviously aware of the story of Colin's brush with the soldiers in the canyon. Still he said nothing.

"But however did you two meet?" asked Colin, apparently unaffected by Michael's indifference.

Gennes smiled shyly and looked down, waiting for Michael to regale his friend with the story of his heroic rescue. But no story was forthcoming.

In a cool, calm voice, Michael responded, "We met in the marketplace this morning. I heard her say she was looking for a place to stay, so I brought her here."

Gennes stared at him, dumbfounded. Once again, she was at a loss, unable to understand what motivated this unusual man. Colin, however, retained his good cheer.

"What am I thinking?" he said suddenly. "After traveling all this way, you must be starving."

Motioning toward a table at the head of the room, he continued, "Let me get you something from the kitchen. You two sit down. Yes, Michael, you, too. I'll get something for all of us."

Colin turned with a relish and dashed off to the next room. Watching him go, Gennes had a moment to look around. The room they were in was long and narrow. Tables and benches sat in two long rows down the length of the room, with one table turned sideways at the far end. A door at one end led to what must have been the kitchen, and another door opened to the street outside. A row of windows on the same wall looked out over a courtyard where small bushes showed off their first soft leaves of spring. A half dozen people walked about the room, apparently preparing to sit down to a midday meal.

Gennes looked up at Michael, hoping that he might soften again in the absence of his friend, but he didn't. He motioned to the same table that Colin had and followed her quietly across the room. She sat on one bench. He walked around the table and stood behind the other. The silence between them deepened.

Gennes cleared her throat and looked at him.

"Why didn't you tell him about the soldiers in the marketplace?" she asked, timidly.

He shrugged.

"Why didn't you tell him about the boy and the carriage?" he responded.

So he had seen that, Gennes thought to herself. She shrugged as well and looked away.

"It didn't seem important," she answered, thinking again about the terrible events of that morning and how unreal it all seemed then.

Michael's words cut in upon her thoughts, his voice soft and gentle again.

"It was important to the boy," he said, "and his mother."

Gennes looked at him again, awed by the speed with which he could change moods. He stood with one foot on the bench, leaning over it a bit with his arms crossed on his raised knee.

"What you did," she responded evenly, "was important to me. And I haven't even said 'thank you' yet."

She smiled at him warmly, but he made no response.

"I do thank you," she continued softly, "for everything you have done for me today."

A light in Michael's eyes flickered and went out. He straightened and returned his foot to the floor. Then he licked his lips and glanced at the far doorway. Looking in the same direction, Gennes saw Colin reentering the room, smiling and balancing three platters in his arms.

Michael turned back to Gennes and nodded his head in a slight bow.

"I believe that Colin has already told you about our work here," he spoke quickly. "If there is anything else that you want to know, I am sure that he will be more than happy to help you."

He marched away then, meeting Colin across the room. Michael took one of the platters, and the two exchanged a few words. Then Michael disappeared into the other room, and Colin hurried to sit beside Gennes, still smiling.

"Well?" he said expectantly, setting the platters on the table and sitting down. "What do you think of him?"

Gennes glanced from Colin to the empty doorway and back again. She thought it best at that moment not to tell him everything she had thought about his friend that day.

"He is a peculiar one," she said, trying to sound noncommittal. "It does seem strange, doesn't it, that he brought me to this place, without even knowing anything about me?"

Colin was eating and didn't seem too concerned.

"He must have trusted you," he said between bites. "Michael always was a good judge of character."

"But surely someone will object," she pressed on. "What if you weren't here to vouch for me?"

Colin shrugged, still unconcerned.

"No one questions Michael," he said. "He is our leader after all. None of us would be here if it wasn't for him."

Gennes looked at him in surprise, but Colin was too busy eating to notice.

"Oh," he continued, "he told me you have a wound that needs cleaning. Do you want me to take a look at it now, or wait until you've eaten?"

Gennes looked down at the scratch on her arm. It had stopped bleeding when Michael held his tunic to her arm in the potter's shop. His grip had been strong, yet gentle. It was then that she found herself trusting him against reason or common sense, before she knew anything about him.

"It can wait," she said.

* * *

For the rest of the afternoon, Colin led Gennes around the buildings and compound of the Roman Hall, introducing her to his friends and telling her about each one in turn. She met Grainne, the young widow of a man murdered by soldiers for smuggling bread to some prisoners. She met Tomas, a large, silent man who had once entered a burning building to save a family of seven. She also met Morgan, an old woman, nearly blind, who had once been renowned for her beautiful woven tapestries.

"These buildings housed a whole garrison of Roman soldiers," he told her proudly, leading her back into the main hall. "One wing fell in completely, and this room was starting to collapse until a wealthy merchant had it repaired. It's large enough to house a few dozen of our people, although mostly women live here. A lot of them are widows who lost everything at the hands of Balchder's men. We're trying to repair more of the building, to house more people, but the work is slow."

"Who is it that had this part repaired?" Gennes asked. "Can he help?"

"No one knows who it is, except Michael," Colin responded. "A lot of people around here are willing to help us, but they do it secretly, to avoid any trouble with Lord Balchder. They trust Michael, but not enough to stand up with us and be counted."

Colin glared out the window where the crumpled remains of a stone wall ran around the compound. Gennes smiled at him.

"Well, I'll stand up with you," she said. "Just tell me what I can do."

Colin smiled back and held out his hand to her.

"First, we have to find a place for you to put your things. After the evening meal these tables are taken down and set against the wall to make room for sleeping mats. When everyone is here, it can get a little crowded. There is another room where a few of the women sleep. It isn't very large, and it's colder than the Hall. But, since you're from the moor and not used to so many people, I thought you might prefer it."

He led her to a small room in a building adjacent to the main hall. It was completely bare, except for two stools, a large chest, and a few rolled-up mattresses against the wall.

"If this is all right, I'll fetch you a mattress from the other room," Colin said.

"Yes, please," she responded, finding a corner to set down her bag.

As Colin disappeared out the door, Gennes looked around the dismal little room. She missed the sweet-smelling herbs that blanketed the floor of Evin and Anna's summer hut at the edge of the moor. She would not have objected to sleeping in the larger room with the others, but the smaller room did at least offer her some privacy and a chance to be alone and think. For a brief moment she wondered where Michael would be sleeping that night. But it was a thought she decided not to dwell on, and she quickly turned her attention to making a comfortable sleeping place for herself. It wasn't until the charm of her bracelet jangled across the stone floor that she realized she hadn't even thought about her real reason for coming to Briallen all day.

* * *

That evening, Gennes brushed out her long red hair and braided it very loosely, leaving it draped over one shoulder. From her bag, she took out her favorite dress, a white gown with wide sleeves and colorful embroidery around the low-cut neck. Although the light-weight material was intended for summer, and the neckline was a little daring, she wanted to wear it anyway.

Supper was a noisy affair, with men and women all over the hall all talking at once. Gennes sat between Colin and another young man who seemed very anxious to make her acquaintance. The two men spent so much time trying to outdo each other with stories that neither of them finished their meal. After supper, Gennes helped the women clear the empty bread bowls from the tables, each taking an armful outside to give to the poor. Then old Morgan took her by the arm and led her into the kitchen where a number of the men were sitting beside the fire enjoying their drink. Colin stood and happily made a place for Gennes to sit. Morgan retired to a comfortable chair in the corner which seemed to be reserved for her. Gennes noticed that Michael was there, too, although she could not catch his eye.

For awhile, Gennes listened to the conversation of the others. A man called Tad told about how he had helped to hide a family's small fortune that day, only moments before some soldiers arrived demanding payment for some fabricated debt. The youngest boy of the family, who was a very smooth talker, convinced the soldiers that they had no gold left and sent them off with nothing but a squealing piglet. Colin said that he heard there was a commotion that morning in the marketplace, but no one seemed to know what had happened. Blushing slightly, Gennes looked at the floor, daring to look up only once across the room at Michael. Expressionless, he was looking down at his cup, slowly swirling the drink inside.

As other stories were told, Gennes realized that she was not the only person in the room who had not spoken. Michael had done little more than look into his cup since she had walked in. The large man, Tomas, had also been silent, sitting still and watching the new-comer through half-closed eyes. Finally he spoke, asking Colin to remind him how he and Gennes had met. Colin told the story with great enthusiasm, but Tomas continued to watch Gennes, a somber look upon his face. When Colin finished, Tomas leaned forward and addressed her.

"You lived near Trevelgue?" he asked. "I suppose you have met his Lordship and his family?"

"Yes, I have," she answered, "many times."

Nodding, Tomas continued his interrogation, "I understand he has a son of a marrying age. Or perhaps he has recently taken a bride. I don't suppose there are very many eligible young men in that territory."

The blood shot up into Gennes' cheeks at the obvious insinuation.

"No, to my knowledge, his son hasn't married," she responded in a barely controlled voice. "And I don't believe I've ever counted the number of 'eligible men' on the moor."

Before Tomas could continue, Morgan interrupted from her corner. With a chuckle in her voice, she said, "Someone at your home must have had marriage on the mind, if your mother let you wear a dress like that."

Gennes gasped in surprise. But when she turned and saw the twinkle in Morgan's eyes, she smiled.

"Why, you're right!" she teased back, putting a hand to one cheek. "She did help me make this dress just before the last festival at Trevelgue's castle. If I had only known what she had in mind."

Smiling coyly, Gennes looked around.

"Ahh," she continued, "but when I told her how many—charming—men I would meet in Briallen, she was more than happy to let me go."

The word "charming" she shot at Tomas, batting her eyelids as she did. Tomas glowered and sat back in his chair. Colin, Morgan, and the others laughed. And Michael—Michael continued to look in his cup. But he smiled, and Gennes could just catch a little twinkle in his eye.

* * *

For the next several days, Gennes helped out wherever she could around the compound. During the day, most of the men were away, doing work around the city. Some of the women remained in the Hall, sewing or weaving or cooking, while others went to the marketplace to trade their goods for food and other supplies. Knowing that she needed to do something to provide for her own needs, Gennes convinced Morgan to teach her how to weave tapestries. The work was challenging and time-consuming, but it gave her something to fill the empty days and provided her with a new friend.

Morgan was very wise, and very knowledgeable about the history of Dumnonia and its people. Although she rarely left the immediate area of the Roman Hall, she seemed to know everything that happened in the city, and she was willing to share her information. So day after day

Gennes sat with her, learning how to make the intricate designs out of threads of wool, and listening to stories about the hundreds of people affected by Balchder's relentless search for King Brenin' crown.

Gennes couldn't hear about the soldiers or the crown without feeling a hard lump in her throat. It stirred the restlessness inside her, reminding her daily that she still couldn't explain the strange vision she'd had the day she met Colin, and she still wasn't any closer to finding out where she had come from or who she was. She wanted to go out into the city and explore it, but each time she asked Colin or one of the other residents of the Hall, there was always some reason for her to be left behind. And she didn't dare ask Michael.

The handsome leader of the little resistance group remained a mystery to her. Although he talked and laughed with everyone else around him, he seemed to avoid Gennes. He was especially kind to Morgan, seeking her out each day to have a private conversation with her and often bringing her a flower or some other small token. But if Gennes was near, he merely nodded to Morgan and passed on by.

One day, about a week after Gennes had come to the city, Morgan announced that she wanted to go the marketplace to buy some special dye for the wool.

"It won't be today, though," she said, looking out a window at the pouring rain. "Perhaps tomorrow I can go."

"I'll go with you," Gennes said, more anxious than ever to see the city. "Or I can go for you, if you tell me what you want."

A shadow of concern passed over Morgan's face, and she drew in a deep breath. Wondering if she had said something she shouldn't have, Gennes looked at her and waited for a response.

"We'll talk to Michael about it this evening" Morgan said, looking down at her needlework.

There was something wrong about the tone of her voice.

"Why do we have to talk to Michael?" Gennes asked, looking at her friend through narrowed eyes.

"Well," the woman began, still looking down, "he did say that he thought it would be best if you remained in the compound for now. It's for your own safety, because of what happened in the marketplace."

"The marketplace?" Gennes repeated. She hadn't realized that Michael had told anyone about what happened in the marketplace the day they met.

"What else did Michael say about me?" she asked, trying to control her rising displeasure.

"He just asked us not to take you into the city, that's all," Morgan answered in a motherly voice.

"Us!" Gennes cried. "You mean he has given orders to everyone that I am not allowed to leave here?"

Furious, she sprang to her feet and spun around. It was still early in the morning, and the rain had kept many of the inhabitants of the Hall inside. But Michael was not to be found.

"He just went out," one woman told Gennes in response to her questions. "There, on the street."

She pointed out a window at the dark figure of a cloaked and hooded man walking away from the Hall. Ignoring the pounding rain, Gennes ran out after him, holding her skirt up out of the puddles of water and mud.

"Michael!" she yelled as she ran. "Michael!"

He was just turning the corner when he heard her and stopped.

"Gennes," he exclaimed as she approached him, "what are you doing? You'll be soaked through."

Gennes ran up to him and stopped only a few inches away.

"Morgan told me that you gave orders that I was not allowed to leave the compound at the Hall. Is that true?" she panted, blinking the rainwater out of her eyes as she looked up at him.

"What?" he asked in astonishment.

"Did you give orders that I was not allowed to leave the Hall?"

He looked at her and drew a breath as if to answer. But no answer came. Gennes felt her heart pounding and the rain splashing on her face. Her body began to shake, only partially from the cold. Still, Michael had nothing to say.

Struggling to control her voice, Gennes threw her head back to look him fully in the face.

"I didn't come to Briallen to be protected or taken care of," she fumed. "I came to help. If you have no work for me to do, perhaps I should look elsewhere."

With that, she turned away and began to march back to the Hall. Moving quickly, Michael overtook her and grabbed her shoulders, stopping her in her path.

"Gennes, wait," he called. "You don't realize how dangerous this place can be. The man you injured is the captain of the local brigade. He's had men all over the city looking for you."

"Then you should have talked to me about it," she said, still angry. "Not given orders about me behind my back."

"You're right," he said, earnestly. "I'm sorry."

For a long moment he held her there, his hands on her shoulders, saying nothing more. Neither of them seemed to be aware of the rain any longer, even though it ran in little streams down Gennes' face and neck. Involuntarily, she shivered, breaking the spell. Michael quickly took off his cloak and wrapped it around her.

"Come on," he said. "Let's get you inside."

Back in the Hall, Michael led Gennes to the fire in the kitchen and found warm blankets to wrap around her. Morgan heated some broth and insisted that they both drink it.

"You're as wet as she is," she told Michael when he tried to refuse.

Michael drank the broth and then retrieved his cloak.

"I have an errand I have to finish today," he said, barely looking at Gennes. "But we'll talk about this tomorrow. I promise."

Gennes watched him leave, and then Morgan came and sat beside her, shaking her head.

"The poor thing," she said, staring at the empty doorway. "In all the years I've known that boy, I've never seen him like this."

"What do you mean?" Gennes asked.

Morgan looked at her and smiled.

"He's in love with you, child," she answered. "Even my old eyes can see that. He just isn't ready to admit it to himself."

Then she stood and went back to her work, leaving Gennes to wonder if what she said was true and why it was he didn't want to admit it.

Chapter Eight

Michael kept his promise. The next morning he took Gennes aside with several others from the group.

"It should be safe now for Gennes to go out," he told them. "But she shouldn't be alone, at least for awhile. Colin, you can show her around today. Introduce her as one of the group." Then to Gennes he added, "We like people to know who we are, so they know who they can turn to when they're in need. However, there are some in the city that we don't trust. Colin will point those out to you so you can avoid them."

"What about the soldiers?" Tomas interrupted. "If they see her and she runs scared, she'll lead them right back here to us."

Michael frowned at Tomas, but he didn't have a chance to respond.

"You needn't worry," Gennes answered for herself in a tight voice. "Even a rabbit being chased by a hound knows not to return to its own burrow."

Tomas glared at her and she glared back until Michael stepped in between them.

"All right, then," he said. "I believe everyone knows what their job is today."

As the small group broke up, Michael stepped closer to Gennes for a private word.

"I know you don't feel like you are doing much," he said softly. "But you have already done a great deal. You hid Colin from the soldiers and nursed him back to health, and you saved that little boy in the marketplace. I know you'll be a great asset to us. Just be a little patient."

He smiled then, that charming, disarming smile that he gave her the day they met. It was that smile that made her trust him from the very beginning, and she knew without a doubt that she trusted him now—trusted him enough to tell him the strange story of her vision and the necklace she had found under the circle of stones. Swallowing hard, she took a moment to think through exactly what she wanted to say.

"Michael," she said, breathing hard, "there's something I need to talk to you about. I probably should have said something earlier, but...."

The slamming of the outside door interrupted her and commanded Michael's full attention. He turned toward the breathless youth who had just run into the room.

"Brogan has been arrested!" the youth called to him. "They're holding him at the barracks outside of town. They say if he doesn't pay three gold pieces by morning he'll be taken away and sold!"

"It's all right, Lon," Michael told the boy as he walked toward him. "I'll take care of it. We'll get the coins and get Brogan out of detention. You go home now and tell your mother everything will be all right."

Gennes saw that Michael's calm voice and sure smile had the same effect on Lon that it always had on her. The boy stared at him for a brief moment, letting his words sink in, then he smiled, shook his head in an excited jerk, and rushed back out the door as quickly as he had come in.

As he turned back to Gennes, Michael's smile faded and he shook his head wearily.

"It's their latest trick," he told her. "They pick people up at random, arresting them on false claims. Then they rough them up and see if they can get any information about us. Apparently, our little band of dissidents is causing the local soldiers some concern."

"But why ask for the gold coins?" Gennes asked.

"It's an added benefit," he answered. "We pay ransom to get the citizens back, which hurts our cause and lines their pockets. I doubt their high command even knows anything about it."

He sighed and looked toward the door.

"I need to take care of this right away," he said. Then to Gennes he added, "Can we talk later?"

Gennes smiled, trying to hide her disappointment.

"Of course," she said. "Unless…well, what if I came with you?"

The thought made her heart flutter with excitement. He had said that she could go out into the city with an escort. Why shouldn't that escort be him? She would stay out of trouble—she knew she could. She would do whatever he told her. And she would finally have a chance to tell him why she had really come to Briallen. But before she could even make her arguments about why she should come, the look in his eyes left her in no doubt that his answer was no.

"Not this time," he answered gruffly as he stepped back away from her. "You had better go with Colin. He's waiting for you at the door."

In the time it took Gennes to turn her head and look for Colin among the group of people who had congregated at the door, Michael had already made his escape. She turned back to see him slipping through the door into the kitchen and out of view. He had managed to avoid being with her again, and this time Gennes knew it was intentional.

* * *

Michael continued to treat Gennes much as he had before. He never sat near her at meals or joined a group that she was in. He never spoke to her directly, sending her messages through Colin or Morgan when necessary. And, although Gennes went out into the city a number of times with other members of the group, she was never allowed into the small band that sometimes went with Michael. She began to doubt Morgan's idea very much, and decided instead that Michael had no use for her. Her consternation was so great that she didn't even realize that May Day was approaching.

It was Colin who first mentioned it, one foggy morning near the end of April. He was walking with Gennes to a farmhouse just outside the city wall to help repair a grain bin knocked down by some soldiers. Colin looked at the cloudy sky and sighed.

"It's going to rain this year, I just know it," he sulked. "She won't come if it rains. It's too far to trudge through the mud."

Gennes had to smile at his sullen look.

"What are you talking about?" she asked. "And who is 'she'?"

"The girl I told you about," Colin responded, kicking a stone out of his path. "She lives outside the city. She said her family won't come to the May Day festival if there's too much mud. And I really want to see her again."

Normally, Gennes would have been more sympathetic to her love-sick friend, but his mention of May Day took her by surprise.

"Is it that time already?" she stammered.

"Next week," he answered. "They're already setting up the festival grounds. Do you want to go down to the river this afternoon and get some oak leaves? We'll have time after we finish at the farm."

"I suppose," Gennes said softly, carefully studying the ground in front of her. "Although, I'm not sure that I'll even go to the festival."

"Not go!" Colin cried. "Gennie, you have to go! Everyone goes! I'll go with you, so you won't be...."

"Alone?" she said, frowning. "Colin, I don't need an escort. And you know you would much rather be dancing with your friend from the farm than with me. It's just that...."

She couldn't think of the words to say. From as early as she could remember—her first years with Evin and Anna—she had disliked May Day. She knew it was supposed to be a time to celebrate new life and new beginnings. But to her, it was tinged with sadness, an annual reminder that she had lost whatever life and loved ones she'd had before she came to live on the moor.

But Colin refused to relent. He even told Gennes that if she didn't go to the festival, he would have to stay home with her. So at last she agreed to go with him to the oak grove and pick as many leaves as they could carry. Later that day, they fashioned them into crowns, pinning the leaves together with strong twigs. Other leaves they made into long garlands to be used for decorations. Gennes promised Colin that she would go to the festival, and he promised that he wouldn't hover about her. She even began to get a little excited about getting her first look at the great festival grounds of Briallen. And a recurring fantasy about dancing with Michael only increased her anticipation.

* * *

May Day morning dawned bright and cloudless. The Roman Hall was full of happy sounds as people put on their best clothes, donned May Day crowns, and gathered up the food and garlands that would be taken to the festival grounds. No one even bothered setting up the tables in the Hall. Anyone who was hungry grabbed a quick bite of bread and cheese while they worked, and, since the party would last until after dark, no one would be eating at the Hall the rest of the day.

Gennes found Colin waiting impatiently at the door.

"I was hoping we could leave early," he stammered. "If you don't mind, that is."

"Colin, you don't have to wait for me," she told him. "Why don't you go on ahead?"

But he refused. So Gennes left him standing in the doorway and went off to the kitchen to help with the food.

Ever since she had left her room that morning, Gennes had been looking for Michael. She was wearing her white, embroidered gown with the wide sleeves, like butterfly wings. Her long, red hair fell unbound down her back in waves, except for two tiny braids that encircled her head. Even in her best dress, she didn't expect Michael to notice her. But she had decided that she was going to seek him out that day and make him talk to her. If only she could find him.

In the kitchen, she found Morgan sitting at the large table in the center of the room. All around her on the table were beautiful spring flowers that she was arranging into a colorful bouquet. Gennes sat down across from her and rested her arms on the table, sighing. Morgan looked up and smiled her patient, motherly smile.

"What is it, child?" she asked kindly. "You don't seem to be in a very festive mood."

"It's nothing, really," Gennes said, trying not to look so glum. "I was just looking for...something."

Even with Morgan, Gennes was embarrassed to admit how she felt about Michael, and how hurt she was that he avoided her so. But very little could be hidden from Morgan's eyes, even if they were almost blind.

"He hasn't come home yet," she said in a low, confidential voice. "When he left the city yesterday, he didn't know if he would return in time for the festival or not."

Gennes shook her head and sighed again.

"You're a wonder, Morgan," she said. Then, afraid that her friend might say more about Michael, Gennes decided to change the subject.

"That's a lovely bouquet you're working on," she said, admiring the woman's work. "Are you taking it to the festival?"

"No," Morgan answered, getting a far-away look in her eyes. "I'm going to deliver this before the festival. It's something I do every year."

Gennes waited, hoping that her friend would explain. At length, Morgan cocked her head over the flowers and met her gaze.

"It's for the grave," she said, in answer to the unspoken question. "Most of the people here are too young to remember. But I can still recall one May Day when there was no festival or celebrating anywhere in Dumnonia. It was the year the king was murdered."

Morgan paused for Gennes to respond, but all she could do was to look at her. After a moment the woman went on, arranging the flowers as she talked.

"It was only a week before May Day that the soldiers came into the city, fresh from the heat of war, and took the lives of the king and queen in their own house—and her already heavy with child."

Gennes took a deep breath, trying to push back the blackness that clouded her vision. Her heart pounded, and her throat tightened, preventing her from speaking.

Morgan dropped her arms to her side and sighed.

"That was a long time ago," she said sadly. "But I remember, and I still take my gift every year to pay homage."

Gennes rose abruptly and left the table. Walking quickly, she headed through the Hall, hoping to escape to her little room before she completely fell apart. She needed to be alone to sort through the feelings of panic and horror that had suddenly enveloped her. Tears unexpectedly filled her eyes, and unable to see clearly, she collided with Colin at the door.

"Gennie, where are you going?" he asked as he grabbed her arms and kept her from falling. "Are you ready to leave for the festival?"

"I'm not going," she said with difficulty.

She tried to go on, but Colin still held her and stood in her path.

"But you promised!" he said. "You have to go! I can't leave you here alone."

Stepping back, Gennes broke his hold on her arms and threw her hair back out of her face.

"You're not my father, or my brother, or my guardian!" she retorted angrily. "I don't need you to take care of me. Can't you just leave me alone?"

She pushed past him and began to run to the next building. Then, suddenly feeling ashamed of herself, she slowed down and turned back to her friend.

"I'm sorry, Colin," she said in a cracking voice. "I shouldn't have yelled at you. I want you to go and have a wonderful time. But I can't go.

I've always spent May Day alone, ever since I was a child. Please don't be angry with me."

Colin nodded his head, but she could see from his clenched jaw that he was still hurt. Gennes walked over to him and put her hand on his arm.

"I'll be fine here alone," she said. "I haven't had a day all to myself since I came to Briallen. Please go and don't worry about me."

Her eyes pleaded with him, and at last he agreed. Calmed then, Gennes walked to her room and unfolded a mattress, sinking down onto it with a sigh. She waited there until all was quiet in the compound and she was certain that everyone had left. Then she walked back to the Hall and the kitchen and sat down among the leftover flowers that lay forgotten upon the table. Her May Day crown that she had put on that morning with great expectations, she took off and laid on the table beside the flowers. Then she sunk her head into her arms and cried until she could cry no more.

* * *

"Gennes?"

At the soft sound of Michael's voice, Gennes swung around on the bench. Her arm caught her crown as she turned, toppling it to the floor.

"Michael!" she exclaimed. "You startled me."

Attempting a pleasant smile, Gennes reached down and retrieved the crown of leaves, placing it again on the table. Michael crossed the room toward her, looking around him as he came.

"I thought everyone had already left for the festival," he said.

"Yes," she answered, with a small sniffle, "a little while ago."

Walking around the table, Michael sat down across from Gennes.

"But you're still here," he said, a kindly question in his voice.

Looking at him, she thought she could see true concern in his eyes. She wanted so much to confide in him. There was no one else that she felt comfortable talking to about her past. But when she had tried to talk to him before, he had walked away, finding any excuse not to be near her.

Before she could decide what to do, however, Michael spoke again. This time, the friendly concern was gone, replaced by a harsher, more direct tone.

"Where is Colin?" he asked.

Gennes looked up in surprise at the sudden change in Michael's voice. She swallowed hard, telling herself that she had imagined his concern for her. Having made his polite comments, he was now moving on to his true reason for speaking to her, to find Colin. Swiftly, she closed the door on her desire to reach out to him and answered him steadily.

"Colin was one of the first to leave," she said. "He didn't want to miss any of the dancing."

Michael's expression was still hard, and his voice deep.

"He didn't take you with him?" he asked, as if in accusation.

Still uncertain about what he was getting at, she was beginning to dislike the turn of the conversation very much. Her back straightened and her chin tilted upward.

"Don't tell me that you think I need a guardian, too," she said. "It's all I can do to get Colin to give me a little breathing space. He's worse than a brother. Just because I helped him in Trevelgue and then came to Briallen at his suggestion, he thinks he has to take care of me. I really am capable of taking care of myself!"

Her agitation had been rising, and with it, her voice. She glared at Michael, defying him to disagree with her. But his expression was not what she had expected. His forehead was creased, and his eyes narrowed in perplexity.

"You mean that you and Colin…," he started. "You aren't…? I mean, I thought that the two of you…."

Gennes' jaw dropped and she found herself laughing when she finally realized what he was trying to say.

"You thought that Colin had feelings for me?" she gasped. "No! Why he's at the festival right now, looking for some girl that he met in the marketplace last month."

She was smiling now, her indignation gone. But she was still a little confused. Had Michael been keeping his distance from her all this time because he thought that Colin had some prior claim to her affections? Was it possible that Michael really cared for her, or was she just imagining things again?

Smiling slightly, Michael reached over and touched her hand, still damp from her tears. Then he looked at her face, kindly again.

"If you weren't crying about Colin," he said softly, "then why were you crying?"

Gennes looked down at the glistening moisture on her hand, and realized for the first time how terrible she must look. Her cheeks felt stiff from the dried trail of tears that had flowed there such a short time before. Her nose was soar and probably red, and her eyes had been moist with unshed tears when Michael had first sat down. Unfortunately, she didn't really know why she was crying, making it rather difficult to explain it to him.

"You will think it's foolish," Gennes said at length, trying to think of some explanation for her behavior.

Michael waited patiently, so she continued.

"I was just feeling a little lonely," she said. "Being away from everything I've ever known."

As her head was still bowed, Michael had to lower his own head to meet her gaze. He smiled kindly.

"You miss your family?" he asked. "Your parents?"

She looked up at him and managed a weak smile. But looking into the depths of his grey eyes, she knew it wasn't true. She wasn't missing her home on the moor, or her adoptive parents, or her old way of life. There was something else she was longing for, something she had known once and then lost. Something that was just out of reach on the verge of her memory.

"To tell you the truth," she whispered, "Anna and Evin are not my real parents. I don't know…."

She could feel the tears welling up again in her eyes again and could not continue for several moments.

"I'm sorry," she sniffled at last. "I'm just not ready for a festival today. You go on. I'll be fine here alone."

She reached for her crown of leaves, but before she could lift it Michael placed his hands on hers, pressing them gently.

"I have a better idea," he said. "We'll both stay here. It's about time you and I got to know each other better."

Since Gennes couldn't agree more, she smiled warmly, wiped her eyes one last time, and set her May Day crown on the floor, out of her view.

For the next hour, Michael and Gennes sat and talked. He told her about his own family, his mother and two sisters still living, his father and grandparents killed in a mud-slide that destroyed half his village. After his father's death, Michael had come to Briallen as a youth, looking for work in Balchder's army. But when he saw the atrocities that the soldiers committed on the townsfolk, he changed his mind. He decided instead to work to protect the innocent, even though the rewards were far less than Balchder could offer. He had found a loose-knit resistance group, perhaps twenty strong. They were mostly merchants and a few old ministers of Brenin's court who had escaped the massacre. Michael helped to organize them and bring in new members, even outside the city. Working covertly together, they thwarted Balchder's men wherever they could and kept resistance to Balchder's authority strong. But over all else, they had one mission that they had failed to achieve—to find King Brenin's crown and to keep it safe from Balchder forever.

As Michael talked, Gennes listened intently. She was thrilled to hear him talk about the Resistance. She was also thrilled to just be there, alone with Michael, finally making some connection with him. She asked question after question, just to keep him going, just to hear the sound of his voice. Her own loneliness and distress had vanished, and she began to wish that May Day would never end.

She was just starting to ask another question about Michael's friends in the country, when he suddenly frowned. It wasn't a very serious frown, but it did stop her in the midst of her query.

"I have just realized," Michael said in mock severity, "that I have been doing all the talking. You have hardly said a word about yourself since we began."

Gennes smiled shyly and shrugged.

"Perhaps," she ventured, "you have had the more interesting life?"

Michael smiled back at her. Through narrow eyes, he regarded her for a moment, as if trying to decide whether he would be successful in getting any more information from her. He must have decided against it, because he yawned and sat back away from the table. For a moment, he gazed out the window. Then he turned to Gennes suddenly.

"Do you want to go out?" he asked.

She raised her eyebrows in surprise.

"To the festival, you mean?" she answered slowly.

"Not if you don't want to," he said with a pleasant smile. "We'll go somewhere else. I have some business I've been needing to tend to. You can come with me."

She was even more surprised at his offer to take her with him on real business, although perhaps this had nothing to do with the Resistance. Still, she didn't want her time with him to end, so she agreed, without even asking where they were going.

"Come on, then," Michael said with enthusiasm, rising from the bench. "Oh, and we don't want to forget this."

Coming around the table before Gennes had a chance to stand, he reached down and picked up her May Day crown. Then he placed it gently on her head.

"It's a disguise," he said. "Now everyone will think that we are just two revelers, looking for a quiet place to be alone."

Frowning, Gennes took his proffered hand and rose to her feet.

"Alone?" she repeated.

Michael explained as they walked to the front door.

"It is best," he said, "if we don't draw any attention to ourselves. We won't be far from the festival grounds, so people will assume that we came from there or are going there."

Michael's tone had changed, and his relaxed and easy manner of a few moments before had been replaced by something more serious. An uneasy knot began to form in Gennes' stomach, as she guessed that they were going to do something important. She wasn't certain whether the knot was from fear, nervousness, or excitement that Michael actually trusted her enough to take her with him. Whatever the emotion was, it intensified when they stopped at the door and Michael stooped low to whisper in her ear.

"Now for the difficult part," he said. "Do you think you can…pretend…to be…enjoying my company? What I mean is, we should…hold hands, laugh…just a man and a young woman who want to get away from the crowd at the festival."

He paused, waiting for her to answer, and Gennes suddenly realized that she was holding her breath. She blinked, and swallowed, and tried to breathe naturally

"Of course," she stammered. "I'll do whatever you say."

Michael smiled and took her hand again.

"Then we should go," he said, holding the door open wide.

* * *

The streets were nearly deserted, but everywhere they went they laughed and held hands like two young people in the first blush of love. Down two streets and then a third they ran, until they could hear the instruments and the singing at the festival grounds. Then another turn, away from the noise, and down a narrow passageway. Between two rows of tiny huts they walked until Michael stopped and pulled Gennes close to him. Playfully, he put his arms around her and locked his hands behind her back. Smiling, he brought his face down next to hers. Her breathing stilled again and her heart raced. His lips neared hers, but they never touched. Instead, his face brushed her cheek and his lips nuzzled near her ear.

"Pretend to be reluctant," he whispered, reminding Gennes abruptly that they were there on real business. "Act as if you don't want to be indiscreet in a public place. Then I'll coax you to come with me someplace where we will be hidden."

Silently, they acted out the charade. Michael nuzzled against Gennes while she, half-heartedly, tried to free herself from his embrace. She pulled back; he stepped closer. She pulled back again, breaking his hold on her. He grabbed her hand once more, pulling her gently out of the passageway and toward the dark window of a large stone building. Beside the wall, he swept her into his arms and placed her gently on the windowsill. Then she slipped inside, and he quietly followed.

Chapter Nine

Gennes found herself in a small dark room. There were no furnishings, and the air smelt old and stale. But the walls were solid and well-made, and underfoot she could feel the firmness of Roman tiles beneath a thick layer of dirt. The flushed feeling that had risen to her cheeks when Michael had held her outside drained slowly from her face. Still breathing hard from running through the streets, she suddenly found herself struggling to take in each new breath. Her heartbeat pounded in her ears, and a line of sweat broke out over her upper lip. When Michael stepped beside her and touched her arm, she jumped and nearly cried out.

"Michael," she whispered, and wished in the same moment that she had not. Even that small sound seemed to echo off the walls and stir the dust of the long-abandoned room.

Michael placed a finger to his mouth, gesturing for her to stay quiet. Then he took her hand and led her to a door at the far side of the room.

Passing through the open doorway, they came into a long hall. The feeling of staleness and strangeness persisted. Perhaps it was the sudden change from the warmth outside to the cool building, but Gennes felt strangely ill at ease, almost as if they were not alone. In the fancies of her imagination, she could hear people busily moving up and down the hall, talking to each other, even whistling a happy tune. And a voice she knew was calling out a name that she couldn't quite hear.

Michael stopped abruptly. Letting go of Gennes' hand, he gestured for her to stay where she was, then he cautiously approached one of the other rooms and slipped inside. For a moment there was silence. Then the low sounds of two voices could be heard from the room. Michael stepped back through the doorway and motioned for Gennes to join him. He was smiling again, and his manner was more relaxed. Gennes followed him into the room, no longer aware of the distant voices in the hall.

There was a small amount of furniture in this room. Several cots, a table with two chairs, and a few wooden chests were scattered about. Then she saw the person who had spoken with Michael. An old man in a tattered brown tunic sat on one cot, away from the small amount of sunlight that filtered through the boarded window.

"Gennes," Michael said quietly, "I want you to meet someone."

Michael brought her over to the man as he continued to speak.

"This is Lanreath. He is one of our best sources of information about Balchder's doings in Briallen. We like to think of him as the guardian of Brenin's house."

At his last words, Gennes caught her breath as if suddenly paralyzed. A cold chill ran up her spine, and the hair on the back of her arms stood up. She blinked twice, trying to clear her thoughts and understand what Michael had just said.

Michael took no notice of Gennes' agitation. He spoke instead to Lanreath, politely turning his attention to the eldest person present.

"I was just about to tell Gennes why we are here," he said. "I understand that Balchder's men were here again, a few days ago. Do you have any news for us?"

The man gave a slow and deliberate nod of his grey head.

"Four days ago it was," he began in a voice as dusty as the room. "They're still looking. But they left with nothing."

Michael turned to Gennes to explain.

"Two or three times every year, Balchder sends some of his elite guards to search the house," he said. "In the beginning they would take items with them, pieces of treasure, large chests, even small pieces of furniture."

Lanreath nodded, adding to Michael's story, "They are looking for the crown. After all these years, they still hunt for some clue to its hiding place."

Michael shook his head.

"They have looked into every corner and cupboard, and behind every loose stone. Surely they can't expect to find the crown here," he said.

"It is not the crown for which they seek," Lanreath scolded. "It is a clue. Balchder has employed a powerful wizard. He tells him that the crown was hidden by means of magic."

Michael scoffed under his breath, but Lanreath must have heard him.

"You don't believe in magic, do you?" he asked.

Michael cleared his throat and inclined his head politely.

"Let's just say, that I have never seen any evidence of it."

Gennes watched Michael as he spoke. He was so certain of himself, so strong and confident. He had probably never needed the help of wishes, or dreams, or magic. She could feel his confidence almost as if he had put his arm around her again, and her own sense of bewilderment began to fade. Absent-mindedly, she fingered the locket on her bracelet and turned her attention back to Lanreath.

Lanreath had turned his full attention to her. He peered at her though narrowed eyes, searching her face, perhaps even her soul. She felt trapped within his gaze like a mouse before a snake. After a long moment, he relaxed and smiled. Still looking at Gennes, he inclined his head toward Michael.

"This one believes in magic, I venture," he said with a twinkle in his eyes. "Perhaps her young eyes may even see something here that we have missed."

Michael turned to Gennes, smiling disarmingly. He didn't appear to be taking Lanreath's comments too seriously. Lanreath, on the other hand, she believed to be quite serious, and she wondered what else he might be able to see in her eyes. Michael took her arm and turned toward the door.

"Why don't we go find out?" he said, motioning for Lanreath to take the lead.

Lanreath shuffled into the hall. Although he moved quietly, he went without the sense of caution that Michael had employed earlier. He appeared to be quite at home in the deserted building and confident that no unwanted company was about. Michael followed, close enough to speak to Lanreath in a soft voice. Gennes followed behind Michael, watching all about her for any ghosts that might inhabit the darker corners.

The hall was quiet except for the low tones of Michael and Lanreath conversing, too softly for Gennes to hear clearly. The walls of the hall were scuffed and blackened by smoke. Many of the tiles on the floor were broken or missing, but Gennes could still make out a pattern of some type among the darker and the lighter tiles. Mentally tracing the lines on the floor, she didn't realize that Michael and Lanreath had stopped at a doorway until she almost ran into them. Following them through the door, she glanced back down the hall, to determine how far they had come.

"They spent a good deal of time in here," Lanreath was telling Michael as Gennes entered. "They have looked here before, but never so thoroughly."

Gennes stopped short just inside the doorway. Light filtered through tiny cracks in the shuttered and boarded window revealing a solid bedframe and a small table with a chair. A large wooden chest sat against the wall, its lid hanging at an odd angle on broken hinges. The tiles in this room were larger and all one color—green, she thought, though it was difficult to see in the dim light.

Michael turned to her and spoke in a whisper, "This was the bedroom of the little princess, Addien."

Gennes tried to answer. She tried to move, but her heart was beating so loudly that she could barely hear Michael's words. He had already turned away from her, joining Lanreath on the far side of the bed-frame. They were crouching down, focused on something on the floor. With a deep breath, Gennes forced herself to go across the room and join them.

"This is what I wanted to show you," Lanreath said, pointing at a large hole in the floor. "The old grate is over there."

Michael reached over and lifted a flat piece of metal crossed with tiny openings barely large enough for a child's fingers to poke through. One corner had been twisted upward, and there were several other marks where something heavy had pounded into it. Michael examined it closely and then handed it to Gennes.

"I don't understand," he said to Lanreath. "Why open the grate? They've already searched the tunnels. And we tried all of the grates in the house. They were all bolted into the floor. No one could have escaped from the house that way, especially not a seven year old girl."

If Lanreath responded, Gennes never heard it. The grate in her hands was all she could see or think about. She had seen it before. She had seen this room before. She had come here looking for something....

Her eyes drifted to the wooden shutters on the window. There were noises outside. Someone was shouting, getting closer to the window. In the hallway, a woman screamed, booted men were running, fighting, clashing swords against shields. She was running out of time....

And then she saw it—on the chest next to wall. Her necklace. Her locket. She moved toward it, to grasp it, to open it....But as she moved toward the necklace on the chest, the heavy metal grate fell from her hands and crashed onto the tile floor. The sudden noise jolted her body like a blow, and she jerked backwards in horror. Then she looked at the chest again, and the necklace was gone.

Through a haze, she heard Michael's voice. It seemed so far away, like a distant sound carried through the fog on the moor. Then he was before her, his hands on her shoulders, pulling her back to the present.

"Are you all right?" he was saying. "Gennes? Are you feeling all right?"

With a sudden breath, she looked up at him. His deep grey eyes were fixed on hers, calming her mind and driving away the torturous vision.

"Yes," she said, barely above a whisper.

He helped her sit down on the wooden frame of the bed.

"You looked as if you were about to faint," he said, sitting beside her.

His eyes still searched her face for reassurance, and she struggled to find some explanation for her behavior.

"I'm sorry I dropped it," she said, looking guiltily at the grate on the floor. "I don't know what happened."

"You don't look well," Michael responded. "We should go home, so you can get some rest."

"No," she answered, quickly. "It's nothing, really. We don't have to leave yet."

In answering him, Gennes realized that she really did not want to leave. She needed to stay and find out more about her visions, about what this house—the house of the last king of Dumnonia—had to do with her.

Glancing at the boarded window, she shrugged and said, "I guess it's just the air in here. I'm used to the open country air. I don't do well in small enclosed places."

She smiled calmly at Michael, hoping that he would not make too much of the incident. After a long moment, he smiled back, but with a trace of concern lingering in his eyes.

"If you're sure you're all right," he said.

Gennes nodded and rose. Turning to Lanreath she asked, "Are there other rooms you wanted to show us. Perhaps if I walk around a little, I'll feel more steady."

Lanreath regarded her through narrowed eyes. Behind his gaze, there may have only been concern for her health, but she doubted it. Once again, he seemed to be looking right into her, sensing that she could see something in the room that he could not. But whatever Lanreath could see in her eyes, he said nothing about it. Instead, he straightened his old back and nodded toward the door.

"Aye," he said, "there is more to see."

Back in the hallway, they walked on past two more doorways, one of which opened into a great kitchen. Then they turned to the other side of the hall where a large wooden door hung on one hinge. The room they entered was tall and wide, and almost as long as the hallway they had just left. A number of heavy wooden tables and benches sat around the room at odd angles, some of them on their sides, many of them scarred by deep cuts into the soft wood. Broken pottery littered the floor, much of which lay deep in dust. It was obvious even to an untrained eye that a battle had taken place there, but a very long time ago.

Gennes would have liked to stop and look around her, but Lanreath moved quickly across the room to a door in the far wall. With Michael walking just behind her with his hand on her back for support, she had no opportunity to explore the strange feelings that the room gave her. Through the far door they marched silently, into another long hallway that stretched into darkness.

Lanreath slowed then, moving more cautiously than he had previously. A wooden door partially barred the way into the first room along the hall. It could do no more, as a large piece of the door had been hacked away. Much of the wood was covered in deep gashes, but across the top could still be seen the remains of an intricate carving. The hinges creaked loudly as Lanreath pushed the door open and entered. He paused for the briefest of moments and took a deep breath. Then he disappeared into the dimness. Gennes stepped into the door-frame after him, but there she froze.

Once again, she felt suddenly paralyzed. Her feet simply refused to carry her into the room. She struggled with all her might to be able to do something—scream, cry, run, anything besides just standing there in the silence. At last, the panic that gripped her released its hold long enough for her to retreat into the hall. But as she did so, she collided with Michael, who quickly put his arm around her waist to steady them both. Gennes looked up at him, uncertain for the moment who he was or why he was there. He looked down at her with a confident smile and eyes that were clear and bright. Gennes' own sense of panic faded once more and she turned back to enter the room.

This room was even darker than the rest of the house. With no windows, the only light came through the doorway from the dim hallway behind them. Attempting to focus her eyes and make some sense out of the shadows, Gennes heard a creaking sound from one corner of the room. A moment later, Lanreath appeared in the far corner of the room with a lit torch.

The light of the torch danced about the still room, driving the shadows into the corners. Moving toward the light, Gennes and Michael met Lanreath in the center of the room. There, they all paused to look at the incredible sight that was revealed. Pieces of wood that had once been tables, or benches, or chairs, had been thrown all over the room. Every piece of furniture that had been in the room had been demolished. Some of the pieces were so splintered and smashed that it appeared as if they had exploded from the inside out. Broken pottery and tattered pieces of tapestries also littered the floor. The devastation was complete, down to the stripping away of the plaster that had been upon the walls.

There was one other thing in the room—an unfamiliar smell that crept up on the senses like a sour aftertaste. Gennes cast about for the cause of the odor, but she could not find its source or even determine from which direction it came.

"What happened here?" Michael gasped as he surveyed the scene.

It was his first display of surprise since they entered the house, leading Gennes to believe that the carnage was recent. Lanreath paused before answering. He cleared his throat twice, as if he as well was bothered by the odd odor.

"I told you," he began at length, "that Balchder has employed a wizard. He was here. I can't tell you what they did in this room, but even I was afraid to come in here for two days afterwards."

"The wizard was here?" Michael asked, astonished again. "We received no report of anyone arriving with the soldiers."

"He came disguised as a soldier," Lanreath answered. "But I saw him later in his wizard's robes. He spent most of the afternoon shut up in here by himself. You can see for yourself the result of his evil magic."

"Potions and incantations, perhaps," Michael mused. "But I don't see what could have been gained by such 'magic' other than the creation of a lot of firewood."

"What they gained, I do not know," Lanreath responded. "I only know that they left here to search the princess' room, as you have seen. The wizard did not seem displeased when they left."

As the men talked, Gennes became more and more aware of the odor in the room. It was almost as if she could see it, a hazy green mist that hung in the air. The mist swirled about her, turning her slowly away from Michael and Lanreath. Parting before her and building behind, it nudged her forward toward a bright circle on the floor. Beneath her feet, she could feel the coolness of the tiled floor, no longer hidden beneath shards and splinters of wood. The whole room was bright with burning lamps, and there were voices yelling, a pounding on the walls, and the crashing of axes at the door.

Unable to stop herself, Gennes moved toward the circle of gold on the floor. The mist parted around it, revealing shiny red stones and engraved knots. She began to reach for it, when suddenly it was grabbed from the floor by a child in a purple gown. The child clutched the circle to her chest, tears streaming down her cheeks. For a moment she knelt there sobbing, then she turned and ran toward a little door in the corner of the room, where she disappeared from Gennes' sight behind a tapestry. An old man's voice echoed off the walls, "*I only know that they left here to search the princess' room...The wizard did not seem displeased when they left."*

The mist thickened again, obscuring her vision, threatening to overwhelm her. With all of her effort, she struggled to see through the fog one more thing. Searching the floor, she followed the line from where the child had been kneeling to the place where she had been looking. A vague outline grew clearer until at last Gennes could see him. Cast upon the tile, covered in blood from his mortal wounds, lay the great king of Dumnonia—her father.

Overpowered at last, Gennes collapsed into the mist. Crumbling at the knees and falling backwards, she impacted, not on the floor, but into strong arms that lifted her upwards. One arm swung under her to support her legs and the other wrapped securely around her back. Her head rested against a shoulder, with her face just touching a sinewy neck. Then she was being carried away from the mist, away from the noise, and away from the crown that had been snatched from her sight. Safe and warm, she closed her eyes and welcomed the darkness.

* * *

Gennes awoke to find Michael kneeling beside her. They were in the servants' room again, where they had first met Lanreath. She was laying on one of the cots, and Michael was preparing to place a damp cloth on her face. Blinking away the last of the mist, she wondered how much of what she had just seen had been real, how much imagined, and how much conjured up by the remnants of black magic in the room.

"Gennes," Michael sighed, relieved to see her eyes opening.

"Michael," she whispered. "What happened in there?"

"Lanreath and I were talking," he answered, "when I saw you begin to fall. Whatever that stench was in there, it must have overcome you."

Half-closing her eyes, Gennes nodded in agreement. The nightmare that had seized her in the King's Court had been hers alone. Michael, at least, seemed unaware of it. For the time being, it would have to remain so. Gennes wished only to leave the house and to find a warm place in the sun to gather her strength and force back the flood of tears that threatened to overtake her.

Michael was agreeable to leaving, but he refused to let Gennes walk.

"At least until we're outside in the fresh air," he said, scooping her into his arms again.

Too drained to argue, she relaxed in his strong grip as he carried her out into the hall and through the small room where they had entered the building. He set her on the windowsill, and she slid through. For a moment, Michael paused inside, speaking a few last, low words with Lanreath. Lanreath waved good-bye through the window, and then Michael slipped outside. Putting his arm around Gennes' waist, he encouraged her to lean on him as they walked. The wall of the King's House disappeared behind them, hidden by the huts that had been built up around it. The ghosts and visions were behind them as well, Gennes knew, but the chilling memories they had drawn out of her persisted, and she clung to Michael for all the security she could find.

Out in the main street, they could once again hear the revelry of the May Day festival. The sun had inched its way a little closer to the western horizon, but it was still high enough to shine down in their faces. Closing her eyes to enjoy its warmth, Gennes breathed deeply and slowed her pace. Michael slowed also, then came to a stop.

"Do you need to rest?" he asked.

Gennes nodded, opening her eyes slowly. What little energy she had seemed to be seeping out of her into the street. She didn't want to walk, or talk, or think. Most of all, she didn't want to remember.

"There's a place over here," Michael said, leading her to a low stone wall.

They sat, and Gennes closed her eyes again, her face tilted toward the sun. Michael remained silent beside her. She could hear the steady rhythm of his breathing and the sound of his boot scuffling in the sand.

She owed so much to him, and he didn't even know. How could he know about the nightmare that had assaulted her in the house? The dreadful memories? The still-present fears? But to tell him about it then would mean reliving it again, and she didn't have the strength to do that. So she closed out the past and brought herself back into the present, back where the sun was shining, and music was playing, and the laughter of the townsfolk drifted down the streets from the festival grounds.

Opening her eyes, Gennes looked down at her hands in her lap. Around her left wrist hung the gold bracelet she had found under the great stone on the moor. The center charm dangled over the palm of her hand, hiding the secret compartment inside. She had gone back to her room to find the locket after her father was killed. She could remember it now, and she could remember why. Like fog burning away in the heat of day, the darkness that had surrounded her past for so long was growing lighter, revealing things she had once wished never to remember.

Drained of energy and emotion, she wanted very much to be alone. She had almost forgotten that Michael was even beside her until she looked up and saw him.

"Feeling better?" he asked her.

She nodded and gave him a weak smile.

"Then let's go home," he said.

Standing, he pulled her to her feet and wrapped one arm protectively around her waist. Together that way, they walked down the street away from the music and the laughter of the festival grounds.

Chapter Ten

Gennes' only thought was to get back to her own little room where she could be alone with her thoughts. The festival would go on until long after sundown, making the Roman Hall a safe and quiet place to retreat. At first, she only wanted to run and hide. But as she walked, her feelings of panic and dismay slowly lessened. She could feel her feet, no longer numb, striking the solid stones of the street. Her chest no longer felt crushed or constricted, and a gentle warmth stole through her body, starting at a low point on her back where Michael's hand still rested.

Consumed by her own emotions, she had almost forgotten again that he was beside her. But as she began to open her mind to the incredible events of that day, she realized that he had always been beside her. It was Michael who brought her out of the fog when she stood in her old bedroom, seeing her necklace on the chest where, of course, it couldn't be. It was Michael who caught her when she passed out in the King's Court after seeing a vision of her father dead upon the floor. And it was Michael who had tenderly carried her out of the building and away from the terrible visions and memories.

As the warmth spread through her to her arms and legs and up to her neck and face, she felt a new sensation, unlike anything she had ever experienced before. Talking with Michael earlier in the day had been pleasant and enlightening. Running hand in hand with him through the streets had been exhilarating. Being held by him had taken her breath away. But nothing had felt like this.

Suddenly, she felt the need to hear his voice again. She rambled through her mind for something to talk about. Not what happened at the King's House; that was too recent. And not her past, which was unraveling inside her mind too quickly for her to clearly understand it. She needed time to think about those things in private and see if she could make some sense out of it all. Glancing around the empty streets, the only other thing that came to her foggy mind was the May Day Festival.

"Michael," she started, her voice dry and strained. "Why didn't you go to the festival today?"

Michael looked at her and raised an eyebrow.

"What do you mean?" he asked.

"I feel bad that I kept you from the festival," she answered. "You didn't need to stay and take care of me."

Michael laughed softly.

"If taking care of you is what I was doing," he said, "I didn't do a very good job of it. Besides, what if I didn't want to go the festival?"

Gennes smiled.

"There must have been a dozen girls there watching for you all day," she said. "One of them will soon be crowned queen of the festival. It isn't too late for you to go."

She wasn't sure why she was telling him to go. She did want to be alone, but she would feel much better in her little room knowing that he was nearby in another part of the compound. She didn't really want him to leave. Perhaps she just wanted to know if he would rather be with her than with some other woman at the festival.

"Maybe I don't want to go," he answered. "Maybe I don't need to go see the crowning of the most beautiful girl at the festival, when I'm already with the most beautiful girl in all of Dumnonia."

Michael smiled and took his hand from her back. From his belt he removed the tattered remains of her May Day crown.

"You dropped this when you fainted," he said.

Folding back some of the crumpled leaves, he formed the crown into a circle again. Then he very gently reached over and placed the crown upon her head.

"Come on," he said, wrapping his arm around her back again. "Let's go home. I'll find something for us to eat from the kitchen, then you can get some sleep. You look as if you need it."

"Still trying to take of me?" she chided.

"Would you let me if I tried?" he asked, turning her toward him.

They stopped in the middle of the deserted street, as Michael wrapped his other arm around her. For a long moment, he looked into her eyes without speaking. Gennes returned his gaze without moving. The strength of his arms comforted her, and the light in his eyes entranced her. It was a light she had never seen there before, and she was drawn toward it like a warm fire on a snowy evening.

"Would you let me…?" he whispered again, as he brought his face down toward hers.

It was a different question this time, she knew, and she answered it in the only way she knew how. She lifted her face, tilting it just slightly, until her lips made contact with his. Warmth, and excitement, and happiness, rushed through her, keeping pace with the swift rhythm of her heart. Her arms embraced him, pulling him closer, feeling the firmness and heat of his sides and back through the thin material of his tunic. Her head spun as she closed her eyes and shut out everything from her mind except the feel, the taste, and the smell of him.

For a long while they remained in each other's arms, until Michael at length drew back. Once again Gennes looked up into his eyes. The fire was still there, but he shielded it with half-closed lids.

"You need to go home," he said with some difficulty. "I'm supposed to be making you rest and take care of yourself."

"I feel better all ready," Gennes murmured with a half-smile.

Michael chuckled.

"You say that now. But wait until tomorrow, when you accuse me of taking advantage of you while you were ill."

Gennes pulled back from his embrace and gave him a serious look.

"You must think of me as a naïve country girl with no more sense or self-control than…than…than Tomas gives me credit for."

"Not at all," he responded. "Sometimes I don't know what to think about you. But you did faint back there, and you've looked ill ever since we entered that house. You need to get inside out of the evening air and get some rest."

She smiled at his authoritative tone and refused to move until he smiled back at her and shook his head in resignation.

"I like being with you," she sighed as they walked together back to the Roman Hall. "I wish it could always be like this."

Michael sighed also.

"We'll find some time alone together," he promised.

"When?" she asked.

"I'll arrange something as soon as I can."

"When?" she asked again.

By the time they had reached the gate to the compound wall, he had found an answer.

"Do you like to ride?" he asked. "I have a friend I need to talk to west of the city. To ride there and back will take a full day. I wouldn't mind a little company."

"You wouldn't?" she teased, taking in the twinkle in his eyes.

"But then I don't even know if horseback riding would interest you," he continued. "Have you ever ridden before?"

"I have," she answered truthfully.

It had been a long time since she had ridden in pony races at the Lord of Trevelgue's castle, but she had always been very comfortable around horses. With fresh insight into her privileged past, she was beginning to understand why. But it really didn't matter. For a chance to be alone with Michael again, she would have ridden the wind.

"When do we leave?" she asked, with more energy than she had felt all day.

"In a few days," Michael smiled down at her. "As long as you are feeling better."

Gennes sighed happily as she followed him into the Roman Hall to find something to eat. She felt better all ready.

* * *

A short while later, Gennes retreated to the solitude of her little room with bread and wine for her supper. She hadn't even wanted to take that, but Michael insisted that she eat something, and nothing else had appealed to her. After shutting the door quietly, she pulled a stool to a corner of the room where she wouldn't be visible from the window or from the door if it happened to open. She collapsed on the stool and put her head back against the cold wall, nearly as weak from hunger as she was from the excitement of the day. Although the thought of eating still did not appeal to her, she forced herself to eat several bites of the stale bread and take a few sips of sweet wine before setting the rest of her supper beside her on the floor.

Cocking her head, she checked once more for any sounds from outside the room. All was still. She bit down on her lip and turned her bracelet around her wrist until she held the locket over the palm of her left hand. With a deep breath, she set her thumbnail beside the little door and popped it open. A small flash of light startled her, and she dropped the locket into her palm. When she had blinked away the little dots before her eyes left by the unexpected light, she looked down at her lap and found a little man sitting on her knee.

He was roughly the size of a mouse. A red cap sat jauntily over mossy grey hair and a wrinkled face. He wore a brown tunic and brown breeches covered to the knees by green stockings. And his tiny black eyes twinkled with reflected light from the one small lamp in the room.

"Trevilian!" Gennes gasped.

The little pixie looked up at her and smiled.

"It was you, wasn't it?" Gennes asked. "That night on the moor? You took me to a cave to escape the storm. But why didn't you appear when I first opened the locket?"

"Who's to say that I didn't appear?" the pixie buzzed. "As I said, sometimes we can't see what is right in front of us. It wasn't until the storm frightened ye that ye began to see with yer heart instead of yer head."

"Then I could see you?" she wondered out loud. "You were as big as me then, I couldn't hardly miss you."

"Was I, then?" Trevilian mused, his eyes twinkling merrily.

Gennes leaned back against the wall again, thinking back to her night on the moor several weeks before. Everything had seemed unreal that night. The storm had come up so quickly and frightened her with its thunder and lightening. In the darkness, she hadn't known which way to go. Then the stone beside her seemed to grow larger, and the grass pushed up around her, and a cave had appeared in a rock wall that hadn't been there before....

"You made me small!" she gasped, finally making sense of her memories. "And the cave that we went in...."

"The very hole that ye had dug under the stone," he finished for her.

"Had you been there all along, guarding the necklace?" she asked.

"Just as ye asked me to," he answered. "Are ye starting to remember it all, then?"

Gazing across the dimly lit room, she tried to work the fractured pieces of her memory back into order.

"I only have a dim memory of the moor," she answered at length, "burying the necklace there. I don't have any idea how we got there. But I do remember that terrible morning...."

Tears filled her eyes as her senses were flooded once again by the sights and sounds of the battle in the King's House. She wiped the tears away, fighting the urge to block out the memories and hide from them once again. She needed to remember.

"I went to my room to look for you," she continued softly, letting the tears fall where they would. "You loved my locket and often hid inside it so we could be together. I asked you to help me hide the crown. And you made me small, like you did on the moor."

"Small enough to go inside the locket with myself," Trevilian added. "Ye and the crown."

Gennes' eyes brightened with the wonder of it all.

"But then what?" she asked.

"We waited while the soldiers searched the room. They were too busy looking for the crown—and fresh victims—to worry about any other little trinkets. Later, when it was quiet, we slipped into the tunnel beneath the room, taking the locket with us."

"And the crown? Is it still…?"

A sudden sense of caution kept her from saying any more out loud, although she had no reason to believe there was anyone around who could hear her.

"'Tis still safe," Trevilian answered, without waiting for her to finish. "Will ye be wanting it, then?"

It was a simple enough question, but one she had no idea how to answer. Now that she knew who she was—or, at least, who she once had been—what was she supposed to do next? As far as she knew, she was the only person in the whole kingdom, other than Trevilian, who knew where her father's crown was hidden. Men would kill to learn that secret. Many had been killed already.

"No," she answered at length. "I would like to leave it where it is. I have to be very careful about what I do now and who I talk to about this."

"Aye, like yer father said," Trevilian droned, nodding wisely. In response to Gennes' puzzled look, he continued: "'Listening ears are everywhere, and an untimely word can bring destruction upon a whole house.'"

Gennes smiled warmly, as another piece of her past fell into place in her mind. It had been on her sixth birthday, when her father had given her the necklace. The locket was a special gift, a place for her "most secret of thoughts" and her "most secret of friends". She had never imagined, though, that it would be a place to secrete herself as well.

Looking back at Trevilian, she smiled and asked, "Do you remember everything you hear?"

"Well, now, pixies live a very long time," he droned, quite seriously. "What may seem a long time ago to some, seems to myself as only a day or two in the passin'."

Gennes was quiet for a long while, thinking about Trevilian's words. Without speaking, she retrieved her bread from the floor and shared a piece with her friend. She followed it with the wine, slowly drinking everything in the cup. When she had finished and replaced the cup on the floor, her eyes were filled with unshed tears.

"Do you think I have been very wicked to forget my own mother and father?" she asked in a bare whisper.

Trevilian cocked his head to one side to answer her.

"I don't know much about being wicked," he said. "That's something yer priests and monks can tell ye about. But as for myself, I can't say I'm surprised that ye would want to forget what happened to ye and yer family. Ye were only a child. It took two weeks for us to get out of the city, hiding by day and moving by night. I had to make ye small again and hide ye in someone's baggage to get us beyond the guards at the gate. Ye wanted to find the remotest part of the kingdom to hide yer father's crown, and that's what we did. But by the time we reached the stones, ye were half dead from starvation and fright. It's no wonder at all that ye put such things out of yer mind after that."

"Anna always said that God guided me to the stones, and guided Evin there to find me. Do you think that's possible?" Gennes asked.

"I suppose anything is possible," Trevilian answered. "Anything at all."

* * *

Late in the night, Gennes sat on her sleeping mat, unable to sleep. The other women had returned from the festival and given her a noisy recitation of the day's events. The festival had ended when the flame of the great bonfire had been passed from one torch to another, one for each household present. Then the assembly had paraded by the light of the torches into the city or away to the countryside, back to each reveler's home.

The women had finally settled down and drifted off to sleep. The room was still, except for the sounds of heavy breathing from one of the sleepers. A full moon had risen, and its light shone through the window, reflecting off the leaves of the May Day crown Gennes held in her lap. For some time, she had ceased to think about the king, or his crown, or even Trevilian. Her mind was more pleasantly employed, remembering one moment of the afternoon, when she had found herself in Michael's embrace and he had leaned down to kiss her.

Very carefully, she lifted her crown and folded it in half, and then in half again. Then she placed it under the rolled cloth she used for a pillow. It was said that the leaves so placed on a May Day night would bring dreams of one's future husband. Then she lay down upon the mattress and finally drifted off to sleep.

Gennes did dream that night. In a dark place, she saw the shadowy figure of a cloaked and hooded man. She ran after him, calling for him to stop. She needed to talk to him, to see his face. Her heart pounded as rain splashed against her face. Her anticipation rose as the man stopped and turned toward her—but his face was not what she expected. His wavy hair was dark, not golden, and streaked with grey, and his eyes were a cool blue. Smiling, he kneeled and held out a closed hand to her. Suddenly, they were no longer on the street, in the rain. They were in a long, lamp-lit hall, in front of a carved door. Gennes' hated enemy, Lord Balchder, opened his hand to reveal a graceful silver ring. He took her hand and began to place the ring within it.

Struggling to free herself from the vision, Gennes tossed and turned until she was in her own room again, panting and sweating on her own mat. She rubbed her eyes and forced the terrible thoughts from her mind. But when she returned to sleep, the vision continued.

Still panting for breath, she was running through the streets and alleys of the city, pursued by some unknown enemy. Suddenly she found herself hiding in a hedge, surrounded by leaves and branches. Peering out from the branches, she saw a man approaching wearing the long brown robe of a monk. His hood was pulled down over his face, but Gennes felt as if she knew him. He stopped by the hedge directly in front of her and dropped something. A silver ring fell slowly to the ground and jingled on the stones at the man's feet. As the man stooped down to retrieve the ring, she caught her breath in horror. Beneath the hood were the same dark hair and the same blue eyes she had been running from for so long. Smiling, he turned to her and held out the ring.

Jolted out of the dream, Gennes wondered if she had screamed out loud. But when she sat up and looked around, the other women who slept in the room had not awoken. The scream instead seemed to be stuck in her throat, forcing her to gasp for air. Impulsively, she pulled the May Day crown out from under her pillow and ran to the window with it. She flung it out onto the dirt and stones, to be trampled under foot the next day. Then, breathing easier and wiping the sweat away, she returned to bed and slept fitfully through the rest of the night.

Chapter Eleven

On a warm and cloudless morning, Michael and Gennes saddled up two tired-looking horses at a stable near the edge of the city. A short while later, they passed through the city's southern gate and turned south-west down a path toward the distant mountains. The two looked at each other and smiled. Then they prodded their horses into a canter and set off to face the day.

For quite awhile they rode in silence, enjoying the spring air and the feel of the wind. They stopped only once, to rest the horses and refresh themselves with water and bread. They talked about the weather, their friends in the city, and the man they were going to visit. Torbryon owned a large tract of land near the city where he kept cattle and did a little farming. Although he wasn't a nobleman, he had several household servants and at least ten hired hands, a sizable force ready to aid Michael and his friends if they ever took up arms. Michael considered Torbryon one of his strongest supporters, and he liked to keep in touch with him.

After their rest, they rode more slowly. They didn't have much farther to go, and Michael assumed that Torbryon would be out until midday. The leisurely ride left Gennes with plenty of time to think, and she had a great deal to think about. Somehow, she had to tell Michael the truth about herself. Again and again she tried to think of a way to tell him that didn't sound completely impossible. She didn't want him to think that she had lost her mind. She began to realize that, unless she showed him the crown itself, it was very possible that he wouldn't believe her.

Gazing at the far horizon, Gennes thought back to the day they had first met and how fate had brought them together.

"Michael," she said, breaking a lengthy silence, "I've been wanting to ask you something."

Michael turned to listen and slowed his horse to a lazy walk. Gennes looked at him and drew a deep breath.

"Why did you help me that day in the marketplace?" she asked.

He answered simply, "You needed help."

She nodded and looked away to hide her frown. It wasn't exactly the answer she had hoped for.

After a moment, Michael continued, "The truth is, those soldiers did me a favor."

Gennes shot a puzzled look at him, and he looked back with a boyish grin.

"I had been watching you all morning, trying to get up enough courage to talk to you," he said. "I saw that boy fall, like you did, but I was too far away to help. Then I saw you throw yourself in front of the horses, and I knew I had to meet you."

"So you saved me from the soldiers," she teased, "and then ran off and left me in the bushes to fend for myself."

Michael looked at her and smiled.

"Knowing you now, I don't doubt that you could have fended for yourself," he laughed. "But the truth is, I was never very far away. I would have come back sooner, but I didn't know what to say to you. You were the most beautiful and enchanting woman I had ever seen."

Gennes caught her breath at the unexpected complement and turned her head away. But whatever he said, it was difficult to think of Michael as being afraid of anything, especially her.

"It must be very dangerous for you now," she said, glancing sideways at him. "You've helped so many people against the soldiers. Surely they know your face. Aren't you afraid that you'll be captured, or…?"

"Killed?" he asked, finishing her question.

He paused for a moment before answering.

"As far as I know, I don't have a price on my head," he said, lightly. "I'm just a minor annoyance to Balchder, not a threat—yet. I'm careful about what I do, and I have a lot of friends that I trust to help me."

He smiled again, full of confidence and conviction. She smiled back, happy for awhile just to be with him. They rode on again in silence until they came to a low stone wall. Michael dismounted and opened a wooden gate for them to pass through.

"This is the beginning of Torbryon's land," he said as he mounted his horse again. "We'll be at the house in time for the midday meal."

The sun above them had nearly reached its highest point in the sky. The day would soon be half over, and Gennes still had not found a way to tell Michael her story. Once again, she tried to broach the subject.

"Michael," she said, looking down at her reins as he mounted again and they prodded their horses into a walk, "what would you do if someone just came to you and gave you Brenin's crown, just like that?"

Michael laughed. But when he looked at her, and saw that she wasn't laughing, his smile faded and he regarded her seriously.

"I think about it sometimes," he said, "what I would do if this ever ends, or if I had never become involved in it. Maybe I would go home and start a farm, or hire on with a nobleman, or even take my chances at sea as a smuggler. That wouldn't be any less dangerous, but at least I'd have something to offer, to someone like you."

"Oh, Michael!" Gennes gasped.

"That is what we're talking about, isn't it?" Michael looked at her again, smiling softly. "I suppose I could find a more stable life if I tried. But I am what I am. I could never just sit back and watch things happening around me."

"And I would never ask you to," she told him earnestly. "I admire you so much for everything you've done, everything you're doing."

They held each other's gaze for a long while.

"I know one thing will never change," Michael said at length. "I will always want to be with you."

Gennes looked at him, wanting so much to believe him. Suddenly, she wanted to know that he would still care for her when he knew the truth, when he knew that she was a princess, when he knew that she possessed the most sought after treasure in all the kingdom—King Brenin's crown—and she had the power to give it to whomever she chose. She thought about the day they had met, when he thought that she was in love with Colin. He had pushed her away then. She needed to know that he wouldn't push her away again when he learned her real name and her title. But, for the moment, it was too late. They were already within sight of a large compound, and Michael had other things to think about. Gennes' confession would have to wait until they began the trip home and were alone again.

As they neared the main house of the compound, something about it stirred a memory in Gennes' mind. She was certain that she had not passed this way on her journey from Trevelgue to Briallen, and she hadn't been this far from the city since her return. Yet there was something very familiar about the place. Puzzled, she scanned the rolling hills of granite and grass. The view was unbroken except for some stone buildings, a few low walls, and the tree-lined brook that ran down from the Tawel Mountains toward Briallen.

It was the brook that she remembered! Some ten years ago, when she fled Briallen, she had followed the brook for the first day. She remembered seeing the compound in the distance and wanting to seek shelter there, but there were too many people around. She was afraid to get any closer. She kept following the brook southward until she came within sight of some soldiers. She had turned west then and climbed onto the moor where she found the standing stones. But she could remember the main house, with the smoke of a cooking fire, the smell of roasting meat, and the distant voices of the servants preparing their master's meal.

While she was recalling this, Michael was dismounting by the door of the house. Gennes was suddenly struck by the quietness of the area. She remembered the compound as having a lot of activity, and Michael had said that Torbryon employed a number of servants. Yet no one seemed to be around. Gennes dismounted while she waited for Michael to check the house. Then she led both of the horses over to the stone wall of the stable. Michael joined her there a short while later.

"There doesn't seem to be anyone about," he said. "The men must be out with the cattle, but I can't imagine where the women are."

"Perhaps gone to market," Gennes answered, looking at a set of deep tracks in the dirt. "Their cart is gone, and from the look of these tracks it was loaded heavily."

"You don't miss much, do you?" Michael asked, looking pleased. "Well, we can wait and see if they return. We'll still have time to get back before dark."

Leaving their horses at a watering trough, Gennes went inside the stable to find some grain for them to eat. As she started out again, Michael suddenly slipped through the door and grabbed her arm.

"Soldiers," he whispered urgently. "Four of them on horseback headed this way. We've got to hide."

Casting about the little building, they both saw at the same time a wooden ladder against the wall that led up to a narrow wooden loft. Michael pushed Gennes toward it as the first sounds of galloping horses filtered into the stable. Holding her skirt up, she climbed the ladder and pulled herself up onto the loft. Michael climbed up behind her and squeezed between her and the wall to hide his bright blue tunic. They laid down together, pressed as far against the wall, and against each other, as they could manage. Gennes could only hope that they would be out of the line of sight of anyone who might wander in.

Moments later, she could hear the horses skidding to a stop outside. The voices of the soldiers rose and then drifted off as they walked away from the stable, presumably toward the house. Gennes sighed, as the sense of immediate danger lessened. After a moment, Michael pushed himself up on one elbow and peered over Gennes' shoulder.

"I can see one of the horses outside," he whispered in her ear. "We'll know when they leave."

"Until then?" Gennes whispered back, fighting a desperate urge to giggle. Her fear of the soldiers was nothing in comparison to the excitement she felt lying so close to Michael. They both lay on their sides, facing each other, with bodies pressed close together. She could feel the heat of his skin, his labored breathing, and the racing of his heart.

"We stay put," he answered, still looking over her shoulder. "I don't think we could make it to a better hiding place. And I don't want to be found here while the rest of the household is away. We might have a difficult time explaining ourselves."

Unable to resist the temptation, Gennes moved one hand and rested it on Michael's side. Gently, she let her fingers explore the solid feel of muscle and bone. Michael turned toward her, and she could see a sudden flashing of light in his grey eyes.

"Gennes…," he whispered as he brought his face down to hers.

"We'll hear them when they come back," she whispered, brushing her lips lightly against his. "Until then…."

His mouth pressed down on hers, pushing her head into the shallow layer of hay that blanketed the loft. The heavy scent filled her nostrils, as the sound of Michael's breathing filled her ears. For a long while, she heard nothing else. His hand found her shoulder, and he turned her slowly until her back was against the boards. He covered her with his own body, chest to chest. Without hurrying, his mouth left hers and continued its exploration, moving hungrily over her cheeks, her jawline, and down to her neck. The hand that held her shoulder groped its way to the neck of her gown and tugged at it until the string that held it gathered together gave way. He tugged again, pulling the gown downward and opening the way for his lips to find the fullness of her breast.

Gennes clutched him to her, wanting to feel his hands, his face, his burning mouth, and the soft caress of his breath. His touch enlivened her. The stroking of his fingers left her skin hot, as the nearness of his body left her breathless. She arched toward him, forgetting all sense of caution in her need of him.

She was gasping for air when Michael abruptly threw his head back and pulled her toward the wall again. She felt his sudden caution, even though she could not see his face, and she remained as still and silent as she possibly could.

A moment later she heard the heavy plodding of boots against dirt outside the stable. The soldiers were approaching their horses. But they didn't stop there and ride away. They came inside. Pressed up against Michael, Gennes could see nothing. But she could hear the men walk in and stop, almost directly below their hiding place on the loft.

"You can look if you like, but you aren't going to find anything," one of the men said testily. "We searched every bit of the stable, and the house, and the lands."

"You said you didn't search the stable," another man replied.

"I said there was nothing here to search," the first snapped back. "There's nothing but dung and hay and wood."

"You should have made that clearer to Cythraul," came the angry retort. "You had orders to search everywhere and to tell him everything that you found. We're wasting time that we don't have coming back here."

A third voice joined in then, calmer than the first two.

"He's telling the truth, sir. We did search everything thoroughly. The only mark we found was down by the brook, the one we already showed you."

"None of us wants to waste any more time here," a fourth voice pleaded. "I say we rejoin the company now."

For a long moment there was silence. Gennes closed her eyes tightly, praying that the men would leave and not search any further. If they found the two of them, there would certainly be questions that would be difficult to answer. And if they recognized Michael, there was no telling what they would do. Apparently in their haste, the soldiers hadn't noticed their saddled horses by the water trough. Gennes could only hope that their haste would send them on their way again and she could finally be alone again with Michael.

"All right," the answer came at last. "Let's go."

For what seemed like an eternity, the men walked to their horses and mounted. Gennes counted her heartbeats as she waited to hear them ride away. The scuffling outside finally turned into steady footfalls and then into galloping hoofbeats, fading away into the distance. Breathing deeply, Gennes listened for any sound from below, any hint that someone was still there. There was nothing.

Finally, Michael moved. His hand still on her shoulder, he pushed her gently away from him so that he could sit up and work his way back to the ladder. Without looking at her, he climbed down and walked away to the door of the stable. Gennes remained on the loft, watching his back, and waiting for some indication from him about what she should do.

"Are they gone?" she whispered.

Michael nodded, then he raised his hands and placed them on the top of his head in an unusual gesture. Gennes' own head was still spinning from the rapid swirl of emotions she had just experienced—from sudden fright, to sudden passion, to sudden fright again. As Michael seemed to have nothing else to say to her, she gathered her skirt in one hand and slowly descended the ladder.

"What do you think they were looking for?" she asked.

Michael still stood with his back to her, and the distance made her reluctant to discuss what had just happened between them. But she wanted to—no, she needed to talk to him and hear his voice again.

"I don't know," he answered at length.

His voice was harsh and ragged, and Gennes recoiled as if he had yelled at her.

"Three of them were locals," he continued, his voice still brittle, but softening as he went on. "I've seen them all before. The fourth was one of Balchder's elite. That means whatever they were doing here has something to do with the crown. The other man they mentioned, Cythraul, I've never heard of him before."

"How do you know this has to do with the crown?" she asked softly, doing her best to ignore his sudden hostility.

"The Elite Corp does nothing *but* look for the crown," he explained, still looking out the door. "They're easy to spot. The capes they wear are different, a deeper red, with a Roman insignia. And lately, they've started painting their faces and wearing gold torqs like the Celtic warriors of long ago."

"Torqs?" Gennes repeated.

"A gold band wrapped around the neck and open in the front. They say the Celts went into battle with the Romans wearing face paint and torqs, and nothing else."

Gennes had to smile at the thought of Michael wearing nothing but a band of gold around his neck. But she sobered again quickly and wondered what he was thinking that had made him so distant and unhappy.

Michael," she said softly, walking up behind him. "What is it? What's wrong?"

He turned to look at her, and she could see the firm set of his jaw and the lines of anguish around his eyes and mouth.

In a strangled voice he asked her, "Do you have any idea what would have happened if they had found us together like that in the loft?"

She wasn't sure what he meant, so she waited for him to continue.

"There were four of them," he said pointedly, "and only me to stand in their way. They would have needed little encouragement anyway, but with your gown half open like that....Don't you understand? I wouldn't have been able to protect you."

On those last words, his eyes grew dark, flashing like lightning from black storm clouds. It was obvious what he meant. He hadn't been worried about difficult questions, or being recognized himself. He had been worried about her, and he felt responsible for putting her in a dangerous situation.

"But, Michael, you can't blame yourself," she pleaded. "We would have been in the same danger no matter how they had found us, you must know that."

Michael groaned and turned away from her again, slamming his fist into the wall of the stable.

"You don't understand!" he growled.

"What?" she asked, walking around him to see his face. "What don't I understand? That they would have raped me?"

Michael groaned again, and Gennes paused, letting her own words sink in. What would have happened then? Was it possible that Michael would never have wanted her again? Would she have been lost to him forever?

"I would have stopped them somehow," he said, his voice low and pained. "I wouldn't have let them hurt you."

"You would have gotten yourself killed," Gennes snapped at him. "And for what? Would you give up all your work, all the good you could do with your life? Would you throw it all away to fight a battle you couldn't win over one woman?"

She was angry, and she felt no need to hide it. But it must have taken Michael by surprise, as he whipped his head upward to face her.

"And then what?" she went on, softer now but still tinged with heat. "You would be dead, and I would be…alone. But perhaps that's better than having to face you again. How could you look at me after what they would have done?"

Her voice faltered, and she dropped her gaze to the ground. Michael was beside her in a moment, taking her shoulders in his hands and shaking her slightly until she looked up at him through tear-filled eyes.

"Do you think that would change how I feel about you?" he demanded, his eyes flashing once again.

Gennes held his gaze for a long moment and let the tears trickle down onto her cheeks.

"Do you think I would care for you any less if you could not always protect me?" she asked softly.

Michael searched her eyes and slowly softened his grip on her arms. The creases around his mouth and eyes melted away, and his jaw relaxed. But instead of releasing her, he pulled her to him and wrapped his arms around her. She embraced him as well and laid her head against his chest. More tears clouded her vision, and she let them fall where they would. At last, he drew himself back and looked at her. His eyes were still cloudy, but no longer dark or flashing with anger. He sighed and managed a faint smile.

"I'm sorry about your gown," he said, fingering the material that hung loosely around her neck. "I'm afraid I broke the string."

"I'll fix it later," she told him, and followed it with her own faint smile.

Still arm in arm, the two walked outside together to their waiting horses. Michael scanned the horizon where the soldiers had ridden off a short while before. Then he turned back to Gennes and frowned.

"I have to follow them," he said, searching her eyes again. "I have to find out what they're after. I don't want to leave you alone, but…."

The scowl on Gennes' face made him stop short.

"I know, I know. You can take care of yourself," he laughed without humor. "But you shouldn't stay here," he added, looking around at the deserted buildings. "Can you get home all right by yourself?"

"Yes, of course," she stammered. "You're going after them alone?"

He nodded, then released her and walked toward his horse.

"Michael," she called after him. "There was so much more I wanted to say. So many things I wanted to tell you today."

He turned back to her and smiled. For a long moment they looked at each other. Then she ran to him and took his face in her hands, pulling him downward until their lips met in a kiss. He held her tightly, then released her slowly.

Clinging to him for one last moment, Gennes closed her eyes and whispered in his ear, "Be safe."

Moments later, he was on his horse with the reins in his hands.

"I'll be back as soon as I can," he said. "You be careful. There's something I want to talk to you about, too."

He gave her one of his radiant smiles, and she felt as if the sun had just come out after a lengthy storm. Then he turned to follow the soldiers' tracks and spurred his horse onward toward the tree-lined brook. Gennes waited and watched until he was out of sight, then she mounted her own horse and made her way home.

Chapter Twelve

Gennes arrived in Briallen just after sunset. She could have made it back sooner if she had tried, but there didn't seem to be any point. What she wanted was not in Briallen. It was far across the hills, riding away from a quiet stable. What she wanted was to be with Michael, that day and every day thereafter. And yet, she let him ride off without telling him the truth.

She had done a lot of thinking on her ride home, mostly about Michael. She had been attracted to him from the first moment she saw him, standing with his hands on his hips in the middle of the marketplace, looking so brave and handsome. But she had known other handsome men in her life, including the son of Lord Trevelgue who had once kissed her during a New Year's feast. She was of marrying age, and her adopted mother had certainly done her best to push her toward one match or another. But to Gennes, the idea of marriage had never seemed right for her—at least, until she met Michael.

Just before reaching the city, she was struck by a memory from her early years, before she had fled the King's House and started a new life on the moor. Shortly after marrying her father, her step-mother had sat her down to discuss their respective roles in the kingdom. Even though Gennes was not quite seven at the time, the conversation had made an impression, and all these years later she could remember it clearly.

"*You know that your mother was the Queen of Dumnonia,*" the woman had said. "*But now that I am married to your father, I am the Queen. You are a princess because your father is the King, and I am a queen because my husband is the King. Do you understand?*"

She had, of course, although no one had ever explained it to her quite that way before.

"*As a princess, your duty is to do as your father and I tell you and to behave with the very best of manners at all times. Then someday, when you are a little more grown up, your father will arrange for you to marry someone. It might be one of the nobles of Dumnonia. Or it might be a king or a prince of another kingdom. Then maybe someday you, too, will be a queen, just like me.*"

Even across the expanse of years, Gennes trembled at the thought. The few things she was beginning to recall about her step-mother were not pleasant, and she had no desire to be anything like her. She had not desired it then, either, and she had secretly hoped that she would never have to marry and she could live with her father in the King's House forever.

* * *

On the fourth morning of Michael's absence, Morgan invited Gennes to walk with her to the marketplace. Although they sat beside each other almost every day working on tapestries, the older woman rarely spoke of Michael. Gennes believed that Morgan knew how much she cared for Michael, but she was waiting for Gennes to broach any discussion about him. As they walked to the marketplace, Morgan held her arm and gave her a motherly squeeze, but they both remained quiet. Gennes couldn't have spoken just then anyway, as they were accompanied by Grainne and Tomas. Grainne had come along to purchase some cloth for a dress, and Tomas was there to provide protection from the soldiers.

The marketplace boasted several booths of woven cloth, but Grainne kept looking for something different. When the others had finished their business, they followed her from booth to booth, exchanging amused glances each time she shook her head and started off toward another merchant.

Set back behind the rows of booths in a granite building, one merchant secretly displayed colorful fabrics from all over the Mediterranean. The hushed tones of the customers inside conveyed the image of an illegally run business full of smuggled goods. The textiles displayed there were enchanting, and Gennes decided it was worth the risk of being caught there to feel the cool, smooth cloth, and to view the intricate designs. With a deep sigh, she ran her hand over one particularly fine piece covered in delicate embroidery. The grey-headed woman behind the table caught her sigh and jumped in to make a deal.

"You have excellent taste, my dear," the woman cackled. "You are looking, perhaps, for something special? Perhaps a wedding gown for such a lovely lady?"

At the mention of a wedding gown, Gennes blushed deeply. Dropping her head to hide her face, she ran her left hand over the cloth one last time.

"No," Gennes answered. "But it is beautiful."

As quick as a wink, the woman grabbed her hand.

"I'd be willing to make a trade," she said, eyeing the gold beads of Gennes' bracelet. "In exchange for this bauble, you'll have enough cloth to make that gown."

Gennes gasped as the woman drew her hand closer, trying to get a better look at the bracelet. Hoping to avoid a scene, Gennes waiting breathlessly while the locket was held up and examined closely.

Then in a soft, far-away voice the woman said, "I know this charm."

It may have been the woman's fascination with the bracelet or Gennes' reaction to it that attracted attention, but when she looked up Gennes realized that Morgan and Grainne were standing beside her watching them. Gennes' eyes darted to the doorway, partly to determine if anyone else was listening and partly to make a plan for a hasty retreat. But there was no way to leave without wrestling her arm away from the woman or waiting for the woman to release her, and she didn't seem ready to do that.

"There should be a little door," the woman babbled to herself, still inspecting the charm. "There it is! It opens like this. Why, I would know this charm anywhere. It was made by my own husband for the king as a gift for his daughter, the princess."

Gennes stopped breathing entirely. From the silence in the room, she wondered if anyone was breathing. Slowly, the woman turned her gaze from the bracelet to the girl and narrowed her eyes. Although Gennes tugged at her arm to free it, the woman's hands held her fast. For one long, silent moment they stared at one another before she finally released Gennes' hand.

"Bless my soul," she whispered, "if you aren't the daughter of Queen Morveren. I spent five years in the King's House serving the queen before I married. I would know those eyes—and that hair—anywhere. And that locket could belong to none other than the princess herself!"

Behind and around her Gennes could hear in soft whispers the names "Morveren" and "princess," and she knew that the others in the room had heard the woman's words. Caught unprepared, she didn't know whether to laugh, to deny what the woman said, or simply to flee. Her long silence did nothing but confirm the woman's words, and it seemed that flight was the only option. Grainne apparently thought so, too. As others in the shop began to gather around Gennes, Grainne pushed her toward the door and out into the street.

Outside in the bright sunlight, Morgan was in a guarded conversation with Tomas. Grainne pushed Gennes toward them.

"Go with Tomas, child," Morgan whispered urgently. "He'll take you someplace safe."

With that, Tomas grabbed Gennes' forearm and turned toward the nearest street leading out of the marketplace. He walked swiftly toward it, almost dragging her behind him. For a moment, she thought they would escape in peace. Then suddenly there were voices behind them calling out for them to stop.

"It's the princess!" a man's voice shouted. "Stop her!"

Other voices took up the call. Twisting her head to look behind her, Gennes saw a small crowd outside the fabric shop, pointing at her. A few of the braver souls started to follow them.

"Come on!" Tomas shouted, as he broke into a run.

Together they darted for an opening between the buildings. Tomas pushed Gennes forward and then turned to dump a cart of vegetables onto the street. The wooden cart fell with a bang, as cabbages and carrots flew out over the dirt and gravel. Tomas rejoined Gennes, and they ran as fast as they could down the narrow street and away from the marketplace.

A few streets away they stopped running. There was no sight or sound of pursuit. Leaning on a wall for a moment, Gennes tried to catch her breath. She looked up to see Tomas staring at her intently. Reading the question in his eyes, she dropped her gaze and tried to think of an answer.

"It's true," she said simply.

Saying nothing, Tomas motioned for her to follow him. They walked in silence, looking about them for any trouble. He took her to a part of the city that she had never seen before. There, he cautiously approached a group of small round huts and peered around them to see if anyone was about. They saw no one. Tomas pushed opened the door to one of the huts, and Gennes went inside before him. He closed the door without a sound and walked to the far side of the room.

"There's a souterrain here," he said, "to store crops. There's a cot and table. You can stay there."

As he spoke, he uncovered a wooden door in the floor of the hut. Pulling it back on its hinges, he opened it wide, revealing a dark hole beneath. Gennes stepped closer to look down into the hole and wondered how many others had taken refuge there. If there was a cot and a table in the little storage place, she was obviously not the first. Tomas stepped down into the darkness with care, apparently using a ladder that rested against the wall of the pit. As he descended, he looked up coldly.

"Your eyes will adjust after a moment," he said, climbing downward. "The sun comes in through a hole at ground level."

Carefully, Gennes lowered herself into the hole, finding the ladder and grasping it.

"How long will I have to stay here?" she asked as she reached the floor.

Even in the dimness, she could see the disapproval and distrust in Tomas' eyes.

"I can't say," he answered. "But it's either stay here or go out there. If the townsfolk don't tear you apart in their excitement, they'll at least hold you long enough for Lord Balchder's men to find you."

An angry shiver ran down Gennes' back. She glared at Tomas and wanted to shout at him. It wasn't her fault that she had been recognized! But the words died in her throat. Instead, she marched past him and stopped before the little cot.

"I suppose I shouldn't do anything until Michael returns," she said.

Tomas remained silent for a moment. Then she heard him cross to the ladder and begin to climb.

"I have to go back to the Hall for supplies," he said, barely controlling the hostility in his voice. "I won't be gone long. After that you won't be left alone again."

Gennes listened as he climbed the ladder and pulled himself up into the room above. The trap door dropped into place with a soft thud, and she heard a scratching noise as something was pulled over it. She was alone. Trying to suppress her sobs, she fell to her knees by the cot and buried her head in her arms. She had nothing to do but wait.

* * *

No one knew where Michael had gone or how long it would be until he returned. The thought of staying in the tiny underground room indefinitely made Gennes' stomach turn. But there didn't seem to be an alternative. So she waited, while Tomas kept watch above. Her only other visitor was Grainne, who brought fresh bread each day. Although they tried to make her comfortable and see to her needs, neither Tomas nor Grainne spoke to Gennes any more than necessary or offered to stay with her underground.

On the third day of Gennes' confinement, Grainne brought breakfast for her as usual. Saying no more than "good morning" and "I hope the porridge isn't cold," she set down the meal and turned for the ladder. Gennes stopped her with a word.

"Grainne," she said, "can I ask you something?"

"Of course," the girl answered, barely turning and dropping her gaze to the floor.

"Why do you hate me?" Gennes asked.

Grainne's eyes darted upward, stealing a glance at the Gennes' face. Then they dropped again.

"I don't hate you," she answered quietly. "You're the princess."

"That's hardly a reason not to hate someone," Gennes said. "For two days you have barely spoken to me. You won't even look at me. Neither will Tomas. What have I done to earn such malice?"

Fidgeting uncomfortably, Grainne looked about her, perhaps for an escape. Gennes' eyes held her as she waited patiently for an answer. At last, Grainne shrugged and looked up shyly.

"It's not your fault, I guess," she said in a timid voice. "It's just that you're not…what we hoped for."

"What do you mean?" Gennes asked, her eyes narrowed.

Grainne paused and looked away again.

"When I was growing up, my father used to tell us stories about the princess and how she mysteriously escaped from the massacre. He said that she—that you—vanished from sight with the help of a mighty wizard, and that someday you would return in a ball of fire and consume all of the soldiers and Lord Balchder as well."

Thinking about her words, Gennes remained silent.

"There are many such stories," Grainne continued. "Some say that the princess fled to another kingdom and married a prince. Others say she lives across the sea—or even in the sea. But all of the stories end the same—with the princess returning someday with the power to avenge the king's death."

Looking down, Gennes nodded her head.

"But here I am," she said sadly, "a mere mortal, with no magical powers, no army, and no way to defeat Lord Balchder. I must be quite a disappointment to you."

"Morgan said that as long as you were missing, we could believe anything we wanted, and we could keep hoping," Grainne answered. "I know you didn't mean to, but you took that away from us."

Grainne turned then and climbed the ladder. The trap door above closed, and Gennes was alone again. She felt sorry for Grainne. She felt sorry for Tomas and Morgan and all the others. She too hoped that the kingdom would be set to rights, that Balchder would be defeated, and that a good king would be crowned. But, unlike them, she had no fantasies about a magical princess to pin her hopes on. She wasn't the one who could help them. All she could do was to give the crown to another and hope and pray that it would be the right person. When Michael returned, everything would be all right. Or so she hoped, as she watched and waited through another solitary day.

* * *

Although the day had been very warm, Gennes found herself shivering that afternoon, alone in her cell. For some time, she had done nothing but watch a small patch of sunlight creep slowly across the room. It was the only direct light admitted into the room, through the one small window above her head. Her supper sat, untouched, upon the table as she focused on the ray of light, waiting for the exact moment when she would be able to see the sun. Her legs ached and her neck felt stiff from standing still for so long. She stretched her back and stood on tip-toe, trying to relieve the tension, trying as well to extend her face upward just enough to feel the unadulterated warmth of the sun. As she had already learned from her two previous days in captivity, the sun would only be visible to her for a few moments before it dipped again toward the western horizon.

Although she heard the trap door above open, Gennes kept her face toward the window. She didn't want to be robbed of this moment that she had been waiting for so long. As the sun moved into position before the window, she closed her eyes and breathed deeply. It was the closest she had come to freedom in three days.

So intent was Gennes on the sunshine, that she almost forgot about the open door. Eventually, she realized that whoever had come down into the room had done so very quietly. Listening carefully then, she could hear steady breathing across the room—deep, hard breathing, like a man's. Slowly, she dropped from her toes and pulled her attention away from the light.

Gennes turned hesitantly toward the ladder. Although the man's face was in the shadows and her eyes were still adjusting from the sunlight, she knew him in an instant.

"Michael," she sighed.

"Princess," he responded with a slight bow of his head.

Not Gennes, not even Addien. In an instant her hopes vanished, like a flimsy bubble popping in the air. The last ray of sunlight slowly disappeared from the wall behind him. Without the glare, she could see him better, standing tall and expressionless beside the ladder. Gennes drew a deep breath and tilted her head back to speak.

"So now you know," she said.

"Yes," came the emotionless answer. "I've known for several days. I pieced it together in Trevelgue."

"Trevelgue?" Gennes asked, surprised.

"The soldiers I was following led me there," he answered. "They were following the trail of an orphan girl who fled there about ten years ago."

Wondering how such an old trail could be followed, Gennes suddenly realized with horror where that trail would lead them.

"Anna," she gasped, "and Evin. Are they…?"

"They're all right," Michael answered. "Luckily, I had a little more to go on then the soldiers did, and I reached them first. The Lord of Trevelgue has guaranteed their safety, but they will have to talk to the soldiers and tell them everything they know. Not that it matters now. Word is spreading all over the kingdom that you've been found right here in Briallen."

Gennes nodded her head slightly, still thinking about her family and friends in Trevelgue and the danger she had unwittingly placed them in. She wanted to thank Michael for helping them, but she couldn't find the words. As Evin and Anna knew nothing about her past or the king's crown, she could only hope that the soldiers would leave them in peace.

"I suppose I should have figured it out sooner," Michael said, interrupting her thoughts. "You are the right age, and you look exactly like your mother, from the way I've heard her described. Obviously something drew me to you from the very beginning, a sense of loyalty, I suppose, even before I knew who you were."

So that was it, Gennes thought. He was pushing her away again, convincing himself that he had never cared for her. She stared at him for a moment through weary eyes. Then she turned away and leaned against the cold wall, closing her eyes. A shiver ran through her, and she wrapped herself in her arms.

Across the room, she could hear the shuffling of Michael's boots, as he stepped closer to her.

"Are you all right?" he asked.

Turning, Gennes shivered again but tried to smile as she answered.

"I told you," she said, "I don't do well in enclosed places."

"Yes, in the King's House," he said, almost to himself. For a moment he seemed lost in thought. Then he continued, "It was in the princess' bedroom—your bedroom. Then again in the King's Court, at the very place...."

"My father died," she said, ending the sentence for him.

His eyes widened.

"You were there," he said, as his eyes widened. "You saw him die?"

"I saw him murdered," she answered.

For a moment, Michael's head dropped and he stared at the floor. Just then, Gennes would have given the world to be able to run to him and hold him and put things back the way they had been before. But she knew it was too late. Suddenly, she had become a prisoner of war, and Michael was one of her captors, present only to interrogate her.

Michael cleared his throat and looked up at her again. He went on, almost as if he had read her mind.

"There is one thing I have to ask you," he said haltingly. "Since you were with King Brenin at his death, you must have some idea where he hid...."

He faltered again, and once again she ended his sentence.

"His crown?" she offered.

Michael nodded. Watching him, Gennes wondered what he was feeling.

"He didn't hide it," she continued at length. "I did."

Unable to control his surprise, Michael crossed to Gennes and took her by the arms.

"Then you know where it is," he said, searching her face, as if to find there some hidden clue. "Why didn't you ever tell us?"

Gennes swallowed hard and tried to back away from him, but he held her tight. How could she explain to him what she barely understood herself? She hadn't known about the crown until that day in the King's House, and even then she wasn't sure about everything. What was she supposed to have done? She would have sounded like a mad woman, if she had tried to tell him then.

Trying to think of some way to explain, she found herself struggling to find any words at all.

"I couldn't," she babbled at last.

Michael recoiled from Gennes as if she had slapped him in the face. He dropped his hands and stepped back. Every bit of emotion that had been in his face drained away again, and he looked at her strangely.

"No," he said quietly, "I guess you couldn't."

She watched in dismay as he turned and walked away from her toward the ladder. She tried to cry out to him, but her throat was too constricted to speak. At the foot of the ladder he turned back and motioned for her to precede him. Obediently, she climbed up into the hut with Michael behind her.

Tomas was just entering the little hut as Gennes pulled herself out the souterrain. His jaw dropped open, and he seemed ready to shout some order at her, but Michael appeared then and cut him off with a look. When they were both out of the hole and in the room, Michael pulled over a chair and gestured for Gennes to sit down.

"It's all right," Michael told Tomas, who stood glowering by the doorway. "She is, after all, the daughter of our late king. We have no right to hold her like a prisoner."

"You can't be serious," Tomas growled. "If you let her go, every snitch in the city will be after her in no time, ready to turn her over to Balchder. And if you take her back to our place, we're all done for."

Michael looked from Tomas to Gennes.

"I have no intention of telling Her Highness where she may, or may not, go," he said sternly. "But I do intend to offer her protection from her enemies, if she is willing to accept it."

Gennes looked at him, not sure what to make of this new demeanor. She looked at Tomas. He also seemed uncertain about his friend's true intentions. She looked back at Michael then, and narrowed her eyes.

"In return for what I know about the crown?" she asked suspiciously.

Michael didn't flinch.

"You have kept your own counsel about King Brenin's crown thus far, and I expect you will continue to do so," he said. "I have sworn my life to prevent the kingdom from falling into the hands of Lord Balchder. As the only surviving family member of King Brenin's line, I swear my allegiance to you as well."

Gennes almost expected Michael to kneel. Had he done so, she might have burst into hysterical tears. Everything that had been between them was gone, and all she had to replace it was his 'allegiance'. Unless Gennes was very wrong, she had also earned his distrust, his disapproval, and, perhaps, his disgust.

Looking at the floor, she asked in a soft voice, "What do you suggest I do?"

"Leave the city," Michael said firmly, as if he had thought it through already. "There is a valley refuge that we can use. If you're willing, I'll return later with a few men and good horses. We'll start out after the moon sets."

Still looking at the floor, Gennes nodded her assent. Then Michael was gone, and she was alone in the house with Tomas. Unusually quiet, Tomas walked across the room and kneeled to peer into the little cell.

"You really should eat something," he said, apparently noticing her uneaten meal. "We have a long ride ahead of us this evening."

Rising from her chair, Gennes was suddenly reminded of her tired and aching muscles. She stretched and slowly descended the ladder to her room. Pausing at the bottom, she looked around, sensing that something was missing that had been there before. Then her eyes were drawn to the little window, where the last faint glow of the setting sun slowly faded from the sky.

Chapter Thirteen

Much later that night, in the moonless darkness, Gennes rode out of the city with Michael, Tomas, Colin, and two other men, Kelly and Niall. On a small rise outside the city wall, they paused and looked back at Briallen, the great capital of Dumnonia.

Leaning forward in his saddle, Michael sighed and said sadly, "I wonder how long it will take Balchder's army to arrive and start tearing her apart again."

From behind him, Tomas added, "Now that he knows that the princess lives, he won't rest until he finds the crown."

Although no one looked at Gennes, she could feel in the air their unspoken question.

"He won't find it there," she said, looking past Michael at the dark silhouette of the city below.

Michael regarded her for a moment before looking back at the city again.

"At least there's that," he said.

He turned and spurred his horse across the hill, and Gennes followed.

The sun rose that morning into the clutches of a dense fog. The horses walked slowly through the half-light, and Gennes wondered how anyone could tell where they were going. They rode silently, listening for any movement. But they encountered no one. Although the air began to warm, Gennes kept her cloak close about her and prayed that the fog would soon lift.

The little band traveled all that day through woods and fields, over creeks and across valleys. When the fog did lift, a grey bank of clouds took its place, obscuring the sun and any distant landmarks. Gennes felt lost and alone, bringing to mind fresh memories of the last time she had fled Briallen. During her solitary days in the souterrain, she had remembered a great deal about her mother and father and her former life. But now she could not stop thinking about the pain of losing them. That old pain, which had been buried for so long, mixed inside her heart with the new pain of losing all her friends who now saw her as no longer one of them. And worst of all was the pain that she refused to even think about—the pain of losing Michael.

* * *

The second day started out with heavy rain. The group trudged on through the mud, sometimes following the course of a river, and other times climbing away from it to higher land.

"We have to make as much distance as we can," Michael said. "The rain will conceal us from Balchder's men and wash away our tracks."

By midday, the clouds were moving off and the sun began to shine. The landscape ahead climbed steadily to a treeless plain. Michael stopped to check the lay of the land and then turned to the group behind him.

"We have to cross the river here," he said. "If we get any closer to the border, we'll be sure to meet up with some soldiers. We'll rest and eat as soon as we're out of sight of the river."

The others followed Michael without a word. Gennes followed as well, but slowly, trying to piece together everything she could recall about the physical makeup of the kingdom. She knew that the Exe River ran due north from Briallen and that in one part it marked the boundary of the kingdom. If they were near that point, then they were already in the Northern Territory—and not far from Balchder's lands. Turning in her saddle, Gennes' eyes followed the line of the river northward to the high plain. It had to be the North Moor, which ran all the way to the Northern Channel. Cleddyf Castle sat on the edge of that moor, between a river gorge and the sea.

Pulling on her reins, Gennes brought her horse to a stop. The men who were riding behind or beside her stopped also. Michael, who had been riding ahead, wheeled his horse around and trotted back to them, demanding to know what was the matter.

Tired and sore from the long ride and many sleepless nights, Gennes glared at him.

"Don't you think I know where we are?" she asked him hotly. "This is Balchder's land. If we go any further, we'll be practically inside his castle."

Michael glared back at her and brought his horse beside hers. Face to face, he leaned forward and spoke in a low, barely-controlled, voice.

"It's an old military trick," he said tersely. "If you don't want your enemy to find something, you hide it right under his nose."

Gennes leaned forward as well, lessening the distance between them even more.

She responded in a low voice that grew louder with each word, "Did you ever stop to think that Balchder is a military genius, and he probably thought up that 'old military trick'!"

Enraged, Michael pulled his horse back.

"If you have any better ideas," he yelled, "I would be happy to hear them!"

"You seem to forget," she yelled back, "that I hid myself quite well for ten years without any help from you or your friends!"

"That was only because everyone thought you were dead!"

Michael's last words stung her face like a slap. Breathing hard, she blinked away the moistness that came unbidden to her eyes. She paused and tried to bring her voice back under control. She knew that directing her anger against Michael wasn't fair. It wasn't his fault that she was on the run again, forced to hide again from Balchder and his men. Still, she was angry at the way he had been treating her ever since he had returned from Trevelgue, and she had to say one thing more.

"You say that I am not your prisoner," she continued at length, "but you still treat me like one."

Sitting tall in his saddle, Michael regarded Gennes sadly.

"You said that you would accept our protection," he said at last. "But you still do not trust me."

For a minute or more, Michael and Gennes remained motionless, holding each other's gaze. Then Gennes looked away and urged her horse back into a slow walk. Beside her, Colin began to walk his horse as well, looking from Gennes to Michael and back again.

"Are we going then?" he asked.

Gennes looked at Michael.

"Wherever you lead," she said.

Leaving the river behind them, the group rode on toward the western edge of the moor. A short time later they stopped at an abandoned farmhouse for a cold meal and a brief rest. The round stone house had been partially burned, and most of the roof was missing. Nothing was left on the inside except broken pots and scattered debris from the fallen roof. The garden and fields around the house were overgrown with weeds and wild grasses. It must have been many years since anyone had lived there. Michael kicked at some of the broken stones below the garden wall and sighed. Gennes stood beside him, wishing that they could talk to each other like friends again.

Perhaps sensing her desire, Michael looked up. His expression was less than friendly, but at least he was looking at her. After a moment, he looked away at the distant horizon where the forgotten farmland merged with a distant woods.

"They call this the 'Dead Valley,'" he said softly. "When Balchder was unable to find Brenin's crown in Briallen, he left with his troops to return to Cleddyf Castle. Some of the people of Briallen and the vicinity followed and met him here in battle. It's a wonder they weren't all killed. But Balchder let them go, sending them all back to the city. The farmers around here who helped in the fight fared less well. Balchder confiscated their lands and parceled them out to his commanders as a reward for their 'loyalty'. But most of the soldiers didn't want to go back to farming, and Balchder found out that he still needed them to keep the nobles in line, so much of the land in the territory was abandoned."

"Why did the nobles never fight him?" Gennes asked.

"Concerned self-interest, I suppose," he replied. "The best men from all over the kingdom had joined the army to fight the Saxons. Those men still followed Balchder and the Military Stone. The nobles had nothing to match that. As long as Balchder left them alone, they had no reason to risk losing everything by challenging him."

Bowing her head, Gennes turned and walked away. Without the crown, Balchder had never had enough power to take over the whole kingdom, and the people had never had enough courage to stand up and challenge him. So the kingdom lay stagnant, like the 'Dead Valley' before them. Michael and his friends seemed to think if they only had King Brenin's crown, the problem would be solved. But Gennes had slowly come to realize that it wasn't that simple.

*　　　*　　　*

The next morning, the road wound down into a steep river valley that dissected the moor. The vegetation there grew thick and lush, and the path through the trees and scrub was barely visible. The river below could be heard before it could be seen. Slowly they made their way down the slope until the river appeared before them, rushing around smooth, white boulders, and lapping against its narrow beaches.

At the floor of the valley, on the far side of the water, Gennes was soon able to spy an old fortress. At a sign from Michael, Tomas rode ahead across a shallow part of the river to the gate of the fort. While he called out for someone to let them in, the rest of the group waited on the river bank. The breeze in the trees played a mournful melody, and birds chattered incessantly, but there was no other sound.

The fortress itself was a collection of five small buildings, thrown together unevenly of wood and stone. A barricade ran around them, made of thick logs tied together in a criss-cross pattern. It hardly looked formidable, like the great stone castle of Trevelgue or even the St. Petroc Monastery. As a place to defend a princess against her enemies, it seemed doubtful at best.

Michael must have noticed Gennes' expression, because he directed his horse over to her.

"It was built before the last great war," he said. "A small force was kept here to keep an eye on the eastern frontier while the main army trained to the west. It was more of a temporary lodge than a fortress. It hasn't been used in years, except by us."

Looking around at the tree-tops, he continued, "It does, however, have the best defenses of any fort in the kingdom."

Surprised by this remark, Gennes looked at Michael and hoped for an explanation. Michael, however, continued to scan the sky. After a moment, Gennes heard overhead the distant cawing of a bird. She looked up as well until she could see it, a large, black raven circling above them. The cawing grew nearer as the bird slowly descended in wide turns. Suddenly, the bird dipped and dropped toward Tomas, who was still waiting by the gate. It landed lightly on one of the gate-posts and cawed three times. Moments later, a man appeared from one of the buildings of the fort and came out to open the gate.

Michael turned to Gennes and smiled. She looked back at him, perplexed. Still, he did not explain. Instead, he directed his horse toward the open gate. Gennes sighed and followed him.

As the gate was closed again behind them, they all dismounted. The man who had opened the gate whistled once, and the raven on the gate-post spread its wings and rose into the sky. It circled overhead once and then dropped onto the man's outstretched arm. Gennes gasped in amazement. Although she had seen hunting birds trained to come to their handlers, she had never seen a raven behave so.

"I've never seen a trained raven before," she told Colin, who was beside her. "How does he do it?"

"He didn't train it," Colin responded. "He speaks to it."

Gennes wrinkled her nose in bewilderment.

"Don't ask me how he does it," Colin continued. "I only know that somehow they understand each other. That bird would do anything for Aderyn, and Aderyn would do anything for him."

Aderyn walked over from the gate. He approached Michael first with outstretched arms and a happy greeting. He exchanged greetings with the others next, and then Michael brought him over to Gennes.

"Princess Addien," he began formally, "this is our good friend, Aderyn. He lives here at the fort and keeps us informed of any movement out of Cleddyf Castle."

Aderyn bowed slightly but said nothing. Gennes made some polite greeting and then turned her attention to the bird still on his arm. The bird cocked his head and returned her gaze with his beady black eyes. It reminded her of Trevilian, and she smiled warmly at the memory.

"This is Dyn," Michael said, motioning to the bird. "The best lookout in the kingdom."

Gennes understood then what Michael had said before. Apparently, the raven kept watch from the sky to let Aderyn know if anyone was approaching. Although the fort could not be defended against Balchder's soldiers, its occupants could safely retreat from the fort long before any soldiers could arrive. As Colin explained to her, although there were few exits from the valley, there were many hiding places, making it almost impossible for anyone staying at the fort to be caught.

Leaving the horses with Aderyn and Tomas, Michael took a bundle he had brought with him and led Gennes to one of the buildings. There they found a small room with a mattress, a table, two chairs, and a small chest. Michael stood uncomfortably in the doorway for a moment. Then he held out the bundle to Gennes.

"I brought your things from the Roman Hall," he said. "I think I got everything."

"Thank you," she said, suddenly overcome with exhaustion.

Unsuccessful in suppressing a yawn, she turned away and placed the bundle of clothes on the table. Then she sank into a chair beside it and closed her eyes.

Still standing at the door, Michael made a small sound as if he were trying to say something but had suddenly forgotten the words.

"Addien," he began again, barely audible. He cleared his throat, almost as if trying to dislodge the words that had stuck there.

Gennes looked at him and smiled slightly.

"It's all right if you would rather call me Gennes," she said. "It's the only name I've known for a long time."

Michael looked down for a moment, carefully studying the floor. Then he looked up again and drew a deep breath.

Without taking Gennes' suggestion, he continued, "I've been thinking about what you said yesterday, about feeling like a prisoner. I'm sorry that it has seemed that way to you."

This time Gennes looked down, and nodded.

"It's all right," she said. "I understand what you are trying to do. I may not like it," she looked up and tried to smile more bravely, "but I do understand."

Pursing his lips, Michael nodded. He took a step back and reached for the door, ready to leave.

"But you don't understand me, do you?" Gennes called out to him, delaying his departure.

His hand dropped and he looked at her steadily.

Shaking his head, he answered, "No, I don't understand. For ten years you have kept your secret while others have given their lives trying to restore peace and order in your father's kingdom. You knew how desperately we have been seeking King Brenin's crown, and yet you never told us the truth."

Turning in her chair, Gennes placed her elbows on the table and sunk her face into her hands. Once again, she searched her mind for some way to explain, some way to make him understand. Perhaps it was impossible. Whatever had happened, it was all in the past, and it didn't make the future any easier to figure out. For a long moment, she remained still, lost in her thoughts. Then she lifted her head and rested her chin on her hands, still looking away from Michael.

"If you were to find the crown," she asked him seriously, "what then?"

He didn't answer, so she turned and asked again, "What then, Michael? What is that you intend to do with the crown?"

Michael's face clouded over and his eyes flashed.

"If you are suggesting that we intend to use the crown for our own gains…," he stammered.

Gennes cut him off.

"Not 'us', Michael. Not 'we'. Only one man can wear the crown and wield its power. One man." She paused and lowered her voice. "Who will that one man be? And how is he to be chosen? Have you even thought about that?"

The spark of anger faded from Michael's eyes, but his mood remained dark.

"I don't know," he answered. "But I do know that someone will have to wear it. I can think of a dozen good men at least that you could choose from, strong, brave, and loyal. But that would require trusting someone, wouldn't it?"

Gennes narrowed her eyes, ready to lash out at him. He was so determined to think the worst of her, that she just wanted to scream at him. But she couldn't do it. With a great deal of self-control, she raised her chin and stared at him.

"My father trusted someone once," she said sadly.

Outside, the sun was rising higher and casting a brighter light. Colin was calling to Tomas something about gathering wood for a fire. Aderyn's raven squawked from the top of the gate, and a horse whinnied. Inside, Michael remained at the door, waiting for Gennes to continue.

She did continue, spilling out the memories that had become so clear to her in the past few days.

"Did you know that as a youth Lord Balchder was my father's closest friend? They fought together at the Battle of Killarney Springs. Balchder even saved my father's life, almost sacrificing his own. There was no one that my father trusted more. When the war was over, my father gave Balchder authority over the whole Northern Territory, practically creating a separate kingdom. The only thing that kept the two lands together was trust. But when the Saxons threatened a second great invasion, Balchder alone rode to meet them. My father was convinced by his advisors to remain behind and take a new bride. The king trusted Balchder to lead the military wisely and to protect the kingdom from invasion. He trusted him so much, that he gave him the Military Stone to ensure his success." She paused for a moment before continuing. "It was a mistake he paid for with his life."

Michael was visibly less tense now. Even in the shadows of the room, Gennes could see in him again something of the man she had come to know in Briallen. He dropped his gaze and shook his head slowly.

"You were only a child then," he said softly. "How could you have known all this?"

Distant memories sprang again to Gennes' mind. Memories of long summer days following her father around the King's House, hanging on his every word. Memories of cold winter nights gathered in the Great Hall while the bards sang story after story about the king's exploits. She closed her eyes and smiled, basking in the warmth and happiness of these thoughts. Then she realized that she had not yet answered Michael's question.

Opening her eyes again, she told him, "My father talked to me about everything. He told me all about the kingdom and shared with me his every thought. The Captain of the Guard used to say that my father didn't realize that I was his daughter, and not his son."

She smiled deeply again, clinging to the pictures of happier days long past. Then she winced, as a dark shadow engulfed her thoughts, and she remembered another day.

"I was with my father when he learned that Balchder had turned the army against him and was marching on the capital," Gennes said. "And I was with him when Balchder's men cut him down."

Michael moved closer to her. The sense of tension and hostility was gone from his body, and his voice.

"Your father trusted the wrong man," he said. "I suppose that he had been separated from Balchder for a long time, and his friendship blinded him to Balchder's true nature. If he had known, he never would have given him the Military Stone."

"You're wrong," she said, shaking her head. "Balchder never asked for the Military Stone. He was even against having it removed from the crown."

In response to Michael's surprised look, Gennes continued, "He wasn't an evil man, Michael. I think he just wasn't strong enough to hold that much power without being corrupted by it. The crown of King Brenin holds four more stones, each as powerful as the Military Stone. Each with a power that can be just as corrupting. It isn't just a matter of trusting someone to wear it. It's a matter of finding the right person to wear it, someone who will be able to control the power without being controlled by it."

Michael stood still for a long time, his hands on his hips. Sighing deeply, he crossed to the table and sat down beside her.

"And what were you planning to do with the crown?" he asked. "Keep it hidden and hope that no one ever recognized you?"

"No," she answered, frustrated that she still didn't know how to explain. "I never meant to keep the crown hidden. I came back to Briallen because…."

"Because what?" he asked when she faltered.

Searching for an answer, Gennes leaned back and rested her shoulder against the rough wood wall.

"I don't know," she said at length. "When I met Colin and learned about your resistance work, I knew I wanted to be a part of it. And there was so much I needed to learn. I thought—I hoped—that I would find someone that I could confide in, who would help me decide what to do with the crown."

She paused and looked into Michael's eyes. Did he have any idea how much she needed his trust? How much she wanted to be close to him again? For a long moment, they sat in silence, holding each other's gaze. Then he dropped his gaze to the table and sighed.

"I don't have any magical answer, Michael," Gennes continued. "I only know that the crown alone is not it. Will you help me find the answer?"

She reached across the table and laid her hand on Michael's arm. He looked down at it for a long time. Then he laid his own hand on top of hers and gently stroked the back of her fingers. The connection between them lasted only a moment, though, before Michael pulled his hand away. He stood abruptly, scraping his chair across the floor.

"You are the princess," he said, distant and formal again. "I will help you in any way I can."

Gennes closed her eyes and listened as he walked away from her to the door.

"May I ask you one more thing?" he said.

She looked up and saw him standing at the door with his back to her. Without turning or waiting for an answer, he continued.

"What if you never find someone that you deem worthy to wear the crown?" he asked. "Would you rather see Dumnonia torn apart by Balchder and those who will rise up to challenge him?"

"No," she answered firmly.

Gennes waited until Michael turned to look at her again.

"Someone must be chosen," she continued. "I know that. I have been praying that I would be given the right answer, that there would be some obvious choice of who the king should be. Perhaps it will never be that simple. But someone must be chosen, and I will retrieve the crown just as soon as that has happened. I'll do my part, Michael. And maybe someday, you can learn to trust me again."

Chapter Fourteen

For the rest of that day the group rested and did a little work around the fort. Gennes spent most of her time with Colin, who, alone of the group, seemed at ease around her. Perhaps it was his youth which made him more forgiving. Or perhaps he had no expectations about the princess in the first place, and therefore had no reason to be disappointed. At any rate, Gennes was grateful that Colin had come with them and that she could still count him as her friend.

The following morning, Michael met Gennes at her room before breakfast and asked to speak with her alone.

"You asked for my help," he said, "and I'll give it to you. But I don't think we should do this alone. I want to tell the others what you told me about the crown."

"You haven't told them yet?" she asked.

He shook his head and answered, "It didn't seem…appropriate for me to tell your secret. You've never told anyone else, I assume."

"No, never," she answered truthfully.

Gennes looked at him and wondered what he was thinking.

"Michael," she said timidly, "you probably won't believe me now, but I was going to tell you. Do you remember the day we went to Torbryon's ranch? I tried to tell you then, but I was afraid."

"Afraid?" he asked softly, raising one eyebrow as he looked at her.

She dropped her gaze to the ground and wrapped herself in her arms. "Afraid of what you might think of me," she whispered. "Afraid that I would lose you."

For a long moment, they stood together in silence. Then, very gently, he placed his hand below her chin and lifted her face.

With a slight smile, he said, "Addien, I don't know what is going to happen next. We don't have much time. Balchder must know by now that you are alive. He may also know that you've joined our group against him. There's no telling what he might do. We have to act quickly. When it's all worked out, maybe...."

He didn't finish the sentence. He didn't have to. She knew that he couldn't make any promises. They had something more important to think about just then. Gennes smiled at him and nodded her head, and they went to join the others.

After a breakfast of bread and porridge, Michael asked everyone to stay and talk. They sat together, cramped around a little table, with Gennes, Colin, and Kelly on one side and Tomas, Aderyn, and Niall on the other. Michael stood at the head of the table to address them.

"The princess has told me," he began in his most serious voice, "that she knows the location of King Brenin's crown. It was she who hid it, and she is willing to give it to us—as soon as we can provide a person worthy to wear it."

The mention of King Brenin's crown brought gasps and startled expressions to the rest of the men. Several voices at once demanded to know what Michael meant. Tomas rose from his seat, red-faced.

"She's known all along where the crown is?" he stormed. "Why are we wasting our time here, when we could be going and getting it?"

"As the princess has already explained to me," Michael responded steadily, "the crown is useless until someone has been chosen to wear it. That's what...."

"But she knew all along...," Tomas interrupted.

"What's done is done!" Michael snapped at him, sending him back into his seat. "It's time to move on."

Michael paused for a moment and took in a deep breath, while Tomas sat silently, frowning at the table.

"All right then," Michael said at length. "This is what we have been hoping for and waiting for all these years. Now we have to decide what happens next."

Slowly, Gennes pulled her gaze away from Michael and looked at the other men. On each face there was a hint of nervousness, even fear. They were all brave men, dedicated to the fight against Balchder's illegal reign. But they were more accustomed to working with their hands than to discussing weighty matters of politics. Gennes was actually relieved to find that she was not the only person apprehensive about making such an important decision.

Kelly spoke first, breaking the long silence.

"Why do we have to decide?" he asked cautiously. "Isn't this something the nobles should be doing?"

Michael nodded, showing his appreciation for the question.

"There are two problems with asking the nobles to choose the next king," he answered. "First, we would have to bring them all together to talk. That would attract Balchder's attention before we're ready, and it could be disastrous. Right now, his troops are spread out all over the kingdom. We can't give him time to pull them together. Second, it's unlikely that the nobles could agree among themselves. We could very easily end up with a civil war on our hands."

Michael stopped and took a deep breath. He reached for a chair and drug it over to the table. Sitting down, he leaned his elbows on the table and rested his head for a moment in his hands. He looked so tired. Gennes wondered if he had slept at all the night before, or any night since he had learned the truth. He was, without a doubt, the bravest man that she had ever known. He wasn't shrinking away from the responsibility of dealing with the crown. He was meeting it head-on, just like she had hoped he would.

"We have to decide," he said at last, "not because we are the wisest, or the most worthy. We have to decide because we are here, and this may be our only chance."

The others murmured their assent. Even Tomas met Gennes' look without his usual anger or dislike. Colin returned her look as well. He smiled warmly and placed his hand on hers for a brief moment. Then Gennes looked back at Michael and smiled. They were ready.

"There are over a dozen nobles and almost as many large land-owners, but only four of them are strong enough to mount a real challenge to Balchder's army. The trick will be to choose the one who can garner the most support from the others."

"When you've chosen one," Niall said, "you're going to have three very unhappy noblemen. What if they refuse to help, or even decide to fight against us?"

"The nobles have become very independent since the king's death," Michael agreed. "It won't be easy to reunite them. I've already talked to many of them, and I have an idea what it would cost to secure their loyalty. The nobles that are loyal to Balchder may turn when they see the crown on someone else's head. Some won't."

"So what are you going to do?" Tomas asked. "Just give the crown to one of them and hope that everyone else accepts it?"

"Of course not," Michael answered. "We have to plan this carefully. In the ten years since the king's death, Balchder has never used his army against the nobles. I don't think he'll fight now if we can raise a sufficient force to challenge him. Faced with the authority of the crown and a kingdom united against him, Balchder may step down peacefully and relinquish the Military Stone."

"So all we have to do is choose the best man and give him the crown?" asked Niall.

"Aren't you forgetting something?" Tomas asked quietly, looking at Michael. "We have more to offer than just the crown. We have the princess. You said yourself that a marriage alliance with the princess would give one of the nobles a clear claim to the kingdom."

Startled, Gennes glanced sharply at Tomas, feeling the blood drain from her face.

"That was if we couldn't find the crown," Michael answered. "We don't need a marriage alliance as long as we have the crown."

Gennes looked at Michael then. His usually smooth brow was furrowed and his lips were pursed defensively. It gave her the strong feeling that he did not really believe what he was saying.

At the far end of the table from Gennes, Kelly cleared his throat.

"It does make sense, though," he said timidly. "If we're going to get everyone to recognize a new king, having both the crown and an alliance with the princess would give him the strongest claim."

There was a moment of silence, and then Colin cried out in dismay.

"But Michael," he complained, "you can't let Gennie marry someone else! You're in love with her!"

"Colin, please," Gennes whispered, placing a hand on his arm.

Then she turned to Michael, using all her strength to remain calm.

"Is that what you think, Michael?" she asked steadily. "That a marriage alliance would be best?"

Michael returned her look with no emotion on his face.

"I do," he answered in a low voice. "Brenin has no blood relatives among the nobles. No one has a better claim to the crown than anyone else. If you were to marry one of the nobles, or his son, or even a brother, it would strengthen his claim to the crown and the kingdom."

Gennes turned to look at the others. Tomas, Aderyn, Niall, Kelly. Each in turn dropped his head and looked away from her. Only Colin met her gaze. Gennes smiled at him weakly and then turned back to Michael.

"Then you have only to choose," she said. "I'll do whatever you ask."

Gennes stood slowly and walked out of the room. She crossed the courtyard, went out through the gate, and walked down to the riverbank. Refusing to cry, she steeled herself and concentrated on the rippling waves the water made when it beat against the great boulders that edged the river. She felt a little like the water, pushing hopelessly against something too strong to ever be moved. With her back to the fort, she sat down on one of the larger rocks and listened to the rushing of the river and the mournful tune of the wind in the trees.

A great deal of time had passed and she was beginning to get hungry, but she had no desire to go back into the fort. Overhead, she could hear Aderyn's raven bringing some report back to his master. The bird flew down toward the buildings and was silent again. Gennes still sat alone, pretending that she was back in Trevelgue, tending the sheep, before she had ever gone back to Briallen. Before she had ever met Michael. But it was difficult to pretend that the aching in her heart wasn't really there. So she climbed off of the rock, tilted her chin upward, and prepared herself to go back in and face her future.

When she turned toward the fort, she was surprised to see Michael waiting for her a few yards away. Their eyes met, and they remained motionless for a long moment. Then Michael walked toward her across the gravel bank.

"The raven brought news," he said matter-of-factly. "There's a rider coming. One of our own. He should be here soon."

Gennes nodded and started to walk toward the gate. As Michael turned to follow her, she stopped abruptly.

Without turning to look at him, she asked, "Will you tell me one thing truthfully?" Then she turned slowly and looked him in the eye. "Did you ever love me?"

Michael recoiled slightly and blinked.

"Addien, I don't think...," he began, evading the question.

"It's a little too late to be concerned about my feelings," she interrupted. "I know it won't make any difference, but I want to know the truth. Did you ever love me?"

He lifted his chin and said softly, "Yes, I loved you."

Gennes held her breath as he continued, "That's why I was so angry when I returned from Trevelgue. I tried to convince myself that I had never loved you, but I was only trying to protect myself. As soon as I knew who you were, I knew that I had lost you—that you would have to marry another. But the truth is that I do love you, and I always will."

Gennes' breathing quickened and her throat tightened. A thousand thoughts and feelings flooded her mind, but the strongest was a great sense of relief. Whatever else happened, the time they had had together would always be hers to treasure. It wasn't imagined, it wasn't lost. He did love her. And on the strength of that thought, she knew that she was ready to do anything that was required of her. She was ready even to be a princess again—Addien, the daughter of King Brenin, and a willing consort to some future king. Smiling at Michael, she raised her chin and straightened her shoulders. Then they both turned and walked to the fort.

* * *

The rider that the raven had seen arrived just after they finished the midday meal. Addien went out with Michael and Tomas to meet him. The man dismounted, breathing heavily as if he had been riding hard.

"What's the news?" Michael asked, taking the horse's reins.

"Have the soldiers entered the city?" Tomas asked impatiently.

The man shook his head, still trying to catch his breath.

"No," he answered at last. "You told us to prepare the townsfolk for an invasion of soldiers, but no one ever came. I rode out to check the fort north of town. The soldiers have all left. From the tracks and all the reports I can gather, it seems that all the troops have been called back to Cleddyf Castle."

Michael and Tomas glanced at each other before Michael looked back at the rider through narrowed eyes.

"There was a company in Trevelgue last week," he asked tensely. "Do you know if they've come back yet?"

The man nodded.

"I was told by one of the servants at the fort that a group of soldiers arrived from the west and they all left together," he said. "He said something about a man in a white robe that was leading the way."

"Cythraul," Michael exclaimed under his breath.

"Who?" Tomas asked.

"Cythraul," Michael said again. "He's the wizard who has been trying to find the princess. I found out that he was the one in the King's House, and he was with the soldiers I followed who tracked her to Trevelgue. Now he's heading north with two divisions of soldiers."

"To Cleddyf Castle?" asked Tomas.

"Perhaps," Michael whispered. "I think one of two things must have happened. If they're heading to Cleddyf Castle without looking for the princess, they may have found the crown."

"No," Addien said quickly. "They couldn't have found the crown in Trevelgue."

"Then they aren't going to the castle," Michael answered with certainty. "They're coming here."

Michael turned to Addien.

"They aren't looking for you in Briallen because Cythraul knows you're not there," he said. "The soldiers are heading this way, and they probably know right where to find you. We've got to get you out of here now."

As he sent Addien off to pack her belongings, Michael called together the rest of his men. When Addien returned, she found three horses saddled and ready to go. Michael took her bundle of clothes and began to tie it onto the back of her horse.

"Dyn just told us that the soldiers are approaching the valley from the west," he said. "You'll go with Aderyn and Kelly upstream. The rest of us will stay behind to deal with the soldiers."

"You can't fight that many soldiers!" she gasped.

"No," he responded. "But we can lead them on a good chase in the wrong direction."

Addien wanted to argue, but from the look on Michael's face she knew it was useless.

"Don't worry," Colin told her with a smile while he helped her onto her horse. "We'll meet up with you again. We've got it all arranged."

Addien looked at Michael one last time. His face was hard and unreadable again. She wanted to be brave like he was, to face danger and uncertainty without a trace of fear or despair. So she took up her reins and turned the horse's head toward the gate. Kelly moved his horse past her and took the lead. Aderyn came up beside the princess, and Dyn flew overhead, cawing loudly. Through the gate they went and onto the riverbank. Then they turned to follow the winding river upstream. Addien looked back at Michael and the others and wondered if she would ever see them again. Kelly and Aderyn prodded their horses into a trot, and Addien followed, saying a last, silent good-bye.

They rode upstream only a short while. Not long after losing sight of the fort, Kelly slowed to a stop and surveyed the woods around them.

"There it is," he said, pointing to the far side of the river.

Addien's eyes followed the direction of his hand, but she had no idea at what he was pointing. The slope on the other side of the river was very steep and covered in thick scrub. There didn't seem to be any way up the slope or any cover there if someone did try to climb it. Kelly dismounted and walked to the river's edge.

"Follow me single file," he said, as he led his horse carefully into the rushing water.

When they were safely across the river, Kelly walked his horse toward the valley wall. As they neared it, Addien realized that the wall of rock and scrub-brush was not as solid as it appeared. A narrow canyon opened up before them that had been invisible from the other side. They entered it and were soon out of sight of the river. The sounds of the water and the wind slowly died, until their every footfall could be heard clearly, echoing off the stony ground.

Suddenly, a great rumbling erupted in the little canyon, sending loose rocks sliding down to the valley floor. The sound washed up from behind them, bouncing off the walls of the canyon. Gennes jumped and looked back, expecting to see a hundred horsemen descending upon them. But the sound passed, and they were still alone.

"That must have been half a division at least!" Kelly exclaimed. "And they're moving fast."

"Toward the fort," Addien added breathlessly.

Beside her, Aderyn whispered to Dyn who had been riding on his shoulder. The bird flew up into the air and soared back down the canyon in the direction from which they had come. Aderyn turned to the others and spoke in his low, halting voice.

"We'll know soon what's happening," he said.

"Mount up," Kelly ordered, with a determined look on his face. "We can ride for awhile. Then we'll have to walk our horses up the embankment."

Silently, Addien obeyed. Her heart pounded in her chest, and she imagined that every hoof-beat was a legion of soldiers ready to surround them. But they rode on unmolested and without hearing any other riders. At length, Addien began to wonder when Dyn would return and what news he would bring of the men at the fort. Although she tried not to think about it, she couldn't imagine how they would escape. One group of soldiers was approaching from the south, and another from the west. The cliff-wall on the east was too steep to climb, leaving the only escape route to the north. But to the north lay Cleddyf Castle and more troops. Her friends had been neatly trapped!

At the end of the canyon, a narrow path zig-zagged up the cliff wall through the brush. Dismounting, they made their way slowly through the tangled, grasping bushes and up the path. Winded and thirsty, Addien urged her reluctant horse to continue, while she scanned the sky for the raven. Finally, they reached a level place and left the steep path and the scrub behind. Trees surrounded them again, although they were sparser than in the floor of the valley, and a cool wind greeted Addien's hot and sticky face.

Without resting a moment, Kelly mounted his horse.

"This way," he said, nodding toward the trees.

Too tired to complain, Addien climbed on her horse and urged it into a slow walk. Close together, they rode cautiously up the little slope that was all that remained of the valley and the woods. The further up they went, the fewer trees there were to give them cover. After a few moments, Kelly stopped.

"We're almost at the edge of the woods," he said softly. "I'll go on ahead and see if there's anyone on the moor."

He nudged his horse into a walk again, while Aderyn and the princess waited and watched. Kelly cleared the trees not ten yards from them and came to a stop. Suddenly, his head jerked to the right, as if he heard something. A bolt of brown flew through the air, and Kelly's horse reared and snorted in fright. Kelly fell to the ground, a spear in his side. In the same moment, Addien heard men yelling, horses stamping, and then a cawing overhead. Stunned, she looked up to see Aderyn's raven swooping down toward them.

Aderyn waved his arms and shouted, "Dyn! Come!"

Addien could see the soldiers then, running toward Kelly's fallen body. In a moment they would see her and her companion. With a final caw, the raven dropped down onto Aderyn's arm.

"Take the princess to safety," he told the bird.

Then he lifted his arm and set the bird aloft again.

To Addien he said urgently, "Follow Dyn. There's a cave in the canyon we came out of. Go and hide there."

In the back of her mind she could hear another voice also telling her to go.

"*The crown, Addien,*" she heard whispered in her memories. "*Take the crown and go. You must find a place to hide it where Balchder will never find it.*"

"Princess, go!" Aderyn yelled again.

Then he reached over with his foot and pushed Addien's horse away from him. The frightened mare snorted and started to back away. Addien grasped the reins firmly and swung the mare's head around. Then she was racing for the canyon, with the sound of pursuing soldiers not far behind. With a yell, Aderyn drove his horse into the midst of the running men. Then Addien lost sight of him as she neared the sudden drop-off into the canyon.

At the sight of the steep down-hill path, the horse balked and backed away. Not knowing how far away the cave was, Addien guessed that she could reach it better on foot than on a skittish mare. Quickly, she jumped down and turned the horse in another direction, setting it off into a run with a sharp slap to the hind-quarters. Then, hoping the soldiers would follow the horse's tracks instead of hers, Addien scrambled down the path into the windless canyon once again.

Dyn flew on ahead of her, and she raced to keep up with him. When he left the path, she pushed her way through the bushes to follow him. Not far from the path, he alighted on a large rock and cawed. Out of breath, Addien reached him and looked behind the rock. There was an opening in the granite wall, barely large enough for her to crawl through. She dropped to her knees and looked at the little hole in dismay. Suddenly, Dyn spread his wings and jumped skyward again.

"Dyn, wait!" Addien called, but the bird flew swiftly away from her, back up and out of the canyon.

As Addien watched him go, she could see some movement near the top of the canyon wall. With a deep breath, she scrambled through the tiny opening on her hands and knees. When she was far enough in to be out of sight, she stopped to let her eyes adjust. There was enough room for her to raise up on her knees and then sit back against the cold stone wall. Alone again, she sat with her arms around her knees, and waited.

Chapter Fifteen

For a long time Addien heard nothing but her own soft breathing. She hoped that the silence meant that no one had come down the path in search of her. But it was just as likely that the rock outside the cave prevented any noise from reaching her. It was impossible in the dark to tell how much time had passed or to know what was happening outside. But when she finally decided to crawl back out of her hiding spot and take a look, a fluttering sound at the entrance startled her back into her place again.

It was Dyn, the raven. Cautiously, the bird stepped into the cave, cocking his head from the right to the left and back again.

"Dyn," Addien whispered. "Are you alone?"

In response to the question, the bird bobbed its head up and down and backed out of the cave.

"Wait," Addien said. "I'm coming."

Back outside in the bright afternoon sunlight, Addien blinked away the dust and darkness of the cave. Rising slowly, she peered around the large rock to see the path in the canyon wall. It was empty. She looked at Dyn, sitting on top of the rock.

"If only you could talk to me like you talk to Aderyn," she sighed.

Dyn cocked his head and looked at her with his shiny black eyes. Once again, she was reminded of Trevilian and his tiny pixie eyes.

Struck with an idea, Addien surveyed the path once more to be certain no one was there. Then she knelt beside the rock and carefully opened the door of the locket.

"Trevilian," she called softly. "Can you hear me, old friend?"

A soft buzzing sound came from inside the locket. Then, with a quick flash of light, Trevilian was standing on the rock beside her arm.

"Trevilian!" she whispered happily. "I'm so glad to see you. The soldiers are looking for me, and I don't know what has happened to my friends. I have to talk to someone so I can figure out what to do. Can you help me?"

Trevilian made Addien tell him the whole story of how she had come to be lost and alone in the wilderness. When she introduced him to Dyn, her tiny friend walked straight up to the bird and stood before him, not even half the bird's height. For a few moments, Trevilian buzzed pleasantly to Dyn, and Dyn made soft crackling sounds in return. Then Trevilian turned back to Addien.

"You can talk to him?" she asked in amazement.

"Aye," he answered. "And his news is both good and bad. Yer friend that ye saw wounded in the woods is dead. Everyone else has been captured."

"Everyone?" Addien asked. "Michael and Colin? And Aderyn?"

"Aye," Trevilian answered. "Dyn saw them all being taken northward toward the great stone building."

"Cleddyf Castle," Addien whispered. "But they're still alive?"

"Aye," Trevilian answered. "They're still alive."

Certain then that no one was coming to help her, Addien knew that she had to find a way out of the valley by herself. She tried to remember everything that Michael and the others had said about who could be trusted and where they lived. It seemed that her only hope was to find one of the four nobles by herself and to set things in motion. But getting past Balchder's troops and crossing the wilderness alone seemed an impossible task. Then she remembered another day that she had to hide from Balchder's men.

"Trevilian," Addien asked, "can you make me small again, like the day we escaped from the King's House and that night on the moor?"

"Aye, it's possible," he answered. "What did ye have in mind?"

Without answering him Addien turned to the raven

"Dyn, there should be a large cattle ranch south of here. Do you know it?"

Dyn bobbed up and down, which Addien hoped meant 'yes'.

"Trevilian," she said, "if you can get me inside the locket, Dyn can carry the bracelet to the ranch. I can find someone there to help me, and then I can get the crown to the right person."

"Ye know who to give it to, then?" he asked.

"No, not yet," Addien answered. "But surely I'll find someone I can trust. I have to."

Trevilian made a few more buzzing noises to the raven and then turned back to Addien.

"Close yer eyes, then," he told her.

She followed his directions and tried to imagine herself as tiny as he. She thought back to a day long past when Trevilian's magic and her child-like faith had shrunk her down to nothingness and hidden her from the soldiers inside her father's house. For the sake of her friends and all they had worked for, they had to do it again. When Addien opened her eyes, she was on the rock, face to face with Trevilian.

"It worked!" she cried. "Trevilian, you did it!"

Addien turned toward the locket, but was surprised to find herself facing the blue-black feathers of some tremendous monster! She stumbled backwards and covered her face with her arm.

"Dyn," she sighed, suddenly recognizing the now huge raven. "You startled me!"

The bird dropped his head and eyed her closely.

"Are you ready to go?" Addien asked. "Once Trevilian and I are inside, take the bracelet to the cattle ranch, all right?"

Dyn ruffled his feathers and cackled a few small sounds. Somehow this time she understood what he was saying.

"I know," Addien answered. "I wish we could help Aderyn, too—and the others. But we have to take the crown someplace safe, to someone we can trust."

Someone like Michael, she thought to herself. Why hadn't she given the crown to Michael when she had the chance, she wondered. He was so much better suited to caring for it than she was. She should have known that she could trust him with it. If only she could see him again and have another chance.

"Trevilian," Addien said in a soft voice, "if I gave the locket to someone else, would you give the crown to him if I asked you to?"

Trevilian nodded, giving her a curious look.

"Then I have an idea," she said. "We can save our friends and give the crown to someone we trust. Dyn, we're going to Cleddyf Castle!"

After Addien explained her plan to Dyn, she and Trevilian stepped inside the locket and closed the door. There was a sensation of upward movement as Dyn lifted into the air with the bracelet in his beak. If all went well, they would be at the castle before sundown. Dyn had told Addien that the soldiers and their prisoners were walking there, so they should arrive about the same time. All her plan needed was a good place for her to make an appearance and for Balchder to be there.

The breathless feeling of flight finally ended. The locket dropped onto a hard surface, and Trevilian opened the door. When they stepped out, they found themselves on a high ledge that ran along the wall of a room inside the castle. Along the grey stone wall above the ledge ran a row of narrow windows, probably used by archers defending the castle from the inside.

Although she had never seen Cleddyf Castle herself, Addien could recall the numerous descriptions of it that she had heard. The stone castle was built into the side of a cliff that overlooked the Northern Channel at the mouth of the Lyn River. The north wall of the castle was a straight drop with no entrances. To the east and south, the castle descended in tiers, widening at the base. The west side was built right into the cliff, with nothing but a windowless wall rising up to the plain above. The only entrance to the castle was a narrow gate on the lowest level of the southern wall—unless, of course, you were the size of a raven, or a pixie.

From the description Dyn gave, Addien guessed that they had entered the castle from one of the higher windows on the south wall. Creeping to the edge of the archer's ledge, she could see that they were in a large room, probably the main hall of the castle. With any luck, the prisoners would be brought in there to be presented to Balchder. At least Dyn could watch through the window and tell them when they arrived. Since Addien didn't know if they would have to move again, she decided to remain pixie-size until she was certain they were in the right spot.

They didn't have long to wait. The soldiers arrived at the castle with their prisoners while the sun still shone low in the western sky. Addien's luck held as the prisoners were brought into the room below them. Now all she needed was for Balchder to arrive and accept her bargain—herself in exchange for the five men. When the men had been set free, Dyn would take the bracelet with Trevilian and the crown to Michael, and Addien would remain behind to face her fate at Balchder's hands.

With their hands tied behind them, the prisoners were thrust into the center of the room. Two dozen soldiers at least stood around them, many with their faces painted in bright and frightening colors. Another door opened, and a lone man entered. In her tiny size, it was difficult for Addien to see across such a distance, but she was certain that it was Balchder. His hair had begun to grey and he had grown a beard. He had also traded his Roman tunic for a long robe, although it was still black. But he still stood tall and erect like a man in control of all around him. On his forehead she could see the glint of metal, where light from the torches reflected off a bronze circlet. In the center of the circlet, she could just make out a blood-red stone.

Taking a deep breath, Addien turned to Dyn and Trevilian.

"All right," she said, "this is it. Dyn, do you remember what to tell Aderyn? You can go to him as soon as we see that the men have been set free and aren't being followed. Trevilian, you should go back into the locket now."

Trevilian regarded her with a frown.

"Are ye certain ye won't be going with us?" he asked. "There's no reason ye can't go back in the locket and fly away again."

She answered with a firm shake of the head.

"I have to stay here," she said. "It's the only way I can make sure that Balchder keeps his word. If I suddenly disappear, he'll have every man at his command after us with a single word."

The two hugged, as Addien said good-bye to her little friend. Then she closed her eyes and said a silent prayer. When she opened her eyes, she was kneeling on the ledge with her head even with the bottom of the window. Dyn jumped up to the windowsill and ruffled his feathers, but no one else seemed to notice the transformation. In her normal size, Addien could see everyone in the room clearly and could hear the conversation below her.

"So we meet again, Commander," Lord Balchder was saying to Michael, "I have often wondered what happened to you after you left my employ. As I recall, you were a natural leader and were promoted quite quickly. And yet you refused to join my Elite Corp, and then you left us all together. Pardon my bluntness, but you could do much better for yourself if you still worked for me."

"It will be a cold day in hell before that happens again," Michael responded through clenched teeth.

Addien smiled at his bravery. But she was surprised to see that Balchder was smiling, too.

"No matter," he replied. "You have already fulfilled your purpose of bringing the princess into my grasp, even if you didn't know that you were working for me."

"Isn't it a little early to be gloating?" Michael asked. "In case you haven't noticed, you don't have her yet."

"Not yet," Balchder agreed. "But without you and your friends to help her, it's only a matter of time."

Balchder motioned to one of his soldiers and turned to leave. Several of the guards came forward to lead the men away. In another moment, Balchder would be gone, and the prisoners would be taken away to the dungeon, or even to their deaths. Addien knew that her moment had come. She stood up with her back to the wall only a few inches from the window.

"Lord Balchder!" she cried. "I believe you have been looking for me."

Every head in the room whipped up and around, following her voice. Addien heard a gasp that seemed to come from all points in the room. Balchder placed his hand above his eyes to block the light from the windows and stared at her intently.

"Oddly enough," he said, "I never thought to look for you in my own rafters."

The sound of his voice broke the spell that had fallen on his men. Half a dozen soldiers ran for the steps on either side of the room that led to the ledge.

"Stop them, Balchder!" Addien shouted. "If they come any closer, I'll jump. Then you'll never have what you want. If I die, the secret of Brenin's crown dies with me."

Balchder ordered his men to stop and to move away from the steps. Then he looked back up at the ledge.

"No one will approach you," he said. "I should think, however, that you would be more comfortable down here."

With a great flourish of his arm, he comically gestured for her to come down.

"Not yet," she responded. "I have come to offer you a trade. If you will release these men—all of them—I will surrender myself to you and be your prisoner."

"An interesting proposition," he said, stroking his beard. "But why should I bargain with you when you are already here?"

"Because you need me alive," she answered. "And the only way you can have that is to agree to my terms."

Balchder looked down and took a few slow steps forward until he was almost below Addien's position on the wall.

"Of course, you could be bluffing," he said.

He looked up then, with his cool, penetrating eyes. Addien held her breath, not certain if she had the courage to carry out her threat. Looking down at the smooth stone beneath her feet, she inched away from the wall and closer to the edge. When her feet reached the end of the ledge, she peered down at the floor of the hall far below.

"The terms of the trade are acceptable," Balchder said suddenly. "Five petty annoyances in exchange for the long, lost princess of Dumnonia." He swept an arm toward the captives, but never took his eyes off of her. "If, that is, you are the princess. I don't suppose that you are prepared to prove that claim, are you?"

His question took Addien by surprise, and for a moment she had no answer for him. The only thing she had that might prove her claim was the locket, and she had no intention of showing that to Balchder. So she searched through her memory for something she could tell him that only the princess could know. Within a few moments, she had the answer.

"When I was six years old," she told him, "you came to a feast given in my honor, and you took my father away. Some urgent business, you said. You apologized to me personally and gave me a present. It was a silver ring."

There was silence below for several moments before Balchder spoke again.

"Anyone connected with the king might have known about the feast, and about the ring," he said.

"No," Addien answered. "I never told anyone about your gift. I threw it away in the bushes as soon as you left."

A wide smile covered Balchder's face.

"Now that's the Princess Addien that I remember," he beamed. "I accept your terms. Come down safely, and I will release the prisoners."

Michael and the others had been standing silently throughout the discussion. But at Balchder's last words, Michael rushed forward.

"Don't be crazy, Addien!" he yelled. "Get away if you can! It's you he wants, not us."

A small sea of soldiers fell on Michael almost as soon as he moved. As he yelled, they drug him backwards, forcing him to his knees.

"Do not harm him!" Addien cried. "Lord Balchder, please!"

Balchder turned and gestured for the soldiers to stop. Most of the men backed away, but two remained, holding Michael's arms so that he couldn't move.

"Forgive me, Lord Balchder, for not taking you at your word," Addien said, barely able to find her voice as the commotion died down. "The prisoners must be released first. This window looks southward, over your main gate. As soon as I see the men ride out of sight, with no one following, I will give myself up to you."

Balchder murmured a few orders to one of his men and then turned to the others who still surrounded the prisoners.

"Take these men outside and provide them with fresh mounts," he said, clearly enough for Addien to hear.

"Do I have your word that they will be allowed to leave unmolested?" she called out, still fearful that Balchder would attempt some trick.

Balchder laughed slightly. With a great sweep of his arm, he gestured toward the men.

"I have nothing to gain by keeping them," he said with confidence, "and nothing to prove by killing them. As for you, I desire nothing more than what I have always desired—to talk. I am a gentleman, Addien, and I will keep my bargain."

"Don't believe him, Gennie!" Colin yelled.

Swiftly, the soldiers grabbed him and each of the other prisoners and pushed them toward the door. Addien watched them go out and counted the moments until they should have reached the courtyard and had time to mount the horses that were being prepared for them. At last she could see them pass through the gate on horseback, and start up the winding path on the face of the cliff. When they reached the plain at the top of the cliff, they disappeared from her view. Addien turned to Dyn, who had been waiting on the windowsill, and gave him the bracelet.

"You know what to do," she whispered.

Dyn hopped around and turned his head in the direction that his master had gone. Holding the bracelet in one claw, he opened his wings and dropped into the darkening sky. Addien's spirits lifted with him, as he caught the wind and soared upward toward the top of the cliff. The locket with its secret treasure would soon be with Michael, and she would no longer bear that terrible burden. Even if she didn't live to see another day, she could be happy for awhile, knowing that she had finally seen her father's crown into safe hands.

Out of the corner of her eye, Addien saw something streaking across the sky. In horror, she realized that it was heading directly for Dyn! With a loud caw, Dyn dived away from the great falcon that pursued him. But it was too late. The falcon dropped swiftly and grasped Dyn with his powerful claws. Struggling in mid-air, Dyn lost his grip on the bracelet. Addien watched with dread as it fell to the rocks below. Her hopes, her happiness, everything that had ever been precious to her, seemed to crash to the ground in that same moment. She remained frozen to that spot, staring hopelessly out the window, until Balchder's soldiers surrounded her and led her down to the room below.

Stunned and heartbroken, Addien stood before Balchder. He waited silently until she looked up at him. Then a slow smile crept up his face, and his eyes gleamed in triumph. For the briefest of moments she saw in him the man who had once been her father's friend, when they would laugh together and tell stories to her, each trying to best the other with some important detail or funny remark. She had heard him called handsome, and he still was, even with the remnants of a deep scar across his forehead that she didn't remember. She had also heard him called vain, and it was apparent from his satisfied smile and glowing eyes that he was still that, as well. Had he looked the same way the day he had her father killed?

"Princess Addien," he smirked, "that was a noble effort. A useless effort—but a noble one."

"Meaning that your soldiers will pursue my friends and bring them back again?" she asked in a faint voice.

"That won't be necessary," he replied with confidence. "Why chase after them, when they will undoubtedly return in some vain attempt to rescue you? All I have to do is wait until your friends betray themselves. I told you that I would keep my bargain, but my bargain didn't include letting them escape a second time. If they are foolish enough to turn back, my soldiers have orders to kill them."

Addien struggled to control her breathing and to find her voice again.

"But you still don't have the crown," she said, attempting a defiant look at Balchder. "I only promised to give you myself. I'll never tell you how to find my father's crown!"

Balchder laughed softly. He was still so much like she remembered him from her youth—a man of confidence and pride. He seemed to be a man without concern or fear, like a man whose battles had already been won.

"But you see, my dear Addien," he gloated, "I no longer have an interest in the crown. I have found another, more reliable, way to claim the kingdom. And here you are, King Brenin's only heir, handing yourself over to me without a fight."

Addien stared at him, trying to make sense out of what he was saying. Then she remembered what Michael and the others had said about a marriage alliance.

"I will never marry you!" she sputtered.

"You don't have to," Balchder replied with a crooked grin.

He moved closer to her until she could feel his breath on her face. Before her eyes, he seemed to grow in stature, towering above her. He reached for her and stroked one hand along her cheek.

"All I need from you," he whispered, "is a son."

Wide-eyed, Addien stumbled back away from him. A guard behind her blocked her path and grabbed her arms.

"You're insane!" she cried.

Balchder ignored the remark and stepped close to her again. Gently, he laid one hand upon her stomach. The soldier's fingers dug into her arms as she tried to twist away.

"It's your destiny, princess," Balchder said softly. "You are the only one who can create an heir to Brenin, someone who can lay claim to the kingdom without a quarrel. That child will be mine, and you will give him to me willingly."

"Then you really are insane," Addien answered, her anger turning quickly from inflamed to coldly deliberate. "Do you think I would ever give myself willingly to the man who killed my father and stole his kingdom?"

"Your father was weak…," Balchder began.

"My father loved you!" she shouted. "You were closer than a brother to him."

"Is that why he banished me here?" he retorted, still keeping his voice in perfect control. "Is that why he sent me to the one point of the kingdom furthest away from his precious Roman city? Your father knew I was strong, and he feared me."

"You didn't used to think that way," she said, searching his face for some sign of what had happened to change him.

"That was before I was cut down on the battlefield and nearly bled to death," he said, the glint of cold anger in his eyes. "Sometimes it takes a brush with death for a man to see things clearly."

Surprised, Addien's eyes flickered to the scar that ran down the side of his forehead to his left ear. Balchder narrowed his eyes and looked at her closely.

"You didn't know that, did you?" he asked. "That I was wounded and left for dead on the battlefield? I'm surprised you never heard of it. My men regarded my return to camp as something of a miracle. Since they couldn't make me a saint, they decided to make me a king. And I will be king, Addien. And you are going to help me."

Suddenly, he straightened and stepped away from her.

To the guard that was still holding her, he said, "Take her to the holding room." Then he turned and began to walk away. At the door, he turned back with a smile. "Oh, and don't worry about your little bauble you dropped outside," he smirked. "My men are looking for it now. I hope it wasn't anything...important."

Balchder disappeared through the door, while the guard pushed Addien toward another. As they reached the door, Addien strained around to take one last look at the high window where she had watched her friends ride out of sight, and where she had watched her plans dashed on the rocks below. She didn't know if she hoped to see Dyn at the window holding the bracelet or if she hoped to see Michael. But she knew that both were impossible. The only thing she could truly hope was that Michael was far away, too smart to be caught again in one of Balchder's traps. Still, she looked. But there was nothing there except an empty window and the gathering darkness outside.

Chapter Sixteen

A short while later, Addien found herself alone in a small cell somewhere inside the castle walls. The room was barely large enough for the table and four chairs that occupied it. There were no windows, and the light in the room was provided by a single torch. She assumed that the guard who left her there was still outside the door, but she didn't bother to look. Even if the door was unlocked and unguarded, she had nowhere to go.

She wondered if she might be somewhere near the kitchen, as the faint smell of roasting meat tickled at her nose. She should have been hungry. She had eaten nothing since an early midday meal. But the gnawing in her stomach wasn't hunger—it was guilt. She couldn't believe how she had failed so miserably in such a short time. Only a few months had passed since she had left her moorland home with hopes of finding out about her missing past. Less than a fortnight had passed since she came face to face with that past in the King's House. She knew then where the crown was hidden, and she had resolved to bring it out of hiding and deliver it to someone who could defeat Balchder and be a good leader for the kingdom. But now, she had failed the kingdom. She had failed her friends. She had even failed herself. Her locket, with all its secrets, was either in Balchder's hands or dashed to pieces on the rocks below the castle. Michael and his friends would very likely be trapped and killed. And the man she hated most in the world was asking her to be his ally and help to make him king.

The aroma from the kitchen suddenly found its way into the room as the door was opened and a man entered holding a wooden tray and a plate piled high with tempting food. More from defiance than distaste, Addien turned her back on the plate and stared at the empty stone wall across from her.

"You really should eat something," she heard a familiar voice say. "You always were so thin."

Addien's eyes widened as she whirled around to face the large man who now filled the doorway. His plump, pink face looked lined and tired in the torch-light, and his hair seemed more grey than she remembered. But his fatherly smile was exactly as it had been the last time she had seen him—at the Christ'mas feast at his castle in Trevelgue.

"My Lord Trevelgue!" she gasped, unable to find any other words in her surprise.

"Little Gennie," he said, crossing to her with his arms open. "Is it really you?"

Addien stood and let herself be lost for a moment in his embrace. Then he pulled himself away and held her at arms length, looking searchingly into her eyes.

"No," he said softy, "it never really was Gennie, was it? You are the princess."

After another long moment, he released her. Still smiling, he motioned for her to sit while he sat down beside her.

"My lord, what are you doing here?" Addien said at last. "I never dreamed that I would see you at Cleddyf Castle, unless…."

"Fear not, child," Trevelgue said. "I am a guest at Cleddyf, not a prisoner. Because you and I are old friends, Lord Balchder has asked me to come and talk to you."

Simply the mention of that name made Addien's cheeks burn and her breathing quicken. In a gesture of contempt, she sat back and looked away. Trevelgue reached over and took her hand in his.

"You must listen to me," he said. "I came to Cleddyf Castle to meet with Lord Balchder at the request of his wizard, a man named Cythraul. This Cythraul is very wise and very powerful. He told us about your past and about what you had been doing since you left us. And he told us something he has seen from the future."

Squeezing Addien's hand slightly, Trevelgue leaned forward to speak very quietly. She couldn't help but look at him as he spoke.

"Princess Addien," he whispered, "the Saxons are preparing for another assault against Dumnonia. More and more of their pagan race are leaving their homes in the far north and coming to the Island. They need more room and they will not stop until they have conquered every corner of our land."

"Cythraul told you this?" she asked in a small, tight voice. "And what is Balchder's part in all of this? Why has he sent you to me?"

"Balchder is our only hope of defeating the Saxons again," he responded. "He controls the army. He possesses the Military Stone. And he has the training and experience that no one in the kingdom can match."

"And…?" Addien asked, waiting for the real point of his message.

"And Balchder is refusing to use the army to defend any part of the kingdom, except his own lands, unless he is made king."

There was a long silence while Addien tried to understand everything that Lord Trevelgue had just told her. She knew that Cythraul had gone to Trevelgue searching for her. Somehow he knew that she had gone there as a child, and he knew where to find her when she fled Briallen again. Was it possible that he could also see into the future and know that their peaceful kingdom would soon be invaded? And was it possible that Balchder would be so cold-hearted as to let the kingdom fall to the invaders?

The second question was easier to answer than the first. Thinking about Balchder's ruthlessness sent a shiver down her back. She stood and walked away from the table, rubbing her arms. Behind her, she could hear Trevelgue turn in his chair.

"I am an old man," he said wearily. "I don't want to go to war. I don't want to lose my son, or my servants, or my friends to a war. Without a trained army, we have no hope."

"It can't be that desperate," Addien argued, turning back to face him. "The army is just a small number compared to all the other people in the kingdom."

"But without a leader…," he began.

"There must be someone else," she pleaded. "Any one of the nobles could bring the people together to fight."

"Without the crown?" Trevelgue asked, leaning back in his chair. "The crown is gone, Princess, destroyed. The only thing left is the Military Stone."

His chair creaking beneath him, the Lord of Trevelgue pulled himself up to a standing position. Addien watched him in silence, her mind racing over his last words. What did he mean that the crown was destroyed? Who had told him so? And when? But before she was able to voice any of her questions, he spoke again.

"We don't have any choice, Your Highness," he said. "If the kingdom is to survive at all, it must survive with Balchder as its king."

He turned then and walked slowly to the door. When he reached it, he turned his head slightly to talk over his shoulder.

"I don't know what Lord Balchder has asked of you," he said, almost sadly, "but I hope that you will consider it carefully—for all our sakes."

Then he was gone. Addien sat down at the table again, exhausted and confused, and realized that her supper had not yet been touched.

* * *

She managed to finish most of her meal before the door opened again and a servant appeared to take the plate away. Just before the door closed behind him, a second man entered. He was not very tall, perhaps two inches shorter than Addien. His hair was completely grey, but his face was unlined, making him look both very young and very old at the same time. His eyes were grey, like his hair. Instead of a tunic and breeches, he wore a long white robe that appeared to have no seams. He also wore a golden band around his neck, like the soldier Michael and described to her at Torbryon's ranch. He approached her slowly and then made a deep bow.

"Princess Addien," he said in a voice as ageless as his face, "your room has been prepared for you. I am to take you there."

The man motioned toward the door, which still stood open. Dumbfounded, Addien walked through it into the hall. After climbing a flight of stairs they entered a large room with a luxurious bed, a round table with chairs, a rug on the floor, and even tapestries. Three narrow windows lined the far side of the room. Drawn by an unfamiliar sound, Addien walked to one of the windows and looked out. By the light of a half moon, she could see a great expanse of dark water below. Silver lines on the water rose and fell and rose again, moving steadily toward her. She leaned out a little further to see straight down. The castle wall dropped far below to a foundation of white rocks that jutted out into the sea. The waves beat upon the rocks making a sound like distant thunder.

"So this is the sea," she said softly to herself.

"It is more of a channel than the sea," the man said.

Addien turned to find him looking out one of the other windows.

"On a clear day," he continued, "you can just make out the shoreline on the far side."

In curiosity, Addien stared at the man. He wasn't a soldier, and he seemed too sure of himself to be a servant. She narrowed her eyes and leaned against the wall.

"You're Cythraul, aren't you?" she asked.

"You are very astute," he answered, turning to her and smiling.

"Have you come to frighten me with stories of invading Saxons," she asked, "the way you did Lord Trevelgue?"

Cythraul smiled.

"My purpose is not to frighten anyone," he answered. "I am merely a messenger. I tell Lord Balchder the things that I see, and he tells me the messages that he would like me to bear to others."

"And your message to me is?" she asked bluntly.

"That you are destined to have a child," he answered as bluntly, "who is to be the future king of Dumnonia."

He stepped toward her slowly. So intent was she on his face, that he seemed to move without actually walking. Like a vision, he simply floated across the floor. When he stood within arm's reach of her, he stopped, his eyes locked on hers.

"The appointed time is now," he said softly. "I have seen that you will conceive a son before the sun sets tomorrow."

"Tomorrow!" Addien gasped.

"Tomorrow," he repeated. "You will meet again with Lord Balchder in the morning. Until then, if you need anything at all there will be a servant at the door. Good-night, Princess, and sleep well."

Then he was gone, leaving her with even more questions than when he found her.

Addien did not sleep well that night. She couldn't stop thinking about everything Lord Trevelgue and Cythraul had told her. It wasn't completely unbelievable that the Saxons would invade again. Some of Dumnonia's neighbors to the east had already fallen under Saxon rule. And it wasn't inconceivable that Balchder would use the army to defend his own lands and leave the other territories without any defense. This much of what Cythraul said may have been true. But there were still so many questions that she couldn't answer. Why was Balchder suddenly uninterested in the crown, and why did Trevelgue think that the crown had been destroyed? With all of his powers, why didn't Cythraul know about the locket and Trevilian? Or did they know that she had hidden the crown, and they were trying to trick her into telling them her secret?

As the dark hours passed, Addien could only think of more questions. Was Michael still alive, and would she ever see him again? What did Balchder intend to do next if she agreed to give him a child? And what would happen to the kingdom, and to herself, if she refused? As the waves crashed endlessly against the rocks below, Addien closed her eyes tight and prayed that the morning light would bring some answers. Then she finally drifted off into a dreamless sleep.

* * *

When she awoke, the deep darkness of the night had been replaced by the drab grey of a foggy morning. Damp sea air blew in through the unshuttered windows and prompted her to pull her blankets closer. Beside the bed, an old woman was putting a tray of food on a little table.

"Breakfast," was all she said, in a voice that crackled like dry leaves. Then she went and sat down in a creaky chair near the door.

Pulling herself up to a sitting position, Addien noticed something else that hadn't been there the night before. At the foot of the bed, a gown was laid out neatly. The material was dyed a deep blue and had a vague pattern woven into the cloth. The neck and long, wide sleeves were edged with white satin trimmed with pearls. It was the most beautiful dress that she had ever seen—something fit for a princess.

"What is this?" Addien asked the woman in the chair.

"It's your dress," she said simply. "His lordship had it made for you."

Addien's first thought was to wonder when it had been made. It seemed impossible for such an exquisite gown to have been crafted overnight. But she didn't dare to ask. She didn't really want to know how long Balchder and Cythraul had been planning on her arrival.

After she had eaten and dressed, Addien sat down at a small dressing table to fix her hair. She had just started to wind the long tresses into a braid when the old woman stood up and came to her.

"Let me do that, child," she said with a hint of irritation in her voice.

With hands much swifter than seemed possible for her age, the woman pulled Addien's hair back into a tight, straight braid, starting at the top of her head and falling to her waist. She even managed to work in all the little wisps of hair that usually fell about Addien's face. Looking at herself in a hand-mirror made of polished brass, Addien couldn't help but admire what she saw.

"What is your name?" she asked the woman.

"I'm called Mag," the woman said. "I'll be here to look after you and your baby."

Addien put down the mirror abruptly, wishing that she could be back in her old worn dress and loose braid again—wishing that she had never come to Cleddyf Castle.

Later, Cythraul appeared to take her to Lord Balchder's private dining room. The long room held a carved table with ten chairs and a narrow side table for holding extra plates and candles. Lord Balchder was there, and Lord Trevelgue, sitting in a chair against the wall with his head bowed. Cythraul led the princess to the front of the table where a high-backed chair had been pulled out for her. Balchder stood beside it.

As always, he stood tall, with his shoulders squared and his chin raised. He had traded the long robe he wore the previous day for a Roman-style tunic. The dove-grey of the material muted the blue of his eyes, giving them the look of a cloudy sky. As she approached him, Addien could see that he was taking in the slimming lines and low neckline of the blue dress he had given her. His satisfied look sent the blood rushing to her cheeks. Looking down, Addien urged herself to breathe naturally and maintain her composure.

"Princess Addien," Balchder said pleasantly, "you look absolutely radiant this morning. I trust that you rested well?"

Refusing the hand that was offered to her, Addien sat down in the chair and placed her hands together in her lap.

"Would you mind terribly if we dispensed with the pleasantries?" she asked tensely, looking directly at Balchder.

"And get right to the point?" he responded. "If you wish."

He stepped away from the chair and walked in front of her, barely an arm's length away. Cythraul also moved, as silently as ever, to a place somewhere behind the table. Lord Trevelgue remained seated, peering at Balchder cautiously from his place by the wall.

"You know what I want, Addien," Balchder began in a matter-of-fact tone, "what I have always wanted—the kingdom."

"I'm surprised to hear you say that," Addien said boldly. "I thought you were ready to throw the rest of the kingdom to the wolves."

Balchder looked at her through narrowed eyes.

"Let's hope it doesn't come to that," he said quietly.

Looking away, he began to pace the floor.

"I've been a patient man, Addien," he continued. "Too patient. Some say that I should have taken the kingdom by force, attacking every noble, every city or village, that refused to bow to me, and burning them to the ground. Instead, I looked for the crown, believing it would give me the power to claim the kingdom without any more bloodshed. But I waited too long, searching for something that could not be found, while the Saxons gathered on our eastern border. Cythraul tells me that we only have one more summer to prepare for a Saxon invasion. In two years, we will be at war."

Balchder stopped pacing and stood directly before Addien. He leaned over and placed his hands on the arms of her chair, bringing his face very close to hers.

"I will defend what is mine," he said in a low, tense voice. "I cannot force the rest of the kingdom to join me. I don't have the time or the strength to fight the nobles first and then the Saxons. But you," he said, drawing even nearer, "you can give the kingdom to me."

Addien stared at his unblinking eyes, the clouded blue turning to stormy black. Could it be that this was just a ploy to trick her into giving him the crown? But why didn't he just ask for it?

"The kingdom isn't mine to give," she answered, barely above a whisper.

"You can give me a son," Balchder responded, still inches from her face. "Give me Brenin's heir, and the people will have to follow me. And I, in return, will defend the kingdom from the Saxons."

Balchder was so close that Addien could feel his warm breath on her face and smell the strong scent of his skin. She knew that he was waiting for an answer, but she still had none to give. She needed time to think. She needed to stall him. But how could she think with his face, his arms, his eyes so near to her?

She jerked her head away from his probing eyes and blurted out stupidly, "I don't know why you are even asking. Why not just take what you want?"

Balchder reached for her face with one hand. Cupping his fingers under her chin, he turned her back to face him.

"I've thought about that, too," he said, deadly serious.

He released her then and stood back from the chair.

"But then how could I ever convince you, or anyone else," he continued, "that the kingdom will be safe in my hands."

Taking another step back, Balchder crossed his arms casually. Out of the corner of her eye, Addien could see Lord Trevelgue, sitting straight in his chair, his face white as a ghost. Cythraul was out of her view, if he was even still in the room.

Balchder began again, his voice smooth and unthreatening now. "You know what I want. But I haven't asked you yet, what do you want?"

Looking away again, Addien answered, "To see my father's kingdom in good hands."

"Yes, of course," he said, dismissively. "But what do you really want, just for you, Addien?"

Her eyes met his again. The answer to his question was completely clear in her mind, but she wasn't certain that she wanted to share it with him. However, before she could decide what to say, Cythraul spoke from behind her.

"There is a man," he said in a distant voice. "A man that she loves. A man that she is not free to be with because of who she is."

"Then we can help each other," Balchder told her. "Give me a child, and I will give you your freedom. You will have given the kingdom a future ruler who is Brenin's heir, and you will be free to live your life as you choose."

"My freedom you may be able to give me," Addien answered slowly. Then she turned in her chair to look at Cythraul. "But, with all your power, can you make the man of my choosing love me?"

There was a long, silent pause, before Cythraul answered, "He already does, and he would do anything to be with you."

As much as she wanted to believe that, at that moment she could only wish that Cythraul was wrong. Addien knew that if Michael loved her the way she once hoped he did, he would never leave her in Balchder's hands without attempting a rescue.

"Then I hope you have the power to bring him back from the dead," she said, still looking over her shoulder at Cythraul. Turning back to Balchder, she explained, "You ordered your soldiers yesterday to kill any of the prisoners who turned back and attempted to rescue me."

For a moment Balchder stood still, the muscles of his jaw drawn up tight. Then he walked to the door of the room and threw it open. A soldier with a painted face and golden torq immediately appeared in the doorway, standing at attention.

"What is the news this morning of the men from Briallen?" Balchder barked out to him. "Where are they?"

"They camped on the moor last night, sir," the man answered. "At the last report, they had made no move to go on. It appears they may be planning something."

Balchder looked at the princess for a brief moment and then turned back to the soldier.

"Send word at once," he ordered, "that the men are to be captured, unharmed. I want them escorted all the way back to Briallen. And Captain...."

"Yes, sir?"

"They are not to leave there again without my permission. Is that understood?"

The soldier nodded his head in a hasty assent then turned swiftly and disappeared down the hall. In a great wave of relief, Addien breathed easier than she had all morning as she said a silent prayer that the message would be received in time. Balchder closed the door and returned to his place in front of her. Once again, he leaned forward and placed his hands on the arms of the chair.

"You can have it all," he said softly, "your freedom, the man you love, and the assurance that I will defend the kingdom better than any other man could—if you give me what I ask."

Addien looked into his eyes, the fresh blue of a clear sky after a storm, and saw there no sign of deceit or treachery. What she saw was a passionate, determined man who desperately wanted to be king. If she denied him what he asked, it was very possible that he would kill her rather than see her give to someone else what she had refused to give to him. But if she said yes...If she said yes, there would be time to think and plan. It was possible that Cythraul was wrong. She might not conceive, or she might bear a daughter instead of a son. Or Michael might find a way to rescue her before the child was born. So many things might happen if she just agreed to this one thing.

Swallowing hard, Addien answered simply, "Yes."

Chapter Seventeen

Balchder's sleeping chamber was not as large as the room that had been given to Addien the night before. It had no windows and only the one door into the hallway. Several tall, thick candles provided the only light in the room. A large, wood-frame bed filled most of the room, barely leaving space for the cupboard and chest that sat against the far wall and a narrow table that held a number of candlesticks.

Addien stood where Balchder had left her, beside the closed door. Without a word to her, he walked around the large bed to the cupboard and opened one of its doors. Removing a carved box, he opened it, and laid it on the bed. Then he carefully removed the bronze circlet from his head and placed it inside the box.

Addien watched his every movement with fascination. Here was a man in complete control of his body. If he felt any awkwardness about their current situation, he showed no sign of it. Nor did he betray any eagerness or desire for haste. Were it not for the large bed that filled the space between them, she might have thought that he merely intended to talk some more, instead of....

The sudden thought of what was supposed to happen there left her shivering, and she forced her eyes off of the bed and tried to focus on something else. What she noticed was the elegant box that Balchder was just closing with his small crown—and the Military Stone—inside.

Feeling a need to break the silence between them, she said sarcastically, "I was wondering if you ever took that off."

Balchder looked up at her with one eyebrow raised.

"Does it bother you?" he asked.

Disgusted with herself for even speaking to him, she turned away and folded her arms over her chest.

"Sit down," Balchder commanded, then added more softly, "please."

Addien had seen no chairs in the room when she entered, and she didn't want to turn then and look for one. That left sitting on the bed her only option unless she wanted to stand there in defiance of him, and there seemed to be no point in doing that. So, keeping her back turned to him, she found her way to the corner of the bed and lowered herself onto it. A moment later, she felt a movement as Balchder sat just behind her at the foot of the bed. There was a long moment of silence before either of them spoke.

"Will you loose your hair for me?" he asked, placing his fingers gently at the base of Addien's neck where the thick braid started down her back.

A cold shiver ran down her back, and she could feel the small hairs on her neck rise up beneath his touch. Breathing deeply, she tried to control the flood of emotions that was sweeping over her. Slowly, she pulled the long braid in front of her and began to undo it. As she did, Balchder reached over and unfastened the small ties at the back of her gown. When the lower length of the braid was pulled out, Addien reached behind her head to finish. Balchder took her hands gently and moved them away.

"Permit me," he said, as he began to carefully untwist the remaining length of braid. "You should always wear your hair loose. It's a shame to obscure such a treasure."

"It isn't much of a treasure when it's blown and tangled by the wind or plastered down by the summer heat," she replied, trying to ignore the feel of his fingers stroking through her hair.

"I think I should like it even then," he responded, his voice low and husky.

Addien's head swam in dizzying circles. This wasn't what she had expected. She had been touched before. She had been caressed and flattered by men who wanted to seduce her. She understood the games of romance and enticement, although she had never given in to them. But she hadn't expected Balchder to act that way. She hadn't expected him to be cruel with her, not after everything he had said. But she had already promised him what he wanted, so why didn't he just take it?

The small knot of fear that had gripped her stomach when she first agreed to Balchder's demands grew steadily inside her. She didn't want to think about the physical act of joining that awaited her, a joining that she would be experiencing for the first time. But she couldn't put it out of her mind. With each moment that she was forced to wait, her apprehension grew. But competing with her fear was another sensation that threatened to overwhelm her, a sensation caused by strong fingers running down her back and then up to her shoulders and beneath the material of her opened gown.

"You are very like her," Balchder murmured, his face touching her hair. "Did you know that?"

The sound of his voice so close to her ear startled Addien, and she lost the meaning of his words. When she failed to speak, he leaned in even closer, so that his lips grazed against her temple.

In a soft whisper, he continued, "I would have known you anywhere as Morveren's daughter." With a hand on each of her shoulders, he began to rub his callused thumbs into the soft skin below her neck. "I had never seen anything so beautiful, so graceful. You have that same look. You have her intelligence, too. I've seen it. Morveren was twice as bright as Brenin ever was."

At the name of her father, Addien jerked away and broke his hold on her. The door was only a few strides away, and she reached it before she even had time to think. But there she froze, battling her fear, her hatred, and her desire to run. What good would running do, other than to make him run after her and drag her back, and give him cause to triumph over her weakness? So she turned back to face him, summoning every shred of courage she had left to her.

A slow smile crept up Balchder's face until it reached his eyes. Addien glared at him defiantly, but he showed no sign of anger. Nor did he jump up to prevent her from leaving the room. He just nodded at her, with a satisfied smile on his face.

"So you are not entirely like your mother," he said at length. "I can see that you are made of something stronger."

"I am my father's daughter," she retorted between clenched teeth, "and if you still desire my cooperation, you will not mention him to me again. Or my mother."

Balchder's smile froze and then slowly disappeared. The amusement in his eyes faded away as well. He dropped his head in a slight bow to her and then rose from the bed.

* * *

The candles in the room had burned much lower before the two lay on the bed beside each other, silent and spent. Addien had turned her back to Balchder as soon as he had moved away from her. He had reached down for a blanket at the foot of the bed and, unfolding it, laid it over her shivering body. Her blue gown lay on the floor in a heap beside the door where he had come to her. His knee-length tunic had been tossed into a corner of the room some time later. The deed was done, and Addien lay on the bed trembling in her bitterness and anger—not at Balchder, but at herself.

He hadn't moved again after placing the blanket on her and lying back down on the bed. He could have been asleep, but she doubted it. She couldn't imagine that he would ever leave himself so vulnerable. His control over himself was astounding, even in the heat of passion. It was the memory of that passion that tore at her stomach and knotted up inside her chest. Although her throat was raw with unshed tears, Addien forced herself to speak, to find out the one thing she desperately wanted to know.

"Were you in love with my mother?" she demanded in a broken whisper.

There was silence for a long time, and she wondered if he had heard her. But at length, she felt him shift his weight on the bed and move closer to her.

"Every man who ever saw your mother fell in love with her," he answered calmly. "I was no exception."

Addien had to swallow hard and wait for her lips to stop quivering before she was able to ask her next question.

"Had you met her before she married my father?"

Balchder paused again before answering with a simple, "Yes."

"But she chose him, and not you?"

Addien knew she was treading on dangerous ground, but she couldn't stop herself from asking. And she didn't want to. She had felt the passion with which he had held her and become one with her. She had seen the need in his eyes, the aching desire, and felt it in his grip. And in meeting that need, she guessed that she had given him more than the opportunity to father a child. There was no answer this time to her question, which to Addien was answer enough. Her father had bested Balchder in winning her mother's love. But Balchder now had triumphed by winning Brenin's daughter into his bed.

"So next to taking away my father's kingdom, this was the ultimate revenge," she sighed, allowing not a single tear to drop from her brimming eyes.

Balchder moved again, pressing his body against her back and laying one warm hand on her exposed shoulder.

"Addien," he said softly. "Addien, look at me."

But she couldn't. She didn't want to see his face. She didn't want to hear what he had to say. She only wanted to bury her head in her arms and be left alone.

"Addien," he said again, commanding her with his tone to look at him. But still she refused.

At length, he removed his hand from her shoulder and rose from the bed. Addien could hear him moving about the room, but her eyes were clenched shut and her face was covered by her thick hair. After a few moments, she heard him walk across the room, and the creaking of metal hinges told her that the door had opened.

"I'll allow you a few moments alone," he said with only a hint of weariness in his voice. "Your gown is on the bed behind you. When you are dressed, there will be a guard at the door to show you back to your room."

Then the door creaked again, and Addien knew that he was gone.

* * *

It was late in the morning when Addien stepped outside the room and found a solemn guard awaiting her. They walked in silence, and Addien paid little attention to where they were going or what was around her. Except for the sound of their own steps on the stone floor, the castle seemed completely still, as if in mourning for something precious that had been lost.

Eventually, they came out of a narrow hallway and into a large room. Addien probably wouldn't have noticed the room at all, except that someone was there, pacing back and forth before a door in the far wall. In absent-minded curiosity, Addien let her steps slow as she turned to see the man better. It was Lord Trevelgue. Addien had little emotion to spare for anyone, but his frantic pacing, with his hands held together stiffly behind his back, aroused a measure of sympathy in her. Thinking that he might have been concerned for her welfare, Addien decided to stop and speak to him. Her escort stopped as well.

"M'lady," he said, gesturing for her to follow him, "your room is this way."

"Yes," she responded, "but if I may have a moment...."

Turning back toward Trevelgue, Addien saw the door beside him open and two other men enter. One was Cythraul, and the other she quickly recognized as Trevelgue's son, a young man two years older than herself. Trevelgue grabbed his son and held him in a long embrace. Although the guard was gesturing to her again, Addien was becoming even more curious about what she was seeing across the room.

"You are unharmed?" Trevelgue asked his son when he finally released his grip on him.

Cythraul responded for him, "I told you that Lord Balchder would keep his word. You performed your job successfully, and now you and your son are free to return to your home in the Southern Territory."

The three men by the door had taken no notice of Addien, and she was certain she had not been meant to overhear their conversation. Hot blood rushed into her face, and she could feel the muscles around her throat constricting. Her fists clenched, and she stepped away from the guard toward the center of the room.

"You lied to me!" she yelled, looking first at Trevelgue and then at Cythraul. "You used him to lie to me by holding his son captive?"

Wheeling around to face her, Trevelgue gasped and his face whitened. Cythraul, however, showed no evidence of surprise. His impassive look made Addien even angrier, and she wanted to run across the room and scratch his eyes out like a wild animal. She might have done so if Balchder hadn't suddenly spoken from behind her.

"No one lied to you," he said sternly.

Addien swung around to face him, making no attempt to conceal her hostility.

"And you...," she started.

"Everything that Lord Trevelgue told you was the truth," Balchder continued, cutting her off.

"Then why were you holding his son?" she asked through clenched teeth.

"It was necessary for you to hear the truth from someone you trusted," he said. "And I couldn't take the chance that he would refuse to do as I asked."

"So you used him, like you used me?" she shot back at him. "And now you expect me to believe you? I'll never believe it was anything but a trick." Drawing herself up to her full height, she threw her head back and exclaimed, "You better hope that you got what you wanted today, because you will never touch me without a fight again!"

Balchder opened his mouth to respond, but Addien didn't wait to hear him out. She ran past him toward the hallway where the startled guard stood waiting. Passing him as well, she continued to run until she was far away from the room where Balchder and the others had been. Waiting then for the guard, Addien let him take her back to her room, where she dropped down on the bed and let angry tears spill down on the soft blanket.

Chapter Eighteen

For the next several weeks, Addien saw neither Balchder nor Cythraul. She was served all of her meals in her room and was only permitted to walk about the castle and yard a few short times each day. Mag stayed with her always. The old woman ate her meals with her, slept on the floor by her door at night, and rarely took her eyes off of her. She spoke little, except to try to persuade Addien to eat on the days when her stomach felt rather queasy. As Mag tried to make her more comfortable, Addien's despair deepened, for it was becoming apparent that Balchder had been successful and a new life grew within her.

About five weeks since she had last seen him, Cythraul came for a visit. He arrived at the room just as the servants were taking away her uneaten breakfast. Addien remained where she was, standing at one of the windows looking out over the sea. A cool wind blew a few loose wisps of hair out of her face and helped to lessen the nausea she felt. Cythraul walked to one of the other windows and stood there, quietly waiting.

"Why are you here?" Addien asked at length, turning to face him. "Did you come to make sure that your prophecy has been fulfilled?"

"I have no doubt of that," he answered without emotion. "You are carrying Lord Balchder's child, a son, and he will be born in due time."

"And then what?" she asked.

"Then someday he will be king," he answered, returning her steady gaze. "That should please you, since you are the mother of the child."

"I had no part in the making of this child, except by your tricks," Addien said in a strained voice. "It is not mine, and it never will be."

Cythraul regarded her silently for a long moment. At length, he nodded and turned to leave. At the door, he turned back.

"I was sent to make you more comfortable," he said. "If there is anything that you require, you have only to ask. Mag will remain with you and oversee your progress, and I will check on you regularly."

"And Balchder?" Addien asked.

"Lord Balchder will be informed of your progress," he answered, like a well-trained servant. "I do not think it will be necessary for you to see him."

Addien held his gaze for a moment before dropping her head and turning her attention back to the window. She had not wanted to meet with Balchder again, to be in his presence, but she had assumed he would insist on it at some point. Knowing that he did not want to see her anymore than she wanted to see him should have made her happy. Instead, it left her feeling confused, and even a little hollow.

"Am I to stay cooped up in this room for the remainder of my stay?" she asked, venting a little of her unhappiness.

"You may not leave the castle grounds," Cythraul answered. "But if you wish to have more time outside of your room, that can be arranged."

Feeling less than gracious toward this concession, Addien continued to stare out the window. She was in a foul mood, and she would have liked to go on sulking, but she had never been one to give in to her moods before. She certainly didn't want to do so in front of Cythraul. So she turned to face him again, and tried to erase the hostility that had previously been in her voice and in her eyes.

"I should like to have something to do," she stated simply. He responded with only a raised eyebrow, so she tried to explain herself. "I cannot just sit or stand or pace the floors all day. I need to be doing something…with my hands."

Cythraul nodded, and she thought he understood. But his answer was not helpful.

"It would not be fitting," he said, "for you to do any menial work around the castle. Your position, and your condition, are such that…."

"A tapestry!" she interrupted. "I could work on a tapestry. I'll need a loom, and some wool. Any colors will do. I can work here in my room, and it will help me to pass the time."

Cythraul nodded again, in all politeness. He asked for more particulars about what she wanted, and promised to provide the materials the following day. Then he bowed low and showed himself out of the room.

Addien walked away from the window feeling more like her old self than she had since she had arrived at Cleddyf Castle.

"I may be a prisoner here," she said to the closed door, "but I will not live my life in despair and let you think that you've beaten me. I won't give you that satisfaction. The battle isn't over, and you haven't won yet."

* * *

True to his word, Cythraul returned the following day with a loom and all of the materials Addien had requested. He also provided more time for her outside and more freedom to walk about the castle. The blackness that had filled her heart and mind began to dissolve slowly, and she felt more in control of her circumstances—at least if she thought only about the present, and not the future. Even Mag began to speak to her more often, telling her about the changes that her body would go through over the following months. Cythraul returned to visit almost on a weekly basis. He watched Addien work on the tapestry, complimenting her work, and even asking questions about the design. In time, she began to look forward to his visits, as he was the only person around who would speak with her freely.

Addien kept as busy as she could and tried not to dwell on unpleasant memories, but she could not prevent herself from occasionally thinking about Lord Balchder and wondering what he was thinking or doing. She had come to terms with the fact that Balchder had been in love with her mother and had been envious when Morveren chose to marry her father instead of him. But that didn't explain the bitterness and hatred that moved Balchder to have her father killed. They had remained friends for many years after her parents had married. It hadn't been until after her mother died that everything had changed. There had to be some other reason for it.

She was reflecting on these thoughts one morning when a knock came on the door of her room. She had been finishing her breakfast as Mag busily worked her hair into its usual long braid. Thinking that the serving girl from the kitchen had come early, Addien took the braid from Mag and asked her to go and open the door. But it wasn't the timid kitchen girl who stepped inside the room beside Mag, but one of Balchder's castle guards. Seeing Addien, he bowed and then stepped forward to address her.

"My lady," the young man began with an air of authority, "I have been sent by his lordship with a message for you. His lordship has instructed me to ask after your health and your contentment here. If there is anything at all that you desire, if it is within his power it will be granted."

Addien's surprise prevented her from thinking of an appropriate response. Even Mag was standing behind the guard with her mouth open. His whole demeanor was so formal that Addien had to suppress a desire to laugh. But she couldn't help feeling sorry for him. In the ensuing silence, he shifted uncomfortably and even began to blush.

"Was there something else?" Addien asked, wondering why he seemed so ill-at-ease.

The guard cleared his throat and stood at attention.

"His lordship has a request that he would like to make of you." His skin color deepened, and his eyes avoided looking Addien directly in the face. "He would like you to keep your hair loose—unbraided. When you leave your room today and he sees you, he would like to see you with your hair unbraided."

The poor man was so flustered by the end of his speech that he could barely get the words out. And Addien could barely believe what she was hearing.

"Do you mean that I'm to see him today?" she asked, feeling a sudden tightness in her chest.

The guard stared at her blankly and then shook his head.

"No, my lady."

"But you said that when I see him…."

"When he sees you," Mag interrupted in her rusty voice. "He sees you every day, m'dear. He always wants to know when you will be outside so he can watch you from the wall or one of the towers. Just like he commands a full report on you every day. He knows everything that is happening here."

Addien's head was reeling, and she found it difficult to breathe. Her braid, only half finished, was still in her hands where she had been working on it without even thinking. Suddenly, her hands felt numb, and her face and shoulders burned at the memory of Balchder's fingers running through her unbound hair. He had told her then that she should leave it unbound. But doing something just to please him had little appeal for her, especially when he had been spying on her from a distance. She had nothing to gain from it. Unless….

Composing herself, Addien looked up at the guard and smiled pleasantly.

"Tell his lordship, that I am willing to do as he asks—for a price. He has asked if I am content here, and I am, except for one thing. The crown that he wears, with the Military Stone, distresses me deeply. Knowing that he wears it is a daily reminder to me of many painful things. So I am willing to make a bargain. If he will take off the crown and put it away until I have left here, I will unbraid my hair and leave it loose every day that I am here."

The guard's mouth dropped open, but he managed a stiff bow.

"I will deliver your message," he stammered.

"Good," Addien replied. "Mag, will you undo my hair?"

* * *

When Cythraul came for a visit later that day, his face and mannerisms, which were usually unreadable, betrayed an air of uneasiness. Addien's spirits were already high, but the wizard's apparent displeasure gave her an even greater feeling of satisfaction.

"I understand that Lord Balchder has communicated with you today," he said after a polite bow. "And you have sent a message back to him."

"I did," Addien agreed, silently noting that Cythraul had somehow been left out of the exchange.

Cythraul moved past her and stood with his back to her where she sat at her loom. Addien waited for him to speak again, although she had to bite down on her lip to keep herself from asking about Balchder's response.

"Lord Balchder accedes to your request," he said at length. But before Addien could even smile, he turned to face her and narrowed his eyes. "But I must ask you, Princess, what it is you hope to gain by this?"

A sense of power emanated from him. His eyes held hers, and she could not turn away. He seemed to grow taller before her, to make himself more imposing. But though Addien's self-control wavered, it did not break, and she considered her response carefully.

"Why do you think I have anything to gain?" she asked. "Perhaps I was just feeling spiteful this morning. Perhaps I was trying to make him feel as miserable as this will make me." She pulled a handful of her loosened hair in front of her. Then on a lighter note she added, "Mag thinks it's a silly wager, too. But it's one thing I'm going to win."

Cythraul continued to hold her gaze, but the fire that had burned in his eyes the moment before flickered and went out. Addien breathed easier. After a moment, she stood and walked over to him.

"And now I would like to ask you something," she said, feeling quite in control of herself again. "What do you have to gain from all of this? Why are you helping Lord Balchder?"

Cythraul returned her look without betraying what he was thinking. "I serve the future king of Dumnonia," he said.

"But you're not from Dumnonia," she said, although it was more of a guess than a statement of fact. "There are other kings and other kingdoms on this island, any number with more wealth than Balchder can offer. Why do you stay here?"

Cythraul smiled as he replied, "I wish only to serve where I am needed."

Then he bowed low and left the room, leaving Addien even more curious about the man than she had been before.

* * *

Summer descended with a blast of humidity, as a series of afternoon storms kept the air damp and grey. Every night, Addien wrestled with her long locks, attempting to comb out the tangles that the wind had blown into them that day. And every morning, she pushed the clinging strands of hair out of her face and cursed herself for making such a ridiculous bargain. Then she would remind herself that for one more day Balchder would be separated from the Military Stone, and from the evil influence that she had come to believe it exerted on him.

In her fourth month, her stomach began to swell and she could feel small movements within her. Cythraul began to visit more often, hovering over her and smiling as if he himself were the father of the child.

Some days, she could almost get caught up in his excitement. Other days, it frightened her. He began to tell her stories of the great kings of the past, before the days of the Romans or the Christian church. The kings of that day depended heavily on their priests, he said, who offered sacrifices to the nameless gods of the trees, the water, and the sky. The druid priests and their kings were fearless leaders who kept even the Romans at bay for two hundred years. The people they led were fierce and merciless, having no fear of death because they believed that after death their souls could return to live again in a new body.

Talking of these things, Cythraul would often get a far-away look. His eyes would stare, out of focus, out the window or at the ground. His voice would rise and fall in the manner of the bards, and he seemed to forget everything around him.

Addien wondered if he was going mad.

Listening to Cythraul's stories about pagan kings and priests made Addien realize how long it had been since she had talked to a Christian priest. If Cleddyf Castle had a chapel, it was not in use, and Mag told her that no holy man would step inside the castle grounds as long as Cythraul was there. It was useless to ask that she be allowed to go into the nearby village to see a priest, and Cythraul only scoffed when she asked that someone be brought to her.

"Those powerless fools!" he laughed. "What can they do for you that I cannot? Can they tell you the future? Can they hear the trees talk? Can they give you everything your heart desires?"

"They can give me peace," she answered quietly.

"How? By absolving you of some sin that they created with their morbid rules?" he responded. "The Saxons do not know your Church, and see how strong they are. One day they will rule this whole island, taking even what the Romans could not. Your Church will fail, and your son may live to see the day."

At the mention of her 'son' Addien glared at him. It was the first time that Cythraul had said anything about what life would be like for the child after it was born, and his words sent a cold chill through her heart.

* * *

When Cythraul left that evening, Addien couldn't stop thinking about everything he had said. As her body had changed, her spirits had also gone through sweeping changes. Some days she felt incredibly alive and unbreakable, while on other days she could barely move under the weight of depression. She had taken solace in her daily prayers, leaving to God the problems she could not solve for herself. She had tried to hold onto her faith and believe that Cythraul was wrong, but her prayers had not yielded any answers, and she had started to wonder if he could be right.

She was removed from everything that she had ever cared about, from her family, her friends, even her faith. She was alone with her greatest enemy, his grim servants, and a mad-man who believed he could see the future. Finding solace from a man of the Church had been her last hope. And now even that hope was dashed. Even her trust in Balchder, that he would keep his word and release her after the child was born, began to waver. She had accused him of lying to her before. Was she being naïve to believe that he would allow her to live when he had everything that he wanted?

She ate nothing that evening and refused to listen when Mag tried to encourage her. In a corner of her room, under a torch, she worked long into the night on a gown that she had been embroidering. She thought back over all the things that she had done, berating herself for every choice, blaming herself for every circumstance. As the hours passed, she convinced herself that Balchder intended to kill her and raise her child in the ways of Cythraul, his druid wizard. Dumnonia would finally have a king, but he would be a pagan, dedicated to overthrowing the Church and leading the people in barbaric rituals.

Her mind raced with desperate thoughts of escaping the castle, running away and hiding the child from Balchder. But there was no way out. And from the back of her mind, the thought that she had pushed there so often finally worked its way to the center of her attention. If Balchder had not intended to keep her alive, as he had promised, than she had no reason to believe that he had kept his other promise to her: to spare the lives of Michael and his friends.

Silent tears splattered on the gown in her lap as the needle in her hands passed feverishly in and out of the material. In the early hours of the morning, she made a desperate decision. At some point, the light of the torch hit her needle and flashed into her eyes. She laid the gown in her lap and stared at the needle's sharp point. Looking around, she found Mag lying in front of the door, sleeping soundly. Then she looked at her wrist, where her locket had once hung close to her hand. She reached down and scraped the needle hard against her skin. Then again, and again, until a small stream of blood flowed down onto the gown. Again and again she jabbed, deepening the scratch and increasing the flow of blood. The colorful needlework in her lap disappeared beneath a growing stain of red. Whenever the flow began to stem, she scraped the wound again, until her strength began to fade and the light in the room darkened.

Her breathing slowed, and she found it difficult to keep her eyes open. She looked down at her mauled, blood-stained wrist. Blinking back a wave of fatigue, she forced her eyes to focus as a hand reached down and touched the wound.

"What is this?" a kind voice asked.

"It's nothing," she managed to whisper, "a scratch, from the bushes."

"It's bleeding," the voice said.

Addien looked up to see a man standing beside her. Although the torch had burned low and the room was almost dark, she could see him clearly, as if he gave off a light of his own. His golden hair shown like a god, and his eyes flashed like an avenging angel.

"Michael?" Addien whispered. "Are you really here?"

Without answering, he pulled up the edge of his tunic and pressed it firmly against the wound. He held her arm gently, alternately pressing down and then lifting the cloth to inspect the cut.

"You'll be all right now," he told her. "Just hold that and call for help. And don't worry, you'll know what to do when the time comes."

The room darkened again. Addien looked down and found her right hand covering her left wrist, pressing her own gown against it tightly. When she looked around, she saw that she was alone, except for Mag who was breathing noisily by the door.

"Mag," she called out in a hoarse whisper. "Mag, wake up! I need you! Please, please, help me!"

Fighting back her nausea and faintness, Addien held on until Mag awoke and scrambled to her aid. As she drifted off into blackness, Addien thought she could see a light shining through one of the windows, and she heard a sound echoing over the waves like a voice telling her to rest at ease. Then she closed her eyes with a promise that she would never again allow any harm to come to her child.

* * *

Somehow Addien survived the night and woke the next day to find Balchder pacing the floor in front of her bed. It was still difficult to focus her eyes, and thoughts formed sluggishly in her mind. Yet she was aware enough to wonder what punishment he intended to mete out for her. She was also aware that someone stood beside her, next to the bed, but she felt too weak to turn her head in that direction.

"She is frightened and unhappy," a voice said beside the bed—Cythraul's voice. "You should not be too surprised by this."

"You told me that she would have this child," Balchder shot back at him. "She can't do that if she's dead!"

"She is not dead," Cythraul responded evenly, "and she will bear you a son. I have seen it."

"Then what do I need to do to make certain this doesn't happen again?" Balchder asked.

"Nothing," was the response. "I will stay with her myself until she is recovered. Then, I promise you, she will not try this again."

Reaching the door, Balchder turned and followed his own footsteps back toward the window.

"What I want to know is, how did it happen in the first place?" he asked in a rasping voice barely under control. "I told you to make her comfortable, to give her anything she wanted. If she was so unhappy, why didn't you tell me?"

Like a long-suffering father, Cythraul droned on, "You must not make too much of this. The only thing that matters is the child."

"Yes, the child…," Balchder started, the anger growing in his voice.

He turned quickly to face Cythraul, but as he did so his glance passed Addien's face. Suddenly he stopped and looked directly at her. Although her instincts told her to shut her eyes and pretend to sleep, she couldn't react quickly enough. She looked back at him and held his gaze for a long, silent moment. Although there had been anger in his voice, there was none on his face. His look was more of concern, even worry. Addien began to feel ashamed for what she had done. Her eyes dropped to the great bulge of her stomach. With difficulty, she moved her uninjured hand to feel it. Several moments passed before she could be certain, but at last she could feel the tiny movements beneath her hand. The child inside her still lived!

"What is it?" Balchder asked, watching Addien's hand move over her abdomen.

"He's moving," she answered in a weak, dry voice. "He's still alive."

Addien closed her eyes and breathed deeply. The baby was alive, and he was hers. Whatever Cythraul and Balchder had planned for him, she couldn't believe her son would ever be a monster like they were. Not with her blood flowing through him, or the blood of her father. If he was even one tenth the man her father had been, he would be a great king someday.

When Addien opened her eyes again, she found Balchder still watching her. His expression was calm, almost sad. Stepping to the side of the bed, he sat down close beside her.

"I never meant for you to be harmed by this," he said softly. "I don't want any harm to come to you or the child, I swear it. If there is anything that you want, you have only to ask."

Looking into his eyes, she wondered what had happened to the man she had seen so often in her imagination, the horrible beast who had tricked her and imprisoned her and cared for nothing but his own evil plans. Or was she imagining the tenderness that she seemed to hear in his voice?

Rising, Balchder looked at Cythraul, who was just beyond him at the head of the bed.

"Stay with her," he said. "Don't let anything happen to her."

Turning her head with difficulty, Addien followed Balchder's gaze until she was facing Cythraul. As Balchder turned away and headed for the door, Cythraul looked down at her and smiled. There, in his face, was what she had been looking for before—the man who had tricked her and imprisoned her and cared for nothing but his own evil plans. And this was the man that Balchder was entrusting her to again. Suddenly afraid, Addien tried to turn and call out to Balchder, to make him listen to her before Cythraul could once again cut her off from him. But it was too late. As the faint sound of her cry began to leave her throat, the door closed firmly in front of her. And once again she was left with the man whose very presence sent a chill through her heart.

Chapter Nineteen

For the next week, Cythraul rarely left Addien's side. He treated her kindly and still talked to her, but he no longer spoke of the future or of his ancient religion. Addien's strength returned slowly, and she was allowed to sit up in bed or even in a chair by the window. She missed her daily walks outside, but Cythraul promised that she could go out again soon. She also missed having something to do, although she doubted that she would ever again be trusted with needle and thread.

Her left wrist remained wrapped in a tight cloth that covered most of her hand and forearm. It throbbed whenever she moved it and especially when Cythraul removed the bandage daily to inspect it. At other times it felt numb, from the wound to the palm of her hand. Cythraul told Addien that she might never fully recover the feeling in her wrist and she would always bear a scar. But he never asked her why she had done it, or why she had stopped and called for help. She was happy for that, because the vision of Michael was something she did not want to share.

She thought often about Lord Balchder and wondered why he still kept his distance from her. Before, she had believed that he simply had no use for her, other than as a servant to carry his child. But that morning in her room, he had seemed genuinely concerned about her. Perhaps she was still too weak to think clearly, but she no longer felt afraid of Balchder or worried about what he might do to her after the child was born. She was starting to believe that he had always intended to keep his bargain and set her free. But somehow that thought did not bring her the relief she thought it would.

One day, about a week after Addien's injury, when a cold wind blew through the windows, Cythraul seemed particularly happy.

"Do you know what day it is?" he asked Addien after she had finished her midday meal.

"No," she answered, surprised to find that she had completely lost track of the passage of time.

"The last day of October," he answered. "Samhain. The soldiers are already gathering wood to build a bonfire in the yard. Tonight the souls of the dead will rise and seek new homes. I understand that the villagers are planning quite a feast!"

"But not Balchder, I suppose," Addien said. "He doesn't strike me as a man who believes in witches or ghosts."

"No," Cythraul agreed, "he will be making no offering tonight. At least not one that he is aware of."

Addien looked at Cythraul and waited for him to explain, but he said nothing more about the ancient holiday or its rituals. Instead, he turned the conversation another direction and asked her how she was feeling. Then they talked for awhile about the baby, which was due to be born at the end of January.

"In the heart of winter," Cythraul said. "You will have to take care from now on to eat well, as you will need more energy in the colder months. Listen to Mag and do what she tells you. You have nothing to fear. You are recovering nicely, and the child is thriving inside you."

"If I didn't know better," Addien said, "I would think that you weren't planning to be here for the birth."

"Oh, I will be back," he said with a rare smile. "But first I will be going away for a little while. I have left instructions with Mag about your care. She is an excellent mid-wife. And I have already made arrangements in the village to secure a wet-nurse to care for the child."

A sudden picture formed in Addien's mind of a tiny infant being taken from her arms and given to another. She winced and looked away.

"You've thought of everything, haven't you?" she asked in a rasping voice.

"Good planning is essential," he answered.

A short while later, Cythraul excused himself, claiming to have important business that needed his attention. Addien supposed it had something to do with the festival of Samhain, which traced its history back to the ancient druids with whom Cythraul identified himself. He paused a moment when taking his leave and held her hand.

"Good-bye, Princess," he said. "Until we meet again."

Although his face rarely revealed any emotion, Addien had the feeling that something unusual was on his mind, something more than a common holiday celebrated every year over the centuries. For a long time after he left, she sat and thought about what he had told her. He believed himself to be a druid priest, although none had existed since the Romans brought Christianity to the Island. Although he had traveled all over the Island, he had come to stay in the one place that had no king. Instead of using his powers to help Balchder gain control of the kingdom, or to find the crown, he had brought the two of them together to form a new life—a child who would have the undisputed right to rule as king. Then, having seen his plan set in motion but not yet completed, he was saying good-bye to her, as if he wouldn't be seeing her again for a long while. On the day of Samhain, when the souls of the dead rise again....

"No!" Addien cried.

Rising with difficulty from her chair, she waved at Mag for help.

"Mag, we have to stop him," she said, clutching the back of the chair. "You have to help me find Cythraul before it's too late!"

"You shouldn't be walking yet," the old woman clucked. "You're too weak."

"I have to!" Addien shouted. "We have to find him!"

Reluctantly, Mag helped Addien to the door and out into the hall. Gasping for breath, Addien struggled to stay on her feet. Shifting her weight, Mag leaned her against the wall and pulled herself free.

"Stay there," she ordered. "I'll find someone to help us."

Mag shuffled out of sight down the hall. Using the wall to support her, Addien slowly followed. At the end of the hall, the stone floor dropped off into a wide stairwell. Dizzy with fatigue, she stopped at the top of the stairs and rested her head on the cold stone wall. Below her, she could hear footsteps, so she closed her eyes to wait for Mag's return.

"Addien!"

Her eyes flashed open to see Balchder rounding the corner of the stairs into her view. He rushed up the last flight as he yelled to her.

"What are you doing out here?" he barked, with his eyes flashing. "Where is Cythraul? And that servant woman?"

"Cythraul," Addien repeated weakly, beginning to reel.

Balchder threw one arm around her and pulled her to his side. For a moment, Addien's head rested on his shoulder. Then she forced herself to look up at him.

"We have to find Cythraul," she pleaded. "You have to stop him."

Balchder looked into her eyes and furrowed his brow.

"What are you talking about?" he asked.

"He's going to kill himself," Addien answered, feeling her strength return. "He thinks that his soul will rise tonight and he can enter a new body, one waiting to be born. He wants to be a king, and he thinks he can live again in this child."

Addien's hand dropped to her stomach. She looked down for a moment and then back at Balchder. His eyes narrowed, and she wondered whether he believed her. Then the lines on his face deepened as his jaw clenched tight.

"I'll find him," he answered, "just as soon as I get you back to your room."

"No, please!" Addien said. "Let me talk to him. I know what he's thinking, and he may listen to me."

At that moment, Mag appeared on the stairs, followed by three guards. She fell back in fear when she saw Addien with Balchder. Balchder ignored her and yelled at the guards.

"Have any of you seen Cythraul?" he demanded. "Do you know where he is?"

"He was in the yard a few moments ago," one of the men answered. "Putting out an offering for the souls."

"Find him!" Balchder ordered. "And hold him until I arrive."

The men spun around and ran down the stairs. Balchder turned to Addien, still holding her close.

"Can you walk?" he asked.

"I—don't think so," she answered.

He reached down and lifted her into his arms. Following the guards, he swept down the stairs, past the speechless Mag, and out into another hall. One of the guards rounded a corner and ran toward them.

"He's just been spotted on the eastern wall," he called. "He's at the end of the walk. Do you want us to take him?"

"No," Balchder answered. "Tell the men to keep their distance. I'll go up to him myself."

The guard disappeared again, and Balchder carried Addien outside into the castle courtyard. Setting her on her feet, he motioned to one of his men to stand with her.

"Stay here," he told her. "It's too dangerous for you to go any further."

Addien wanted to argue, but his look warned her against it. Instead, she watched as Balchder hurried onto a staircase leading to a wooden catwalk that ran just below the top of the outer wall. Walking out a little further, she could see Cythraul in his white robes standing at the end of the catwalk, where the eastern and northern walls met. Balchder was approaching him quickly, but Cythraul didn't seem to see him. He was pulling himself up onto the top of the wall, where he stood and looked out over the water.

"Cythraul!" Balchder called, his voice flying away from him in the wind. "Cythraul, come down! We have to talk."

Cythraul turned then and looked at Balchder. He was too far away for Addien to see any expression on his face, but he made no move to climb down off of the wall.

"This is insane, Cythraul," Balchder called again. "Come down so we can talk."

"I cannot come down yet," Cythraul called back. "I have not yet completed my offering."

Addien realized then that Cythraul was holding something in his hands, a bowl perhaps, made of a metal that reflected the light of the sun.

"You're coming down if I have to bring you down myself," Balchder yelled, moving forward again.

Cythraul laughed and held the bowl above his head. Then suddenly he threw the bowl down onto the catwalk halfway between himself and Balchder. A dark liquid spilled out over the wooden walkway and dripped over the edge. Cythraul laughed again at Balchder's startled expression.

"Are you afraid?" Cythraul yelled, still holding his arms high in the air. "It is merely an offering of fragrant oil that I intended to give to the sea. But it is only the beginning of the sacrifice. The rest must be made in fire and in blood!"

"Your blood?" Balchder asked, stepping closer to the spilt oil as if to try again to reach the wizard.

"My fire!" Cythraul roared.

Suddenly, his hand came down and something flew out onto the catwalk before him. The oil ignited into a ball of flame. A moment later it exploded, sending pieces of wood spiraling into the air and down to the ground below. The soldiers around the princess covered their heads or ducked behind walls to avoid the debris. Addien also ducked, as the man beside her threw himself forward to protect her from the falling wood. As soon as she could, Addien looked up at the catwalk where Balchder had been standing. He was still there, although he had been thrown back against the wall and seemed to be struggling to stay on his feet. Addien guessed that if Cythraul had intended to kill him, he could have made his aim better. But he had been successful in destroying the walkway between Balchder and himself, keeping Balchder from getting any closer.

With his robes fluttering in the wind like a flag, Cythraul turned to look down at the princess. He made a deep bow and saluted her. Then, before anyone could utter a word, he turned swiftly and threw himself off the wall toward the sea and the boulders below.

In horror, Addien looked back at Balchder who was still staring at the place where Cythraul had been. No one seemed to be moving, as if everyone had been caught in a terrible spell. Exhausted and out of breath, Addien started to drop her eyes from the wall above when something else caught her attention. Only a foot or two from the hole that had been blown in the catwalk, a small fire was still burning on one of the triangular supports set into the wall. If the support gave way, one whole section of the walk would collapse, taking Balchder with it!

"Lord Balchder!" she shouted as loud as she could, pointing upward. "The support is on fire! The walk is going to fall!"

Balchder barely had time to look down before the burning wood began to give way. With a shudder, the walkway dropped an inch, then another. Balchder scrambled to grab hold of the wall and pull himself halfway up before the support finally collapsed in flames and the catwalk fell out from under him. As a dozen soldiers rushed up the stairs to the remaining length of walkway, Balchder dragged the rest of his body onto the top of the wall. A short while later, he was back on the stairs, surrounded by his men, on his way down.

In shock, Addien waited silently until he reached her. Unable to find any words, she could only look at him through wide, frightened eyes.

He stepped closer to her, wrapped his arms around her, and pulled her close. She closed her eyes and rested there, wondering what unbelievable thing could possibly happen next.

"Bring me his body," Balchder ordered someone beside him. "I want to see with my own eyes that he's dead."

Then he lifted Addien gently and carried her through the castle back to her room. He laid her on the bed and sat next to her. Through a stream of tears, she told him everything that Cythraul had said to her, all the stories of the past and of his own life. She told him about the druids and Cythraul's prophecy that pagan kings would one day rule all of the Island. And she told him of her fear that Cythraul expected his soul to rise from the dead that night to inhabit her unborn child.

Balchder listened silently while Addien poured out her heart to him.

"He must have been mad," Balchder said when she finished. "He never confided to me his true intentions. But I can promise you this, wherever his soul goes tonight, it will not return here. Cythraul was wrong. So rest at ease tonight and fear no spirits. Tomorrow, if you like, I will find you a Christian priest and bring him here."

Addien looked at Balchder as if she had never known him. His comforting words and strong presence reminded her of her father, when he would sit on her bed at night and chase away her bad dreams. She thought of Balchder in his younger days when he had been charming and handsome and her father's best friend. If the Military Stone had influenced him toward evil, perhaps Cythraul had also influenced him. She couldn't help but wonder what kind of man he would have been if he had not been caught up in a desperate quest for power—his own and Cythraul's. Then she thought again of Cythraul and imagined his broken body dashed upon the rocks beside the sea. Addien looked toward the windows and realized that the sun was already setting and the witching hour was close at hand.

At that moment, there was a knock at the door. Mag rose quickly and opened the door to Balchder's Captain of the Guard.

"What is it, Captain?" Balchder asked, his voice strained and tired.

"I'm sorry to interrupt, my lord, but there is news," the man said.

Balchder looked at him and waited for him to continue.

"We were unable to retrieve Cythraul's body from the rocks," the Captain said. "A group of men was waiting below on the beach. They reached the body first and removed it. I had my men follow them to see where they were taking it."

The Captain paused and glanced down for a moment.

Balchder's eyebrows raised as he murmured a gruff, "And?"

"If he wasn't dead before, there is no doubt of it now," the Captain continued. "His body was taken to one of the old sacred groves in the valley—and burned. My men are certain that he was placed in the flames, and the fire was so great that we could see the light of it from the castle wall."

Glancing in Addien's direction, the Captain bowed slightly, as if in apology for bringing such appalling news. But his message did not surprise her. Cythraul had indeed planned everything, and his body had been sent to his gods the way he had wanted.

"A sacrifice of blood and fire," she murmured, with a small tremble in her voice.

Balchder looked at her and took her hand.

"It means nothing," he said. "Anyone can arrange their own death, even their own funeral. But managing to be reborn is quite another thing. I give you my word that Cythraul is gone, and he will never haunt you again."

That night, after Balchder had left, Addien dreamt about Cythraul. She could see his twisted and contorted body dancing among the flames of a huge bonfire in the castle yard. Terrified soldiers fell to the ground on every side as his fiery form jumped upon the castle wall. She cringed in terror as he ran toward her room, throwing his head back in wild laughter. But at the door he was stopped by two men, one dressed in a grey tunic with dark hair, the other shining with a light from within, with hair of gold. Together they fought him with swords of iron and flame, until Cythraul fell to the floor with a great wailing. His fire was extinguished until nothing remained but blowing ashes on the floor.

* * *

The next day, Addien rested in her bed all morning and into the afternoon, lacking the strength or the will to get up. For most of the day, she thought that Balchder had forgotten his promise. But he hadn't. Just as the torches were being lit that evening, Mag opened the bedroom door to a young man in brown robes. He told the women that he was a monk who had been traveling to a monastery across the sea. Although he had had his heart set on a pilgrimage, he had agreed to come and live for a time at the castle to see to the spiritual needs there. Addien had to smile when he confided to her that he alone was asked to come out of a number of traveling companions because he was a foreigner and had never heard of the lord of the castle.

When Addien was feeling well enough to resume her daily walks, she began to visit Brother Peadar every day in the little room that Balchder had given him for a chapel. They talked about his travels and his religious training in Ireland and debated current issues about the Church and the priesthood. Addien told him about the people of Dumnonia and a little bit of its history. But she found herself reluctant to tell him about her role in the kingdom's most recent history. He assumed that Addien and Balchder were married and that she was the Lady of the castle. She decided not to dispel that assumption. Although she wanted to confide in him and seek his guidance, she was never left alone with him, even in the chapel. Ever fearful that anything she said would be reported back to Balchder, she kept her secrets to herself.

Addien was very surprised one day, only a week after Cythraul's death, when Balchder himself came to visit her. He requested that she have supper with him that evening in his private dining room.

Although they barely spoke to each other during the meal, he asked her to come again a few days later. Eventually, it became a routine. A guard would be sent for her each evening and would escort her to Balchder's private dining room, where they would dine alone. Over the meal they would discuss the daily affairs of the castle, Addien's discussions with Brother Peadar, and even the petitions of the villagers and farmers who lived near the castle. Balchder even granted Addien's request to plan a feast for Christ's Mass for the servants and soldiers at the castle. Although Christ'mas was still a month away, it had always been one of her favorite holidays, and she hoped that planning a celebration would help to take her mind off of Cythraul's death.

The short days of winter seemed endless. Most mornings, Addien looked out her windows to see heavy grey clouds lying low over the water. Her extra bulk left her tired and uncomfortable, and she was afflicted with numerous aches and pains. Mag listened to her daily grumbling and put her moodiness down to a fear of the pain of childbirth. But it wasn't that. Addien knew that she wasn't afraid of having the baby; she was afraid of having to say good-bye to it after it was born.

Balchder still had not told Addien what he intended to do with the child after its birth. She wondered how the child would be raised, and when Balchder intended to present him to the kingdom, and who would take care of him if Balchder marched off to another long war against the Saxons. As the day of the birth approached, these things weighed more and more upon her mind.

With Balchder, Addien attempted to hide her feelings. They dined together every evening, even when she was sore or depressed or simply not hungry. Usually, she was able to confine her conversation to trivial matters or to eat in silence. But as her uneasiness about the future grew, Addien's ability to control her emotions diminished. One evening, in mid-December, she sat staring at her plate, unable to eat or to talk.

"Addien," Balchder said at last, when his meal was finished and hers still sat untouched. "You seem unhappy this evening. Is there something troubling you?"

Addien sat for a long moment, breathing deeply, before she could trust herself to answer.

"It's nothing, my lord," she answered, looking down at her plate.

"If you are ill, I should send for someone…."

"I'm not ill," she interrupted rudely.

Balchder regarded her silently. She could feel his look and could imagine him sitting there feeling sorry for her. At that moment, it was more than she could take.

"If you want to know the truth," Addien said, looking up to meet his eyes, "I'm angry. I overheard some of your soldiers talking today, and what they said made me very angry."

Balchder looked at her through narrowed eyes, but he said nothing. Addien took a deep breath and continued.

"Three of the men were boasting to the others about how they had been in the village today and beat a man senseless. The three of them dragged him from his cart, threw him to the ground, and kicked him in the head and stomach until he couldn't move. And the reason for this brutal assault was because the man 'insulted' the soldiers by not moving his cart out of their way fast enough."

"Was that all the men said that made you angry?" Balchder asked.

"There were a few other bloody details," she responded, "but that was the general story."

Balchder sat back in his chair and nodded.

"I'll have a talk with the men tomorrow," he said evenly. "I'll let them know that that kind of behavior is unacceptable."

Addien stared at him in disbelief. All the things she had ever heard about the cruelty and callousness of his men flooded her mind. A tiny voice in her head warned her to hold her tongue, but it was too late.

"Unacceptable?" she shot back at him. "Your men have roamed the kingdom for years terrorizing everyone they come into contact with. They steal what they cannot have and destroy what they cannot steal. They are bored and unruly and undisciplined. You use them as a weapon to maintain your power through fear. And you have been successful. The kingdom fears them, and it fears you. But the people will never accept you as their king, even if you sire a hundred bastards that can claim to be Brenin's heirs!"

In a rage, Addien pushed away from the table and stormed out of the room. In the hall, Mag rose swiftly and held out a cloak to her. Addien blew past her and marched to her room without looking back. When the door finally closed behind her, she dropped down on the bed in an angry tantrum and sobbed uncontrollably. She couldn't decide if she was angry with Balchder because of all the years of harm that he had done to the kingdom, and to her own family, or if she was really angry at herself because she had begun to believe that he could change. She wished with all her heart that the day would come quickly when she would be free to leave Cleddyf Castle and never have to see Lord Balchder again. Then she thought again of the child who grew within her, who would have to grow up without a mother and without any kindness or happiness in his life. And she cried again, until she fell into an exhausted sleep.

Chapter Twenty

For the next two weeks, Addien received no word from Balchder. No guard came to escort her in the evenings to his chambers. Instead, her meals were once again brought to her room where she ate alone with Mag. A relentless rain pounded the coastline, keeping everyone indoors and inactive. With too much time on her hands, Addien's thoughts began to mirror the gloomy weather more and more. When she tried to distract herself from thinking about her baby, she could only think of more distressing, unanswerable questions.

Addien thought about her locket and wondered what had happened to it after Dyn dropped it outside the castle. Did Balchder find it? Had Cythraul used his magical arts to unlock the secret inside it? Or had he, perhaps, hidden the truth from Balchder to further his own, mad scheme?

She thought about Trevilian and wondered if he was all right. But most of all, she thought about Michael. It had been such a long time since she had seen him that sometimes he seemed like a dream. Although Balchder had promised to set her free so that she could be with Michael, Addien had never really believed that such a thing would be possible. Michael would more likely consider her a traitor to his cause, and he would never be able to forgive her. So she passed the days trying to keep busy, but never really able to escape her fears about the not-so-distant future.

Christ'mas morning dawned cold and windy, but without a cloud in the sky. Addien rose early and combed out her hair, then waited for Mag to help her dress. With the baby due in a little more than a month, she had required some new clothes with more room in the middle. Mag had personally chosen a woman to sew a few heavy woolen gowns to keep Addien warm through the short, chilly days. One gown, died emerald green with gold embroidery at the neck and sleeves, she had saved for that special morning. Addien was determined to enjoy the Christ'mas feast with the others in the castle, even if Balchder refused to join them. And she had promised Brother Peadar that she would be at the chapel early for a private mass before he went out to the castle yard to hold services for the others.

Since Cythraul's death, the soldiers had become much less hostile around the castle. Most of them had given up painting their faces, and they all treated Brother Peadar with respect. Addien was never certain, though, if it was because of his holiness, or because of the large, thick staff he always carried with him.

"Good morning, Brother," Addien said as she entered the chapel.

"And a fine morning it is," Peadar said, rising from a bench to greet her.

It was then that she noticed that Peadar was not alone. Sitting beside him on the bench, wrapped in his black cloak, sat the lord of the castle. Balchder rose also and bowed his head to Addien politely.

"I hope you don't mind," he said. "I asked Brother Peadar if I might attend mass with you this morning."

After a brief, stunned pause, Addien was able to respond.

"Of course not," she said, returning Balchder's polite bow.

When the mass concluded, Peadar left Addien and Balchder alone in the chapel. Even Mag stepped outside to wait in the hall. Addien sat for a moment in silence, waiting for Balchder to say something, or to leave. But he did neither. At length she stood and gathered her cloak about her to go out into the drafty hall. Balchder stood also and walked with her to the door. As they crossed the small distance, he cleared his throat and looked at the floor.

"I believe it is the custom at this time of the year," he began, his voice halting and uncomfortable, "to give gifts. I am not very knowledgeable about these things, as I have not had any family of my own for a very long time. It is not a practice I have kept up with. Still, I thought it would be fitting to present you with something—something to make you a little more comfortable while you are here."

He reached down and retrieved a bundle of brown cloth that had been sitting beside the door. Unrolling it, he pulled out a long, ivory-colored cloak trimmed all around in rabbit's fur. It was the most beautiful thing that Addien had ever seen. She couldn't help but reach out and run her hand down the soft folds of cloth. In wonder, she looked up at Balchder, who was neither smiling nor frowning.

"Is this for me?" she asked, unable to fully understand what was happening.

"You need something to keep you warm," he answered.

He pushed the cloak into Addien's arms unceremoniously and turned to open the door. As he walked out, she finally overcame her shock enough to whisper a hoarse, "Thank you." Balchder continued on down the hall as if he had not heard, while Addien stood in the doorway, holding the fabulous cloak and watching him go.

Balchder did join the festivities that day in the Main Hall. The servants had helped the princess hang evergreen garlands all about the room, and savory meats and puddings had been cooking all morning. The soldiers were in a merry mood as they crowded into the Hall, although they quieted when they saw Balchder take a seat at the front of the room. Addien knew that Balchder did not often eat with his men, and she hoped that they would greet it as a special occasion and not as an interference. The seat on Balchder's right was given to Addien, and the Captain of the Guard sat on his left. Then the food was brought in, and the uneasiness lifted. Everyone ate and drank and sang silly songs as the hours passed and the day grew old.

As the sunlight through the upper windows began to fade, Balchder turned to Addien with a contented sigh.

"It's been a long day," he said.

"It's been a good day," she responded with a happy smile.

For a long moment, Balchder just looked at Addien, searching her face. He seemed almost sad. But then he smiled and pushed his chair back away from the table.

"A good day, but a tiring one," he said pleasantly. "And you need your rest. Come, I'll walk with you to your room."

He took Addien's hand and helped her to rise. Then they walked alone down the long halls and up the stairs to her room.

"Addien," Balchder began as they walked, "there is something I have to tell you. I had hoped there would be something I could give you today, but I don't have it yet to give."

"Another present?" she laughed, pulling her new cloak closer about her. "It can't possibly be nicer than this one. And I wasn't expecting anything at all."

"No, it's not a present," he answered seriously. "It's something that I promised you a long time ago."

Addien slowed her pace and looked at him.

"I sent some of my men to Briallen last week to—invite—your friends to Cleddyf," he said, looking at the floor ahead of him. "You'll be leaving soon, after the birth, and I thought it might make you happier to have some of your friends around you in this last month. Then I suppose you will want to leave with them as soon as possible."

In amazement, Addien stopped and turned to face Balchder.

"You mean Michael is coming here?" she whispered. "Now?"

"As soon as he is found," he answered. "I received a message today that the Commander has apparently left Briallen, but as soon as he is found he will be brought here."

Addien's gaze dropped to the floor as she tried to understand the strange feelings that overwhelmed her. She felt more sad than happy and more apprehensive than excited. And she felt very much afraid, though she didn't know why.

"You do still love him, don't you?" Balchder asked after a long pause.

"Yes, of course," she answered in a faint voice.

"Forgive my impertinence," Balchder continued, "but you don't look very happy."

Looking up at him, Addien tried to conceal her uncertain emotions.

"I'm just surprised," she said, managing a little smile. "It's been a long time since I've seen him—or any of my friends. I suppose I'm not sure what to expect."

Balchder nodded his head, then he turned and continued down the hall. When they reached Addien's room, he went inside with her and asked her to sit down in the chair by the window. He stood before her, looking very serious.

He took a deep breath and began, "I was hoping to wait until after you had seen—your friends—before talking to you about this. But, with time growing short, I'm going to say this now. When you agreed to give me a child, I promised you your freedom in return. I still intend to give you that, if that is what you want. But I want to give you another choice as well."

Balchder straightened his shoulders while Addien sat still and waited for him to continue.

"I've been thinking about the child," he said. "I know that you have, too. I can see it in your eyes every time the baby moves. You're his mother, Addien, and it's only natural that you should care about him."

The rush of emotions that had first hit Addien in the hall finally overwhelmed her. She looked down at her swollen stomach and let the silent tears begin to fall.

"But you have a choice," Balchder continued, softly now. "You can stay here with the child—if you want to. I'm asking you to stay, as my wife."

Through damp eyes, she looked up at him in wonder. She couldn't believe what she was hearing. But Balchder didn't wait for a response.

"I don't expect you to give me an answer now," he said. "You should think about it. But, for the sake of the child, it would be best if the ceremony was held before the birth."

"But that's only a few weeks away!" she cried.

Balchder nodded. Looking around him, he stepped back and sat down on the edge of the bed.

"This isn't a trick," he said, as if responding to some argument she hadn't made. "It was never part of the plan. In fact, Cythraul was quite adamant about having me raise the child alone. This has nothing to do with the kingdom or with anything else. I want you to stay because you can give this child what no one else can. And…I want you to be here with me."

Unable to respond, Addien closed her eyes and had to remind herself to breathe. She heard Balchder stand and walk to the door. There was a moment of silence before the door opened.

"Good-night, Addien," he said softly. "I hope you enjoyed your Christ'mas."

Then Addien heard the door close, and she knew that he was gone.

* * *

The next day Addien took refuge in Brother Peadar's chapel. She desperately needed to talk to someone, and there didn't seem to be anyone else who might understand her plight. Her first thought had been to tell Peadar everything, even about Trevilian, and the locket, and the crown. But a lifetime of protecting that secret made her cautious still, and she decided that she would not risk having their conversation overheard and reported back to Balchder. If he had the locket, she could not take the chance that he would find the crown and use it unwisely. So the story that she told Brother Peadar that day was an honest one, but not a complete one.

"So Lord Balchder was responsible for the death of your father?" Peadar asked, trying to understand the incredible sequence of events that Addien related to him.

"And the queen and everyone in the house," she responded.

"But you escaped from harm?"

"Yes," she said. "But I can't tell you how. Anyway, I was adopted by a shepherd named Evin and his wife, Anna, and I lived in Trevelgue in hiding—until last spring."

Addien told him how she had returned to Briallen after meeting Colin in Trevelgue, and how she had met Michael and fallen in love with him, and how she was recognized in the marketplace as the missing princess. Peadar continued to listen in silence as she told him about her flight from Briallen with Michael and their short stay at the valley fort. But Cythraul and his men were right behind them, and Michael and the others were captured, leaving her alone in the wilderness.

"So I decided to give myself up to Balchder in exchange for the men he had captured," Addien said.

"And that is how you came to be here?" he asked.

"Yes," she answered, setting one hand on her stomach. "I didn't know what he had planned. I thought he was looking for my father's crown. I didn't know that I would be helping him by coming here."

Fighting back a wave of sobs, Addien paused and tried to find the words to finish her story.

"Balchder promised me my freedom if I would agree to give him a child," she continued through her tears. "He told me that there would be another war with the Saxons and that he would not use the army to defend the kingdom unless the people accepted him as their king. With a son who is Brenin's grandson, and his only rightful heir, Balchder will finally be able to claim the kingdom."

Peadar looked at her through tender eyes.

"But you told me that no one could claim the kingdom without your father's crown," he said. "Isn't that what Lord Balchder had been looking for all those years?"

"But he couldn't find it," she answered. "He believes that it has been destroyed. So he decided to use me instead."

For a long while, they sat without speaking. Although Addien wiped the dampness from her face again and again, she could not stop the flow of tears. At length, Peadar moved closer to her and placed his hand on hers.

"Lady Addien," he began, "or, should I say, Your Highness? What is it that brings you to me today? Why are you telling me this now?"

With eyes lowered, she answered, "Balchder has asked me to marry him. He has given me a choice between staying here to raise the child or leaving with Michael."

"Do you still love Michael?" Peadar asked. "Do you want to be with him?"

Sobbing softly, Addien nodded her head yes.

"Do you think he still loves you?" he asked, hitting upon the true cause of her pain.

Addien dropped her face into her hands and sat there until she could control her voice again. Then she lifted her head and stared at the distant wall.

"If he doesn't, it will make my decision much easier," she whispered.

Standing, Addien began to pace the small area of open floor at the front of the chapel.

"I don't want to see him," she said, watching her feet as she tread back and forth across the floor. "I'm not ready. He may hate me for what I've done. He'll say I'm a traitor, and he'll never want to see me again."

"What if he doesn't?" Peadar asked softly. "What if he still loves you?"

Addien stopped pacing and stood still, just looking at the floor. Her breathing quickened, but she was no longer crying. At last she realized what she feared the most.

"Then I will have to choose," she said.

The next day, Addien rose early again and made her way to the chapel. For most of the morning she sat quietly, thinking about her short time with Michael and praying for guidance. Peadar came and went, attending to his duties, and leaving her to her thoughts. It was there that Balchder found her, late in the morning. He was accompanied by a soldier who looked as if he had just come in from a long ride. His muddy boots scraped across the stone floor, and his red cloak was still damp from lying on wet ground.

"I thought I might find you here," Balchder began in a subdued voice. "My men have returned from Briallen, although only partially successful. They have brought with them three of your friends, but not Commander Michael. They are being taken to my dining room. I thought you might like to join them there for the midday meal."

For a moment, Addien sat without answering or even looking up. Then she turned to face the two men.

"May I ask you a question?" she said, looking first at Balchder and then at the soldier. "How where they 'brought' here?"

Balchder looked at the soldier to let him answer.

"We found the men at the Christ'mas feast and told them that the princess wished to see them," the man responded formally. "They agreed to come with us peacefully."

"And the Commander of the Resistance?" Balchder asked. "Is there no news of him yet?"

"According to the local division, he hasn't been seen in Briallen for over a month," the soldier answered. "If any of his men know where he is, they aren't saying. But if anyone is communicating with him, we should know soon."

"What do you mean?" Addien asked.

The man looked hesitantly at Balchder, as if he was not certain whether he should answer. Balchder nodded slightly, so he continued.

"We left word around the city that the men were being taken as hostages. We told the townsfolk that we would hold the men until the Commander of the Resistance surrendered."

Addien's eyes flashed wider, but she saw that Balchder was smiling and nodding.

"A creative ploy," he said. "Let us hope that the Commander receives the message before his men decide to go home. Even then, he may not come...."

"He'll come," Addien interrupted. "If he is able, he will come."

Suddenly, she knew in her heart that he would come, and she would have to face him. It couldn't be avoided. She pictured him in her mind, standing before her with his radiant smile and his golden hair. She imagined his touch on her arm, like the day they met—and she remembered the vision she had seen of him on the night she cut her wrist. She remembered the soft voice of the vision telling her, "*You will know what to do when the time comes.*" And in that moment, Addien finally knew what she had to do.

"I'm not very hungry right now," she told Balchder. "I'll let the men finish their meal and then I'll join them."

Balchder nodded and turned to leave.

"I'll be in the yard with my men if you need me," he said as he walked out the door.

How long she sat there after that, Addien didn't know. Time seemed to have stopped for her. But at some point she did get up and leave the chapel in search of Balchder. Although he had invited her to join her friends, it seemed presumptuous for her to go to his private rooms alone. So she went out into the castle yard to tell Balchder that she was ready.

"You may want to wait a little while longer," Balchder told her. "We've just received a signal from an outlying post that a single rider is approaching the castle. He's coming fast, and should be here in less than an hour."

"Is it Michael?" Addien asked.

"Assuming that he got the message, I would say that it's a fair guess that it's him," he answered.

Balchder reached over and put his hand under her chin.

"You haven't eaten, have you?" he asked. "I'll have something sent to your room. You can rest until the Commander arrives."

Addien did as she was told and returned to her room. She even managed to eat her meal, although she tasted none of it. She sat quietly, listening to the crashing of the waves on the rocks below her window, until a servant came to tell her that Commander Michael had arrived.

Following the servant, Addien stepped into the Main Hall and paused under the window where she had first entered the castle. Michael stood in the center of the room with his back to her, waiting for Balchder who was talking to a guard on the far side of the room. It had been eight months since Addien had seen him in that exact spot, but so much had changed since then. Unable to move or speak, she stood in the doorway and watched as Balchder approached him.

"Commander," Balchder addressed him pleasantly, "we meet again."

"Where are my men?" Michael asked.

Balchder smiled at his directness and waved toward another door.

"Safely waiting for you in another room," he answered.

"You said that you would release them if I gave myself up to you," Michael said.

"I am more than willing to release them," Balchder replied. "But, you see, they are not my prisoners. They came here willingly. My men made up the hostage story in hopes of bringing you here." He paused before asking, "Now, don't you want to know what I want with you?"

"You want to kill me?" Michael answered.

"No," Balchder laughed. "You are more valuable alive than dead. You have proven yourself to be a man of integrity, someone the people will listen to and trust. I am still hopeful that one day you and I will find ourselves on the same side."

"You made that offer to me before," Michael said.

"And you soundly refused it," Balchder recalled. "But sometimes people change their minds—when the circumstances change."

"What are you up to, Balchder?" Michael asked in a tight voice.

Balchder smiled. Glancing over Michael's shoulder, his eyes met Addien's.

"Let's just say," he responded, looking at Michael again, "that the kingdom will soon be coming to me."

With a sound like a low growl, Michael sprang forward. His arms flew up toward Balchder's neck, and he might have made contact had not three soldiers fallen on him from behind. The four men hit the floor in a tangle of arms and legs. In the same moment, Addien finally found her voice.

"Michael, no!" she screamed.

The struggle on the floor ended in a heart-beat. Michael twisted away from the soldiers, spinning around to look for Addien. Their eyes locked, and she saw the shock that covered his face.

"Addien," he whispered.

The expression on his face changed swiftly from shock to something like relief. Then it changed again as his eyes dropped to the great swelling beneath her dress. His skin burned with a red heat, and his eyes, when he looked up at hers again, flashed like lightning. Behind him, Balchder stood with an unreadable face.

"Perhaps I shall never be king of Dumnonia," he said, looking at the princess. "But my son shall."

Half on his feet, Michael turned and lunged at Balchder again, almost dragging the soldiers along with him. Balchder stepped easily out of his reach as the three men wrestled Michael back down to the floor. Addien ran to Balchder and grabbed his arm.

"My lord, please!" she pleaded. "Promise me that he will not be harmed."

Balchder motioned to his men. Holding tight to their prisoner, they pulled him to his feet. Michael's eyes darted from Balchder to Addien and back again.

"What about the princess?" he asked, still panting from the fight. "What happens to her when you have what you want?"

Balchder looked at Addien and placed his hand on top of hers where she still held his arm.

"I have already promised to release her," he answered. "She may leave here with you, if she chooses, as soon after the birth as she is fit to travel. Or I have given her another choice. She can tell you about that if she wishes."

He released Addien's hand and backed away.

Looking again at Michael he said, "Now, I am certain that you would like to see your men. Addien will go with you. You should all have a great deal to say to each other. I have arranged for you to speak privately in my dining room."

He turned then and walked away, leaving Addien alone in the room with Michael and a half-dozen soldiers. Two of the soldiers turned Michael roughly and led him out of the Main Hall and toward Balchder's rooms. Silently, Addien followed, praying that she might find the right words when she was left alone with the men who had once been her friends.

Chapter Twenty One

By the time the soldiers reached the door to Balchder's chambers, Addien was several yards behind them. They opened the door and pushed Michael into the room. Inside, Addien could hear startled voices—Colin, perhaps Tomas, and someone else. Michael was asking them if they were all right and assuring them that he, himself, was unharmed. Addien stood out of sight in the hall listening to them, reluctant to intrude. The two soldiers watched her, standing out of the doorway so she could pass through. One even cleared his throat and gestured as if he was going to close the door. Short of making a scene, Addien decided that her only option was to go in.

As soon as she stepped into the room the door closed behind her. The men inside were gathered beside the long, wooden table where Addien had so often sat with Balchder for the evening meal. A few of the chairs around the table were pulled out, where the men must have been sitting while they waited. No one else was there.

The four men turned at the sound of the closing door. Seeing Addien, they stood still, as if suddenly frozen in their places. Addien also stood frozen in her place, glancing slowly from one face to another—Colin, Michael, Tomas, and Niall. Each returned her look, although Michael quickly looked away. Colin recovered first from the spell and crossed the room to Addien's side.

"Gennie," he said with a smile.

He gave her a careful hug and then took her hand in his.

"The soldiers told us," he said, looking down at her huge stomach. "We didn't want to believe them at first. But we decided we had to come and see for ourselves."

"I'm so glad you came," Addien said, with a cautious smile. "I've missed you so much. But I want you all to know that you are not prisoners here. You can go whenever you want. I'm not even sure why Balchder brought you here."

"Well," Tomas said gruffly, "we can see for ourselves why he's kept you here."

Unable to look at any of them, Addien dropped her gaze to her bulging stomach and tried to control her breathing. Beside her, Colin inched closer.

"How much longer?" he asked in a low voice.

Addien looked up to see him looking down at her stomach.

"Four weeks," she answered. "It could be sooner."

"You should sit down," Michael said, pulling out a chair for her.

His voice was low and difficult to hear, and still he did not look at her. Addien walked to the chair and sat down. Beside her, Michael leaned against the table, his jaw clenched and his face down. Tomas sat beside the table, further down. Niall and Colin still stood, glancing around the room. No one spoke. After several tense moments, Addien edged to the front of her chair again, preparing to rise.

"I should go," she said, feeling the tightness in her voice. "This is too difficult."

As she began to stand, Michael suddenly pulled himself away from the table.

"No!" he said. "Don't go."

He placed his hand on her shoulder, then pulled it away slowly. Although the contact between them lasted only a moment, that gentle touch sent an unexpected shock through Addien's whole body. When she was able to breathe again, she looked up at him, as one solitary tear found its way down her cheek. Unable to take her eyes off of him, she finally found the words she wanted to say.

"I've thought about you so many times," she said, "wondering what you were doing, whether you were safe, whether you knew…what had happened."

She closed her eyes and sank back into the chair.

"I never dreamt that something like this would happen," she continued. "I only gave myself up so that you could on and finish the mission. I tried to send you a message to tell you everything, but Dyn was attacked and couldn't reach you…."

"Dyn did reach us," Colin said.

Addien gasped as she glanced up at him, but it was Michael who explained.

"The next morning," he said, looking at Addien with a puzzled expression. "We were camped not far from the castle, trying to figure out a way back in. When we found the bird, it was badly injured. Even Aderyn couldn't make any sense out of what it was saying."

"He didn't tell you any of my message?" Addien asked, hopeful that at least some of her secret might have been revealed.

"No," Michael answered.

It was as she had always feared. She had risked everything that night coming to the castle so that her father's crown might find its way into Michael's capable hands. She had trusted him enough to give him her greatest treasure and share with him her greatest secret—and he didn't know. So much had happened since then that she wasn't certain herself where the crown was or whether it had, in fact, been destroyed. Although she longed to explain everything to her friends and beg their forgiveness, once again she found herself wondering how much Balchder really knew, and how much she could risk him finding out about.

"Poor Dyn," Addien said softly, as a second tear dropped down into her lap. With a deep sigh, she went on, "That first night, I wondered if you would return and try to rescue me. Balchder expected you to, and he ordered his men to kill you."

"Then why did they take us back to Briallen unharmed?" Tomas asked sharply.

"It was part of the bargain," Addien answered, looking down. "Your safety, the safety of the kingdom, and my own freedom—in exchange for a child."

There was a long silence in the room before Michael finally asked the question that hung ominously in the air.

"You gave yourself to him—willingly—because of a bargain?" he asked in a strangled tone.

Addien nodded her head, still looking down.

Suddenly, Colin threw his arms up in dismay.

"I knew we should have come back!" he exclaimed. "We never should have left here without her."

"No," she told him. "You couldn't have helped me. Balchder knew that I would come to him. His wizard foretold it. He also knew that I would conceive a male child the very next day. If you had tried to come back, you would have all been killed. There was nothing you could have done."

Michael turned away abruptly, walking across the room. Tomas stirred also, pulling himself forward in his chair with a grunt.

"What about you?" he asked, placing his arms on his knees as he leaned toward her. "Even if you felt trapped into making this child, you can't tell us that you couldn't find some way to stop it afterward?"

Michael turned on Tomas, angrily gesturing to him to be quiet. But it was too late. Addien knew exactly what he meant. All of the months of loneliness and self-doubt she had suffered erupted within her. Her face burned, and her eyes felt like darts of fire, ready to strike.

"What are you suggesting, Tomas?" Niall asked. "That she should have found some way to terminate her own condition?"

"It's possible," Tomas retorted angrily.

"I tried!" Addien cried, barely able to find her voice.

She knew that everyone was looking at her, but she kept her eyes, still hot with anger and pain, on Tomas. She had to look at him—for if she turned she might see Michael's face, and then she knew she couldn't go on.

Reaching down to the wrist of her left arm, Addien pulled back the sleeve of her gown, revealing the ragged scar that was all that remained of the deep wound she had inflicted.

Holding it out to them, she said, "I thought that by killing myself I could defeat Balchder's plan to take my father's kingdom with my own child."

Colin knelt beside her and took her outstretched arm in his hands. He examined it gently and then released it.

"What happened?" he asked softly.

Addien laid her hand on her stomach, feeling the movement within her.

"I couldn't do it," she answered. "I stopped the bleeding and saved my own life." Then she continued, directly to Tomas again, "No matter what evil Balchder has done or plans to do, and no matter what I have done, the penalty of death is too great for an innocent child to pay before he has even been born."

Tomas took a deep breath and opened his mouth again to speak. Michael crossed to him and spoke in a low voice. After a moment, Tomas relaxed into his chair and Michael stepped back away from him. Addien relaxed as well, carefully pulling her sleeve back down over her wrist. As she did, she thought again about the locket that had once hung there, and she wondered if she would ever see it again.

For quite some time, no one spoke. No one moved. The men of Briallen all had a great deal to think about. Although Addien knew there was something more she needed to share, she didn't want to intrude on their thoughts too soon. She would have chosen to remain silent indefinitely, had not her own body betrayed her.

"Ahh!" she gasped suddenly, reaching for her stomach as a strong contraction pushed the breath out of her.

Michael turned and crossed the few steps between them before the contraction had even ended.

"Are you all right?" he asked, reaching for her right hand where it gripped the arm of the chair.

As the pain subsided, she nodded her head.

"It's all right," she said, when she could find her breath, "the pains are coming more often now and are getting stronger."

Colin stood and scrambled for the door.

"Should we call for help?" he asked.

"No, it's all right," Addien repeated lamely. "The midwife tells me I still have three or four weeks. The pains are nothing to worry about now."

Michael kneeled beside her and placed her hand in his. His touch caused less of a shock this time, but it was no less warming. Addien wrapped her own hand around his and grasped it tightly.

"At least there is this," he said, "you can leave with us as soon as the child is born."

Slowly, reluctantly, Addien released her grip on Michael's hand and pulled her hand away. It was the moment she had been dreading the most. She had made her decision, though, and it only remained for her to state it out loud.

"I'm not leaving," she said firmly.

"What?" Michael gasped. "But Balchder said...."

"Balchder said I could leave if I choose," she interrupted him. "Or...or, I may stay."

"Stay here? At Cleddyf Castle?" Michael stiffened, and his voice turned cold. "You aren't seriously thinking about staying here, are you?"

Addien could hear Colin and Niall as well, pleading with her to listen, but she shook them all off.

"I can't leave my baby," she said firmly, staring at the floor.

Michael took a deep breath and leaned closer to her. Addien kept her hands clenched together, but he laid his hand firmly on top of them.

"Addien," he said gently, "you can't believe that Balchder will ever let you be a mother to this child, someone who could have an influence on it. At best, you would be nothing more than a servant in his castle, until he decides he has no further use for you. Then what do you think will happen?"

She knew that Michael could be right. If she stayed, Balchder would have complete control over her and could take her life at any time. But she had come to trust him, and she felt certain then that he would never harm her.

"You're wrong," she said. "Balchder has asked me to stay here—as his wife."

After a stunned pause, Michael stood and walked away from the table again. Niall turned away, and Colin dropped to the floor, burying his face in his hands. Addien looked at each of them and then back at the floor again. Finally, she lifted herself out of her chair and turned toward the door. Halfway there, she stopped and turned back.

Speaking to no one in particular, she asked, "If I went back with you to Briallen, do you think I could have any 'influence' or usefulness there? I would never be taken back into your confidence, because you would always wonder where my true loyalty lay—with your cause, or with my son."

Michael turned toward her then. Pain etched his face, and his eyes were clouded over with sorrow. He said nothing, but it wasn't necessary. She knew he understood.

Addien turned again to leave, but it seemed that Tomas was not finished with her yet.

"There is one way that you can help us," he said tersely, "if that is really what you want to do."

Addien turned back and looked at him, waiting for him to explain. He rose from his chair and stepped toward her.

"You can tell us how to find King Brenin's crown," he said.

All eyes turned to Addien, and she swallowed hard. Straightening her shoulders, she looked back at them, remembering the unseen ears that she suspected were near.

"I only wish I could," she said simply, and she left.

* * *

Out in the hallway, Addien had no idea where she was going. She let her feet take her where they would. Without intending to, she retraced her steps from the dining room back to the Main Hall, where supper preparations were being made. The large room always seemed so much smaller when the long tables and benches were set out. Servants walked in and out, bringing pitchers and goblets and spoons. As soon as the men were all seated, the bread bowls would be brought in, bearing that night's concoction of meat and vegetables. But it would be a simple meal, with only the raucous voices of the soldiers to fill the room. There would be no singing or merriment as there had been only a few days before when she had sat beside Balchder at the head table, surrounded by evergreen garlands and holiday puddings.

Slowly, Addien walked between the tables and the curious servants until she reached the head table. She reached for one of the carved wooden chairs and ran her hand over the back of it. She wondered what it would be like sitting there night after night as the Lady of the castle—sitting beside Balchder, who would be her husband—having their son sitting on his other side. Drawing her hand back, she turned to leave. But when she looked up, she was surprised to find Balchder only a few yards away, watching her.

"My lord," she said with a quick breath.

"Addien," he answered politely.

Pulling herself up to her full height, Addien regarded him without emotion.

"I have decided to accept your offer—of marriage," she said.

Balchder held her gaze without any change in his expression or demeanor.

"I'll make the arrangements at once," he answered at length.

Addien nodded and dropped her gaze. Then she fled from the Hall and made her way to the calm and quiet of her own room.

* * *

That night Addien declined to join Balchder and the others for supper. She simply couldn't bear being in the same room with the four brave resistance fighters and their sworn enemy, knowing that it was her actions, good or bad, that had brought them together. She assumed that the evening would be cordial—if Tomas was able to hold his tongue—but such quiet civility seemed worse than a desperate battle. It was like admitting that there was no longer any reason to fight. So she ate alone and wished the next few weeks would pass quickly.

The next morning, she found Michael and his friends in the castle yard. It had rained during the night, but the sun was shining through the broken clouds. The light reflected off of the smooth stones in the yard, making the ground seem even brighter than the sky. The men were walking several horses, and Addien wondered if they had decided to return to Briallen. As she approached, Michael waved and came over to her.

"You're leaving then?" Addien asked, trying to keep her voice calm and unemotional.

"No, not yet," he answered. "Tomas and Niall want to get back. But, if it's all right with you, Colin and I will be staying for awhile."

"Of course," she answered, almost choking on the tension in her voice. "Whatever you want to do."

"Colin is going to ride with them a short distance," Michael told her. "He wants to give his horse some exercise, and…it will let him talk a little to Tomas and Niall before they go on."

Michael's voice had dropped very low on his last words, so that Addien had to strain to hear him. They had been walking while they talked and had almost reached the others. Colin looked up and smiled, then he quickly came around the horses to join them. Michael mumbled something and excused himself, leaving Colin and Addien to walk the final distance alone.

Addien walked carefully through the mud beside Colin and held his arm.

"Tell me," she said, "whatever happened to that farm girl you were so fond of? Do you still see her sometimes?"

Colin smiled, looking at his boots.

"Sometimes," he answered shyly.

"And?" Addien asked. "Have you told her how you feel?"

Colin shrugged.

"It wouldn't be fair," he answered. "She'll be wanting to get married soon, have a home of her own, and a family. I can't give her those things."

"Colin, don't say that," she told him, grasping his arm tighter. "You have your whole life ahead of you. You should live it to the fullest. If you can find someone to share it with, someone who will bring you some happiness, you shouldn't let that slip away. We have a new life to live every day, but it's not everyday that we have a chance to make our lives better. Don't miss this chance, Colin, please."

Colin smiled and gave her a long hug. She smiled back at him and watched as he mounted his horse.

"I've missed you, Gennie," he said.

"I've missed you, too," she answered. "Hurry back so we can talk some more."

A few moments later, Colin, Tomas, and Niall were heading through the gate and up the winding path to the top of the cliff. As she waved good-bye, Addien turned to see Michael watching her, his face once again devoid of emotion.

"Is there someplace we can talk—privately?" he asked.

"I know of a quiet spot in a corner of the yard," she answered. "If you don't mind the dampness."

As she spoke, Addien began to walk across the muddy courtyard toward a secluded area next to the outer wall which might once have been a garden. A few old fruit trees stood there, waiting for the warmth of spring to bring new life to their branches. The other bushes and plants in the garden all seemed to have died long before, although no one had bothered to remove them.

"This is as private a place as I can offer," Addien said. "I have found inside the castle walls that I am never really alone. I can't even guarantee it here."

She looked at Michael and hoped that he understood her meaning.

"So I shouldn't say what I really think about Balchder, should I?" Michael asked.

"No, you shouldn't," she answered.

Addien found a stone bench beneath one of the barren trees and sat down, pulling her cloak about her. Michael walked past her, looking up at the high castle wall.

"Balchder told us last night about the Saxons," he began in his usual direct manner. "Cythraul predicted an invasion in less than two years, and Balchder's spies have confirmed the possibility. He told us that he intends to bring all of his troops here in the spring to start training. He mentioned something about the men being 'bored and undisciplined'—your words, I believe."

Addien nodded and smiled slightly, feeling rather pleased. Balchder had listened to what she said about his soldiers, and he had taken it seriously. Michael, however, was not smiling.

"Is that why you did this?" he asked. "So Balchder would defend the kingdom against the Saxons?"

She nodded again and dropped her gaze to the ground.

"He told me about Cythraul's prophecy," she said. "And he said that he would only defend his own lands, unless he was made king."

With a short, hard laugh, Michael stepped further away from her. "And this is the man you're going to marry?" he asked.

Addien shot an angry glance at him but said nothing. The look on Michael's face softened.

"I'm sorry," he said. "I shouldn't have said that."

He came to her and sat down on the bench.

In a very low voice, so as not to be overheard, he asked, "And the crown?"

She had to smile again. Michael wasn't quite as blunt as Tomas had been, but somehow she knew he would end up asking her the same thing. It was strange that it was Balchder who had never asked her about the crown.

She stopped smiling and answered, "He never even asked for it. All he wanted was this."

Addien placed her hand on her stomach and started to rise, assuming the conversation was over. But Michael took her arm and stopped her.

"Addien," he whispered, "you don't have to do this. Let Balchder have the child. Let him have the crown. You've done enough. You should leave while you can."

"And go where?" she asked, looking away.

"With me," he answered simply. "Addien, I'm asking you to come with me."

"So you can protect me and take care of me?" she asked in a tight voice.

"So I can be with you," he answered. "I told you once that I would always want to be with you."

Addien looked at Michael then. She could see in his eyes that he was sincere. It was the same look he had given her the day they rode to Torbryon's ranch, the day he held her and kissed her. The day there was nothing between the two of them—but lies.

"That's when I was Gennes," Addien said, choking on the words, "not Addien. As Addien, you were willing to see me married off to some nobleman who could claim the crown and challenge Balchder. As

Addien, I have nothing more to offer than a title and a womb. I see now that I was destined to be nothing more than a pawn in this game, on one side or the other."

"If this child is a boy, the game is over," Michael replied. "Balchder wins." Taking her hand, he pleaded with her, "Leave with me. We can go anywhere and do anything you want to do."

"And you will stay with me, lead a quiet life, and just watch things happening around you?" she asked. "You couldn't do it. And neither can I. I may just be a pawn in the game, but I'm right in the middle of the board. I can't walk away. If my child is going to be the next king of Dumnonia, I have to stay and do what I can to prepare him. Tell me you wouldn't do the same thing if you could."

Addien's eyes held Michael while she waited for him to answer. Still holding her hand, he drew his shoulders back, increasing the distance between them. The silence lengthened. No sound of wind or sea-bird found its way over the castle wall, and the soldiers and stables were too far away to be heard in the little alcove of the yard. For a long time, Michael said nothing. At last, he released Addien's hand and stood wearily.

Looking away from her, he said, "Balchder told us last night that you had agreed to his marriage proposal. I suppose the ceremony will be very soon."

"Yes," Addien whispered. "I suppose so."

"It's cold out here," Michael said, quickly changing the subject. "We should go inside."

"Yes, I suppose so," she whispered again, as she rose slowly and walked with him back inside the castle.

Chapter Twenty Two

For the rest of the morning, Michael and Addien walked and talked together. They spoke no more of Addien's decision to marry Balchder or about their own past together and the many decisions that had brought them to that point. Michael told Addien about her friends in Briallen and what they had been doing since she left. Morgan was well, although her sight was growing weaker. Aderyn had gone into hiding for awhile to grieve for his friend Dyn, but he had returned to the fort in the valley before winter set in. Michael had also been to visit Anna and Evin in Trevelgue, although it meant sneaking out of Briallen against Balchder's orders. They were doing well, although they had been saddened by Michael's news of Addien's capture by Lord Balchder. It seemed that the whole kingdom had been in a state of shock since the princess' unexpected discovery in Briallen, followed by her sudden, unexplained disappearance. Except for their closest allies, Michael and the others had not told anyone what had really happened to her, and apparently neither had Balchder.

Addien told Michael about Cythraul and his strange beliefs. Although her talks with Brother Peadar had reassured her that it was impossible for Cythraul's spirit to inhabit her child, Addien was still bothered by a lingering doubt. It wasn't something that she could discuss with Balchder, but with Michael she found herself disclosing her secret fear.

"It's not just his spirit," she said, trying to explain. "He was so certain that he had everything planned. I can't believe that he just expected to die and come back anyplace he wanted. He was too careful for that. There must have been more to the plan than that."

"You said he had followers," Michael said, "the men who took his body and burned it. Do you think he left them with instructions to do something to the child?"

"Perhaps," Addien said. "I don't know. It all seems so preposterous. I just don't think that we've heard the last of Cythraul."

Colin returned to the castle just before the midday meal. As Balchder had not given any other instructions, Addien invited Michael and Colin to dine with her in her room. The day passed quietly and quickly, as they talked and laughed together. For Addien, it was almost like being back in Briallen again, before her identity had been discovered, before Michael had pushed her away, before Balchder had taken her and asked her to be his bride.

That evening at dinner, Balchder announced that the wedding date had been set.

"I have sent riders to the Western Territory to invite my neighbors to the ceremony," he said. "It will take no more than four days for them to arrive. We will plan on five days from now, if that is acceptable?"

The tone of his voice sounded more like he was planning a military assault than a wedding, but Addien nodded politely. Balchder turned then to Michael and Colin.

"Of course, you are invited to stay for the ceremony," he said. "I'm certain that Addien will want you to be there."

Addien looked at her friends and smiled slightly. In her heart, though, she wasn't at all certain that she wanted them to stay. The easy friendship that they had shared that day would grow tenser each day as the event approached. Her decision to marry Balchder was going to be hard enough on her. It would only be harder if she had to watch her two dearest friends hurt by it as well.

"We thank you for the invitation," Michael said politely. "And we accept, although we needn't tax your generosity. I'm certain that we can find lodging in the village."

Michael's first words caught Addien by surprise. His last words surprised her even more. Even Colin seemed a bit perplexed. But Balchder waved him off.

"Nonsense," he said. "You came this far to spend time with the princess. You should stay here, where you will have plenty of time to talk."

Michael nodded his agreement, and the conversation turned to other matters. But after dinner, Addien was very glad when Michael arranged to escort her to her room alone.

"Michael, I've been thinking," she said in a low voice as they walked down an empty hallway. "I don't think you should come to the wedding ceremony. I know Balchder won't mind if you leave before then."

"Why would I do that?" Michael asked softly.

Addien shrugged and looked away.

"To see the woman you once professed to love married to your greatest enemy...."

"You're the woman I still love," Michael interrupted. "And I want to be there, for you."

Addien looked at him and caught her breath. For a brief moment, he reached down and touched her hand. Then he faced forward again and continued walking.

"As for Balchder being my greatest enemy," he continued, "that's something that may have to change."

He slowed to a stop and leaned against the stone wall. Crossing his arms, he regarded Addien with a faint frown.

"Addien, do you remember what you said at the fort, about wishing that there was an obvious choice for who the next king should be?" he asked. "I think we both know that now there is. It's not a choice either of us would have made, but it's been made. If you're willing to stay here and raise this child, he has every chance of being a good king someday. And if it means having Balchder as king until the child is grown, at least we know that there are limits to what he'll do for power. He could have fought the other nobles for power. He could have killed you. He could have even stopped our resistance group, if he had really tried."

"I don't think he's afraid to fight," Addien mused. "He's never been accused of that."

"No, he hasn't," Michael agreed. "And if the Saxons do invade, we need to have all of our people fighting on the same side. Maybe it is better being in the middle of the board, as you said, instead of fighting from a distance an old battle we can't win."

"Then what are you planning to do?" she asked cautiously.

Michael took a deep breath and pulled away from the wall. Addien could tell that he was still struggling with his thoughts and probably didn't have a clear answer yet. At length, he shrugged and started walking again.

"Stay close," he said. "Stay close and do anything and everything I can to help you and support you."

Thinking to a day long past when Michael had first pledged his allegiance to her, Addien smiled.

"Because I'm the princess?" she asked coyly.

"Because you are the most courageous person that I have ever met," he answered seriously, "and I would do anything for you."

* * *

For the next few days, Michael, Colin and Addien spent much of their time together. Addien enjoyed being with them so much that she ignored Mag's warnings to take it easy, and she didn't even mind the sudden pains that wrapped around her waistline several times each day.

During her afternoon rest time, which Mag vigorously enforced, the two men would ride into the village at the bottom of the cliff or travel up the river valley away from the sea. Addien made them tell her everything about what they saw, as she had not been allowed to leave the castle grounds since she arrived eight months before. She envied them their freedom and wondered if she would ever again be able to wander freely or make her own decisions about where she wanted to go.

On the day of the wedding, Addien asked to be excused from their usual meetings. She spent most of the morning alone with Brother Peadar in the chapel and spent the afternoon preparing herself for the ceremony that would be held just after sunset. She decided to wear the green gown she had worn for Christ'mas. Mag said that the color brought out the brightness of her eyes and made her hair shine like fire. Addien combed out her hair and braided a small strand on either side of her forehead, circling them around her head like a crown. It wasn't the look she would have chosen, as she had always preferred her hair braided. But Balchder had never broken his promise to her to leave off his crown, and she couldn't break her promise to him on that night of all nights.

Mag stood behind her and gave her shoulders a squeeze.

"You look lovely," she said.

Looking down at her stomach, Addien realized that her hair was not the only thing that was depressing her.

"It's not exactly how I planned to look on my wedding day," she sighed. "I'm fat. I walk funny. And I don't even have any flowers to wear in my hair."

Mag nodded, knowingly.

"Ah, but I have something for you," she cackled in pleasure.

From a small box she had hidden beneath the bed she took out what at first appeared to be a circlet of perfect white blossoms. But as she lifted it up, Addien realized that the crown was solid, not flimsy like flowers would be. With great pride, Mag placed it in Addien's hands. It was a wedding crown made of seashells, fastened together to resemble tiny flowers!

"Mag," Adien whispered in awe, "it's beautiful!"

"I thought you would like it," she beamed. "There's a man in the village what makes them. Girls who marry in winter ought to have the same beauties as girls who marry in the spring, he says."

"Thank you, Mag," Addien said. "Will you help me put it on?"

Mag helped her arrange the crown and finish dressing. At last Addien was ready. She looked down at her wedding gown and sighed again. She had never expected to have a joyful, carefree wedding like the ones she had witnessed in Trevelgue or in Briallen. Only once in her life did she let herself imagine she might be able to marry for love, instead of political necessity. But she had hoped that the wedding experience would at least be a pleasant one. Yet there she was, in a cold, dark castle, on a cloudy day in January, preparing herself for a simple ceremony in a tiny chapel with only a few people even present. She sighed, bit her lip, and walked to the door.

In the hallway outside her bedroom, Addien was surprised to find that the torches had not been lit. Instead, there was a soldier standing beside the door, holding a tall candle. A few yards down the hall was another soldier, holding another candle, and another beyond him. The men stood at attention as she walked past, eyes straight forward. The candlelight continued down the stairs, through the next hall, and all the way to the door of the chapel. Balchder himself was waiting there. He smiled warmly when he saw his bride. Then he took her hand and led her inside.

The chapel, like the hallways, was lit only by candlelight. There were three men there that Addien didn't know, and Peadar, Michael, and Colin. The men all bowed when she entered, three of the men wearing bright plaids and jeweled rings, Peadar in his brown robes, and Michael, as she had never seen him before, wearing a pure white tunic with a brown belt and brown breeches. Raising his head, he looked at Addien and gave her one of his radiant smiles. It reminded her of the first time that he had smiled at her, in the bushes in Briallen, and it made her heart flutter.

"Princess Addien," Balchder was saying, "permit me to introduce you to Lord Daimhin and his son Conall and Lord Gorman, both of the Western Territory."

Addien greeted each politely and then turned with Balchder to greet Michael and Colin.

"Colin, of course, you know, and Commander Michael," Balchder continued, pleasantly. "I want you to know that I offered him a position of rank in my army, but he refused. He tells me that he still has work to do in Briallen."

"Not stirring up a rebellion against our future king, I hope," Daimhin suggested gruffly. "Isn't that what you are known for?"

"I have decided to step down as the Commander of the Resistance," Michael answered evenly. "Although I can speak only for myself, I will fight no longer against Cleddyf Castle. The one I have sworn my loyalty to is here."

He looked at Addien again and bowed low. Feeling the eyes of the nobles upon her, she tilted her chin upward and walked with Balchder quietly to the altar and knelt with him there.

In lovely Latin phrases, Brother Peadar called down the blessings of Heaven upon Lord Balchder and Princess Addien and bound them together as husband and wife. As the ceremony proceeded, Addien became aware of a great tension in her shoulders and back. She was holding Balchder's hand so tight, she thought he might try to pull it free. Breathing deeply, she loosened her grip and tried to relax a little. But the tension spread to her legs and sides, making her heavy stomach feel like stone. She could no longer hear Peadar's words. It took all of her concentration to keep breathing and remain still.

When the ceremony concluded, Balchder rose slowly from his knees and helped Addien to her feet. For a moment, his eyes searched her face.

Suddenly donning a smile, he turned to his guests. The usual applause and well-wishing from the audience were omitted.

"I would like to thank you all for your presence this evening," Balchder told the men. "If you would be so kind as to wait for me in my chambers, I will be with you shortly. I believe that Princess Addien is tired and would like to retire."

Without another word, he led his bride through the room and out into the hall. When the door had closed behind them, he leaned over to speak in a low voice.

"I hope you don't mind," he said. "You looked very tired, and I assumed that you would want to go to your room and rest."

Addien only nodded.

"I'll walk you there," he said.

Still holding Addien's hand, he turned and walked with her slowly to her room. Neither spoke. Addien's body was shivering, and she found it difficult to breathe. It was almost as if something was squeezing her and pushing the air out of her lungs. She felt sick, and she wondered if she would be able to make it to her room without completely falling apart.

What's wrong with me? she thought to herself. *This is what I wanted. This is what I chose. So why have I suddenly become so unnerved? Why are my legs shaking and my heart racing?* Stealing a glance at Balchder, Addien wondered if he could feel her hand shaking and see the tension in her face.

When they arrived at the room, Balchder held the door open for his bride and waited for her to enter. For a long moment, he stood still with his back against the door, as if trying to find the right words to say. When at last he spoke, his voice was low and halting.

"I'll say good-night then," he said, bowing his head slightly.

Addien waited a moment to see if he might say something else. She didn't know what to expect. She didn't imagine that anything would change between the two of them before the baby came. It made sense for Addien to stay in her room and for Balchder to stay in his. But she hoped he might say something about what he intended to do in the future. They had, after all, just married. It would be very naïve of her to think that nothing would change.

Balchder cleared his throat and looked down, as if he had been waiting for Addien to say something. He started to turn then to go out the door. Realizing that she hadn't spoken a single word since the ceremony, Addien opened her mouth to say good-night, but the words never came out. They were strangled in her throat by another spasm that grasped her and forced the air out of her. The door closed slowly, and he was gone.

Addien wasn't alone. Mag had been waiting in the room, crouched down in the little corner where she usually slept. As soon as the door was closed, she popped up and came to Addien. Her old eyes surveyed the young woman carefully as she placed skillful hands on Addien's stomach. Mag dropped her head down until her ear touched the top of the bulge. Then she looked up at Addien with bright, expectant eyes.

"How close together are they?" she asked.

"What?" Addien responded, as her lungs relaxed and she found her voice again.

"The pains, child," she answered, still feeling Addien's stomach with her hands. "How far apart?"

Addien looked down in amazement, suddenly realizing what was happening. The tension she had felt in the chapel hadn't been from the ceremony—at least not entirely. She had been having contractions! And this time, they were for real. Mag's words confirmed it.

"Yes, indeed," she cackled, "this baby's coming tonight!"

"Now?" Addien gasped. "Do you mean right now?"

"No, child," the old woman answered. "These things take time. Lie down on the bed and let me see how far along you are. Chances are, you'll be at this all night."

Mag confirmed that the labor was in full progress, but she guessed that it would be several hours before Addien would be ready to push the baby into the world.

"You should get some rest now, while you can," she told her charge. "You'll need all your energy later when it's time to push."

Mag helped Addien change out of her fancy dress and into something more comfortable. The crown of seashells was placed safely back in its box. Then Addien settled down on the bed to try to rest.

When Mag left to send word to Balchder, Addien realized that he was probably still entertaining the wedding guests. She wondered if he would share the news with them. She hoped so. Although she had often hoped, for his sake, that Michael would be far away when the event happened, Addien suddenly wanted him as near as possible. She had to admit to herself that she was afraid—afraid of the pain, afraid of the thousand unknown things that could go wrong, and afraid of Cythraul, whose ghostly image seemed to fill her thoughts more and more as the pain increased. Even if Michael couldn't be with her, it comforted her to know that he would at least be thinking about her.

The hours passed slowly. When lying down became unbearable, Addien would walk around the room or stand in front of the windows and listen to the waves. And when the pain made standing too difficult, she would lie on her side on the bed and cry. Servants came and went from the room, bringing clean cloths and water. Balchder came, too. Most of the time he stood out of the way against a far wall, but sometimes he would come to Addien and hold her hand for a little while.

At last, Mag said that all was ready. She looked at Balchder expectantly until he came and sat beside his bride, taking her hand.

"Now, it's time to push," Mag said. "Be ready when I tell you."

Already exhausted from the stressful day and the long hours of pain and contractions, the pushing seemed to drain all of Addien's strength. The light in the room darkened, and she had difficulty focusing on any one thing. Addien could hear Mag telling her what to do, but it seemed that there were other voices as well, coming from somewhere in the room. Once again, fear gripped at her, and she cast about the room, looking for any sign of Cythraul's unwelcome spirit. At last, Addien's eyes rested on one of the torches, burning on the wall across the room. The light took on a familiar glow, and she seemed to hear a voice saying, "*You'll be all right now...You'll know what to do when the time comes.*" The vision that had saved her from her self-inflicted wound several months before filled her thoughts, and she clung to it as if she were drowning.

"Michael," she whispered. "Don't leave me, Michael."

"Push!" Mag ordered.

With all her strength, Addien bore down, raising her head and shoulders upward as she did. When she relaxed again, the darkness had lifted somewhat and the strange voices in the room were gone. She looked at Balchder, who still held her hand, and was surprised by the strange look on his face. He held her gaze for a moment and then turned and motioned to one of the servants.

"Yes, my lord," the woman said as she approached him.

"Our guest, Commander Michael," he said quietly, "find him at once and bring him here."

The woman bobbed and immediately left on her errand. But Addien had no time to even wonder at the reason for the command, as Mag was yelling at her to push again, and another great wave of pain was crashing through her body.

Again and again Addien pushed, each time swearing that she could never do it again. She had almost given up hope that the baby would ever be born, when Mag suddenly gave out a little cheer.

"I see him!" she cried. "Gently, now. Gently. One more push, and I'll have him."

Addien pushed—in relief, in triumph, in complete exhaustion. Then she could hear it, the lusty, high-pitched cry of a tiny newborn babe!

"Your son, my lord," Mag said, holding out the small, wrinkled form to his father.

Balchder went to her to take the child. Taking his place beside the bed, Michael suddenly appeared, smiling warmly.

"You did it," he said. "You really did it."

"It's not quite over yet, child," Mag said. "A few more pushes for the remainder, and then you can rest."

Those last few pushes seemed even more difficult to Addien than the dozens that had come before. Every inch of her body ached, and she felt too tired to move. But at last Mag had what she wanted, and Addien could rest. After taking a few sips of a drink that Mag offered, the new mother shut her eyes and listened to the commotion around her, as the baby was taken from Balchder to be cleaned and wrapped in warm blankets. Addien hadn't held him yet, or even touched him, but she didn't mind. She only wanted to rest her weary eyes for a moment, and then....

"What is it?" Michael asked in a low voice. "What's the matter?"

Forcing her eyes open again, Addien realized that Michael was talking to Mag. Her first instinct was to look for the baby, but Mag was examining her, not the baby, and looking rather serious.

"She's still bleeding," Mag answered, speaking quietly to Michael. "She has to keep contracting to cut off the flow of blood. But she's stopped."

Breathing in painfully, Addien looked at Michael. He looked back at her with a reassuring smile and took her hand. Then he looked back at Mag.

"Can't you do something?" he asked.

Although he still smiled, the look in his eyes was deadly serious. From across the room, Balchder must have noticed something of the concerned looks and whispered words, because he crossed the room frowning.

"What's going on here?" he asked. "Is anything wrong?"

"The bleeding hasn't stopped like it should," Mag explained.

"Is it dangerous?" Balchder asked, in his straight-forward manner.

Without answering, Mag looked at Addien and then back at Balchder again. The look on her face must have been answer enough, because Balchder's own face suddenly turned very grim.

"There must be something you can do," he said gruffly. "You can't just stand there and let her bleed to death! There must be some way to stop it."

Mag's eyes darted nervously from Balchder to Michael to Addien. Suddenly she reached for the cup Addien had sipped from earlier.

"The draught," she said in a shaky voice. "Master Cythraul said it would help her."

As she brought the cup down to Addien's lips, Michael grabbed her arm.

"No!" he shouted.

"It was Master Cythraul's orders," she shouted back, almost in hysteria.

"Don't you see," he said, turning to Balchder. "It's part of Cythraul's plan. Addien told me that she was afraid that Cythraul had arranged something else to ensure the return of his spirit. She thought it involved the baby, but it must be this."

Searching through her own, desperate thoughts, Addien could see Cythraul standing on the castle wall only moments before he jumped to the sea. That night his body had been devoured by flames, but was he really finished with them yet?

"The fire and the blood," she mumbled, fighting to stay awake. "A sacrifice of blood…my blood."

Barely a heartbeat passed before Balchder grabbed Mag by the shoulders and shook her, knocking the cup to the floor.

"Forget what Cythraul said," he commanded. "Whatever you have to do to save her, do it now!"

Mag glanced about fearfully for a brief moment. Then she turned to Michael with a determined look.

"Give me your hands," she ordered. "You'll have to push on the outside while I push on the inside. We'll have to do the work until her muscles take over again."

In a cloud of fear and pain Addien screamed, struggling to free herself from their hands. Balchder quickly came around to the head of the bed and held her arms down at her sides.

"Don't ease up!" Mag yelled at Michael, as Addien let out another cry of pain. "Push harder!…That's it.…That's it.…It's easing up now.… That's it.…"

CHAPTER TWENTY THREE

When Addien opened her eyes, the room was very still. The torches were extinguished, and a half-light glowed in the windows. She had no idea if it was morning or evening, or if more than one day had passed. Somewhere in the room, she could hear the sound of water dripping, as if it was being wrung out of a cloth into a bowl. She wanted to look around for the source of the sound, but her head wouldn't turn. So she just laid still and listened.

As her senses slowly recovered, she tried again to move her head. A feeling was growing inside her that something was missing, something very important. Slowly, she turned her face one direction and then the other. The only person she could see in the room was one of the servant girls, wringing out a washing cloth near the bed. Addien's first distinct thought was to wonder where Mag had gone. As her thoughts became clearer, she could remember Mag being beside the bed. Balchder had been there, too. And Michael. And something had been wrong. But what?

"My baby," she whispered.

Addien forced her head to turn again. She looked about the room, searching every corner for some sign, some clue.

"My baby," she said again. "Where is he?"

The girl on the floor looked up from her task.

"What is it, m'lady?" she asked shyly.

"I want to see my baby," Addien murmured, barely finding the strength to speak.

The girl looked at her through frightened eyes. For a moment, her mouth hung open, as if she couldn't speak. Then she bobbed in a little curtsey and moved away from the bed.

"I'll get Mag," she squeaked, running toward the door.

A short time later, Mag was beside Addien's bed, trying to convince her that the baby was well and was being cared for in another room.

"I want to see him," Addien said.

"It's too soon," Mag told her. "You lost a lot of blood last night. You've been asleep all day. You need to rest and drink some broth. Perhaps tomorrow, when you're feeling better…."

"I want to see him now," Addien said stubbornly. "And if you don't bring him to me, I'm going to get out of this bed and go find him myself."

Mag shook her head and pursed her lips. Then she left the room without another word.

It was very difficult for Addien to stay awake. Breathing seemed like a monumental task, and keeping her eyes open seemed almost impossible. But she refused to rest until she had seen her child. When the door finally opened again, she turned to it slowly, expecting to see Mag. But it was Balchder who stood there. And in his arms he held a tiny bundle of white cloth.

"I understand that you're being difficult," he said with a teasing smile. "Refusing to follow orders?"

Addien was too tired to think of a response. All she could do was wait while he crossed the room with his precious bundle. Balchder sat down on the bed beside her very gently and turned the bundle until she could see among the folds a tiny face, the face of her son. His eyes were closed, and one delicate little hand rested against his chin, but Addien could see the rise and fall of the cloth around his chest in a healthy rhythm.

"Mag asked me to come talk some sense into you," Balchder said. "She thinks you shouldn't have any disturbance until you're stronger. But I think," he said, turning the bundle to hold it in one arm, "that you need a different kind of medicine."

Very carefully, he took Addien's arm out from under her blankets. Then he laid the bundle beside her, between her arm and her chest. As she stared at the perfect little face beside her, Balchder moved her other arm and laid it across her so that she could just touch the infant and stoke his round cheeks. After several moments of wonder, she looked up at Balchder with a warm smile.

"How is it that you know me so well?" she whispered.

"I've watched you," he answered.

For another long moment, he let her hold the child in silence. Then he reached over and took the bundle from her arms.

"I'm afraid we can't stay any longer, though," he said. "You do need your rest, and babies make very noisy roommates. But, if you drink your broth and sleep well tonight, he can stay with you longer tomorrow."

With a twinkle in her eyes, Addien asked, "Is that another bargain?"

Balchder's eyes returned the twinkle.

"Do you accept?" he asked.

Addien smiled and breathed deeply.

"Yes," she answered.

"Good," he replied. "Then shut your eyes for awhile, and we'll see you tomorrow."

It was several days before Addien was able to move her head or arms without difficulty. She couldn't sit up or roll over without assistance, and her legs still felt like stones. But it was obvious that she was recovering and that the worst was past. Mag even started braiding her hair again, to make her more comfortable. Balchder only smiled when Addien stole a cautious look at him.

"You can resume your side of the bargain when you're feeling better," he told her. "I won't hold this against you."

* * *

Michael and Colin came to visit her every day, staying only a short while each time. Almost a week after the birth, Michael came to visit her alone one day. As Balchder had promised, Addien had been given more time each day with the baby in her room. Although she wasn't able to nurse him, she loved just holding him and stroking his soft skin. Michael sat beside her while she lay on her side, holding the tiny hand of her son.

"Isn't he beautiful?" Addien murmured. "He's to be christened tomorrow."

"Yes, I know," Michael answered. "Lord Balchder invited Colin and I to attend."

Pulling her eyes away from the baby, Addien looked up at her friend. Something in his eyes told her something that his words had not.

"And then you'll be leaving?" she asked.

Michael smiled.

"I wish I could stay longer," he said. "I'd like to know that you're going to be all right."

"I'll be all right," Addien said, smiling bravely. "I have to be. I have a job to do now."

For a few moments they sat in silence. They watched the baby as he squirmed and squeaked and pulled his mother's fingers toward his mouth. Addien laughed softly as he sucked on one fingertip. Then she looked at Michael again. He was looking down at her, his eyes soft and tender.

"It's good to see you happy," he said.

A few moments later, he rose to leave.

"There is something I've been meaning to tell you," he said. "It might help to ease your mind. Ever since Colin and I arrived at Cleddyf, we've been looking into things around here, talking to people in the village and the nearby farms. We found some of Cythraul's followers."

Addien's eyes widened as she looked up at him.

"You don't have to be afraid any longer," he continued. "Cythraul left no other instructions. It was only Mag—and the drink she was to give you to relax your muscles. If Cythraul's followers had any ideas of their own to cause trouble, I think Colin and I took care of that. We even took Brother Peadar with us to put the fear of the living God into them."

Addien had to laugh at the thought of Peadar, Michael, and Colin terrifying a group of misled pagans with threats of eternal damnation and hell-fire, not to mention Peadar's large stick. She smiled at Michael again and thought of simpler times.

"Still trying to take care of me?" she asked.

"Still wishing I could," he answered simply.

Addien smiled, but she could not stop her eyes from filling with tears. Balchder had set a date in the spring when their son, Prince Brion, would be presented to the kingdom. It was agreed that Michael and Colin would return for the ceremony, but the five months in between suddenly loomed large in Addien's heart. Michael sat down again beside her and silently took her hand.

"How will I ever manage without you?" Addien whispered, as she tried to dry her eyes with her free hand. "No, don't answer that. It isn't fair."

Michael squeezed her hand tighter.

"You know I would stay if I could, but…."

"Don't say it," Addien told him. She shut her eyes and let the tears fall. "I don't want you to worry about me. You know I'll be all right. I have Brion now. And you have to have your own life. It's just that…."

"I know," Michael answered. Then he kissed her hand and said good-night.

* * *

Only five weeks had passed when Addien was surprised to receive a message that Colin had returned to the castle. She was spending the afternoon, as usual, in Brion's room. Taking her infant son with her, she went down to the main entrance of the castle to see her friend.

"I didn't expect to see you again so soon," Addien said, giving Colin a warm hug.

He smiled at her and took a moment to look at the baby before explaining.

"Before we left, Lord Balchder asked us to visit some of the nobles and landowners we know personally to invite them to the prince's presentation. I've just finished all of my trips, and I've come to give him a report."

Addien drew in a breath and looked away.

"Will Michael be coming, too?" she asked.

"No," Colin answered, "not until the feast. But I have a message from him to deliver to his lordship."

"Come, I'll take you to him."

As they walked together toward Balchder's private rooms, Addien asked Colin how the news of Brion's birth was being taken.

"With mixed emotions," he answered. "But mostly positive, I think. Most of the people I know are just happy to finally have things settled. It may mean more freedom in the land and a reopening of trade and commerce. That will mean a lot to the people."

Colin asked Addien how she was feeling, and they talked about Brion and how big he was getting. Addien was just going to ask her friend how long he would be staying, when they were interrupted by a commotion in the hall in front of them. A woman was standing in the hall, yelling and crying, and two of Balchder's guards were trying to move her out of her spot.

"Please, please," the woman begged, "let me see him! I can't wait until tomorrow. It has to be today!"

As the men lifted the woman and started to remove her, Addien rushed to stop them.

"What is the meaning of this?" she demanded. "What are you doing to this woman?"

The guards stopped and looked from Addien to Colin and back again. Although the woman's cries made talking difficult, one of the men tried to explain the situation.

"His lordship does not receive petitions today," the man said, struggling to keep the woman from breaking away from him. "We told her that she will have to return tomorrow. She never should have been allowed this far into the castle."

"Tomorrow is too late!" the woman wailed. "He'll be dead by then! They'll all be dead!"

"Put her down," Addien commanded in frustration. "Let me talk to her."

Handing the baby to a surprised Colin, she took the woman by the shoulders and held her tight.

"What are you talking about?" Addien asked her. "Who is going to be dead tomorrow?"

"My husband," the woman said, panting for air. "All the men on his boat. They went out yesterday and never returned. Today, one man came back on a raft. He said the men of Cambria captured them because they were fishing in their waters. They won't let them go unless a ransom is paid. And it has to be paid first thing in the morning!"

The woman began to wail again, burying her face in her hands. Addien looked up at the two guards who still stood beside her.

"Where is Lord Balchder now?" she asked them.

"In his dining room, m'lady," came the answer, "meeting with Lord Daimhin."

"Keep her here," Addien ordered. "And find her a chair so she can sit down. Colin, come with me."

Without waiting for anyone to answer, Addien walked off toward Balchder's rooms. When she reached the dining room, the guard outside hesitated only a moment before knocking on the door to announce her presence. A moment later, she was inside with Colin at her shoulder, still holding the baby and still looking perplexed. Balchder sat at the head of the table with Daimhin, in his usual green and blue plaid, siting beside him. They both seemed quite surprised at the interruption.

"My lord," Addien began, "please forgive this intrusion. A matter of some urgency has been brought to my attention, and I think you should know about it."

She explained to him everything that the woman had told her in the hall. Then she waited in breathless silence as Balchder considered the matter. After a long moment, he looked at Lord Daimhin and then back at Addien.

"This is, of course, a tragedy," he began in a low voice. "The winter storms were very hard this year. Many of the fishermen from the village were lost at sea, and the rest are having a difficult time finding enough food for their families. However," he said, leaning forward in his chair, "I cannot agree to a ransom. Undoubtedly, the people of Cambria suffered as much as we have. If we give in to a demand for ransom, it will only encourage them to capture more of our men and demand the same again."

As if to dismiss the matter, and his wife, Balchder sat back in his chair and turned to face Daimhin.

"Besides," he said over his shoulder, "it's very possible that these men were fishing in Cambrian waters and only got what they deserved."

Although it was obvious that Balchder was finished with the discussion, Addien was not. She walked to the end of the long table and put her hands on it, leaning over it to look directly at Balchder.

"Are you telling me," she said, "that a man who is trying to feed his family deserves to die just because he crosses some imaginary boundary in the middle of the sea?"

Balchder turned back to her, looking a little annoyed.

"No," he said, "I didn't intend to say that. But the point remains that we cannot encourage lawless behavior by paying a ransom. It will only make the lives of the villagers more difficult and dangerous."

"Then there has to be another answer," Addien pressed on. "If the Cambrians were hurt by the winter just like our people, maybe we can encourage cooperation instead of competition. What if you agreed to not enforce the boundaries and let the Cambrians fish wherever they want?"

Lord Daimhin sat forward in his seat, snorting in disgust.

"There still wouldn't be enough fish to go around," he said. "The villagers all along the coast have been hurt by the lack of fish. Sharing the waters would only make things worse."

"You talk as if fishing is the only thing these people can do," Addien said. "Isn't there something else the villagers can do to survive if they can't get enough fish?"

"This conversation is pointless!" Daimhin said, growing red in the face.

Addien glanced at him briefly and then decided to ignore him. She could only imagine that he wasn't used to having anyone disagree with him, especially a woman. But she was not a mere woman. She was still the princess, and she wanted to do what she could to help the people of the kingdom.

"If fishing in the channel isn't enough to support our village and theirs," Addien continued, looking away from Daimhin's glare, "let's give them something else to cooperate on. Colin, you said it before," she said, turning to her friend. "The reopening of trade will help all of our people. Why not offer the Cambrians an agreement of free trade?"

Balchder paused a moment before answering. His face was calm and unreadable. But when he spoke there was a hint of interest in his voice.

"Even if the Cambrians agree," he said, "what do we have to trade?"

"Drop your travel restrictions and taxes," Addien said confidently. "People from all over the kingdom will bring their goods here to trade for goods from Cambria. The villagers will receive a share of the profits for handling the trading, and the Cambrian villagers will do the same. They'll never have to resort to abduction again!"

Speaking for the first time, a quiet Colin mused, "It could work. But what about the other nobles? What if they don't drop their restrictions?"

Still looking at Balchder, Addien concentrated her arguments on him.

"There are goods being smuggled into Briallen all the time, much of it from the continent and the Far East. If you open up the Northern Territory, people will flock here for a safe place to trade. The other nobles will follow your lead when they see how profitable it can be."

Balchder seemed to be softening to the idea, but Addien decided to make one last point before letting him speak.

"And," she said, "this would be a good time to improve our relations with Cambria. We may need their help someday in the fight against the Saxons."

For a long while, Balchder sat still, saying nothing. It was obvious that he was giving the matter serious thought. At last, he looked up and sighed.

"Someone will have to bear the message to the abductors," he said. "I don't think my soldiers will be greeted warmly. And it is possible they will refuse to release their hostages in exchange for a mere promise."

"I'll go," Colin said unexpectedly.

Addien looked at him in surprise, wondering if he understood the dangerousness of the mission. He smiled at her confidently, and she smiled back.

"Then I have an idea," Addien said.

Grabbing Colin's arm, Addien made her way back to the place where they had left the distraught woman.

"Stay here," she ordered Colin. "I'll be right back."

Colin looked at Addien in dismay and held out the sleeping baby he was still holding.

"But…," he started.

"I'll be right back," she promised, leaving him holding the little bundle.

A short while later Addien was back, holding a wooden box in her hand. Opening it, she took out the beautiful crown of seashell blossoms that she had worn on her wedding day.

Turning to the village woman, she asked, "Are there very many of these wedding garlands in the village?"

"I don't know," the woman stuttered in surprise. "Perhaps a dozen."

"Gather them all," Addien told her, "and meet Colin at the cliff road tomorrow morning. Tell the women that you need the garlands to save your men and your village."

Walking up behind her, Balchder took the garland and examined in curiosity.

"Do you think they'll accept these for trade?" he asked.

"They would be fools not to," she answered. "If the women of Cambria are anything like the women of Dumnonia, they'll be lined up on the beach waiting to have one of these."

He handed it back to her, and she returned it to its box.

Watching how carefully she handled it, he asked, "Are you certain that you want to give that up? Besides, giving them a boatload of these things is almost like paying their ransom demand."

"We aren't going to give them to them," she said.

Addien turned to Colin and traded him the box for the baby.

"Tell the Cambrians that these are not a gift," she said. "We will expect full payment for them in due time, when they have had time to trade them. Tell them we have many other fine works of craftsmanship to trade if they, in good faith, will release our men."

Balchder sighed and gave his wife a somber look.

In a low voice, he asked, "And what if they decide instead to kill the fishermen and the messengers, and simply take the treasure?"

Addien's eyes widened, and she drew in a quick breath. Turning to Colin, she knew that she had no other answers. She couldn't ask him to risk his life, but she knew of no other way to save the captured fishermen. But she didn't need to say anything.

"I'll make them take the trade," Colin said with a smile. "They can't eat shell garlands. But if we promise them trade in all kinds of goods from Dumnonia and the continent, they'll be able to feed their families even in the worst of circumstances."

The next morning, Colin took Addien's garland and went to the village to meet the woman and a few fishermen who would take him out into the channel. All day, Addien kept watch out the windows or along the castle wall, praying for his safety. He returned to the castle just after sunset that night. She could tell from the look on his face that his mission had been successful.

"The Cambrians were suspicious, to be sure," he told her after they embraced at the castle gate. "But there was more than one husband among them, and they were anxious to get their hands on the shell garlands. They released the village fishermen and let us all return safely—with the promise of more garlands to come, and anything else we can find to trade. And Gennie, the villagers have even promised a new garland for you to replace the one you gave away."

"Colin, I don't know how to thank you," Addien gushed as she embraced him again.

"It was your idea," he replied. "The whole village is singing your praises. When word spreads that the old trade routes will be reopened, everyone in the kingdom will have you to thank."

Addien blushed slightly. Although the compliment pleased her, she felt uneasy about receiving too much credit.

"They should thank Lord Balchder for that," she responded, gazing at the stones beneath her feet. "He'll be their king soon. It's only right that the people should look to him to restore peace and prosperity in the kingdom."

Colin took her arm in his as they walked through the castle yard.

"Do you think the people will ever accept him as their king?" he asked softly.

"I think they're going to have to," Addien replied with a sigh.

Chapter Twenty Four

At last the day of the presentation arrived, the twenty-fifth of March, the first day of the New Year's Feast. Balchder had sent invitations to every nobleman and large landowner to attend the presentation and to remain at Cleddyf for the eight days of the feast, ending on the first day of April. Supplies for the festival had been arriving for weeks, and a large camp had been erected in the valley behind the castle, complete with tents, tables, and a large area for dancing. The presentation itself would be held in the Main Hall of the castle, with the lords and ladies and greater landowners in attendance. The rest of the guests and the servants would celebrate outside under the moon and the stars.

Alone in her room that afternoon, Addien dressed for the evening's festivities. Since the baby's birth, she had lost a considerable amount of weight, especially during the first two weeks when she could barely eat. But she still retained something of a motherly figure. Her hips were wider, and her breasts fuller. She had decided to wear the blue gown with white trim that Balchder had given her the day after her arrival at the castle. Mag had given her a matching blue bow to tie back the great expanse of her hair. But once she put the gown on, she wondered if it might not be too tight and—well, revealing.

Twisting around to get a better look at herself, Addien didn't realize that her door had opened.

"You look beautiful," Balchder said, standing just inside the doorway.

"My lord," Addien replied, blushing slightly.

She turned to face him, holding her arms out to her side to show him the gown.

"I was just wondering if this would be appropriate," she said. "It seems rather tight."

Balchder looked at Addien for a long moment without answering. Slowly, he crossed the room until he stood within reach of her. His blue eyes had a soft, far-away look.

"I've often pictured you in this dress," he said, as his eyes traveled up and down the clinging lines of the gown. "I've also pictured you out of it."

Addien felt her face blush again, deeper this time. Her gaze dropped to the floor as she crossed her arms in front of her.

"To think," Balchder continued, "that I once dared to dream that you would come to me again some day, willingly."

Confused, Addien looked up at him.

"My lord?" she asked, searching his face for some clue to his meaning.

"When you agreed to be my wife, I hoped that some day you would be able to give yourself to me freely," he explained.

Still uncertain of his meaning, Addien lifted her chin and regarded him seriously.

"My lord," she said, "I am your wife. I have given you my vows, my obedience, my self. If there is anything you wish, you have only to ask."

"But not your heart," he answered, as the muscles around his jaw tightened. "That will always belong to another."

He turned then and stepped past her to look out the window at the sea.

"Did you know that on the night of Brion's birth," he continued, "in your pain, you called out for Michael and begged him not to leave you. It was I who held your hand that night, but Michael who held your heart."

He turned again to face Addien. His eyes stared into hers like a hungry animal. He stepped closer and then gently wrapped one arm around her waist and pulled her to him. With his other hand he reached up and stroked her face and chin. His hand moved downward, along her neck and onto the swollen flesh of her breast that pushed above the low neckline of the dress. Barely breathing, Addien remained still and let him hold her. His fingers sent a sensation of heat through her body, as his hand dropped still lower and pressed against the fullness of her breast. Then his eyes rose to hers again. His hand wrapped around the back of her neck, and he pulled her to him in a long, demanding kiss.

Very slowly, he released her. His eyes scanned her face as she gradually pulled back from him. Whatever he had hoped to see must not have been there, for his eyes clouded over and his jaw clenched tight again.

"Even now, it is him you are thinking of, isn't it?" he demanded.

Feeling a calmness she couldn't explain, Addien looked back at him.

"I told you that I am your wife," she said. "I will do anything you ask of me. But if you ask for my love, that is something I cannot give. And it has nothing to do with Michael. It is because of everything you took from me the day you took away my father."

The tension in Balchder's jaw seemed to spread to his neck and shoulders as well. But the darkness in his eyes softened. He took a deep breath and stepped back away from her.

"I do not ask for your obedience," he said at last. "You are free to do whatever you choose. I know that you will stay here to be a mother to our son, and I trust that you will rule with me as a leader of the kingdom. But a wife to me you will be in name only."

As he turned to leave, Addien stared, unseeing, at the wall. When she heard him stop and turn back to her, she continued to look away, unwilling to meet his gaze.

"At least until the past has been forgotten," he said softly, "and the unforgivable has been forgiven."

When he left, Addien sunk down into the chair beside her dressing table and tried to still the fluttering of her heart. She hadn't expected this, and she wasn't certain how she should feel about it. She should have been happy that Balchder was going to keep his distance from her.

She had never wanted an intimate relationship with him, although she had expected it as one of her wifely duties. But happiness wasn't exactly what she felt. Instead, she felt a heavy door closing inside of her. Every hope she had of ever being held again, or kissed, or caressed, or treated like a desirable woman had just been shut away, just one more thing to hide away in the secret place in her heart.

* * *

As Addien left her room to take her place at Balchder's side in the Main Hall, she thought of something else that made her heart flutter. She would soon be seeing Michael again. Balchder had personally invited him to sit with the nobles and landowners at the presentation, and she knew that Michael would not refuse. She had not seen him since Brion's birth, and the time and distance that had been between them once again made her nervous to be near him. For a moment she stopped and closed her eyes, willing her mind and body to be calm. She would not let Michael see her upset or unhappy. She had chosen her course in life, and he had to be free to choose his. So she donned a smile and walked the rest of the way to the Hall with her head held high.

Inside the Hall, the guests were already assembled. Balchder was waiting for his wife at the door. Addien took his arm, and together they walked into the room and took their places at the head table. The guests rose and waited for them to sit, although Addien guessed it was more out of respect for the occasion than for Balchder. Then, as everyone was taking their places again, Addien had a brief moment to look around.

Balchder's neighbors, Lords Daimhin and Gorman, were sitting near the front of the room with their families. She could see Lord Trevelgue with his wife and son, and one or two other men she had seen in Briallen. Near the very back of the room, she finally spotted Michael, in a closely guarded conversation with another man about his age. She wondered if it was Torbryon, who owned the large ranch west of

Briallen. Before giving it much thought, she forced her eyes to move on, taking in all the faces in the room, lest she be caught staring too long in one direction.

When all was still again, Balchder stood and raised his arm.

"Lords and Ladies," he began, "freemen of Dumnonia, I thank you for your attendance today. This is a great moment, with all of the people of Dumnonia—represented here by you—reunited again in peace."

There was a slight commotion in the room, as some of those present shifted in their chairs and others murmured under their breath. Balchder quickly surveyed the room, but then continued as if nothing had happened.

"For too long our kingdom has been without a king," he said. "But today I call upon each of you to join with me in greeting a new king—Brion, son of Addien, grandson of Brenin, the last king of Dumnonia."

There was another wave of murmurings, and Addien steeled herself for what she expected to come next. Balchder had not yet declared himself king, as she had always assumed he would. But before he could continue, Balchder was interrupted by one of the men in the room that Addien didn't know.

"You say that this child is Brenin's heir," the man shouted as he rose to his feet. "But what proof do you offer us other than your words?"

"I am that proof," Addien answered clearly, rising to her feet before Balchder had a chance to speak. "I am Addien, daughter of Morveren, and the only child of King Brenin. What evidence would you ask of me?"

Quickly, Balchder reached over and touched her arm. She looked at him and saw a shadow of concern in his eyes.

"I can do this," she whispered to him.

As Addien turned back to her audience, she saw Balchder out of the corner of her eye sitting down. All eyes in the room were focused on her.

"You have demanded proof," she said to the one man standing. "What do you ask of me?"

Silenced for a moment, the man looked about him for support. When no one else spoke, he finally turned back to the princess.

"If you are Princess Addien," he said, "then tell us how you escaped from the King's House on the night of the massacre?"

The room remained silent while Addien quickly thought over her answer. If she told the truth it was possible that no one would believe her, and it would only lead to more difficult questions. But she didn't want her son's heritage to be based on lies either. So she decided that a half-truth would have to do.

"I was hidden during the fighting by a friend," she said, "someone that I promised never to reveal. That night I left the house with only the clothes on my back and the necklace that my father had given me on my sixth birthday. It was by a charm on that necklace that I was eventually recognized when I returned to Briallen ten years later. A woman in the marketplace had been the wife of the man who made it especially for me."

"Then you have the charm still?" the man asked. "Will you show it to us?"

Addien paused for a moment, trying to decide what to do. A movement beside her caught her attention, and she turned to see Balchder unfolding a cloth on the table. Out of the cloth he took the bracelet that she had given to Dyn and that Dyn had lost, and he handed it to her. In amazement and relief, she held it tight and then lifted it up high so that everyone could see it.

"When my father gave this to me," Addien said, "it had four garnet stones inlaid on teardrop pieces of mother-of-pearl. I removed the garnets and some of the gold beads and made it into a bracelet when I returned to Briallen. I'm afraid it is the only proof I have."

"Then perhaps I can add some more," came a deep voice from the center of the room.

It was Lord Trevelgue, standing to address the room.

"I learned of the reappearance of the princess in Briallen at the same time as the rest of you," he said. "But I learned something else about her that most of you didn't. It seemed that she had been growing up right under my nose the whole time. I have personally investigated this young woman's past, and I can tell you this. She came to the Western Territory only a few days after the death of King Brenin. She was about seven years old at the time and was found wandering alone in the wilderness by a family in my employment. I have known her and watched her grow since that time. And I can tell you that anyone who has ever known this woman knows that she is who she claims to be."

The voices in the room rose again, as people discussed among themselves all that they had heard. For a long while, Trevelgue remained standing, holding the gaze of the man who had begun the challenge. At length the man sat down, and Trevelgue sat also. Balchder rose then and hammered his cup on the table to call for the room's attention.

"I suggest we end the suspense," he said with a smile, "and let you see what you have come here to see."

He turned and motioned to a servant at the door. As the door was opened, Addien went to meet the nurse who waited there. A moment later, Addien held a bundle of white cloth in her arms as she peered into the wide blue eyes of her little boy. It was her job to take the prince around to each of the guests. Each man and woman would stand, as was the tradition, and touch the child on the forehead, symbolically identifying with the child and accepting him as their future king. As Addien walked to the first table, she placed her bracelet on top of the cloth, under Brion's arms, where it could also be seen.

From table to table Addien walked, from person to person. Each rose in turn to see the little prince. Each reached out and touched him on the forehead, some reverently, some reluctantly, some fearfully. But no one refused. There were even a few moments of laughter, whenever Brion would start to cry, for it was an old tradition that anyone who made the baby cry at a presentation would owe twice the normal tribute when the child became king.

Slowly, the somber mood in the room lifted as the guests seemed almost enchanted by the perfect little being in their presence. When Addien reached Trevelgue, she looked up at him with a smile of thanks and appreciation. He touched the child and then reached up to touch Addien on the cheek.

"Bless you, child," he whispered. "Bless you."

Addien could tell from his look that he was thinking of another day, a day when she had accused him of lying to her and helping her enemy. She smiled again to let him know that all was forgiven, and then she moved on to the next person.

She had made her way down one row of tables and back up the other side, and she was nearing the end of the second row. When she started back up the other side, the second person she would encounter would be Michael. She was trying to not think about him, and forcing herself to look away from him. So great was her concentration, that she wasn't fully aware of the rising voices at the other end of the room. But when she came around the end of the last table, her attention was drawn to the far end where Daimhin and Gorman were in a heated debate with several other men.

Concentrating on her duty, Addien waited for the man beside Michael to rise and meet his future ruler. Then she stepped beside Michael's chair and held her breath as he stood up beside her. Unwilling to meet his gaze, she kept her eyes on Brion's face. Very gently, Michael touched the baby on the forehead.

"Welcome, little prince," he whispered.

Then he moved his hand down to touch the hand that rested on top of the baby. With a quick breath, Addien looked up at him.

"No!" boomed a voice at the far end of the tables. "It is not agreeable! You can't expect us to just roll over and...."

"Gentlemen!" Balchder's voice echoed over the room, leaving complete silence in its wake. "This is not the time for quarrels. What you have to say can wait until after the presentation."

The group of men quieted, but the look on their faces remained grim. Addien had not yet reached their end of the room, and she was becoming very reluctant to go there.

"You'll be all right," Michael said softly.

He gave Addien a reassuring wink and then gently squeezed her hand. Addien suddenly realized that she had been standing there for some time with his hand on hers. She looked down and saw that Michael's hand was also being held, by the tiny fingers of her son. As Michael carefully removed his hand, Addien smiled, took a deep breath, and moved on.

From person to person she walked down the room until she had reached the end of the table and the man who had been arguing with Gorman and Daimhin. From his bearing and the look of his clothes, Addien guessed that he was a nobleman, perhaps one of the four lords that Michael had said was strong enough to challenge Balchder. From the look on his face, she wondered if he was ready to make that challenge right then.

The man stood slowly and looked at the baby in Addien's arms. But instead of touching the child, the man turned around to face Balchder.

"Lord Balchder," he said in a loud voice, "I am prepared to recognize this child as Brenin's heir. And when he is old enough to rule this kingdom, I will accept him as my king. But do not think that I will ever bow before you or serve you."

The threat in the man's voice was clear. Addien's eyes darted to Balchder, where he still sat at the head table, and then back to his challenger.

"Granted," Balchder said. "I do not ask to be your king."

The swiftness of his answer caught Addien by surprise, but not as much as what he had said. She was not alone in her surprise, as she could tell by the many gasps and other startled sounds around her.

Balchder stood and looked around the room.

"For too long our kingdom has been divided," he said. "With the Saxon menace approaching us again, and the need for trade and commerce, we must reunite if we are to survive. If you will not all follow me as your king, then I ask you all to join with me as neighbors and fellow countrymen to put aside our differences and do what is best for the kingdom. I do not stand here today to name myself king, as some of you have feared. By my position as Brion's father, I name myself Regent only—co-regent in fact, for I must share that responsibility with my wife, Addien."

With his arm stretched out wide, Balchder pointed at Addien. Eyes wide with shock, she looked back at him. Then, breathing deeply, she looked around the room at all of the faces that were looking back at her. Most of the expressions were blank, neither happy nor angry, not even registering the surprise that they must have felt. As Addien met each look, she continued to turn until she could steal a glance at Michael. He alone of all the group wore a radiant smile. Addien smiled to herself then and turned back to the man who still stood beside her.

"We're waiting," she said softly to his back.

The man turned and looked at Addien searchingly. At last, his gaze dropped to the baby's face and he reached up and touched him lightly on the forehead. With her head held high, Addien walked past him and waited for each of the remaining people at the table to stand in turn and meet their future king. Then she returned to the head table and sat down in her chair. Beside her, Balchder still stood. Placing his hands on the table, he leaned over it to address his audience again.

"As Brion's Regent," he began, "I swear to you that I will do all I can to defend this kingdom and to see it united and prosperous once again. I know that Addien joins me in that pledge. Under the leadership of Princess Addien, there has already been a renewal of trade in the Northern Territory and a dialogue of peace begun with the kingdom of Cambria. I invite each man here to join with us in planning for the future of the kingdom. During the remaining days of the feast, I will hold council every day to hear your concerns and your wishes, to work together with each of you to restore to Dumnonia what has been lost."

Coming from Balchder, it may have been a poor choice of words. There wasn't a person in the room who didn't recall that it was Balchder who caused the rift in the kingdom when he tried before to make himself king. Was it possible that he could now restore the kingdom by refusing to become its king? Looking about her, Addien wondered how many other people were thinking those very thoughts. Men and women all around the room were in hushed conversations or just sitting silently, looking down at their hands. But there were no more open challenges to anything Balchder had said.

After a few moments, Balchder sat and turned to his wife.

"I think that went rather well," he said with a little smile. "If you want to take the baby to his room, I'll have the food brought in as soon as you return."

"No, that's all right," Addien said, starting to rise. "You had better give them something else to chew on now, before they start chewing on each other again. Start without me. I'll be back in a little while."

As she walked to the nearest door, Balchder stood to announce the beginning of the feast. Soon the room would be full of servants carrying great platters of meats and breads and mulled wine. The voices of the many guests would rise over the noise of plates and platters and cups. The Feast of the New Year would begin, with many new things to think about and to discuss.

Addien was glad that she had an excuse to escape for a little while, to be by herself to think. As she walked toward Brion's room, where she would leave him with his nurse, she thought about Balchder's promise to restore to the kingdom what it had lost. He had already given the kingdom an heir to Brenin, who would be the future king. He had promised his protection and his leadership until Brion was old enough to be the king. But there was one thing that he could never restore. Only she could—if it is was still physically possible.

When she reached the bedroom, Addien asked the nurse to wait outside while she said good-night to her son. Placing him in his bed, Addien leaned over it to be very close to him. Then she took her bracelet in her hands and opened the secret door on the locket.

"Trevilian!" she whispered happily as her little friend appeared on the bed in a flash of light. "I'm so glad to see you. I was so afraid that I had lost you forever." She reached down a finger to her little friend and stroked his arm gently. "I have someone I want you to meet. But first, there's something I have to ask."

In hushed tones, Addien told Trevilian about how Dyn had been attacked and had dropped the locket onto the cliff rocks.

"I haven't seen this again until today," she said, touching the locket. "I thought I would never see you again, or—the crown."

"And now that ye know that the locket is safe, and myself, you want to see yer treasure, too, don't ye?" he asked with a grin.

Addien nodded, and Trevilian turned and opened the door of the locket. Inside, she could just see the outline of something round and shiny, and dotted with several blood-red stones.

"It's all right!" Addien gasped in relief. "Then Trevilian, let me introduce you to the one who will someday wear that crown—my son, Brion, the next king of Dumnonia."

Chapter Twenty Five

The week passed very quickly. Every day the lords and landowners met with Balchder at the castle in an open council. Most of the time, Addien was there, too. Although at first she had to fight to be heard in the room full of loud, strong-willed men, she eventually earned some measure of respect, and her opinion was even sought after in certain matters. By the end of the New Year's Feast, there was a definite feeling of hope and anticipation as they all looked forward to a time of cooperation and unity.

Balchder announced that he would be recalling immediately all of the divisions of the army so that they could train together at Cleddyf under his command. Small companies would be dispatched on a rotating basis to keep watch on the borders and to deter smuggling and stealing along the coasts. Another company was requested by the merchants of Briallen to keep open the major roads in and out of the capital.

"A lot of good that will do us," one man scoffed, "asking the wolves to guard the sheep."

There seemed to be a general consensus about distrusting the military, so a suggestion was made to have a civilian commander oversee the army's operations in the Southern and Eastern Territories. The group unanimously chose Michael for that position. The lords and landowners even agreed to pay an annual amount of 'support' for the army's provisions. The word sounded better than 'tribute,' although no one attempted to define it.

At last the feast came to an end, and Addien walked with Michael to the gate of the castle to say good-bye. It was the first time she had been alone with him since his last visit to Cleddyf, and she wondered how long it would be before she would see him again.

"I have some news for you," he said, as they were finally left alone in the yard. "I was waiting to have a moment alone to tell you. Colin is getting married. He wanted you to know."

"Oh, I'm so happy for him!" Addien smiled. "Will you give him my best wishes? I don't suppose I'll be seeing him for awhile."

"Well, it may be sooner than you think," Michael responded. "I'm planning on using him to send my messages to Balchder, at least until I can find a few people within the army that I can trust."

Looking down, Addien bit her lip softly.

"Then I won't be seeing you here for quite awhile," she said.

"No," he answered with a sigh. "I think it would be best if I stayed in the south for now."

Shyly, she looked up at him. She was certain that he meant it would be best to stay away from her, but she decided to give a less painful meaning to his words.

"You'll have a lot to do," she said, looking away again, "keeping track of all of Balchder's men down there. It's a tremendous responsibility."

"And that's not all," he said. "Balchder has given me another job. If the Saxons attack us in force, our army may not be enough to stop them. Balchder wants every able-bodied man who can find a horse ready to ride to the border if needed. And he wants me to be in charge of this 'reserve cavalry.'"

Addien stopped walking and turned to face him.

"He couldn't find a better person for the job," she said.

They smiled at each other, and Addien reached up to give him a brief hug.

"Be safe," she whispered in his ear as she pulled away.

Then they said good-bye, and Addien watched as Michael directed his horse out through the gate and up the winding cliff road away from Cleddyf Castle.

* * *

Summer arrived with a whirl of activity. The holiday camp in the valley was turned into a military training camp. Balchder spent most of his time there, drilling the soldiers and teaching them the ways of the Roman infantry. Addien saw him only briefly on most days, for an occasional meal together. Some days, she didn't see him at all. He never changed his mind about their relationship. He continued to sleep in his room, and Addien slept in hers. And the room next to Addien's was made into a nursery so that she could always have Brion close by her.

Even with Balchder away so much, Addien was not alone in the castle. Directing the daily affairs of the servants and castle guards fell to her as Lady of the Castle. She also started receiving the petitions of the villagers and neighboring farmers, which Balchder no longer had time for, and she met with the nobles and landowners who began to visit Cleddyf more frequently. The roads into the Northern Territory began to fill with merchants and pilgrims and even families seeking a better life. Obviously, Michael was doing his job well, because none of the travelers ever complained about trouble on the road or difficulties with the soldiers in the south.

But, as the cold months of winter approached, travel into the territory lessened. Balchder closed down the camp in the windy valley and dispersed the soldiers. Those with families or property to care for were sent home. Others found temporary work in the growing villages along the coast. The rest were assigned to permanent camps around the kingdom where their job would be to maintain the peace. With Michael and the other nobles keeping an eye on them, the kingdom settled in for a quiet, uneventful winter.

One evening, late in January, Addien sat in a quiet room in the castle working on a tapestry. Balchder sat near her on a bench against the wall, and Brion, now a year old, toddled back and forth between them. During the less hectic winter months, Balchder had spent more time with his wife and son, and they enjoyed his company. On that night, however, he was very quiet, and Addien wondered what was on his mind.

"May I ask you a question?" he said at last, breaking a lengthy silence.

"Yes, of course," she answered, still looking down at her work.

When he didn't speak again, Addien laid the tapestry in her lap and looked up at him.

"What is it?" she asked softly.

Balchder paused and then reached down to help Brion, who had just tumbled onto the floor.

Without looking up, he said, "I was wondering about the bracelet that you always wear, the one your father gave you. Cythraul told me it was nothing, just something to remember him by. But I have always wondered if there was something more to it."

He glanced up at Addien and held her gaze.

"Will you tell me the truth?" he asked. "Does the locket on the bracelet bear some clue to the hiding place of Brenin's crown?"

For a moment, she held her breath, trying to decide how to answer him. He waited patiently, holding Brion's hand as he tried to regain his balance and strike out on his own again.

"Yes," she said at length. "The locket holds the key to finding the crown."

Balchder took a deep breath and sat back again. Brion released his hand and wandered across the room to explore something shiny that had caught his attention. Addien sat still with the tapestry lying forgotten on her lap.

"Then Cythraul lied about it being destroyed," Balchder sighed, staring at a window on the far wall. "I wonder what else he lied about."

Watching him, Addien guessed that his real concern was not the crown. Something else was bothering him.

"Do you think he lied about the Saxon invasion?" she asked. "You told me before that they have shown no sign of preparing for battle."

"That's what I'm afraid of," he admitted in a low voice. "It was the threat of an invasion that brought the nobles back together. If they find out it was all a lie, they may reconsider their pledge of loyalty to their future king."

Balchder shot a glance at his little son, who was playing happily in the corner. He had given up his quest for the crown to have this child, and he had given up his desire to be king so that his son would be accepted as the future king without a challenge. Addien had to admire him for that.

"It wasn't your lie," she said, trying to encourage him. "You were tricked by Cythraul, just like everyone else."

"Do you think anyone will believe that?" he asked, shaking his head.

"I do," Addien answered.

Balchder looked at her, searching her face as if he were trying to read her thoughts. She smiled at him softly.

"So much that is good has come from this," she said. "There is peace in the kingdom again, and cooperation, instead of fear and backbiting. The roads are safe to travel, trade has increased, and people are building homes and starting new farms again. Why would anyone want to give that up? And even if the Saxons don't invade this year, they will before long. And you're going to be ready for them."

Balchder stood and walked slowly across the room to stare out the window. For a moment, Addien left him to his silent thoughts. Then she stood and walked over to him.

"My lord," she said softly, "are you sorry that you listened to him?"

He turned to face her and looked deeply into her eyes. Then he looked past her at Brion, who was toddling after some other prize in another corner of the room. Looking back at Addien, he attempted a slight smile.

"No," he answered. "I'm not sorry. But I don't think I'll ask you that question."

They spoke no more about the past, as they waited to see what the future would hold. As spring approached, they began to receive conflicting reports from Balchder's spies and from their neighbors to the east and north. Balchder decided to recall the troops to Cleddyf Castle to prepare for a Saxon assault as originally planned. The camp was raised again in the valley and regular shipments of provisions began to arrive from all points of the kingdom. Balchder even brought in allies from the east to teach him the Saxon language, in case an opportunity ever offered itself for diplomacy instead of battle. Addien learned it also.

One morning, Balchder asked Addien to join him as he rode out to the encampment in the Valley of the Rocks. Brother Peadar rode along to escort the princess back to the castle when she was ready.

Although the valley lay only a short distance from the castle, Addien had never been there before. The plateau between the sea-cliff and the river gorge fell off gently as one traveled inland to the south. Green grass and red bracken grew thick there, sheltered a little from the harsh sea winds. Once into the valley, the ground on one side sloped back upward toward the high moor, and on the other it rose abruptly in towers of rocks giving it the appearance of some ancient fortress.

As they rode, Balchder turned to face Addien.

"I don't know what is going to happen this summer," he began in his usual blunt manner, "but I don't want you to be in the middle of it. I've sent a message to Briallen to have the King's House prepared to be reopened. I want you to take Brion and go there."

"But my lord," Addien answered in surprise, "we would be so far away from you. I don't think...."

"I've already decided," he said curtly. "Commander Michael is relocating all of the people who have been living in the royal compound.

Some will be given farmland or new homes in the city. Others will be asked to work as servants in the house. You will also need guards there. I'll send some of my own men with you. But I still have to choose a Captain. Of course, there is always Michael."

He paused and narrowed his eyes, searching Addien's face. She didn't know what he expected to see there, or what he hoped to see. The entire conversation had taken her by surprise, and she didn't know what to think about it. But she was certain that one thing he said was not a good idea, for her sake, or for Michael's.

"No," she answered after a moment. "I wouldn't want to take Michael away from the work he is already doing. It suits him so well. But there is someone else that I could suggest. Colin. I know that he's young, but he's the kind of man that people trust implicitly, and I believe he would be a good leader. I know that I trust him with my life."

When Balchder didn't answer immediately, Addien wondered again why he had suggested Michael and whether he was testing her loyalty to him.

"Besides, Colin is recently married," she continued. "And I don't think he is enjoying working on his father-in-law's farm. Deirdre is expecting soon, so Brion would have a playmate when the baby is older."

Balchder nodded, but his look remained serious.

"I'll send a message to him at once," he said. "I want you to be on your way before the New Year."

Without another word, Balchder spurred his horse and hurried away. Addien sat quietly for some time, listening to the sea birds that circled above the tents. Then she turned to the monk who sat silently beside her.

"And what about you, Brother?" she asked at last. "Will you go to Briallen with me? Or will you finally finish that pilgrimage you started so long ago?"

When he didn't answer, Addien turned to look at him. He smiled slightly.

"I think I'll stay right here," he said. "My services are still needed."

Addien looked away again and sighed.

"Will you go with them to the battle?" she asked softly.

Peadar paused again before answering, and again Addien turned to look at him.

"Aye," he said, "I suppose I'll be there, too. The men will need me there. Both the living and the dying."

"You're a brave man, Brother Peadar," Addien replied, realizing that she would miss him very much when she left. "This isn't even your kingdom, but you would risk your life for it?"

"We're part of the same kingdom, you and I," he answered with a smile. "The Kingdom of God."

The two rode back to the castle in silence, but when they reached the back wall Peadar brought his horse to a stop. It was truly an amazing sight. A single low wall ran along the side of the cliff, like some forgotten line of defense, concealing the rest of the great castle that was built on layers of rock descending toward the sea. It was built even before the Romans came to the Island, and it was a testament to the great intelligence and imagination of the Celtic people.

"Your Highness," Peadar began, "I know that you are anxious about what might happen here—what might happen to your kingdom. I cannot promise you that everything will be all right. But I do know one thing. The Kingdom of God will not be brought down by these heathens."

Staring with unseeing eyes at the castle wall, Addien remembered another prophecy made to her, by a very different kind of holy man.

"What if we can't stop them?" she asked with a shiver in her voice. "What if they do take over the whole Island?"

"You've heard me talk of my homeland in Ireland," he replied. "There is a place there called the Hill of Tara. Ever since the ancient days, the people celebrated a great feast there every year. There the king would decree that the night should remain dark. But one year, the night of the feast was not so dark. A huge bonfire blazed on a hill some miles away.

The druid priests turned to the king and told him, 'if this fire is not put out tonight, it will never be put out.'"

Peadar paused a moment and took a deep breath. Addien watched him in silence, unable to take her eyes off of his face.

"The man who lit that bonfire was a man named Patrick," he said at last. "And the light of that fire has never gone out. After that, the druids lost their magical powers, as Christianity came to Ireland. The druids couldn't put out the fire, nor could the early Romans. The Saxons will not be able to either."

Swallowing hard, Addien blinked away the moistness that came to her eyes. It was reassuring to think that part of what they were would continue, even if they lost the battle, and their lives. The land would continue. Not all of the marks they made upon it would be permanent, but some would. Perhaps even their stories would live on, passed down from parent to child again and again, as they had been for countless generations. As Addien urged her horse into a walk again, she promised herself to tell Brion the story of Patrick and the bonfire that night, and to start telling him the stories of his grandfather as well, the last great king of Dumnonia.

*   *   *

Colin arrived at the castle a few weeks later, excited about his new position as Captain of the Guard. He brought a message from Michael that the royal compound was almost cleared and that the King's House was livable, although it still needed a lot of work.

"Well, that will give me something to do this summer," Addien said.

Since Balchder had first told her that she would be returning to Briallen, she had suffered from mixed emotions about it. Her father's house still held a lot of terrible memories for her. They were less daunting now, since she no longer feared or detested the man who had caused those memories. Balchder was trying to make up for the damage he had caused, and giving Addien some freedom from him was probably part of that plan. Briallen was her real home, after all, and she had many good memories there, too. So when the time came to pack up and say good-bye to Cleddyf Castle, she did so with happy expectations.

It was not as easy to say good-bye to Balchder.

"If the Saxons do invade this year…," Addien began, realizing how much he had come to mean to her.

"Don't worry about me," he said with a smile. "I can take care of myself. I'll send you regular reports so that you'll know what is happening here. And if all remains quiet—perhaps you and Brion will decide to come back in the fall."

Trying to force a smile, Addien blinked back frightened tears.

"My lord," she said, "before I go, I want to give you something. It's the crown—my father's crown. I think you should have it."

Balchder looked at her for a long moment, until the surprise in his eyes was replaced with a soft look of contentment.

"No," he answered. "I've finally discovered that being a good soldier isn't the same thing as being a good king. I think I'll stick to what I do best and leave the rest to you."

"But you'll wear the Military stone?" Addien asked with a sniffle. "When you go to battle, you will wear it, won't you?"

Reaching up to touch her cheek, Balchder sighed and shook his head.

"No," he said. "Every good thing I've done in my life, I've done without the stone. I should have trusted myself all along, instead of trusting in a power that wasn't mine."

As the tears fell silently down her cheeks, Balchder wiped them away. Then he reached around her and ran one hand through her unbound hair.

"I do thank you for this, though," he said. "If you don't mind, I would like to remember it as a gift, instead of a wager. You do look very beautiful like this. It's the way I will always remember you."

Gently, Addien reached up and kissed him on the cheek. She closed her eyes and rested her face against his for a long moment.

"Be safe," she whispered, then she turned and left.

Balchder said good-bye to Addien again in the courtyard. He held Brion close and kissed him on the forehead. Then he handed the child to the nurse who was just climbing into a covered carriage. Colin gave a command to mount up to the dozen soldiers who would be traveling with them. One of the soldiers held open the carriage door for the princess, but she walked past him and began to mount one of the horses.

"But, my lady…," the soldier stammered, uncertain of what to do.

Balchder laughed.

"I wouldn't argue with her, if I were you," he told the man. "I suggest that you go find another horse."

With a final wave behind her, Addien followed Colin out of the gate. Behind her came the carriage, the soldiers, and a few wagons full of provisions for the King's House. When they reached the plateau and the road widened, Colin fell back to ride beside Addien. She looked at him and smiled.

"I'm going home, Colin," she said. "I'm finally going home."

Chapter Twenty Six

The enthusiasm Addien felt starting out on that journey stayed with her as they eventually reached their destination. Even though they arrived in the city late in the evening, many of the people came out of their homes and lined the streets to see them. Some cheered. Most waved. A few even bowed or curtseyed. When they passed near the old Roman Hall, Addien even thought she saw Grainne and Tomas in the crowd, waving happily. At last, the company reached the King's House, and they brought their weary animals into the sheltered area that had once been the garden. The rose-bushes were gone, and most of the fruit trees, but through the windows they could see torches burning, and the welcome odor of roasting meat wafted out the open door to greet them.

Michael was the first to come out of the house. It had been almost a year since Addien had seen him, but the sight of him still set her heart to fluttering. Dismounting, she reminded herself to remain calm and friendly, although what she really wanted was to run to him and embrace him. A few other men also came out of the building to help unload the wagons and lead the horses to the stable. Then they all went inside to rest and eat a hearty supper.

While Addien ate, Brion lay in his mother's arms resting his head on her chest. Before long, he was breathing deeply, with his eyes closed. Michael came and sat down across from them.

"I wasn't sure how you would want things arranged," he said in a low voice, so as not to awaken the child. "Deirdre has been here since Colin left. She set up some of the rooms in the west wing. I can take you there when you're ready."

Addien smiled her thanks at him and finished her drink.

"Someone is definitely ready," she said, lifting Brion to carry him.

"I can do that," Michael said, holding out his arms. "You must be tired."

Very gently, he took the sleeping child from Addien's arms. Without another word, she followed him out of the Great Hall and into the west wing. As they approached the door of the King's Court, Addien lowered her eyes and looked at the floor. Michael led her to a cozy room next to the room that had once been occupied by her father and mother. A small bed had been prepared there with a comfortable mattress and soft blankets. Michael laid Brion on the bed, and Addien covered him up. Whispering 'good-night', she kissed her son on the forehead. Then she extinguished the one candle that had been left burning in the room and went back into the hall with Michael.

"He's a handsome boy," he said softly, as Addien pulled the door partially closed.

"Yes," she said, "and very sweet."

Addien looked up at Michael, but had to look away again quickly as her breath caught in her chest.

"Do you want to see the other room?" he asked after a quiet moment. "Deirdre said you should have the largest room, but she moved things around so that it wouldn't look like…."

His mouth hung open, but the words would not come out. It took a moment for Addien to realize that Michael was concerned about what she must be feeling, being in her old home again after such a long time. Ironically, Addien hadn't been thinking about the house at all, only that she was alone in a hallway with a man who made her heart race and her cheeks warm. Turning away from him to hide her emotions, she nodded slightly.

"That was very kind of her," she said, almost choking on the huskiness of her voice.

With a deep breath, Addien started toward the next door in the hall. The truth was that she had very few memories of that part of the house. She had been only six when her own mother died, and she had almost never gone there when it was occupied by her step-mother. Inside, she surveyed the room briefly and then turned to Michael again.

"This will be fine," she said. "You've all done a wonderful job of making things welcome for us."

As they stepped back into the hall, Addien noticed a shadow of uncertainty pass over Michael's face. Very slowly, they started to walk back toward the Great Hall. As they neared the end of the hall, Michael slowed and came to a stop.

"This must be very difficult for you," he said, turning to face Addien. "I keep thinking about the last time you were here...when we were here together. I always thought that if I had known...well, I might have been able to make it easier for you. But, here we are again, and I still don't know how to make it any easier."

Addien laid her hand softly on his arm.

"You're here," she said. "That helps, more than I can possibly tell you."

For a moment, they stood there just looking at each other. At length, Addien dropped her hand back to her side and looked away. She also remembered the last time they had been there together, before she fully understood who she was, before her life had been so drastically changed. She had been afraid then to tell him the truth. And in that hallway together again, she was still afraid.

There were so many things that she wanted to say to him, so many stories she wanted to share with him about her life. It was the first time in years that they had been truly alone, far from the watchful eyes of Lord Balchder. She didn't have to be afraid of anyone overhearing them, or of revealing any great secrets. But still there was a wall between them, a wall of her own making, and she feared what might happen if she ever tried to cross that wall. So she said nothing, telling her heart that its secrets that longed to be spoken would have to remain silent still.

As they continued to walk down the hall, Michael pointed ahead of them.

"There is one thing I accomplished," he said, waiting for Addien to look where he was pointing. "I made sure that the King's Court was completely cleaned out, and we had a new door hung. I'm afraid it's not as nice as the original. We haven't had time yet to find a wood carver."

For a long moment, Addien stared at the large, smooth door that barred the entry to the King's Court. The mangled, ax-hewn wood that had stood there before was gone. With a calm assurance, she knew that the ghosts that had been inside were gone, too. Blinking back the moistness that filled her eyes, Addien whispered the only words that she could think of at that moment.

"Thank you."

* * *

Michael stayed in Briallen for the next few days and visited the King's House often. He discussed security with Colin, helped Addien to find new servants, and even took time to play with Brion. Although Addien greatly enjoyed his company, she had a feeling that it wouldn't last long. She was right. One afternoon Michael found her in the garden, discussing the positioning of some new trees, and told her that he had to leave.

"I want to get a final headcount," he said, "to know how many men I can count on if we're called to the border. I might be gone for several weeks, longer if Lord Balchder needs us right away."

"Do you think it will come to that?" Addien asked, walking with him toward the road.

He shrugged and looked at the sky.

"I don't know," he answered softly.

"Michael," she said after a long moment, "I probably shouldn't be telling you this, but Lord Balchder is worried that the people will lose faith in him if the Saxons don't invade this year. He's blaming himself for ever listening to Cythraul. And I think he wants a chance to prove himself again, so the people will respect him, the way they did when he was young."

"I guess I can understand how he feels," Michael mused, kicking a few stones out of his way as he walked.

Addien stopped then and took his arm.

"When you're visiting the nobles, you'll tell them, won't you?" she pleaded. "Tell them that he's doing the right thing. If the Saxons don't invade this year, we still have to be ready for them. It might be next year, or the next."

Michael laid his hand on hers and smiled softly.

"I'll tell them," he said.

Impulsively, Addien reached up and gave him a brief hug and then stepped back away from him.

"Be safe," she said.

For a long moment, Michael stood motionless, almost as if he was trying to decide about something. At length, he smiled and bowed politely.

"I'll be back," he said pleasantly. "I still have to get a wood carver for that door of yours."

When he had ridden out of sight, Addien walked back into the house and stood before the great door of the King's Court. She rather liked the smooth surface of the plain oak. It wasn't the way it used to be, but then so many other things had changed as well. It wasn't Brenin's house any-more. It didn't really seem to belong to anyone. She couldn't imagine Balchder ever wanting to live there, even if the kingdom was at peace. And she had difficulty thinking of herself living there without him. Like the crown, the King's House was a symbol of authority that was lifeless until possessed by the right person.

Turning away from the door with a sigh, Addien wondered how long it would be before the house would live again the way it still lived for her in the memories of her youth. In those memories, there was not only a king in the great house, but a family. There was music and merriment and stories by the fire. It was a place where she had belonged to someone and someone belonged to her. It was this more than anything that she wanted to give to her son—a happy home, with a mother and father who loved him. But, at least until the present danger had passed and there was time to think about the future, the King's House would remain a temporary shelter, and their home would still be at Cleddyf.

* * *

As the summer passed, Addien received regular reports from Balchder. They were always the same. No definitive information had been received that the Saxons were preparing for war. The army marched up and down the eastern border, drilling and looking for an enemy that never came. At length the first frost appeared, and Balchder began to disperse the troops once again. No one said it out loud, but everyone knew that they had been duped. Cythraul had lied to them all.

Addien and Brion returned to Cleddyf Castle for another long, dark winter. For the first month, Balchder paced the floors like a caged lion, barely speaking to anyone. In time he softened, perhaps realizing that time with his young son might be short. In the spring he insisted that Addien and Brion return to Briallen while he stayed with his troops in the north to wait out another quiet summer. North in the fall, south in the spring, Addien traveled with her son for two more years. But in the months after Brion's fourth birthday, the word finally came. A large force of Saxon warriors was gathering on the frontier east of the border, within easy striking distance of Dumnonia. Balchder ordered all the troops to assemble at Cleddyf and sent a message to Michael to prepare his reserve cavalry. Once again Balchder said good-bye to Addien in the courtyard, as she and Brion prepared to return to Briallen under Colin's guard.

"This is something I should have done years ago," Balchder told Addien as they walked to her horse.

Opening the box he was carrying, he pulled out the shiny brass circlet that held the Military stone. Holding it out to her, he waited while Addien slowly reached for it.

"The stone should be returned to the crown," he said. "I would like to know that it's where it belongs. I know you'll keep it safe for Brion."

Holding the little crown in her hands, Addien wondered for a moment if she should try to persuade him to keep it and to wear it into battle. But in her heart, she knew he had been right before. It wasn't the Military stone that had made him a great warrior, and it wasn't the stone that made the army follow him. They followed him because they trusted him to be a good leader, and she knew he wouldn't let them down. So she held the crown tightly as she mounted her horse.

"I'll take good care of it," she said. "I promise."

* * *

The journey to Briallen that spring was far from exciting. From the reports that had been recently received, the Saxons would not wait until summer to attack. A group of mercenaries from Cambria had informed Balchder that a wagon camp of women and children waited behind the Saxon army, ready to follow their men into the country to settle it immediately. They intended to sweep over the entire kingdom and be ready to farm the land by summer. The men of Dumnonia they had vowed to kill, and the women and children who survived the assault they intended to make into slaves. All along the route to Briallen, Addien and her companions found farmhouses empty and villages abandoned, as the men went to join the army and their families fled inland, away from the border.

At the King's House in Briallen, Colin tried to devise the best possible plan for evacuating the city if the need arose. If the army was defeated at the border, the few armed men in Briallen would have no hope of defending the city, or even the royal compound. So the wagons were kept ready with provisions for the road, and a number of escape routes were planned to be prepared for any contingency.

Michael was not available to help. He had already left Briallen before Addien and Colin arrived. In the years since the invasion had first been predicted but had failed to occur, some of the nobles had become reluctant to support Balchder's army. A few even refused to send any men away to battle, claiming that they were needed to defend their own lands. It was up to Michael to convince them that their only hope was fighting together under one leader. As soon as he had received word that the Saxon's were gathering, he had started traveling all across the southern half of the kingdom, trying to pull together a sufficient cavalry.

Two weeks after Addien arrived in the city, Michael rode into the royal compound at the head of a sizable group of mounted men. Dismounting, he gave orders to the men to ride on to the army camp north of the city to rest for the night. A short while later, he was sitting with Colin and Addien behind the closed door of the King's Court.

"You don't look happy," Addien told him bluntly, realizing that time was short.

Michael shook his head sadly.

"Four years ago I had twice as many men," he said. "Some have already left their houses and can't be found. Some say they'll follow us as soon as it's convenient for them. Others simply refuse to leave their homes. I've done all I can; I can't wait any longer. I have to go with what I have."

"When will you leave?" Addien asked.

"In the morning, at first light," he answered. "Riding hard, we'll reach the border by midday and meet up with Balchder before dark. Let's just hope the Saxons can wait a few days before attacking."

As Addien sat silently and listened, Colin told Michael about his plans to evacuate the city if the Saxon army broke through. Michael nodded his head and made a few suggestions, but most of the time Addien knew he was watching her out of the corner of his eye. As they talked, Addien realized that she had never really taken an interest in the evacuation plans, as if it had nothing to do with her personally. At first she thought that it was just a sign of faith, that she believed that the army would be victorious and that no retreat would be necessary. But as she thought about it more, she realized that her feelings went deeper.

Hearing her name brought Addien's attention back to the conversation of the two men.

"The most important thing," Michael was saying, "is to get Addien and Prince Brion out of here at once. The wagons can wait until later. If you have enough warning, you'll be able to use the South Gate and head directly for the port."

"I'm not leaving," Addien said suddenly.

Two heads turned quickly toward her. Colin's jaw dropped open, but no sound came out. Michael started to speak, but Addien raised her hand to silence him.

"Twice in my life, I have fled from Briallen in fear," she said steadily. "I will not do so again."

"Addien, be serious," Michael said. "You can't stay here. What would you do?"

"Help with the evacuation," she answered. "Colin and Deirdre can go ahead with Brion. He'll be safe with them. But this is my city, and I'm not going to leave it as long as one person is here who still needs my help."

"Gennie," Colin began.

"I'm not going to change my mind," Addien said, cutting him off. "Make whatever other plans you will, but I will take care of myself."

Afraid that they would still try to talk her into leaving, Addien decided to call an end to the meeting. Leaving Colin to rethink his plans, she walked with Michael to the garden to say good-bye.

"You're worried, aren't you?" she asked in a low voice as they walked toward his waiting horse.

"To tell you the truth," he answered, "this would be a lot easier if I knew for certain that you would be safe. If we fail...."

"You won't," she said, turning to face him. "You have to have faith—in yourself, in your men, and in those you leave behind."

For a long moment, they stood still, just looking at each other. At length, Michael smiled and looked away.

"You would think I would have learned that lesson by now," he said.

At last they reached his horse, but before Michael could mount, Addien took him by the arm. Fumbling with her thoughts, she looked down at the ground. Gently, Michael placed his hand under her chin and lifted her face until their eyes met. His clear grey eyes calmed Addien's mind, and she smiled.

"I was going to say something," she told him, "but I've said it so many times that it's starting to sound weak."

"What is it?" he asked softly.

Suddenly, Addien reached up and placed her hands on Michael's shoulders. She pulled herself up to her tiptoes and placed her face close to his.

"Be safe," she whispered in his ear.

Then, as she started to pull away, he wrapped his arms around her and held her close for one long, breathless moment.

"I'll be back," he whispered. "I promise."

Releasing Addien slowly, Michael turned and mounted his horse. In another moment, he was pulling away from her, leading the horse in the direction of the army camp, the border, and the battle. Addien waved good-bye to his unseeing back as he rode away.

"I'll be waiting," she whispered out loud.

Then she walked slowly back into the house to do just that.

Chapter Twenty Seven

Addien found herself alone in the Great Hall. With so many men having left for the battle and the servants busy preparing to leave the city, the house seemed strangely quiet. The long tables sat empty, waiting for the evening meal that would be set out later for the remaining occupants of the royal residence. No guests were staying there, and those servants who had families nearby had already been released to go home. Quietly, Addien searched her mind, wondering if there was something that she should be doing as well. She had just turned to walk to her room when the door from the west wing opened and Colin's wife, Deirdre, came in.

"Your Highness," she said, her soft voice echoing in the empty room, "I've been looking for you. Prince Brion is hiding in your room again, and he won't come out until you come and find him."

Addien laughed as she started toward the door.

"I always loved to play hide-and-seek when I was little, too," she said. "I'll go find him."

Remembering her childhood days and her favorite game suddenly reminded Addien of something she had hidden herself, and a promise she had not yet kept.

"Deirdre," she said, coming closer to her friend, "I need you to do something for me. I need a jeweler, a fine craftsman, someone who can be counted on to keep a secret. Do you know someone in town?"

"I suppose so," she answered, shrugging her shoulders.

"Go get him now, please," Addien asked. "I know it's late, but I have something I need to finish. Have him bring his tools, and bring him to my room. I'll be waiting there."

Deirdre looked at Addien with wide, puzzled eyes, but she didn't ask any questions. She bobbed in a slight curtsey and disappeared through the garden door to do as she had been asked.

A short while later, Addien was in her room with her victorious son sitting beside her on the bed.

"Did I fool you, mother?" he asked amid his giggles. "I hid from you good, didn't I?"

"Yes, you did, my love," she told him. "I would never have found you if that table hadn't toppled over. But now, my dear child, I have to ask you to do something for me. Deirdre has gone into town to find someone for me, and I need to be alone for a little while. Do you think you can play quietly in your room until supper is ready?"

"All right," he agreed, wrinkling his lips into a tiny frown. "But it would be more fun if I had someone to hide with."

"I know," Addien said, helping him off the bed and toward his room. "Someday you'll find a special friend to play with, you'll see."

When Brion had finally moped into his room, Addien returned to her own room and shut the door. From a locked chest she removed the box with the brass circlet that Lord Balchder had given her only a few weeks earlier when they had said good-bye at Cleddyf Castle. Fingering the red stone in the center of the circlet, Addien placed it gently on the bed. Then she reached down for the locket that still hung on the bracelet on her left wrist and attempted to open the little door. It had been several years since she had opened it, and the door seemed to be stuck. Working with only one hand, Addien couldn't budge it.

The knot on the bracelet wouldn't come free, either. With time passing quickly, Addien decided to cut the band with a small knife that she kept in the chest. The bracelet sprang apart, and gold beads bounced noisily across the floor, but at last she was able to hold the locket in two hands and force open the door. Kneeling beside the bed, Addien held the charm gently in both hands and called out for her little friend.

"Trevilian," she called in a low voice. "Trevilian, can you hear me? I need to see you."

In a tiny twinkle of light, Addien's old friend appeared before her on the bed.

"Trevilian!" Addien whispered in relief. "I need your help again, dear friend. I have the Military stone, and I want to return it to the crown. It will finally be whole again, the way it was meant to be. Will you bring the crown to me, please, so I can have the stone set in it again?"

Trevilian buzzed pleasantly and then disappeared into the locket. A moment later, there was a larger flash of light that made Addien blink and turn away. When she turned back, her father's crown was sitting on the bed in front of her. The soft light of the setting sun shone through the window and reflected off the shiny circle of metal, casting a glow of golden light onto the blanket. Slowly, Addien reached for it and turned it in her hands. One, two, three, four red stones clung to the sides, surrounded by twisted knots engraved in the metal. A fifth setting sat empty, waiting for its long-lost stone to be returned.

"I had forgotten how beautiful it is," she said, running her fingers over the interlocking knots. "Thank you, Trevilian."

Setting the crown down again, Addien looked around for the little pixie.

"Trevilian," she called. "Trevilian?"

He was nowhere to be found on or near the bed, and there was no answer to Addien's call when she opened the locket to look for him. Her friend was gone. He had returned the treasure that he had protected for so long, and then he vanished, back to a world that only exists for children and those in need. Gently, Addien closed the locket and said a silent good-bye to her long-time companion. Then she laid it aside and waited for the jeweler who would restore the missing stone to her father's crown.

Deirdre returned just as the household was being called to supper. Asking the craftsman to wait for her in the hall, Addien shuffled Deirdre off to the Great Hall with Brion. Not even to her closest friends was she ready to show the crown. When the jeweler was finished, Addien paid him handsomely for his work—and for his silence. Then she placed the crown in the box that had held Balchder's circlet and locked it away in the chest. If and when the time came to evacuate the city, she would give the box to Colin and Deirdre and ask them to keep it safe for her until Brion should be old enough to claim the crown, and the kingdom.

Later that night, when the lamps in the hall were being extinguished, Addien could still hear soft sounds coming from Brion's room next door. Impulsively, she got out of bed and retrieved her locket, which was still attached to its broken string. Wrapping it in a small cloth, she took it into Brion's room and sat down on the side of his bed.

"There's no use pretending to be asleep," she said. "I know that trick too well. Besides, I have something for you."

In a soft rustling, the blanket moved downward and two blue eyes peered out at her.

"I have a present for you," Addien said. "My father gave it to me when I was a little older than you are. It's a place to keep your most secret of thoughts, and your most secret of friends."

As Brion emerged further from the blanket, Addien held the locket out to him. His eyes widened in awe as she showed him the little door that would open and then snap closed again.

"It's for me?" he whispered in childish wonder.

"Yes," she answered. "And I want you to keep it with you always. There is magic in here. It may even save you from harm. Someday I will tell you the story of how it saved me."

Addien leaned down and kissed him good-night. Then she walked slowly back to her room. She knew that the locket was empty. But she also knew that Brion had heard all the talk about the Saxon invasion and the plans for evacuation. It was the only thing she had to give him that might offer him a little hope. For a moment, she stopped and looked back, wishing that she might be a child again with childish hopes and dreams. But she wasn't a child, and she needed something more substantial than blind hope to help her.

Straightening her shoulders, Addien turned back and continued on her way. She might not have a magical friend to help her anymore, but she wasn't afraid. She had her faith, and it had seen her through a lot. In her lifetime, she had been a princess, a shepherdess, a hostage and a prisoner, a mother, and a leader. If the next day she found herself a Saxon's slave, she would find a way to live that life as well, without regret. But she wasn't ready to go to that life without a fight. So she closed her eyes and prayed for guidance and then went to bed and slept soundly.

The next two days passed slowly and painfully. Addien started at every sound, expecting any moment to hear the trumpet blast that would signal a messenger arriving from the border. But no message came, and she passed the days pacing the floors and praying for deliverance.

The third day, after the breakfast dishes had been cleared from the tables and morning chores were being finished, the trumpet finally sounded. Colin and Addien ran out into the garden together to await the news. Before long, a single horseman galloped onto the garden road toward them. Nearly jumping from his horse, he saluted Colin weakly and stumbled forward. Colin caught him and supported him while another guard reined in the tired mare and led her away.

"Take him inside," Addien ordered, leading the way and opening the door to the Great Hall.

The news that the soldier brought was not good. His message came, not from the northern reaches of the border where Balchder stood opposite the Saxon army, but from further south, along an unprotected stretch of wilderness.

"A great company of men crossed the border this morning," the soldier said breathlessly. "At first we thought that they had divided their forces, intending to come around on our army from behind. The first message we sent was to Lord Balchder to warn him. But they didn't march northward. They're heading directly for the capital. If they march all day, they'll reach the city by nightfall!"

"They won't attack at night," Colin said. "They'll probably camp just out of sight and attack in the morning when they're fresh. That gives us the rest of the day and the night to get everyone out of the city."

Addien was amazed at how quickly Colin had recovered from the surprising news and sprung into action. He seemed confident and assured, much more so than she felt. The thought of abandoning the city to those merciless pagans to pillage and destroy still disturbed and angered her, but there didn't seem to be any other choice. So she watched while Colin summoned his men and began to give orders about evacuating the city. The household servants gathered around as well, casting frightened looks at one another, while even the children sat silently on the floor listening to the serious discussion that took place over their heads.

Near the back of the group, Deirdre stood, holding Brion with one hand and carrying her own young daughter in her other arm. Carefully, she worked her way through the little crowd until she stood behind her husband. At the first break in the discussion, she leaned over and whispered something in his ear. Swiftly, he turned to face her.

"What?" he gasped in disbelief. "Deirdre...."

"I don't want to go," she said, apparently repeating out loud what she had already told him. "This is my home, and I don't want to leave it. If you're not going, I'm going to stay, too."

"I'm only staying until the evacuation is complete," he said. "I have to stay with the princess and protect her. That's my job."

"Then why is the princess staying?" Deirdre asked stubbornly.

Amid a soft murmuring of whispered questions, Addien answered, "Because this is my home, too, and I don't want to be run out of it."

A heavy silence fell over the room. All eyes were focused on Addien. Looking from face to face, she remembered a day long past when frightened townsfolk had stood before her father in that exact spot, seeking his protection from an approaching enemy.

"*Go to your homes and stay there,*" he had told the people. "*If you offer the soldiers no resistance they will have no cause to harm you.*"

That wasn't true this time. Every person that the Saxons found would be either killed or enslaved. This time there would be no hiding and hoping that things would get better. The only alternative was to run—or to fight!

Addien looked again at the people around her. They were waiting calmly for directions, prepared to do whatever was necessary. Lifting her chin, she addressed them bravely.

"Deirdre and I would rather stay and fight then be run out of our homes," she said. "How many of you feel the same way?"

After a brief, stunned pause there was a sudden exclamation as nearly every voice in the room rose in assent.

"We can do it!" rang out one voice.

"Fighting is better than running," another called out.

"Those heathens can't scare us away," cheered a third.

"This is insane!" Colin's voice rang out above the others. "There aren't a dozen fighting men in the whole city. How are you going to stand up to a whole army?"

Pushing her way through the crowd, Addien found the soldier who had brought the message from the border.

"You said that the division approaching us was smaller than the main army, isn't that right?" she asked.

Colin interrupted and answered for him.

"It's still enough men to sack the city," he argued.

"Not if we fight back," Addien answered. "We have the day and the night to prepare for them. By morning we'll have every man, woman, and child in the city waiting for them at the gate. They won't be expecting that!"

In a rush of excitement, she whirled around to face the group again.

"I want every one of you to head out and find as many people as you can," she said. "Tell them to be at the gate at dawn and to bring any kind of weapon they can find—swords, knives, pitchforks, even sticks and rocks. Any archers that we can find we'll place on the wall. The rest of us will stand before the wall and defend the gate."

Ignoring Colin's attempt to take her aside, Addien turned to one of the stable hands.

"Niles," she asked, "how many horses do we have left—good ones that can ride a distance?"

"Only five," he answered.

"Colin," Addien said, turning to face him directly, "take your best riders and go at once to every farm and homestead within a half-day's walk of Briallen. We need everyone we can find at that gate by sunrise."

For a long moment, Colin held her gaze without replying. At length, he sighed and looked away.

"All right," he said softly, "if that's your command. What else do you want me to do?"

"First things first," Addien said, looking around her at the expectant faces. "You all know what to do. Let's get started!"

Quickly, Colin pulled aside several of his men to give them specific orders. A few moments later, they were filing out of the room after the servants who had already left to spread the word around the city. Addien took Deirdre aside to ask a special favor of her.

"Do you remember the big white horse that the miller uses to turn his stone?" Addien asked her. "Does he still have it?"

"Yes, I think so," Deirdre answered.

"I want you to get it for me," Addien told her. "When you come back, I want you to stay here with the children. I'm going out into the city myself."

Quickly, Deirdre unloaded her child and Addien's into Addien's arms and then ran for the door, excited to have something useful to do. Pulling a child in each hand, Addien started for the door to the west wing. In a moment, Colin was behind her.

"I thought you would be taking one of the horses," Addien called over her shoulder.

"I'm still the Captain of the Guard," he called back. "My job is to stay close to you."

"Not today!" she said. "We have too much to do and too few people to do it. I have another job for you. Last year you told me that the wheel-wright was hoarding weapons. Do you think he still has them?"

"Probably," he answered, marching along behind her.

"Then go get them," Addien ordered. "Take someone with you to help carry them. Oh, and make sure someone tells the brothers at the church. I think even they will join this fight."

"Gennie," he said, finally overtaking her when she stopped at Brion's bedroom, "are you sure this is what you want to do?"

For a moment, Addien paused and looked at him. Then she knelt down beside her young son.

"All my life, I thought that my father's greatest mistake was trusting someone too much," she said softly. "I realized today that his only real mistake was in not trusting enough. He never gave his people a chance to fight for what was theirs—their freedom and their way of life. He tried to save them by telling them not to fight. But he didn't really save them at all. All these years they've lived in uncertainty and fear, just waiting for someone to lead them. Don't ask me to lead them into hiding and despair. I've been there. And I'm not going back."

Colin dropped his head and sighed.

"So you'll lead them into battle?" he asked.

"Everyone who will follow me," Addien answered. "Now go and do what I told you. Deirdre will be back soon with the horse, and there's something I still need to do."

Shuffling the children into Brion's room, Addien listened to Colin march to the end of the hall and go out the door. Alone at last, she walked to her room and unlocked the chest that held her father's crown. Removing it from its box, Addien held it up and examined the stones and the engravings once more. For a moment, she thought about putting it back and walking away, but she knew that that would be the cowardly thing to do. The people needed a leader, someone that they could believe in and trust with their very lives. If the crown might give them the courage to follow her, then she had to have the courage to wear it.

Slowly, Addien lifted the crown and set it on her head. Then she marched back to the Great Hall to wait for her horse.

Chapter Twenty Eight

All that day Addien rode through the city on the great white horse. Cheers went up around her when people saw the crown, and she could see looks of despair and doubt turn into wide, excited smiles. Never before in her life had she been so certain that she was doing the right thing, and she refused to think about what would happen to all those brave souls if the Saxon forces that arrived the next day greatly outnumbered them.

When the sun had set and darkness began to fill the sky, Addien returned to the royal compound. Brion ran to meet her in the garden, and she carried him inside. In the Great Hall, another messenger was waiting.

"They're in the woods just north of here," he told the princess in a serious tone. "We haven't been able to get close enough to number the foot soldiers, but there aren't more than a dozen men on horseback."

"Thank you for your message," Addien responded calmly. "Rest here tonight. Tomorrow you'll be standing eye to eye with them. You can count them then."

That night, Addien never left Brion's room. After singing him to sleep, she rested her head on his bed and fell asleep there. But she needed no one to awaken her in the morning. She was up well before dawn, rousing the servants and calling everyone together in the kitchen.

"Take some food and water with you," Addien told them. "We don't know how long we'll have to wait, and we don't want to meet them on empty stomachs."

As she took up her own water flask and some bread, Addien walked over to the woman who had become a dear friend to her.

"Deirdre," she said, "I want you to stay here with the children today. I know that you would rather be with Colin outside, but I need to know that Brion is safe. If we fail out there, there won't be anything you can do. But even if we win, we're going to lose a lot of people. I don't want Brion to be in the middle of it."

Addien could tell that Deirdre wanted to argue, but apparently she couldn't think of anything to say. Nodding slowly, she worked her way around the room to find the two children. Addien followed her to give one last, long hug to Brion.

"Do you still have the locket?" she asked him after giving him a kiss.

Silently, he opened his hand and showed it to her.

"Hold on to it," she told him. "It will always remind you of how much I love you."

With another kiss to his forehead, Addien rose and pulled herself away from him. Then it was time to mount what few horses they had left and to begin the march to the gate.

By the time the sun had fully risen over the eastern horizon, Briallen's northern wall had virtually disappeared behind the mass of people who stood before it. A dozen archers, half of them women, knelt on top of the wall near the gate. A few stragglers from the city pressed through the small opening that was left, while at either end of the wall reinforcements from the countryside took up their positions. At the center of the brave army, Addien and Colin sat on horseback with three other men, waiting.

They didn't have to wait long. Even before they could see the invaders, they could hear them. Drums pounded, and harsh voices rose up in a devilish war song, praying to foreign gods for victory in battle.

At the wall, all was silent, as the people of Dumnonia steeled themselves to face the enemy. As the Saxon soldiers appeared over a ridge to the north, Addien could hear Colin to her right trying to number them under his breath. When the soldiers were in full sight of the city wall, they slowed to a stop and ceased their horrible song. A prepared defense was not what they had expected, and at least for the moment Addien and her followers had the upper hand.

"We outnumber them," she said in happy relief. "It looks like it's almost two to one."

"If you count the children," Colin said sourly. "The difference is that they are heavily armed and we have little more than sticks and stones."

"Sticks and stones may be enough if your fighting for your home," Addien told him. "But maybe it won't come to that. I want to try something first."

Turning to the men and women around her, Addien motioned for their attention.

"Hold your position here," she told them. "Wait for the Saxons to come to you, so the archers can take some of them out before you engage them. They will probably hit in the middle in force, so our people at either side will be able to come around from behind them."

"What are you going to do?" one of the guards asked.

"I'm going to talk to them," she replied.

With the sword Addien had chosen that morning balanced across the saddle in front of her, she prodded her horse forward. Colin stayed at her side. When they were out of earshot of the others, Addien leaned over a bit to talk to him.

"I want you to stay back behind me, where you can see everything," she told him. "If I'm struck down, you mustn't try to save me. You have to get back to the wall and lead the defense. I'm counting on you, Colin."

Addien expected an argument, but she didn't get one. As they neared the waiting ranks of enemy soldiers, Colin fell back and she continued alone. A little more than half-way between the two armies, Addien stopped. With her head held high, she waited, praying that she would be met by a single emissary from the other side, and not by a full onslaught of attacking warriors. After several long moments, three men on horseback detached themselves from the group and rode slowly out to meet her.

"I am Addien," the princess called out in her most royal voice, in the language that they would understand, "daughter of Brenin, the last king of Dumnonia. You are foreigners who have come here with weapons and hostile intentions. As such, you are not welcome here. The day may come when we may meet as neighbors and talk of trade and ways to help each other. But that day is not today."

Moving her horse forward a few more steps, Addien raised her voice higher, hoping that her words might carry to the foot-soldiers still waiting behind their leaders.

"Today you stand before a Celtic queen in her wrath!" she shouted. "And if you decide to fight, not one of you will live through this day to return to your homes again."

Angry glances passed among the three men who had ridden out to meet her. They glared and growled, but they made no move forward and sent no signal to their men. Addien's heart pounded in her ears, but she made no move either. The weight of all the lives of the men and women behind her pressed heavily on her shoulders, but she kept her back straight as she looked from one man to the next, steadily holding each one's gaze.

The incredible tension was broken at last by a distant sound. Uneasy murmurings broke out among the Saxon forces. A fourth rider came forward to meet the three who still waited before Addien.

"Sir," the fourth man said in restrained excitement, "riders are approaching from the northeast, a large group of them."

One of the leaders looked at Addien and smiled a wicked smile.

"Our men have been victorious in the north, and they are sending reinforcements to help us," he said.

"Sir," the messenger continued, "they are still too far away to see clearly. We cannot be certain...."

The messenger was silenced by an angry glare from his commander. Still unmoving, Addien smiled her own slow smile as she kept her face forward, refusing to turn to look for the approaching riders. The Saxon leaders remained still as well, but their confident expressions were fading, and they couldn't help but glance over their shoulders from time to time as the sound of pounding hoof-beats swept ever nearer.

The time of uncertainty probably only lasted a few moments, but it seemed like a lifetime. At last, from the eastern edge of the field a cheer went up—from the townsfolk at the wall! The cheer spread down the full length of the wall, as the horsemen thundered into the open area between the two armies. Startled exclamations spread through the Saxon forces, and the ranks swayed in fear and uncertainty. Although she still did not look, Addien knew that the men who rode up behind her were not Saxons. They were men of Dumnonia who had ridden out of Briallen only three days before under Michael's command. From the great amount of noise they made, she guessed that their numbers had not decreased in size. With a silent prayer of thanksgiving, Addien lifted her chin and waited for the commotion to die down.

A single rider from the cavalry came forward to join her. Turning, Addien saw Michael's face, covered in dirt and sweat from the hard ride, but smiling his radiant smile. Together they turned back to face the enemy.

"Throw down your weapons and you may leave peacefully," Addien said firmly. "Take your families and go back to your own homes. There is no place for you here."

For another long, tense moment, there was silence. Then one of the Saxon leaders removed his sword from its scabbard and held it out to his side. From the wild look in his eyes, Addien thought that he might raise it above his head as a signal to attack. But at last he looked down and threw the sword to the ground in disgust. The other men beside him threw down their swords as well. Michael's cavalry fanned out around the edges of the Saxon army and watched as spears, swords, knives, and arrows were dropped onto the ground. Another great cheer went up along the wall, and Addien finally felt as if she could breath again.

Turning to Michael, she smiled.

"It seems you were just in time," she said. "Will you and your men escort these soldiers to the border and see them safely, and swiftly, out of Dumnonia?"

"As you wish," he answered with a slight nod.

Colin had ridden up to them, and Michael turned his attention to him.

"It may not be over yet," Michael told him in a low voice. "We encountered a large force at the edge of the northern moor at Setta Barrow. That battle was still going on when we left. Keep your guard up until we come back."

Michael directed his horse toward his men to give them their instructions. Addien and Colin returned to the wall, where Colin quickly gave orders about gathering up the Saxons' weapons and posting guards north and east of the city. Addien left him there and rode back into the city, surrounded by a crowd of celebrating townsfolk.

"Hurrah for the crown!" one woman shouted.

"The queen! The queen!" others cried, amidst cheers and applause.

Addien accepted their thanks and well-wishes with happy smiles, but their praise only reminded her of the presumptuous decision she had made to take up the crown. In light of their great victory, no one seemed to mind just then. But would they still feel the same after the passage of time, she wondered. Or would she be accused of stealing what was not rightfully hers, just as Balchder had been accused and detested when he kept the Military stone and tried to take the crown?

When she returned to the King's House, Addien greeted Deirdre and the children happily and told them everything that had happened. The crown she took off and held in her arms until she would have a chance to put it away safely. As the rest of the servants returned to the house a quiet celebration was planned for that evening. Addien excused herself and went to her room to return the crown to the locked chest.

*   *   *

The next two days passed very slowly. No news was received from the army, although reports trickled in slowly from merchants and farmers that a great battle had been fought at Setta Barrow and that many had been killed on both sides. Addien remained in the city, filling the days by meeting with grateful townsfolk and a few disgruntled souls who wanted payment for lost provisions. Addien personally invited the miller to the King's House and offered to buy his white horse. He was reluctant to part with the animal after it had become famous by being ridden into battle by 'Queen Addien', but he promised to retire it from milling work and to find it a comfortable home.

On the evening of the second day after the Saxons' surrender, Addien sat alone in the King's Court with her father's crown sitting before her on a small table. She couldn't get out of her mind the excited looks on the faces of the people when they saw the crown. Many had never seen it before, but they seemed to know in an instant what it was, and it lifted their hearts just to see it. Over the years, she had begun to wonder if the garnet stones in the crown really held any magic. It seemed more likely that the stones were merely a symbol of the power that was inherent in any good leader. For so long the people had desperately wanted, and needed, a real leader. It seemed wrong to lock the crown away again and tell them they had to wait another ten years.

A knock at the door brought Addien out of her somber thoughts. A moment later the door opened and Colin stepped inside. He stood with his back against the door, as if waiting for someone else to enter. The solemn look on his face made Addien catch her breath and wonder what news was being brought to her now. But it was not a messenger who stepped through the door. It was Michael. Colin nodded to him slightly and then stepped back into the hall, closing the door behind him. Michael stood alone at the far end of the room. Addien stood to greet him, but remained beside the table.

"Your Highness," he began with a slight bow, "the Saxon army has been escorted to the border, as you directed. I left most of my men there to set up camp within sight of their army, just to be sure they don't try anything else. The rest of my men I dispatched to help round up the survivors of the battle at Setta Barrow."

"And that battle, how did it go?" Addien asked breathlessly.

"The Saxons threw their main force at us there," Michael responded, "and they probably outnumbered us two to one. But even against those odds, Balchder ordered me to take the cavalry and ride to Briallen as soon as he heard that a second band had entered the kingdom south of us. When we left, the battle wasn't looking good."

Realizing that Balchder's desperate decision had probably turned the tide and saved the city, Addien shut her eyes and took a deep breath. Michael waited until she looked at him again before continuing.

"As soon as I could, I headed back to Setta with some of my men to help. We met a messenger on the way. I decided to send my men on ahead and deliver the message to you myself."

Trying to control her voice, Addien asked, "And your message is?"

"Lord Balchder is dead," he said softly.

As Addien sank back down into her chair, Michael took a step forward and continued.

"He fought very bravely," he said. "If it hadn't been for his planning and quick thinking, the army wouldn't have had a chance. The messenger told us that, after the cavalry left, Lord Balchder led a full assault right through the middle of their forces. They broke rank and ran before our men, but Balchder was hit though the chest by a spear. He was dead before anyone could reach him."

For a long while, Addien sat in silence, thinking about the man who had been her husband, the man who gave his all on the battlefield to protect his family and a kingdom that could never really be his own. At length, she looked up at Michael again, still standing in respectful silence at the far side of the room.

"There should be an appropriate memorial for him," Addien said, barely above a whisper.

"His body is being brought here to Briallen," Michael responded. "The wagon should arrive by nightfall tomorrow."

"I'll notify the church in the morning," she said sadly, "and put the word out through the city. I'll wait for him tomorrow at the gate. Will you do me the honor of going out in the morning and escorting the wagon the rest of the way?"

"Of course."

With a deep sigh, Addien sat forward in her chair and looked at the crown that still sat before her on the table. Reaching for it, she turned it slowly in her hands.

"For so much of his life, all he wanted was this," she said, running her fingers over the intricate designs pressed into the metal. "I offered it to him, before I left Cleddyf for the first time. He refused it. He even gave me back the Military Stone and asked me to return it to the crown—for Brion."

Addien stopped turning the crown and held it tightly in both hands. Then she looked up at Michael.

"For most of my life I've been hiding this away, or trying to give it away," she said. "What do I do with it now?"

Michael smiled softly.

"I think you already know the answer to that question," he said.

Taking strength from his smile, Addien stood slowly, still holding the crown. Gently, she placed it on her head, then let her arms drop to her sides.

"I never thought it would fit me," she said, glancing upward.

"You've grown into it," Michael responded.

Stepping around the table, Addien took a few steps toward him.

"Have I changed very much?" she asked. "In your eyes?"

Michael thought for a moment before answering.

"You seem more confident now," he said. "More assertive. You've always been courageous."

"Not always," she corrected him. "Too often, I've been afraid to say what I felt. I kept waiting for a better time, when it might be easier."

"And now?" he asked, a soft light filling his grey eyes.

"I don't want to wait any longer," she answered, walking slowly toward him. "I don't want to miss another moment of happiness because I'm too afraid to trust myself, or someone else."

Stopping in front of him, Addien struggled for a moment to find the words she had hidden inside of her for so long.

"I want to be with you, Michael," she said at last. "I don't want you to stay with me because I'm the queen who is commanding you, or because I'm a princess who needs your protection. I want you to stay with me because I'm Addien, and I love you."

Addien paused briefly to let Michael respond, but a sudden wave of fear and doubt rushed over her, and she babbled on.

"I know that it's been a long time since you said that you loved me. And you've had your own life to live. You don't have to say anything...."

Suddenly, Michael stepped closer and threw his arms around her waist. He pulled her close to him in a strong embrace. Then his lips found hers, in a long, hungry, searching kiss. After a stunned moment, Addien wrapped her arms around his neck, and let her hands wander through his hair and across the hard muscles of his neck and shoulders. Her body burned with a heat from within, and for awhile she forgot everything around them. There was no room there for fear, or doubt, or questioning. She felt as if she was finally where she really belonged.

Slowly, Addien pulled herself away from the kiss so that she could see Michael's face. Although part of her wished to never be separated from him again, she knew that their time together would have to wait a little while longer. She dropped her eyes to his chest and moved her hands down the strong arms that still encircled her.

"Will you come to me again—after the time of mourning?" she asked softly.

Michael said nothing, but his hold on her loosened, and she could see his chin drop in a quiet nod.

"There's something I want you to know," Addien said, shyly stealing a look at his face. "I will grieve for Balchder, because, in the end, he was a good leader, and a good father, and I respected him. But I could never give him my love. There was nothing between us since the day that we created Brion."

Softly, Michael swept his fingers across her cheek and onto her neck. His eyes searched hers, and his forehead creased sadly.

"You must have been very lonely," he said.

"Not in my heart," she answered. "I always had you there."

Once again, Michael brought his face down and kissed Addien softly. Reluctantly, she pulled away. Stepping back away from his arms, she straightened her shoulders and stood tall.

"You should go now," she said softly. "I'll see you tomorrow when the wagon arrives with Lord Balchder. Right now, I have to go and say good-night to my son."

"Are you going to tell him tonight?" he asked.

"No," Addien answered, looking at the floor. "It's late. It can wait until morning."

Hesitantly, Michael asked, "Do you want me to stay? I can go with you in the morning to talk to him?"

Addien looked up at him with a soft smile.

"No," she answered. "This is something I have to do alone."

Michael turned and walked to the door. Before he opened it, he looked at Addien one last time.

"May this be the last thing you ever have to do alone," he said.

Then he opened the door and walked out. Before the door had a chance to close, Colin stepped inside and waited patiently for any orders. Moving slowly, Addien walked over to him. She removed the crown from her head and placed it in his hands.

"Take this to my room, please, Colin," she said. "Put it beside my bed, where I can find it in the morning."

A great smile spread over Colin's face as he looked from Addien to the crown and back again.

"Yes, Your Highness," he said with great satisfaction. "Do you need anything else?"

"No," she answered. "Not tonight."

When Addien reached Brion's room, she thought at first that he had already gone to sleep. Entering quietly, she sat down on the side of the bed and pushed his hair away from his closed eyes. Then she reached down and kissed him on the forehead. A slight shiver of movement rustled the blankets on the bed, making her wonder if he was really asleep or only pretending.

"It's late, Brion," she whispered. "Go to sleep now."

Touching his forehead one last time, Addien stood and walked to the door. As she started to go out, she could hear stifled giggling in the bed behind her. There was another familiar sound there, too, like the soft droning of a bee. Peering cautiously over her shoulder, Addien could just make out on the bed beside her son a little shape the size of a mouse. Two tiny black eyes twinkled at her from under a jaunty red cap. Addien smiled and walked out into the hall.

"Good-night, mother," a little voice called to her from the room.

"Good-night, Brion," she called back. Then under her breath she added, "Good-night, Trevilian. Sleep well."

The End

Afterword

The faith that sustained Addien through all the challenges that were thrown at her can belong to anyone. The Bible says:

"We rejoice in the hope and glory of God. Not only so, but we also rejoice in our sufferings, because we know that suffering produces perseverance; perseverance, character; and character, hope." Romans 5:2-4

"For I know the plans I have for you, declares the Lord, plans to prosper you and not to harm you, plans to give you hope and a future. Then you will call upon me and come and pray to me, and I will listen to you. You will seek me and find me when you seek me with all your heart." Jeremiah 29:11-13

"Be strong and courageous. Do not be terrified; do not be discouraged, for the Lord your God will be with you wherever you go." Joshua 1:9

0-595-20810-X